3 2

MW00827197

Other books by the author:

A Bad Piece of Luck, novel
The Drinking of Spirits, story collection

Goya's Head

a novel

Tom Abrams

Livingston Press
The University of West Alabama

Acknowledgments are listed on page 238.

for Jane

This is a work of fiction.
Any resemblance
to persons living or dead is coincidental.

Livingston Press is part of The University of West Alabama
and thereby has non-profit status.
Donations are tax-deductible:
brothers and sisters, we need 'em.

first edition
6 5 4 3 2 1

Goya's
Head

Eloy Tomás Martinez:

Why does history have to be a story told by
sensible people and not the delirious raving of losers?

A storm last evening dragged a cool rain across the city and this morning is cool and windswept, and it's a nice change. The only air I noticed moving lately came from ladies in black at the terrazas fanning themselves. I took my morning walk, which I began early, woke early. I wore my flat cap, a flannel shirt, black jeans. I stop in Plaza España on my way home and sit on a wooden bench. The trees around the Cervantes monument sag with green olives. A woman I often see walking an antique dog at all hours is at the moment bumping a garbage pail along the cobblestones. Two pigeons squabbling over a bar napkin pause to blink at her. There's a little person who sells lotto tickets over this way. She walks past. I'm sitting and still taller than her. She wears a built-up shoe on one foot, looks like a grown-up child, has bangs, dresses in pink most days, wears bottle-lensed eyeglasses. Even with these she has a hard squint. Because of this, just by some quirk of her features, she always appears to be smiling. Or maybe she is always smiling. I take the letter from my back pocket and read it again.

I received it yesterday from a woman I knew several years ago. I've had some trouble remembering her face. I do recall that she was indescribably well proportioned but had no vocation for tragedy and, consequently, paid me little mind. At any rate, here's some of it:

> *Starting over is always the worst part. A new outline for a new life. It's all very ridiculous, so lofty and never followed. What I'd really like to do at the moment is suck all the cocks in this town. I am in a horny mood. However, perhaps I don't want to do that to all, just an elite few dozen. I never would, of course, you know me, but it's good fantasy material for long drives. Being surrounded by all those soft heads. Brushing my face over them one by one. Maybe I shouldn't be writing this in Starbucks.*
>
> *I have feelings of pain and sadness but almost as*

if it doesn't relate to anyone. Or it relates to me, but I'm make-believe so that it doesn't count. Joey from the meat department asked me out. That started the turbulence. My boyfriend had a fit. I've been molded all my life to be a victim. I do not know how else to act. I think maybe it's chemical, what controls some women to make them so crazy and loyal. An ancient survival skill. In dreamy romances and the Bible, this blind love is considered a virtue. Women should have it for their husbands as men do for God. But why must you be pulled in so close before they cut you loose?

I have begun to talk to myself. I've started to verbalize the more unfathomable aspects of the situation, speaking to myself like a madwoman on the streets. At least so far I talk quietly. I am not giving speeches on the corner. My boyfriend said I am totally orientated in physical beauty. You should see how hideous I look.

Humidity, damp thick hair of storm, red clouds brewing on the horizon. Streaks of lightning make a skeleton of temple and stairs. My man leaving me, and in the distance then, so small it's like he walked along my windowsill ...

The letter came from Tampa. I'm curious as to how she got my address here. She signed her name, and it don't mean much to me. She went by a nickname when I knew her. She was a photographer then and made her living taking pictures of food that Kash & Karry supermarkets used in their newspaper and magazine ads. She was amused by the job. We were in an AA group together. My attendance was sporadic at best, and I went there heavily drugged in order to bear the humanity. But then, too, whenever I get any communication from a woman, a phone call, note, or something even more complicated, such as a smile, Megan starts cleaning her pistol. I hate it when she does that. Consequently, when she asked if we happened to get any mail I said, Just an advertisement. I don't ever lie to her exactly you see.

Megan heard from Emilie that the ATM machines are down because of Hurricane Floyd in the States. But there's money in the kitty, she tells me. It's what she calls the little safe in my bedroom. I went to the panadería at noon to get bread. The sun had warmed, a lovely Madrid autumn day now. Yet the crowd on the sidewalks appeared to be on speed, bouncing off one another like pinballs as if some ludicrous power surge had garbled the town. English is rare in our neighborhood and I'd not come across it for some time, but then I heard it spoken twice. I was walking by a fish market—the market's open at the front, the produce on ice, good work in the summer, but already the mongers are rubbing their hands—when a young American said to her companion, Big fish! I winced and raised an eyebrow. I thought momentarily that she was referring to me, but it was the merluza she had in mind. And down on Calle Princesa, I noted a long, thin woman on a bench. She had on high-top, rather heavy shoes. She wore a fur stole, draped across her shoulders, one with the heads still attached. It was hard to imagine these button-eyed foxes mousing in a field; they were going bald. I was about to ask her, Madam, are those feral dogs you have about you? But, then again, that's not quite true. I speak to no one on the streets. I did, however, begin to add up the words in Spanish—I do this often and, for the most part, unsuccessfully—when she abruptly pointed a finger at me and spoke as if we were perhaps in London. I say … excuse me, she said. Yes, you old boy. Would you mind not inspecting me as though I were a piece of cod? I retreated from her with instinctual horror. I might usually mark it as a bad sign and go into hiding, obviously there's something fishy about the day, but I felt no loss of good humor. I am in some kind of lark mood. I tucked the long baguette under my arm and walked home quite happily down the sidewalks mottled by the shadows of the restless leaves on this cool autumn day.

Sommelier! Megan called to me just as I was hanging up my cap in the hallway. I sense some advice on my drinking is on the way. She's seen me from the balcony coming home with my purchases.

She has to put in a couple hours at school today tutoring. She doesn't normally go in on Saturdays and isn't pleased about it. It's fouled her mood the last several days, and it's not like her. She's not very good at being sour.

Lucas, she said, you must slow down a bit.

I'm holding a bottle of wine in one hand and two in the other, a promising young rioja I'd purchased at the corner store for 310 pesetas each.

Let me put these down, I said. I placed the bread and wine on the kitchen counter.

You have that cyst on your liver, don't forget. And you're not getting any younger … you can't do it like you used to.

She persists, for some reason, in trying to keep me alive.

I can still hold my own, I was about to say, but she went on.

Honey, really, I mean it. You're up to three bottles a day. That's too much. And look—she patted my stomach. You're gaining weight again. Then she kissed my cheek and left.

What could she mean by that remark? I am holding steady at 228.

Monday—Our apartment consists of five small rooms, plus bathroom, and a water closet. Three rooms face the street and open onto balconies. The two on the outside are bedrooms. In the middle of these, the computer sits on our dining room table. I take my place there, turn on the screen, stare into the wilderness for awhile. I often have jack to say, and if I don't drink heavily before I present it, have little to add. Some wine is in order. Today I'm sampling a bottle of ten-year-old Irache from Navarra. It costs the equivalent of five dollars American and is quite good. I've discovered that if I play Mozart's Violin Concertos 3 and 5 as I compose, this too is of help. Turn up the volume, the music acts as a muffler on the traffic noise below. I think I would like this town better if I were deaf.

Half a block away, workmen are tearing up the calle. They're installing natural gas lines. The jackhammers are at it. They are powered by gas generators. I walked by there earlier, my dark glasses jumping on my nose. It has been raining off and on today. The rain and strong wind have cleared the air. As late as Friday certain streets would choke you, especially those connected to the bus lines. Occasionally it will rain hard enough to stop the jackhammers. When this happens, the quiet throws you.

The roadwork has exasperated the drivers in the neighborhood. Some side-streets are shut down completely and traffic funneled to our street, which has taken on the properties of an enigma. I stood on the middle balcony this morning observing the scene below. Traffic had bottlenecked and stopped. One driver became so enraged at a truck up ahead of him five-six cars, he jumped out of his vehicle—I could see beyond the truck, it had nowhere to go just then—ran to the truck and threw a punch. The truck driver, however, was rolling up the window at the time. The punch caught the windowpane and bounced. Traffic ahead of the truck had started up. Now the truck and the cars behind it were moving. The fella with the damaged hand hustled back to his own car, which, in the meantime, had stalled. All this accompanied by a great deal of honking and the word *coño* repeated like an echo.

At the moment, I am on the lookout for a bombona truck. I check the street every twenty minutes or so. We have to purchase butane canisters to heat the apartment and for cooking. The canisters, about two-foot tall, fat in diameter and bright orange, are called bombonas. Appropriately so, as they tend to detonate from time to time, usually taking an old lady along. One of our canisters is empty. When you see the truck, you yell down from the balcony. They bring a bombona up to you. A man carries it on his shoulder, no small feat, as we live on the fourth floor, no elevator. The whole operation is from another time. Or you can simply phone their office and put in an order. Sometimes they write this down, sometimes not.

Below, on the ground floor, one of the shops is called Carbones la Criba. They sell cordwood and small pieces of coal. The boss of this operation goes by the name of Nacho. Short for Ignacio. He's a pinch-faced man, a man you see on the street, you want to walk up to him and punch him in the head. Say hello to him, I get nothing back but the dead-eye. It's difficult to understand this. Even though I'm not fit to be around people and the less interaction the better, on the surface, at least, I must seem a likeable sort. I say Good Day in Spanish, I try to be pleasant. I have a disagreeable side, but it's hard to get that number; you have to know me awhile. I don't believe Nacho is that perceptive. And even worse, I note in his look the malice of fools.

He and his extended family live in the apartment above the shop and stand around in front of the shop on the sidewalk most of the day on the lookout for customers. In other times they would be called peasants. Our landlady, Ana Dolores, says the family came from the countryside after the Civil War. The shop is small and cluttered and dusty. Inside there, it could be the 1930s again; it could be the Middle Ages.

There are any number of motorcycles and scooters around. With these, I suspect, you can regain some personal sense of control over time and space in the gridlock. Many of them are nothing more than dirt bikes and have no mufflers whatsoever. I mention this because one just went by. It's very much like somebody riding a chainsaw past your windows. The Spaniards have a term for this, which translates as *That son-of-a-bitch mounted on noise*. I've started dropping ice cubes on these assholes in the vague hope that I'll get lucky and maim one.

On the weekends, all-night street parties take place in our neighborhood, Argüelles, and the noise level increases dramatically. There are young people about, many from the *Universidad Complutense de Madrid*, 130,000 strong, where Megan is an exchange student. Revelers stop and go throughout the night below our balconies. There's a good spot down there to drink and smoke *porros*, a tobacco and hash cigarette. They like to break into song. They're loud and not adept at carrying a tune. It angered me at first, until I realized they were just having a good time, a thing I've spent my life at.

For all the thousands of revelers, however, the streets are safe. The Madrileños, young and old alike, live on the streets. Walking

Goya's Head

about is one of the main occupations of this town. And you can walk anywhere, night or day, and not be bothered. This in itself, coming from America, was for a long time something quite different.

We don't have a car. If I owned a car here, then I would have to find a place to park it; and there are no parking spaces left in Madrid. My neighbors correct this problem by double-parking. Calle Meléndez Valdés, where we live, is a one-way street. There are cars parked bumper to bumper on both sides of it. Often, the right side of our block is completely double-parked. When someone who's trapped on the inside wants to leave, he'll lay on his horn until the other party comes and moves his vehicle out of the way. For the most part, those double-parked are fairly quick to retrieve their cars. If one of them has dropped in on his girlfriend to catch a piece of ass though, maybe he's not in such a hurry to respond. No matter. The horn blows till he gets there.

By 4:30, 5 a.m. on the weekends, delirium has set in among the merry-makers, and soon after, the neighborhood clears. If you rise early, the quiet is spooky, as if you're the only one awake, which is, often as not, exactly the case. This town gets up late. You'll see some of the revelers unconscious on the sidewalks.

One Sunday morning not long ago I woke early and went out to inspect the casualties. Next to Carbones la Criba is a churro shop. The shop opens at 6:00, but it wasn't open yet. A young girl was passed out, sitting down, leaning against the door. She was beautiful there, an angel slumped against the building. Fifteen, sixteen, I can't tell anymore. She cradled an empty bottle of wine in her arms, her face tilted up toward me. In an act of spontaneity and gentleness that confounded me even as I did it, I bent down and kissed her on the forehead. I watched a few seconds more. She grimaced in her sleep. I had the distinct mental impression she was at that moment dreaming of being kissed by a very large frog.

Megan wants to have a party at our place.

Who's coming?

Emilie, she says. Kevin Ray. That new guy who's working with

Kevin—

Chelo, I said.

Yes … Some folks from my Spanish Lit class …

She appears to be considering who else she might add but, not coming up with anyone, after awhile says, Lucas … is there anyone you'd care to invite?

Who could that possibly be? I hardly know a soul in this town. It's difficult to make friends when you speak like a two-year-old. My bar Spanish is impeccable, but otherwise I'm picking up the language slowly. Most of my vocabulary is profane. I fear my learning curve is in a constant trough. Whenever I say something aloud, the Spaniards I'm addressing immediately answer with their hands and whatever sign language comes to them in its turn.

I'll make a list, I say.

I want seven hunchbacks and seven limpers. If any one of the latter is clubfoot, give me Lord Byron if you would. Seven fatsos who dance light on their feet. I want seven deaf men and many mute women. Give me a dwarf to consult and canine mascots with large heads. Eight spades and albinos, mix 'em up till they answer to piebald, and throw in a trollop for good measure. I walked to the estanco while I composed this to purchase Cuban cigars.

Emilie Dessommes is a graduate exchange student Megan has befriended. She was born in Paris, grew up in New York City. I'll speak more of her a bit later. Kevin Ray is from Fort Myers. He's sometimes known as Queerboy. I'll get into that later, too.

Chelo Cruz and Kevin Ray are attached to a posh school here, Luis Vives, but they work out of the university in Tampa. That's where the paychecks come from. They teach English as a Second Language. ESL. Chelo is newly arrived. Luis Vives has enrolled a large number of new students this fall. Chelo is emergency help. He'll be staying the year, a concession he gained to come to Madrid on short notice. This is how he puts it. In Tampa, Kevin Ray reports, they're quite happy to have him off their hands.

I knew Chelo when he was going to college, but that was awhile ago. I had to ask Kevin Ray what he looked like now.

He seems younger than you, I think, he said. Though not by much. Kind of got a strut to his walk. He's a little short. Not a bad looking guy at all, really. Dark eyes. Bedroom eyes, we used to say …

Let's not get carried away, I said.

Dark hair, he continued. His hair is thinning slightly, maybe a little silver in it, but he appears to have aged well … if that's what you were wondering, Luke. He's also quite full of himself. And so full of shit at the same time.

You're on the money there, I said.

In the old days in north Tampa, Chelo and I drank in the same bar, Morgan's Pub, a great afternoon bar. I was working construction around the university, and he was taking classes during the day and driving a cab some at night and during the weekends. When I got off work, drained by the sun, I'd go to Morgan's. It was freezing in there and the drafts ice cold and the barkeep cool and pretty. We'd drink for a couple hours, then be on our way. Sometimes we'd still be there later on when the college girls came in. Neither one of us could quite imagine what you might say to them, though Chelo would give it a shot occasionally. He was a good man to drink with I remember. He could hold his own. But I never could quite figure him out then, and I'm having no more luck with it at the moment. He has joined a gymnasium that is only a block away from us and dropped in after a workout today. We shook hands. He sat down in my chair. He brought along some questionable red wine, which we started in on.

He worked here three winters ago, actually rented the apartment we're in now. Our landlady has some arrangement with Tampa. He stayed that semester and did not find Madrid to his liking. He didn't have any money, was the problem. He would work, come straight back to the apartment and read detective novels. The winter passed this way, and it got damned lonely, he says. This isn't like him. He likes to talk and be out on the town. He didn't much care for Madrid then, but now he's back for another go, and he's out of debt.

There's some talk about the program expanding next year to Barcelona. He wants to get a leg up on this assignment. He worked in Barcelona for awhile ten years ago. He was married to a Venezuelan then. I met her one time at a party in Tampa. She was younger than Chelo, lively and pretty, as I recall, really a very nice girl, and I wondered at the time what the hell she was doing with such a rascal.

They broke up after Barcelona, but he was happy there. He has good memories of that place. Barcelona is the finest town in the world he's told me several times already. I'm thinking maybe he wants to recapture something he no longer has. The world takes in a big area though. It takes in Prague, for example, and even Amsterdam, two cities where I would live, given my druthers. I might have argued the point if it hadn't originated from such a high authority. We've only been to Barcelona once, for a long weekend, much of it wiped out by a torrential downpour. I liked it well enough, the Gaudí creations, Park Güell especially. The town seemed more cosmopolitan than Madrid. We stayed in a hotel on the Ramblas but in a rather sorry room. The rain made me sleepy. I slept 15 hours that Saturday night, during which time Megan was, often as not, twiddling her thumbs. I hear her mutter in the kitchen, Fuck Barcelona.

But Chelo likes to make such inclusive statements. And he can talk through his hat, too. Kevin Ray had it right—he has a strut about him. He's a Tampa Cuban banty, a cock of the walk. And women fall for it, this spark in him. I recall that when I knew him before, he went through them pretty fast. The only time he's ever settled down I know of was during his marriage. Otherwise, he lived his life as if the bars were about to close. I'm trying to get an angle on him once again, obviously, but he's hard to pin down. He's one of those guys you can't help liking, though you don't know why exactly, and in some other indefinable way, you can never trust him.

I note that he likes to pass off his comments as wry wit, this interspersed with an occasional touch of stand-up comedy. A canny silence whenever you say anything remotely stupid. He amuses me. Sometimes at my own expense, sometimes at his. Beneath the facetiousness, however, he seems still the bumbler I remember. He has a curious absent-mindedness and is forever losing things. He's managed to lock himself out of the place where he's staying twice already and today somehow demagnetized his bank card so that he can't get any money out of the machines. He came to us to borrow some.

He is dressed casually, a sweatsuit, tennis shoes, his T-shirt on inside out. A trace of aftershave when he moves about the room. He smokes relentlessly, a cigarette emphasizing at all times the constant ironic twist to his mouth, a mirth there, hint of some secret amusement.

He looks around the apartment in a proprietorial manner. Same furniture, he says. Dreadful. Nothin's changed. I liked it here really. Even though I was miserable.

In my opinion, the place is cramped, a bit ugly and, as I've said, loud. We've been here far too long. I'm actively plotting to break the lease; I just haven't come up with a good enough scheme. It's hard to dislodge Megan once she's in place and even remotely happy. She's not good with obstacles, however. She'll give them a gentle push, and if that doesn't move them out of the way, she'll walk.

Chelo wonders now if I might want to sign up at the gym, too. I've got some dumbbells. I work out on my own, I tell him. My dumbbells weigh eight pounds apiece. I'm no longer worried about muscle mass; I'm just trying to keep the circulation going. Yeah, I say, and I'm doing some push-ups, things of that nature. How many push-ups can you do he wants to know. I'm at 11 now, I reply. It's all adding up … I fear that I'm beginning to suffer from good health. I don't mention that I enjoy a cigar while I work out and, afterwards, a towel draped over my head and a glass of absinthe.

Trying and not succeeding well to suppress a smile he says, And now you call yourself …?

A poet, I say. And wine taster to boot.

Ah, well, I see, yes, indeed … He raises his eyebrows and looks around, whistles a couple barely audible notes.

But you have to call yourself something, right? is how I look at it. People ask my mother what I'm doing, she can say—He's a writer. He lives in Spain. It sounds better than having to tell them— Oh, Luke … he's a wastrel. It's going on a good long while of that, and he does such a bang-up job of it. And truth be known, you tell somebody here you're a writer, it has meaning to them.

Are you getting a lot of work done? Chelo asks.

Not exactly. The last poem I finished was in '95. I don't tell him it took me six years to complete or that it wasn't very long.

He goes, 1 9 9 5, as if the number is shrouded in the smoke of a distant age. Morgan Pub days, he says. His curiosity about poetry allayed for the moment, or possibly for all time, he can't quite think of anything to add.

What else are you up to? he says eventually.

I'm doing some cooking, I say.

This seems of interest to him. He has a sudden glint to his eyes.

Right now I'm working on how to correctly move the food about. You ever see the cooking shows how they're so careful with it, put the food on the plate like rare jewelry? I'm working on that part now. Being attentive to how it's handled and all.

Presentation, he said.

What?

It's called presentation.

Just then the building groaned. He looked around and smiled.

I remember that … it sort of grumbles from time to time.

It's a talker, I said.

And you can make it all right? he asks. What he means is, Who's working around here?

I gesture with my hand, displaying our hovel. We live in genteel poverty. While he looks for an apartment, he is, for the time being, staying in a rat hole down in the Lavapiés barrio with an Irish friend named Enda he met in a bar last weekend. It's a cellar apartment, and apparently all you can see out the window are peoples' shoes going by on the sidewalk.

Kevin Ray tells me you've not quite gotten the hang of Castilian.

True, I answer.

Have you thought of taking a Spanish class?

I did for awhile, but … I never liked school, I say. I'm not one for sittin' around remembering verb forms. And I'm not very talkative to begin with, you know that. I don't even speak English very much, let alone Spanish. I've got so I can read some … I have to use the dictionary a bit, but … I can understand it. When they talk, though, it's too quick. I can't seem to listen fast enough.

You have no hope with the Madrileños then, he said. Talking is their life. I have the idea even food means little to them. That they don't care what they eat, whether it's good or bad. Meals are more a way to get together and talk. And they all talk at the same time. Listening isn't part of the deal. Even drinking … they frown on getting drunk here. It's bad form.

But I don't know about the Madrileños, really, he went on. They'll let you in on their scene, but then eventually they dead-end on you. No one else quite exists but themselves. You certainly don't need to worry what they think of you. They're not thinking about you at all. Though, not being able to speak Castilian, then you're no more than a plant to them … and they don't have a sense of green things in general. You notice the old parts of town, in Austrias, say, there's nothing but stone. That's their true way of living. Them and stone and their elegantly shabby little cafés.

The Madrileños, he said, you treat them like shit and they think—Hey, we've really got something here. It's the best way to handle them.

The ones I like are from elsewhere, he continued. And some of them are hardly Spanish. The Catalans, they're good people, and they don't care much for Spaniards. My daughter, we named her Montserrat. I like the Basques, too. They're less fussy. More direct. Up in Basque country on top of the mountain ridges, there are old lookout towers. You can see everything up there. See who's coming to fuck with you I guess, and far as they're concerned, somebody's always on the way with those intentions. I can't help thinking … if they ever did get their own nation, it would be a fine one, though that's not likely to happen.

Changing the subject on a dime he said, Remember that ole gal you was goin' with back when, danced at the Alibi Lounge?

Megan came in from the kitchen with tuna and tomatoes.

Let's not get into that just now, I said.

Y'all want colas? Megan asked.

We're fine, I said. Thanks.

Chelo inhaled his portion. I'm wondering how much he's had to eat lately. Then he started reminiscing about his college days. He had long hair back then and rode a bedraggled bicycle around campus and to the bar. He was famous in some quarters for being the guy in the clown suit who threw a banana cream pie in the face of the college president during a ground breaking ceremony for a new parking lot. At registration that fall, Chelo had been handed a batch of long unpaid parking tickets, which, of course, he thought unjust. So he retaliated. Local TV was there and caught the incident for the 6 o'clock news. The president was apparently a loathsome twit and well deserving of the pie, on general principle perhaps, but his only comment was that he preferred lemon meringue. This response saved the day for him, making light of it. But Chelo denies any involvement when I bring up the subject, which I can't help smiling about. He acts as if they're even now out to get him, that it's still a hot item in the Tampa police files.

Like I say, we used to frequent the same bar back then. He says, You remember so-and-so at Morgan's? and goes off about him, what a cockhound he was, always good for a laugh. Listening to Chelo, this guy was all but royalty, a prince of the good ole boys. Unfortunately, I remember him well; he was bullshit. And our conversation ended there, as Chelo and Megan started talking.

When they finished, Chelo's eyes followed her out of the room. Women don't wear shorts out on the street here, but in the apartment, like just now, she's wearing cutoff jeans, cowboy boots, a chambray shirt, her hair plaited in a long braid. Her hair is the color of pecan shell.

Where'd you come across her? he said.

Does she look like a Gatins?

She don't look like you, he said, if that's what you mean. She must be from the pretty side of the family.

She's my niece, I said. My brother's girl.

She's adopted, but I made no mention of that.

She's a Cracker beauty, he said.

Yes.

Megan came and went from the room once more. He was just looking at her a bit too hard for my liking.

Che, I said, don't even fucking think about it.

Afterwards, some days pass wherein I don't know what became of me. I make only a single entry: One of our neighbors in the building died. I saw an ambulance pull up out front. No lights, no siren. No hurry. I didn't watch any more. The next day his name was posted on the wall opposite the mailboxes. Evangelista. He was 61 years old. One of the tenants described him to Megan. She remembers him. I don't recall ever seeing him in person, though I might have at one time or another. I knew him only by sound. I heard him cough all summer. A consumptive, empty hacking, the lungs no longer elastic. Just wracked him to the soul sounded like. Go well wherever you go, Evangelista.

Then a curious dream toward morning. I was a waiter in a bar restaurant, and it was my first shift. The bar itself was small and horseshoe shaped, and behind it a very small barmaid with a poker face—she wasn't giving anything away there. Beyond this, however, were tables and chairs which, possibly because of mirrored walls, or maybe not, stretched to infinity, but very few customers when I started. I was slightly concerned about this. I had neglected to ask how much I was being paid. I might be working for tips. I waited on several tables, explained the menu, mostly simple fare, and took orders. A customer asked me soon enough, How's the goulash? How should I know? I felt like telling him. I began to notice that each time I took an order back to the woman behind the bar, she'd gotten a little shorter, until after awhile I had to stand on my toes and look over the bar wood to find her. She didn't seem to be so interested in the food orders. They piled up. But she drew the beers okay. They would appear on the bar in my brief absences, although the location of the taps was a mystery. The next time I went out on the floor, I approached a table with two women sitting there. I noticed they were crying, and none too softly. I recognized one, a girl I had gone out with long ago; somehow she had not aged. Her companion also seemed familiar, though I couldn't quite place her. Maybe she just had one of those faces that remind you of someone else. I was hoping the one wouldn't remember me—after all, it had been many years—and stayed in my waiter mode. Could I help you? I asked politely. She started bawling her eyes out. You loved me, didn't you? she said. Just for a little while you did. Being the sensitive type I replied, How about a couple large Cokes? On the house. She sort of tossed her hand over, like—Why not, you fucking prick. I went and got the Cokes, and when I delivered them kept my face turned far to the right so as not to know these people any further. In the meantime, a show had let out, perhaps a flamenco, as several groups were singing like Arabs in mourning, making noise with castanets made of shells, and the tables were filling up. I took orders like a madman for a while and gave them to the little thing behind the bar. I had to shout down to her. She'd take the food orders to the kitchen now, she said, it was time to do that. Past time, I had it, but I cupped my hands and shouted O k a y ! even though, I realized, there didn't appear to be a kitchen or even a door one might be behind. I turned around momentarily—it seemed the star of the show had entered the restaurant, or else was leaving, I couldn't make out which, a woman doing something with a hat, a commotion of some sort—and when I turned back and looked for the barmaid again, she was gone. A remarkably gaunt young lady grabbed my wrist just then and drew me aside. She said, The service here is appalling, don't you think? She spoke as if I were a confidant, or possibly her date. I felt sorry for her really, she looked to have been waiting on her food for several weeks, but, I don't have time to discuss it, I told her and abruptly pulled away. I'm sold! she bellowed. I turned and saw that she had spoken through a bullhorn like those used by cheerleaders. Trying to fathom what that was all about, I went out to take more orders but discovered I had lost my order pad and had to write on my hand. Now there was a new crowd stampeding into the place, and those who had been at their tables awhile were looking at me with something close to hatred … I woke then and was happy to do so. It is 29 September 1999. El Veranillo de San Miguel.

Our first autumn in Madrid, the weather turned cold at the very beginning of September and stayed that way throughout the month. I wondered if it was always so, as it seemed winter almost upon us, and asked a British friend, who was living here then, about this. She told me that soon enough good weather would return, and it would do so on the feast day of San Miguel, or so the Madrileños claimed, and that they called this phenomenon *veranillo*, the little summer. I found it all hard to believe, honestly, but exactly on that date the weather turned for the better and stayed that way a good long while. It's not been so exact since, but close enough. Warm days when it should be cold are known as Indian summer in America, but those are random events. The regularity by which the veranillo comes around is somewhat fascinating to me and, of course, no one has offered an explanation except that it's the saint's doing.

My grandmother called this Michaelmas Day. Her name was Tillie Gatins. She would buy a young goose from a Mex farmer she knew, usually in mid-August, and feed it well on scraps from her garden and kitchen. She would cook on the Sunday closest to the 29th. The day before, my uncle Harlen and I would go into her orange grove and shoot three or four rabbits, and grandma would stuff the goose with rabbit legs and backs, and oysters.

Her groves covered 200 acres at one time and went down in the first hard freeze of the 80's that hit central Florida, at Christmas in '83, when the oranges froze solid on the trees. There were two more hard freezes that decade, which finished the job. Tillie was gone after the first one. The family had it that she died of grief, but she was old by then; she was from another age.

About half of that land is still in the family, planted with pines now, this for tax purposes. The pines have covered over the dead orange trees, which are white and skeletal. A few of the old trees came back from their rootstock and make sour oranges. I'd pick one or two of these occasionally to marinate pork. They're a fine marinade for pork but are otherwise useless. Orange wood is the best wood for smoking mullet. In order for me to smoke mullet, however, somebody has to deliver a mess of them to my door, which sometimes happens but not often. The pines have grown large and should be harvested, but that won't happen as long as my Aunt Sylvia is alive, unless such a move became too profitable to ignore.

Grandma's house still sits beside one of her groves, a white, wood, two-story affair, three large rooms and kitchen on the first floor and four bedrooms on the second. Nothing of hers has been touched inside, though from time to time, things are added. It's become a storage place for my family. The son of the Mexican she bought her geese from, Sixto Aponte, now a grown man, owns a yard service, and he cuts the lawn once a week. Grandma's is the only lawn he cares for himself anymore; he has his help do the rest. This was his first job of work and, he maintains, his last. For a long time, the newspaper kept on being delivered, this went on for years, as my father believed it would make burglars and vandals think the house still occupied. He would pick up the paper at noon each day when he came home for lunch from his liquor store in Dade City. On Sundays, he'd walk down to the house, sit on the green swing on the front porch and read the financial pages and the sports section. There are only 500 people who live in San Ann, a good many of them at least shirt-tail relatives of ours, and all of them knew the score to begin with. But the old man wasn't concerned with locals so much. He worried on outsiders. None of these happened to steal so much as a newspaper, however.

Still, he thought it clever and maintained the practice far beyond common sense would dictate. He grew up in this house. I saw him there on the porch some Sunday mornings when he didn't see me. He would read the paper, one leg crossed over the other, lick his thumb before he'd turn a page. But he'd be looking around, too, taking in the place, taking deep breaths of it; and he would smile now and then for reasons all his own. It struck me on those occasions that I had never seen him more at ease in the world.

A brief from the *International Herald-Tribune* that interested me:

> *Basques Suspected in Explosives Raid*
> *Paris—Armed men stole Tuesday eight tons of dynamite from a depot in Brittany in a raid believed to have been orchestrated by the Basque guerilla group ETA, judicial sources said. Anti-terrorist investigators are leading the inquiry. The sources said that between six and eight men stormed the explosives cache owned by a private company in the northern village of Plevin. The robbers spoke Spanish and drove a type of Citroen van often used by Basque guerillas operating in France.*

Yea, though I walk through the Valley of Beauty and Bloodshed …

There's an odd, anonymous feeling to city life. There are so many people in Madrid, but you rarely see the same ones twice. So many they seem to cancel out somehow, and you're left alone. If you don't enjoy your own company, you're in trouble.

Everyone lives in apartment buildings. The entire population, except the King, who has quite a house down the street. But I don't think he's home much. I haven't seen him around the neighborhood.

I'm not even certain who all lives in our building. People come and go. There's a piso directly across from ours. The front doors face one another. Just by chance last week I happened to open our door at the same time this old couple opened theirs. Until then I had no idea anyone lived there. I'm not sure when they arrived. I heard no furniture being moved in, so I assume they lived here before, have simply been away, although it had to be a lengthy absence. The old couple, for their part, seemed not at all surprised to see me, nor in the least bit curious as to who I might happen to be. That's how it is here.

This building was pretty much demolished in 1939 by Franco artillery during the siege of Madrid. It wasn't rebuilt until '43. The entire neighborhood was heavily bombarded during the Civil War, by artillery and plane, and inspired Pablo Neruda, then an Argüelles resident, to write his poem *España en el Corazón*. These lines caught me:

> …I lived in a quarter
> of Madrid, with bells
> with clocks, with trees.
> From there one could see
> the lean face of Castile
> like an ocean of leather …

One tenant I can positively identify is an old lady who lives on the next floor, the 5th. By the vagaries of Spanish floor counting, it is actually the 4th. They don't count the bottom floor. She's 89. It takes her a good half hour to get down, then go back up the stairway after she does her shopping. She has to rest quite often. For being 89, she's in good shape I guess, walking these stairs, I'm sure, having much to do with it. But anyway, I see her around a lot. Also, I've noticed, during her shopping trips, she lingers at the little bar across the street named Cara Y Cruz and plays the slot machine.

Often she will nab me on the stairs and talk my ear off. She can't hear all that well and speaks somewhat loudly. I never have a totally clear picture of what she's saying. But, far as I can understand this one part of it, she lived in this building before it was destroyed in the war and moved back into the same apartment after it was rebuilt, and so has lived in the building off and on for some 60 years now.

She reports to me last week that a transvestite has moved in across the hall from her.

Transvestites interest me, as do all things odd. I tend to like that which confounds my sense of reality. I wanted to get a look at this person. The pursuit of someone who changes disguises in this city, however, made the whole thing difficult at best. The old lady doesn't see very well either. Or, it crossed my mind, she might have simply hallucinated the whole idea, which turned out to be the case. A couple days pass and then one morning she points the guy out. He went by us on the stairs. He's just some schmo. Plus he's about 70. The thought of him in a skirt is out of the question.

I know one fella in the neigborhood, this little guy I drink beside down at Kiko's Bar. He stands out in that he's so short. He's jockey size. Now he's getting on in years. He stands at the same spot at the bar each night, always wears the same suit. The old gents in the neighborhood wouldn't think of going out on the street without a suit and tie, their flat cap, a cane, maybe, or umbrella, a sweater and topcoat when it's cold. They dress up, doesn't matter if they're only out for a loaf of bread. Shorty's duds are a bit shabby, but he looks dignified … except when he tips back sometimes, gives himself away a little there.

But I go stand by him at the bar, order a caña. We exchange pleasantries. I offer him some of my tapas; he cordially declines. I've never seen him eat a thing. Then we don't speak much until I leave, when we say so-long. Sometimes, say a woman walks by in a tight dress, he'll shake his hand: Hot stuff. Otherwise, we watch the football match, or the bullfight, whatever happens to be on. I've noticed that, at times, when I have a slight jag on, I can listen a little faster, and, on TV or in a personal conversation, pick out individual words and meanings. But in the bars at night, the Madrileños get that deep guttural rasp going, mixed with their thick-tongued theta accent, and it doesn't sound like human language anymore. I hear instead a lion huffing and drawling, and there is not but one long catarrhal word that does not stop until the speaker tilts his glass again.

Shorty is a man of few words to begin with. When it's crowded in there, I don't think he can actually see the TV, being so little. He just sort of faces that way and drinks steadily.

Maybe I'll invite him to Megan's party.

Since it appeared that I might soon have an anxiety crisis over this, the party has been canceled Megan tells me. To make it up to her, as compensation, she puts it, I have agreed to start cooking again during the week. It is my job when she's going to school. I'm off during the summers. I have been slow to get at it again, as she is a great cook. So I'm the weekday cook from here on out, though it's a manner of speaking more than fact. What I cook up mostly are sandwiches. But I'll start tonight, Friday, which is her long day.

This place is too small for a party anyway, I said.

She grins and sets those oversize hazel eyes on me, all innocence and easy playfulness.

There's an alternate plan, Lucas … we're going to a bar instead.

We are?

Yes. With some Brits from my Spanish Lit class. To an Irish pub where they celebrate Halloween.

Since this is some weeks in the future, I put it out of my mind.

I walk with her to the metro, kiss her good-bye, and continue on to the Rosales Paseo, to Montaña Park. I'm wearing a short-sleeved shirt, as it has turned warm these last few days. Montaña is the highest spot in the city. It is soaked in blood. It figured prominently in the fighting at the very start of the Civil War. The battle for the Montaña barracks on the 18th of July 1936, when the people of Madrid stormed this stronghold of the military rebellion, marked the beginning of a three-year-long defense of the capital, known to history as the Battle of Madrid. From here you can see the Royal Palace, the Casa del Campo, Parque del Oeste and the distant Sierra de Guadarrama mountains, which today are marred by haze.

Montaña is one of the most peaceful locations in the city now, one of the few places where the Madrileños in this neighborhood seem to relax. I see a large biker thug walking two teacup Yorkies. There are black and white magpies on the lawn croaking like frogs. People taking their shoes off, tipping back their hats. A slight breeze comes and goes, leaves falling down the autumn light. There are solitary wanderers here. There are pairs of lovers holding hands. A girl with chestnut-colored hair, a braided pigtail all the way down her back. A young man in red jeans. Another fella scuffing one of his soles on cement, then looking at it in disgust. If you've ever been to Madrid you know what that's all about. The pleasant noise of water from the fountain hitting on the reflecting pool.

On the way back to the apartment, I stop for several moments to marvel at the woman who has taken up residence at a bench on Princesa. All the comforts of home. She seems to have simply moved everything she owns to this bench. Close by, a man who appears to have just come in from the wilds, in a knee-length lady's fur coat, no socks, his ankles black with grime, turns in a tight circle on the sidewalk, giving himself a good talking to. When I return home, I look in the freezer. There's nothing in it but a rabbit head.

When you buy rabbit here, the head is left on, apparently to demonstrate that you're not getting an alley cat. We had rabbit stew some time ago, and Megan has saved the head, for reasons beyond me. In the icebox there are three six packs of San Miguel beer, a rind of Manchego cheese and a very dispirited stalk of celery. I throw that out. I open a beer and work off several thin slices of the Manchego. We have nothing to compare with that at home. It's delicious. I contemplate my dinner menu. An exceptionally thin gruel would be nice, I'm thinking. A small turnip to the side, perhaps. Some Zwieback toast.

Megan had seen me working on this and was curious. What is it? she wanted to know. A journal, I told her. That I thought to record this winter, it being the millennium and all, and that I did not want it to disappear into the years.

She read what I have finished and commented:

But it's not completely true, is it? That's not really you. It's like a character who is something like you, but different. You are much nicer, she said.

She's a sweetheart.

Anyway, she said, I hope you put in more about our family, Lucas. It interests me.

I nod. But there are things she doesn't know about our family, and things I don't want her to know.

I go to the bathroom, look at my face in the mirror. What a battered ornament. How could so many thousands of generations have merely added up to this?

I have never been good-looking, but I used to be young and ugly. There's a difference. The mirror is now an area of damage assessment.

I'll tell you about one of my relatives I liked, a cousin named Sally. To speak of those I don't care for would take too long.

Back in high school the older boys called her Sailboat Sally. The name had to do with how she filled out her britches, I think, as she had a big ass on her, like hard wind in a sail, though it probably held some other implications, too.

When I was twelve she taught me some things. I was big for my age. She had been teaching the boys in our family for awhile, especially at family reunions, and it just happened to be my turn. She was four years older than I. She told me she had a secret under her dress. She called it her *well* and taught me how to drink at it, though I found the water somewhat fishy and only drank there once.

Several years later, when she was a senior in high school, one of my friends told me that his brother and three others partook of Sally one late night on County Line Road. They laid a horse blanket on the road behind the car. By the third boy, Sally's head was under the bumper and they couldn't see her face anymore, which made it better. She wasn't much of a looker.

I had started to drink beer and smoke cigarettes by then. I was hanging out with 16-year-olds who had cars. Back in those days we were called hoods. One night Billy Jenks and I ran into Sally down at the town square. We were going rabbit hunting, and she wanted to come along. In the winter we hunted with .22's late at night on country roads. Rabbits will freeze when headlights hit them. Sally bought two six-packs of Miller, and Billy purchased some Red Man chewing tobacco.

By the end of the hunt, somewhat excited by the shooting and the blood, perhaps, Sally told Billy she'd like to give him a blowjob. He got in the backseat with her. He had a beer in one hand he was drinking of, and an empty can in the other that he spit into. He was a romantic type when he was younger, and all the girls fell for it. Sex was old hat to him, the way he told it, but everyone lied so back then. Tobacco juice was somewhat new to him, though, and after awhile he happened to swallow some. Then he threw up on Sally's head.

Toward the end of her senior year, Sally had acquired a steady boyfriend. I can't even remember his name now, but he was a fella who liked to walk on his hands. You'd see him upside-down walking on his hands often as you'd see him right-side-up on his feet. At night sometimes in bed, knowing Sally as I did, this would bring pictures to my mind.

She had also by this time caught the eye of her male teachers, those who were still young enough to be on the look out, including, by all accounts, the head coach of the football team. Before graduation, she suddenly moved to Tallahassee and stayed up there for months. She had a baby, apparently, but she didn't bring the child back with her. She brought back a weight problem. Our family, which was numerous throughout the community, tried to keep all this quiet. But one day toward the end of summer, Dad came home from work at noon and said to my mother, Even the priest knows!

There was much speculation around as to who the father was. Her boyfriend was mentioned, of course. People said he'd stopped walking on his hands, but no one knew quite how to interpret that. And there were rumors, many and sundry, which is the way of small towns.

The talk behind her back finally got to Sally. One day she packed a suitcase and left and never returned. Never so much as sent back a postcard as to her whereabouts. Her mother was religious and said publicly any number of times that she thought Sally had gone to hell. But she didn't go quite that far. Ten years later I saw her at the Cadillac Lounge in Tampa, down on Florida Avenue. It was late, and I was on my way toward the door and home when I noticed her. She looked at me. I'd caught her eye. She sized me up a moment or two, then went on about her business. Though I didn't get the sense she truly recognized me, she was at the time obviously very high.

The 12th of October was a national holiday. I'm not sure what the occasion was. Many of these holidays are unfathomable to me. This one was on a Tuesday. Monday then is called a puente, or bridge, which connected the weekend so that the Madrileños had four days free. They started pouring out of town Friday, and that night and several that followed were surprisingly quiet, the streets ghostly, empty of cars. There were a few people around, mostly of the street and dodgy sort, who stood out, not having so many others to blend into. Even the beggars were absent. The guy with the hands growing out of his shoulders, the fella with no legs who plays the violin badly. They had no one to beg from and wisely stayed home. It was very much like August, when the town is eery, no one about at all, and the Cerrado por vacaciones signs are up everywhere. I notice that the swallows are gone now, too; they won't be back till May.

Saturday on TV, I watched the King review troops on Paseo Castellana. It's a tree-lined street usually chaotic with eight lanes of traffic.

Some rain early on in the neighborhood, gentle and brief and then just one of those days the sun, like it had been facing the other way, turned and saw you again, the lovely flat light of October. For reasons unknown to me, I could barely allow myself to enter it. This has happened several times lately. I consider it no less than criminal behavior on my part, the wasting of a good day. It is a small way of losing your life. On my deathbed, I know, I'll want these days back. But there's no getting them back, no one to bill.

When this kind of inertia strikes, I resent that it's nice outside. I don't want to see the sun then. I want cold and rain. I'd like it black as a widow's dress, but it doesn't work that way.

Megan took off with Emilie. They went to lunch, shopping, who knows what they do, but she was gone all afternoon. I moved the geranium pots off one of the balconies. I swept and mopped it. I cleaned the wrought iron with a dishrag. Then I sat down on the tiles of the balcony, my back against the bars at one end. The balconies jut out only two feet. This was as far into the day as I got. My geraniums endure there in the shade and don't seem to mind. They put out a flower occasionally as if remembering how to do it from some older time and place.

At this particular time, as I sat on the balcony, the canaries on our street started singing. There are a number of canaries about, and in good weather their owners hang the cages out on the balconies. There's a kid a building to the left who whistles to them. He knows their songs a bit, and it provokes them.

I notice now a new canary directly across the street and down one floor. A very bright yellow bird. That apartment has been empty since we've been here. The canary is obviously pleased with his new surroundings, maybe he's not been outside for a long while or heard others of his kind.

The bird's owner comes out and speaks to him several times, a young woman with a great mane of black hair. She's wearing dark glasses, jeans, a black t-shirt. Tough looking face. A nice ass, though, an abundance there. Her balcony is much larger than ours. She can walk around, has several folding chairs on it, a line; now she's hanging clothes out to dry. The canary sings in ecstasy beside her, the song built around her movements perhaps, the sway of her hips.

Then Megan and Emilie came back with a whole bunch of food for the long weekend, rented some movies to watch. Later she'll spend three hours cooking shrimp and okra gumbo. That's for tomorrow. Salmon for tonight and fried green beans. She bought a six of Kronenbourg and a bottle of Marques del Romenal, Gran Reserva 1983, a rioja. The three of us got to work on that right away, and it turned out to be quite good.

She's also brought back a small wreath of rosemary.

Where'd you get that?

A gypsy, she said.

Emilie was smiling.

She's afraid of those assholes, she said.

She was kinda scary, Megan said.

So what happened?

This crone started reading my palm over in Retiro. Told my fortune. She kept sayin' how lucky I was going to be. Read my palm, read up my arm and back down it. On and on. I'm not wantin' to be mean to her. It might jinx me. I don't want to lose all this luck that's coming my way. She hands me this bracelet when she's finished. She called it romero. Put it under your bed she says, it'll prevent bad dreams.

Then she wanted 40 bucks American, Emilie said.

Godamighty, I said.

We just looked at each other, Emilie said, like, Did we hear that right?

Rosemary's supposed to ward off witches, too, I said. I guess not, though, if the witch is handin' it to you.

That bitch did have some weird eyes, Emilie said.

How'd you get rid of her?

I gave her a cien, Megan said. Which made no impression on her at all. But then Emilie told her off.

I didn't either, Emilie said. I dropped to one knee, held the gypsy by her wrists and asked if we could share a brief prayer there on the sidewalk, rather than discuss money. I asked her, Do you have room in your heart for HEY-ZEUS?

She hightailed it, Megan said.

Let me try this another way. The person writing this is developing a gin nose. He has a disproportionately large head and brown-black eyes. Time has cut up his face. He is beginning to resemble what his father looked like. He's overweight, smokes Ducado cigarettes, Cuban cigars, swallows hard and often loses his speaking voice. Though he doesn't talk to many people to begin with, the voice is one of his defining aspects, an odd quaver to it, a thinness, as if it will not much longer have a thing to do with him. He has a diagonal scar on the left side of his forehead that is quite noticeable, a white line straight as a razor cut. A hat covers it most times. He wears a hat indoors as well as out. His hair is short, cuts it himself, smallest attachment, convict/boot camp result. A three, four day beard. He drinks, because wine is so very inexpensive here, one bottle in the morning, most often dispatched before noon, a second split between lunch and dinner. And sometimes a third bottle for good measure, consumed slowly through the evening, which, because it is not uncorked until after dinner, he thinks of as dessert. His drinking has been on the increase of late. He doesn't count the beers. He is composing this on a dilapidated Packard Bell, purchased cheap, undoubtedly stolen, from a gypsy he will see, some days later, walking a billygoat through the neighborhood. His back is to the balcony. The sun doesn't shine on this side of the street and lends to what he writes a shadowy cast. Below him the sidewalks of Madrid are crumbling from the mass of humanity boiling along them. When he works, this loud world disappears. He views the screen always with a somewhat puzzled expression, in wonder at what will come up next.

Some blocks down from our apartment is Parque del Oeste. The Western Park. It's a fine place where the city starts falling away, many trees, and a stream winding through with small waterfalls. There's a rose garden, I measure it two acres, and just below this is Goya's tomb in the chapel of San Antonio de la Florida. They call this the Florida part of town. The old guys in their flat caps play cards on picnic tables. Lately there's been a fella blows a tenor sax—a slow blues wandering through the rust on the horse chestnut trees. You know what that can do. It moves you like a wind moves the leaves. The Madrileños walk about arm in arm how they will. And at dark, the flowers of the night appear.

When it's warm in the evenings, as it has been lately, they might wear nothing at all. Maybe a garter for effect. Stiletto heels. A piece of black silk tied at the neck.

I was once assured by a Tampa street preacher that the first whore was the seventh child of Cain. He said he could prove it, but I was already tired of listening to him. And I don't know about any of that. I know the profession has changed little or none in the millennia since work itself began. As nearly everything in my lifetime has changed so very much, I take comfort in that which has not.

But last night, two of these daughters of the sidewalk crossed my path out of the blue to speak to a gentleman who had politely stopped his car for them, perhaps he wanted directions, and I, a man who thought he'd seen damn near everything in his day, was so taken aback I felt myself all but turn to stone, like the many statues in the park. So frozen had my countenance become watching it that, when these nude angels piled into the guy's car and the car drove off, I had to literally tear myself away from the scene, and frayed one of my sleeves in the process.

The veranillo appears to be coming to an end, but early Friday afternoon, the 15th of October, was one of its small perfections. I walked the length of Retiro Park, a warm sun and haze in the air.

From the southern end of Retiro I took the metro back to Argüelles and came up from underground at the corner of Princesa and Alberto Aguilera, to the big Corte Inglés store, bought a *Herald Tribune* at the kiosk there, and went inside the market.

I wanted bananas and wine. I noticed soon enough the strange power surge that electrifies the population from time to time throughout any given day had torched the old ladies there. The market was frantic.

A rather large one with bright hair came barreling toward me. I sidestepped her like a matador. I thought momentarily that there was some emergency. As it turned out, she was simply in a hurry to get to the carrots. She grabbed each bunch by the hair and shook them, trying to ascertain some quality or other.

I look around: The entire market is full of old ladies it seems, just them and me. It is one of my versions of hell, and I'm not at all clear on the reality of the situation. I note that many are quite birdlike in structure. Some of them no more than wrens. This does not in any way, however, stop them from abusing you. When you get into a line in this neighborhood, you have to make sure you are close to the person in front of you. If there's any space at all between, one of these old birds will surely cut in front of you and begin speaking to all and no one at once, as if she'd been there quite some time and owned the spot to begin with.

I'm convinced they wake up talking in the morning and don't stop until they pray themselves to sleep at night. If they can't find another of their kind to converse with, they'll talk quietly to themselves, to a can of chick peas or bonito. If they're not birdlike, they're somewhat burly, wear short-heeled black pumps, their ankles mushy.

It's such a strange scene, I check the feet of those around me for webbed toes or hooves.

Many of them are dressed in black, their husbands, mercifully I take it, gone to a quieter place. And many have red hair, though it is not a shade of red often found in nature, only in certain mushrooms or rusted iron. One has just tried to cut in front of me in line, but I have blocked her. She stands behind me muttering about the indignity of it all. I notice another, at the head of the line, having bagged and paid for her goods, takes a beer from a six-pack, opens it, and quaffs the entire can before leisurely moving along.

Off to my left a clerk has apprehended another one shoplifting. A manager comes and empties her coat, which looks much too heavy for the weather. The pockets contain an amazing variety of bounty, much of it candy. She turns her head slightly and spits on the floor. Another manager arrives and starts dressing her down. He's really giving her hell. She begins to mock him, repeating his words in a childish rendition, though her voice comes out in octaves unnatural to humanity, more like a bullfrog's. I remember that I have seen her before, at a small bar in the neighborhood, engaged at the time in a heated argument with a slot machine.

I am in the line I usually go to. The checkout girl is slow but very pretty. For the past month I have been trying to get her attention by displaying at every turn how attractively my stomach hangs over my belt. When I put down money to pay for my items, the old bird behind me, the one I had successfully blocked before, gives me a shove in the back. Ándele! Time to move along. I start to protest in Spanish, but, as usual, it comes out so appalling and confused, not even I know what I've said.

Out on the street afterwards, as I wait to cross, a wino approaches me. He wants a light off my cigarette. He has two cigarettes in his mouth, very short, both just recently purchased from the curb. He's a little shaky. He takes my cigarette and stabs himself in the face several times trying to get his lit.

As I turn away from this, I'm confronted by a cup held forth by a tiny old crone who has somewhat magically appeared there. She is dressed entirely in black, including a hood that nearly covers her face. She very much resembles a Biblical leper or perhaps a symbol of the Plague. I give her the coins I have in my pocket, which she neither scoffs at nor acknowledges. No movement whatsoever. She leans so far forward, it appears she might soon tip over. I take it she is some curious weathervane, at rest in the dead calm area immediately surrounding her, a still point in the flashing, discordant world of the street.

I make it another block and stop on the corner to admire a Great Dane a man is walking. The Dane's coloring is unusual. Patterns of black, gray, white, some black spots scattered around. Almost like a puzzle someone has put together to make a dog. These thoughts are soon interrupted by a lady who wants directions to Calle Fernando el Católico. I know exactly where it is, three blocks straight west, but I can't for the life of me remember the Spanish word for straight and begin moving my arm like a traffic cop, pointing the way. I bring my hand up to my shoulder and extend my arm out, bring it up, extend it. The third time I do this a short young woman cuts in front of me, and I smack her on top of the head, knocking her dark glasses cockeyed. The glasses are so large as to resemble blinders on a horse. She allows them to sit askew on her face a moment while she purses her mouth and throws off a look meant to destroy me. I have to laugh at this. However, I've had enough. I decide to pummel her about the head a bit, but … then again, that won't do. I quell that thought and glance up the street as if friends have just called out my name. I wave. I start toward them … I try not to make it appear as if I'm bolting.

20 October Slept till 9. Woke to cold and rain. Pale autumn day.
For several hours in the morning, I am so absent-minded I can't complete even the most simple task. I unaccountably discover the salt shaker in the icebox. I head for the bathroom to brush my teeth; five minutes later I find myself staring vacantly at the closet in my bedroom. The closets are short on depth. You hang up a shirt, a third of it is sticking out in the room. Since I was in the area, I decided to retrieve my winter clothes from the cedar chest, see which are still viable, and hang them up. This is basically taking stock of my rags. At home, I shop exclusively at Goodwill and other second-hand stores. Megan buys me new clothes occasionally, but I never wear them right away; they have to age. From the looks of my heavy shirts and jeans, I may have to sew some of them back together. Several items have mold. I throw them all in the wash. I'll end up wearing only a few of these clothes, my favorite and most comfortable, which become my winter uniform. Unfortunately, these are exactly the ones Megan tends to look upon with some disappointment. Take, for example, my blue/green flannel shirt. It is scored with rents and burn holes, I somehow spilled bleach on it, iodine, has one small patch, plus the collar is going thin. But it's perfect in many ways. It fits just so. I can button it at the neck, the only shirt I own that this is possible. I want it to hold together one more winter. It has such good character, almost like someone I know very well that just happens to spend a lot of time in the closet, for reasons I don't question.

I folded my short-sleeved shirts and put them away. They seemed grateful I wouldn't need them for awhile, all but jumped into the cedar chest. Somewhat later I took the metro to the Ópera exit, walked up to the International Bookstore and traded some books. One I got in return is a short story collection called *Love of Fat Men* by Helen Dunmore. What a title. Several of the others, I had to glue and scotch tape back together.

While I was doing this, Chelo Cruz stopped by. He stayed with his Irish friend, Enda, only a week or so, then took a room at Hostal Lido on Echegaray, while he looked for an apartment. He's found one finally, in the Lavapiés barrio, and moves in tomorrow.

You need help moving?

No, he said. I don't have that much. I'll take a cab … You fancy a pop? he asked, taking a bottle of wine from a bag. It turned out to be quite nice. Montestir del Tallat. A merlot rosado from Cataluña.

It tastes like cherries, I said.

It does, doesn't it, he said. I mean you read those wine reviews, some asshole sayin' the plonk has a nutty complexity with a plum backbone, a note of bramble and a hard finish, and you just want to murder the fuck, but … this tastes like cherries. There's no getting around it.

How's the hostal? I said.

Basic. Spartan. My room's pathetic, really. I took the cheapest one. 2000 pesetas a night, which … isn't cheap to me, but that's what you pay around Santa Ana. A bed. No window. The landlady says there's a room to come open at the beginning of the month with a view of the clothesline.

Hard not to jump on that, I said.

I mean to tell you. But there's some beauty passing through … especially on the weekends. They're from all over. Come into town a couple, three nights, get high, get laid, don't sleep … though, for some reason, my tally was nothin' to brag on.

It's all young?

Yeah, Chelo said. Pretty much. But … so what. This woman from Iceland … she found me amusing. There's people in the hostal, just live there, rent by the month. She's here for the winter. Not going home right now, for obvious reasons. She thought of Florida as an exotic place. But the way she described her country, it had the same effect on me. Talkin' about fairy stones, volcanoes … rivers of hot water under the ice. Some firewater drink they're fond of called Black Death. I guess it's a kind of schnapps.

She's working on a book. Has a grant for the project. I forget what she told me how much. Something outlandish. Says her grandfather won the Nobel Prize in '53. Hemingway used to call him up. I'm thinking, Can any of this be true? And if it is, why's she staying in this dump. Not that I care … it don't mean a thing to me, one way or the other. She laughed at everything I said like she was on acid. Didn't matter how corny. And also, I'm just overcome by her breasts.

They're big, they take up a lot of room in your thoughts. We sit down to eat, and it's like maybe they're gonna spill out on the table. They make you think of loaves of bread, of fat trout … I can't concentrate on the menu. I'm cramming rolls into my mouth … but it's not food I want. I understand the nature of my starvation.

As Chelo talks, I remember one of the characteristics I like about him; he's a story teller. It makes up for a lot with me.

She explained her novel one night, he went on. I lost track early on. I'm sure the plot was riveting. But she's wearing this white halter-top at the time that's so low-slung, half her nipples are showing. Like these big eyes trying to see me … you know … if eyes happened to be some other color than they are. Apricot, say. He shot down the last of his glass. Damn, that's good, he said. I shoulda got two bottles. There was a little left in the bottle. He tipped it, and the wine was gone. What was I saying?

Iceland.

Right … the Viking. Only problem was, she has this slight beard under her chin, which … I don't know about you, but … You'd only see it when she threw back her head and laughed. After awhile I tried not to be so funny.

I escorted this Australian girl around last Friday night. She was a knockout. Drank like she was in a hurry. I couldn't keep up. She likes Guinness, so I take her to a couple of the Irish pubs. O'Neill's over on Príncipe. And that one by Plaza Mayor. Moore's. She's knocking back pints left and right. Which ... don't seem to be affecting her that much. Not nearly so much as it's gettin' to me.

I'm sort of taken by her mouth. She's a bobber, got to be, I'm thinkin', with a mouth such as that. But I'm not helpin' my own cause much. I was so fucked up, every once and awhile, for no reason whatsoever, I'd babble like a mental patient. Of course, at the time, I'm not hearin' it that way. It sounded to me somewhat lyrical.

Then, at some point, I happened to look into her eyes. Nothin' doin'. No drama there. She had something else on her mind. She thought me a good drinkin' mate, she said finally, but she was in love with a boy and felt kind of true to him at the moment.

I'm thinking the guy's in Spain or ... I don't know what I was thinking. No. He's back in Sydney. Just about couldn't get any farther away ... but love's not on the maps. How could I compete with that? Then she goes on about something else real quick, like, that's settled ... let's have another pint. It didn't set right with me. How about some head? I asked her. That's innocent enough. We can go into one of the stalls ... I point toward the Gents. She takes exception to this and walks. All I end up with is the bill. And the Irish consider their beer a luxury item, so it cost me a bundle.

So ... I'm walking out of Moore's, look in my wallet one last time, unbelievable. I'm damn near broke, and I got heartburn like crazy, and they don't even know what a Tums is here. When, about just then, I run into this very attractive woman from Argentina who's staying at the hostal. I mean I actually ran into her, looking in my wallet so nostalgically, not paying attention to what I was doin'.

She's at the hostal but just passin' through. She speaks Spanish with an odd accent that sounds vaguely Italian. I had no idea the Argentines talked that way. It's musical. Especially if the speaker is so exotic as this woman.

I came across that once, down in ... I started to say, but, if you're going to talk when Chelo's like this, you have to be fast.

We decided we were both hungry, he went on, and ducked into Trucha for a tapas. When she takes off her coat, she's in this outfit that emphasized things well, the legs, her slender arms. All in white. The pants are the kind you can see through, and it's clear she was wearing a tiny pair of black panties … that tucked neatly into the crack of her ass. Well, I thought, maybe this is to be my adventure tonight, and the Aussie was just a detour. Then I ordered a glass of wine, but she said she'd have a tonic water. What? I say. Yes, just a tonic. I have to meet friends at Plaza España in a little while.

We had asparagas a la plancha. She picked up the tab. I put her in a taxi, walked back to the Lido alone and never saw her again.

Quite a night, I said.

Nearly perfect, he said.

The next night, two American girls took the room beside mine. 19, 20. Both of 'em sports and pretty to boot. The partition walls are thin. You can hear everything. The first night they're in there, one of them gets it good. Some Spanish guy's over there blasting her. After this, what I've got in mind is, I'll just stand by the door … soon as something nice checks in at the desk, come gallivantin' out there with cock in hand hard as a doorknob, ask politely can I be first in line. What do you say, Luke?

Well, long as you're polite about it.

That's what I'm thinking.

You say you're going to gallivant?

I'm considering it. Anyway, that was 3:30, 4, Chelo says. They wake me up, and I get to hear the whole shebang. They're slapping away at each other. The springs in the bed are goin' oink, oink. On and on with it. I get to wonderin' where the other girl is. Is she observing? Maybe lending a hand? But … that was it for me. Time to move on. I'm not into vicarious pleasure. I found an apartment by Monday afternoon.

He looked around our place.

It's not as nice as this.

You found it pretty quick.

I lowered my expectations, he said.

Tonight's one of those nights you can put out on the street whatever you want to get rid of, old furniture and such, and the city picks it up. The first time I saw this I thought a good many people on our street were moving. There's good stuff along with the junk, and it becomes a free bazaar. Folks empty out of the apartments and shop around, and nearly everyone you see walking is toting a prize. I found two nice, very old 10 gallon wine jugs covered in wicker.

The next morning I walked down to the Velázquez dig one block from the Royal Palace at Plaza de Ramales. The dig is taking place in the middle of a traffic circle.

It's the 400th anniversary of Velázquez's birth. They've lost him, however, and are trying to find his bones in the remains of the razed medieval Church of San Juan. He was entombed in the church a day after his death in 1660, in a black cape and hat, along with his sword. The church was demolished in 1809 in a matter of days to make room for a plaza ordered by Bonaparte's brother, who ruled Spain then and wasn't particularly interested in art unless he happened to be sitting for a portrait, nor in Spanish genius. No record has been found that Velázquez was moved at that time.

In the plaza there are four tile street signs depicting Velázquez's face with long black hair and mustache, as he painted his self-portrait in the masterpiece *Las Meninas*. Ladies in Waiting. There are three open-pit sites. The dig started last April and is proceeding in the Spanish way, slowly, if at all. There wasn't anybody working when I was there.

I like very much his paintings of common people going about every day life in Madrid. For the court painter, it was a revolutionary concept, and over a century later Goya took to the idea.

from the *International Herald Tribune*
Popular Poet Wins Top Spanish Prize
Madrid—Jose Hierro, a gravel-voiced bard who uses verse to speak out against social injustice, has won Spain's National Poetry Award. The Madrid native, 77, received

the prize for a collection entitled 'New York Notebook,' which was published last year and has gone through eight printings and sold 25,000 copies, a rare feat for a work of poetry in Spain.

In April, Hierro won the Cervantes Prize, considered the Spanish-speaking world's top honor in literature. Hierro backed the Republicans in Spain's 1936-39 Civil War and was imprisoned for four years after they lost and Franco seized power. Some of his most acclaimed works dealt with his experience behind bars.

Hierro is said to do most of his composing in a café near his home in Madrid. He says that contrary to what people might think, writing is a tortuously slow process for him.

Seven days of rain. I listened to Pedro Iturralde's 'Jazz Famenco' much of the time; it seemed to go nicely with the weather. Or I listened to The Doors. Great music anytime but Morrison and the rain mix especially well. The rain didn't bother me, or the raw gloom. A prisoner don't mind losing bad days so much as good. The moon, however, had me addled—a pressure in the head as though wearing an ill-fitting skull. What is the purpose of this shit? I questioned myself. What's the meaning? And I hate when I do that, know I'm in trouble then.

There is no meaning. I worked that out one summer when I was 14 and moved quickly to other mysteries that caught my attention just then, such as The Immaculate Conception and Day Light Saving Time. I tried to solve the immediate problem by drinking through it, hashish for breakfast and so on, which seemed to work toward the end, or else the moon phase merely clicked past my danger zone.

The first day of rain, umbrellas sprouted on the sidewalk like black mushrooms. I looked over some of the poetry I'd written 10 years ago. I was doing violence to the language then, in a pretty sort of way. The image drove those poems, and I like them still. Reading over it all again, however, had a soporific effect. I'd read a poem or two and then felt like I had to lie down soon. That's probably not what you're looking for; that's not good.

The second day I made spaghetti.

The next two days, I seemed to be waiting until something important needed done.

The day after that, I polished one shoe. I didn't want to overdo it. I might run out of projects.

The following day, I had an intense desire to lower my head to the floor. A feeling that I wasn't getting enough blood to my brain. That night I took a walk down in Santa Ana, a film crew there. Somebody spoke of Almodóvar, but I looked around and didn't spot him. They were filming in Casa Alberto, the doors closed, so I couldn't see very well. Four hundred years ago, in the rooms above this bar, Cervantes wrote the second half of *Don Quixote*.

On the seventh morning of waking up to rain, I cleaned the glass on the french doors in my bedroom and the computer room.

The rain never seems to pour down like in Florida, an off and on drizzle instead and maybe winter hidden behind its skirts. The neighborhood ladies hang out their wash in the building well, then put sheets of clear plastic over it.

Saturday night, obviously an odd-numbered day of the month, the 23rd of October in fact, there was a break in the clouds and the sky unaccountably cleared a few moments as I stood on the balcony, the full moon a limestone coin over the buildings on our street. I saw the man in the moon, his face tilted and bemused. Then he was gone just as suddenly, and the rain came again.

Later on, things got curious.

Ana Dolores, our landlady, Megan and I and an insurance agent, this woman with a three-pack-a-day cigarette voice, were sitting in the living room close to midnight discussing an insurance policy on the apartment. The Madrileños conduct their affairs later than anyone on this earth.

Megan thinks we need these things, as I have a tendency to set fires after I've fallen asleep. I personally wasn't much involved in the discussion. I was sitting there making my leg shake. But the policy is inexpensive, $150 a year. When Megan gets something like this in the crosshairs, even though I rarely understand the purpose or need, it's best to go along. No harm comes of it. So I went into my bedroom, where we keep money in the little safe.

I happened to glance out the window, to the apartment across the street where the new tenant lives, the canary cage on a table and covered with dark cloth. All the lights were blazing over there. And momentarily, into the living room walked the girl with the mane of black hair, and a boyfriend, both of them buck naked. They seemed to have just gotten out of the shower and were drying each other off with their hands. It was some show, I'll tell you. I had my face pressed flat to the window for a while taking it in before I remembered I was supposed to be doing something. I lurched back into the living room with the money, sat down, the insurance conversation going forward. And let me interject here, insurance is the last thing I've got on my mind, this day or any other; if I'm lucky enough to wake up in the morning, I figure I'm covered.

I'm situated in the room so that I can see into my bedroom and the lights of the street beyond, and this beckons to me. So while they're dealing with some paperwork, I just leave and go back to the view. And they're still at it over there, right in the middle of the big picture window.

As I watch, she takes a large steak out of the oven and sets it on the dining table. She has put on white socks since I left. She slices into the steak, spreads the cut apart carefully with knife and fork, shows her boy the pink meat on the inside. She points down to his ol' turkey neck and says something, and they both laugh like hell. I can't hear it, of course; it's as if I'm watching mimes.

Once again I'm entranced by this, but now Megan is calling me. They need my signature. So I return to the living room. But now I'm bent over. I've never had a steak affect me in quite this way. I'm bent at the waist like a little old man bent double by age and just get to my chair and sit down before anyone notices it.

Megan carries the papers to me, I sign my name, and just then the business at hand is done it seems, our visitors about to stand up and leave. But I need a few moments to compose myself. I blurt out, my voice a bit strangled and peculiar, Would you all like some cheese and olives?

I don't know what I'm saying really. I don't even know if we have any cheese and olives. Luckily, they politely declined the offer, sat back awhile and we all relaxed.

25 October
from the *International Herald Tribune*
Spain Denies Getting ETA Offer

MADRID—The Basque separatist group ETA said on Sunday it had proposed resuming peace talks with the Spanish government, which quickly denied receiving any such offer and dismissed the gesture as propaganda.

ETA called a cease-fire over a year ago but has yet to announce a definitive end to its 30-year guerilla campaign of bombings and assassinations.

Representatives of the government and ETA held an initial meeting in May, but a second session was suspended.

In a statement to Basque media on Sunday, ETA said it had sent a letter to Prime Minister Jose Aznar stating its willingness to hold a new meeting.

Madrid responded with a flat denial that any proposal of new talks had been made by ETA.

No one knows exactly who the Basques are or where they came from. They may trace back to the original Iberians. The country of Spain is only a small part of their history.

Sheep were driven through the center of Madrid today, seven, eight hundred of them I'd guess. The sun was out, the sheep packed in among farmers riding horses and donkies and carts drawn by oxen. It's an annual demonstration, urging the protection of ancient grazing routes. Spanish farmers have been doing this for a thousand years, the right to cross all of Castilla, both León and LaMancha, given to them by kings of old, an association of herders and shepherds called the trashumante de la mesta por la cañadas real. The arroyas of old Madrid are these same cañadas, or washes. They've been doing this, in other words, since before Madrid was here. When the city was built, it just happened to be on their route.

There was a ton of sheep shit after they passed. Street sweepers, then the heavy equipment went by with whirring stiff-bristled spinning brooms, followed by water trucks. I'd stood by a rail to get a good view, the horses and sheep passing inches from me. A couple of attractive peasant girls among the riders, wearing chaps. I was looking at one of these closely, she had a gentle face, when suddenly her horse took a nip at me. She slapped the horse upside the head.

Coño! she said. Cunt.

Hijo de puta! Son of a bitch.

Later Megan and I went to the Rastro, the flea market that occupies several streets in La Latina, claustrophobic with humanity. I bought my mother a Christmas present, a hand-embroidered tablecloth.

Sunday night, the 31ˢᵗ of October, we went to the Halloween get-together. We ended up at an Irish bar eventually, but first we went to a flat in the Estrecho district. There were three Brits, a Japanese girl, one fella from Coruña, in Galicia on the northwest coast of Spain, Megan and me. I took some detailed notes on these people, but I've, in the meantime, lost or misplaced them and so will concentrate on the Spaniard, Ramiro, who is a refrigeration repairman. He had an earring, wooden beads around his neck, sideburns, a good sense of humor, and he taught me how to make Quemada.

Now here's what Ramiro did: He had a liter bottle of aguardiente his grandfather had concocted. He poured it into a wide-mouthed crockery bowl, about a foot in diameter, maybe three inches high—you can use anything that will withstand heat. This was placed on the living room floor, which was tile. You have to do it somewhere that is easy to clean up afterwards. Aguardiente is clear liquor, distilled from what remains of the grapes left over from making wine. It's very much like what we call moonshine. He put about a half handful of coffee beans into the pot, maybe a quarter pound of sugar, and a lemon he peeled down on an angle about three quarters of the way to the bottom of it, and then threw the whole thing in. The coffee beans turn the liquor a light brown. He stirred all this around awhile to dissolve the sugar. Then he took a tablespoon full of the concoction and lit it with a match. He took a long-handled dipper full, and transferred the fire from the tablespoon to the liquid in the dipper. Then he eased the fire into the bowl. And the bowl of this concoction was on fire. As I said, the drink is called Quemada. This translates to burnt or burning and, figuratively, means burnt-out. The fire at this point is ghostly. It is like a small, wild sea there in the bowl, diaphanous and constantly changing.

Ramiro started taking dippers full and, pouring it out as he lifted, raised the ladle two or three feet above the bowl. The fire in the bowl had turned yellow, but the burning liquid pouring down descended as blue flame. We had turned the light off by this time, and you have to do it in the dark to get the full effect, which is hypnotic. He did this ladling and pouring for 20-25 minutes, and we all had a turn at it, until the fire in the bowl had burned down to almost nothing. Then he blew it out and served up the drink, really quite delicious as drinks go, and it got you high very quickly. The room we were in was small, and the fire made it warm. A good thing to make on a cold night. It's a recipe from where the Druid/Celts settled in Spain and came down to Ramiro through the generations.

After we finished off the Quemada, we took taxis to an Irish pub in Bilbao—Molly Malone's. There are many Irish pubs in Madrid, and in the last decade they have brought Halloween to the attention of the young Spanish bar crowd, who have taken to it. Corn stalks and yellow gourds decorated the bar. There were drunken witches and goblins, and laughter behind goat head masks. One of the barkeeps had dyed her hair half black, half orange. I don't recall much else. Megan and I didn't get home until 4. I couldn't go to sleep even then, maybe the coffee beans in the drink. I lay in bed and ran cartoons on the back of my eyelids. I don't remember falling asleep, but at 9:30, I was awakened by the man who goes through the neighborhood calling out—A F I L O O O ! It is a hard and haunting O on the end. The sharpener. He's saying—I sharpen knives.

Halloween started with the Celts. Their year ended on October 31st. Between the old year and the new, they thought there was a crack in time through which spirits could travel and haunt the living.

The things you notice when you're alone in the morning, the odor of certain hours. This particular one is geranium and leather. I seem to have a brain cloud today. Thinking of my friend Billy Jenks, gone to ground now, taken out by his own hand last Christmas Eve. I had an odd experience recently. Just on the brink of sleep one night, I had an overpowering feeling that he was close by. I don't believe in heaven or hell or everlasting life. I don't believe in ghosts; you must have very keen eyesight to see them I think, and my eyes aren't that good. I'm not sure what they're supposed to be. No more than bugbears to keep children well behaved. Celestial drifters. But this feeling was so strong, I couldn't deny it. One of the most remarkable sensations I've ever had. And a pleasant one. I spoke to Billy awhile in my thoughts and then, sooner than I would have liked, he no longer seemed to be there.

Death is one of the few things still capable of shocking me, the order of the harvest, especially, beyond any reckoning.

I grew up with Billy, and he was different from anyone I've known in this life, and smarter, though his intelligence was of a kind that could think around corners but could not in the least gain purchase on the workings of day-to-day existence. It was one of the particulars of his madness later on that he was forever studying maps, memorizing routes, looking for the shortest distance between points, though in truth he never went anywhere. It crosses my mind that he has found his way somehow through the backwater on the other side of life—a thought I dismiss a moment later.

I was angry with him for awhile. But he'd sort of told me what was coming. He said, I'll know when it's my time, and when I know that I don't want to idle. I want to run fast as I can. I want to be completely out of breath when I speak to God.

The Monday after Halloween, the 1ˢᵗ of November, All Saints Day, is a national holiday. On long weekends such as this, large segments of the population pour out of Madrid like molasses. Traffic out of town inches along, bumper to bumper. A destination that normally takes one hour may require three. Then they repeat it coming back in as the holiday ends. Cars going by in the street, the clang and push of rush hour traffic, long after midnight. Drivers trying to parallel park in impossibly small spaces. Watching a Madrileño attempting this is painful to witness. The noise of the traffic reverberates, shakes the walls, the windows. The sound magnifies as it rises against our building. The vibration creates a chemical change in me. It turns me irascible. All but violent. I am not accustomed to noise. In Florida I had a small house on 11 acres, much of it woods. It is out of the way and quiet. The only noise I dealt with were my own dogs barking, hoot owls in the yard at night, whippoorwill, tree frog … I don't think I will ever get used to the city, the heavy energy of it, the beehive glass-pack hum.

5 November

Friday morning I am up early and out on the streets before the sun has risen above the buildings. I am wearing a coat, can see my breath, as it is in the low 40's, the wind hard against me turning certain corners, I'm walking fast. I have no idea why I'm doing this, except that sometimes I like to change my routine. I walk to Puerta del Sol, even at this early hour busy with people and traffic, past the statue of the bear and the madroño tree. I've heard said of this statue that the bear is kissing a strawberry tree. There are a number of live madroño trees planted out front of the statue in large wooden containers, the trees themselves ten feet tall, which have berries on them now, and these resemble strawberries. I understand that, in the statue, the bear is raiding the tree. I've tasted ripe berries that have fallen; they don't taste as good as they look, sort of nondescript.

I should have known that. If they were any good at all, the great pigeon flock at Sol would strip the trees.

I move on to Plaza Mayor. The terrazas made their last appearance Monday. They're gone now until spring. It is the town's first step toward bleakness. Soon the leaves will fall and the cold set in for good, and I can't say I'm looking forward to it. I take my first sun stroll through the plaza, following the black cobblestone pattern, three times around. The square is full of light. I've already started readjusting my walking routes, looking for light now instead of shade. There are some terrific buskers on Calle Postas, as you leave Plaza Mayor heading back toward Sol. A man and woman on violin and another fella on bass. They play classical arrangements, sheets of music on stands before them, a hat on the ground to drop your coins in, the best music I've heard on the streets here.

There's a junkie-beggar hangs around our neighborhood. He's usually to be found at his residence on the cement outside a posh clothing store on Alberto Aguilera, which I'm sure they're pleased with, but he's a happy-go-lucky sort, different from most. Even the begging, you can tell his heart isn't in it. He stays too high to take it seriously. Today he was in Plaza Mayor near the statue of Philip III, wearing a Superman cape and with a pacifier in his mouth, arms upraised as if to soon fly away.

On the way back to my quarter, the sun warming by then, I'm reminded over and again that Madrid is a city of odors. The streets smell of diesel exhaust and spilled beer and tripe stewing and garbage and fish on ice and old men's cigars and fried sardines from the hot griddles of cafés as their doors open and close and coffee steam and dog piss and hashish and wino swill and hot olive oil and the competing perfumes of a thousand women. I purchase a bottle of wine at Corte Inglés, exit the back of the store and cross over Calle Serrano Jover. There's a large building on that corner, a crossed cannon/carbine emblem on one door, so it's military, or was once. Somebody connected to it keeps a fish pond to the rear of the structure. It's a decent size pond, there are water lilies and many bigheaded goldfish. There are rose bushes planted next to it, and their canes spill into the water. The roses are yellow, deep red, lavender, and petals of these colors float on the surface. I look at this for a while through the tall bars of a wrought-iron fence. Though I have walked for hours this morning, my feet have not touched bare earth or grass, only cobblestone, cement, asphalt.

I go home. I've had a good long walk and I'm hungry and eat some hard-boiled eggs and later I fall asleep for a little nap, and then the afternoon follows a normal pattern. It could be any other, and I don't remember it at all.

Just past the musicians, on the corner of Postas and Calle Mayor, I had come across the first vendor of the season selling roasted chestnuts and sweet potatoes and corn on the cob, and bought chestnuts from him. I've always entertained a romantic notion of these, I guess from that Nat King Cole song. If you eat them hot off the brazier, out of a little cup fashioned of newspaper, they're really good. Let them get cold, you might as well have a tablespoon of dry corn meal instead. Those I brought home today I'm using to stretch out my left shoe, as my little toe on that foot, by some painful miracle, has started to grow again.

That night, Megan and I and Emilie went out. Emilie is cool, lanky, 29. She has light brown hair streaked with blonde that falls to the middle of her back, and this evening wore a long, camel hair coat and black leather. She's looking good, as usual, and she has fun at it.

Emilie is engaged to a fella back in Tampa, who she speaks well of and seems to truly love—she's not going out with anyone here nor appears inclined to—but I take it she needed some time to be sure about this marriage business.

We went to Malasaña and bought two grams of hash on the corner by Café Manuela from a young man who was wearing clown pants, then drifted over toward Chueca. There were many gays and punks about, many young people in general, thousands of them, glassy-eyed, so much studded jewelry attached to some they appeared to have bees on their lips and ears, hair spiked and dyed. Greenish black seems to be in vogue, like the head of a mallard. Very sharp, I thought. We stopped at a place called La Tetera de la Abuela. Granny's Teapot. Megan had read about it recently as a café writers and actors frequent. That and the name should have warned me off. Sadsacks all around, very existential. Everyone in mourning over the tea.

But we hit the jackpot at a restaurant called Cambalache. It's an Argentine place on Calle San Lorenzo we stumbled across. We were the only ones there, other than the cook and a waitress named Mónica. We got there at 10, which, I took it, was early for them. They weren't too crazy about letting us in.

Now Cambalache is a tango place. They only dance there on Thursday nights, however, so we missed that. The place is small. I can't imagine the tango in there. Even with the tables and chairs pushed back against the walls, it doesn't seem there'd be enough room. But we order wine and food, and Megan and Emilie got to talking with Mónica. She had long ginger hair, wore a puffy white shirt, black pants and shoes, and a red apron from her neck down to below her knees. She was a very robust woman. A barrel of a woman. She's from Buenos Aires, she tells us, as is the cook and everyone else connected to the restaurant.

She made a phone call and soon enough this fella came in with an accordian type instrument he called a bandoñeon, a big young guy with a pair of black handlebar mustaches. He's wearing a black, soft felt hat with the brim pushed up in front, a black tie that hangs like a swallow tail on his chest, a powder blue shirt and baggy trousers.

He starts playing these sad, dramatic tango songs. He plays a couple numbers and begins on the third when here comes Mónica running toward us, slides to a stop, spreads her arms and starts belting out a tune. She has a full range to her voice, and the song was a beauty. Later I have her write it down for me, about a gaucho, out of place in the city, who returned to the Andes and left his love behind; he had a long silver dagger and soft, pointed boots and a dream that didn't include her. It was a heartbreaker, and Mónica sang as if she took it personally.

From 10 to 12:30 we were the only customers, and I'm glad that no else showed. We were given a private concert, and the musicians, even the cook singing in the kitchen, seemed to take as much pleasure from it as we did. Mónica sang once more, after dessert, and I didn't want it to end; but we were drunk going on punchy by then and decided to move along.

Outside, while we waited for a cab, Emilie said, Did you catch that last song? Emilie is fluent in French, but she wants to be a language teacher, and one of the reasons she came to Madrid was to get her Spanish down.

Something about horses and boats, Megan said.

Well … far as I could understand, Emilie said, there was a shipwreck. The ship ran aground, I think. And this guy's horse fell on deck and broke two teeth.

She looked at us. She said, Could that possibly be it?

Saturday through Tuesday, 6-9 November, was another puente holiday, this one for Almudena, the female patron saint of Madrid. The holidays are numerous here and, as I've said, somewhat unfathomable to me. But this one is for the priests and widows and the religious, who seem to be mostly older people. Almudena's float is out downtown, decked in flowers and a big doll, as Catholicism here strikes an equal balance between cross and carnival. Chelo came over at noon today and stayed for awhile; we watched the parade on TV news. He says of the doll representing Almudena, It's not like they believe in God or anything like that.

I spent the early morning swabbing the kitchen. Our washing machine broke. There seems to be a hole in the bottom of it. All of its water content discharged onto the floor.

Megan has such a sweet disposition … and also a sense of direction, not only that she knows where north and south point, but for life in general, and she takes these things calmly.

Look at it this way, Lucas, she said, the floor wanted a cleaning. It would have been awhile till we got around to it otherwise.

Some nights back, one of my fillings crumbled. This is a bit more serious. I not only don't like going to the dentist, I get psychotic about it. The only time I've had dental work done in Madrid, I had to get my front teeth worked on. One had turned gray. What happened was, years ago, it had been cracked by a blow to the mouth. It happened over a game of pool. I made the eight ball but didn't call the pocket. My opponent disputed the shot. The other tooth was moving away from it, perhaps in embarrassment. Needle in hand, the dentist says, First, we're going to put your nose to sleep.

Dental humor. But what I'm noticing is a woman leaving the next room in a wheelchair. It gave me a start, since I'd seen her in the waiting room earlier walking around just fine. The dentist was a Brit and a handball enthusiast, photos all around of him and various competitors on the court. I asked him about the game, handball being a subject I find endlessly fascinating whenever my mouth is full of cotton. Over the next hour, while he ground my two teeth down to stumps, he tells me about losing a recent tournament, 21-20, still angry about a referee's call on a hinder, and sends bits of enamel flying. I left with temporaries and later got a shock looking in the mirror. Only a son of a bitch sends another human being into public with teeth like those were. All jutting about at different angles. For two weeks I don't smile or laugh so as to keep them hidden. With great reluctance I informed Megan that we needed to cut back on our social calendar. Using my new lisp I told her, I don't see nobody and nobody sees me. She gave me a blank look.

You got a bird in your mouth? she said.

As for the washing machine, it will have to be fixed or replaced. It is a small one located beneath the kitchen sink. I'll have to wash my rags by hand for awhile. I've never seen a laundromat in this town. We dry our clothes on a tintadora in my bedroom, or in the building well where there's a clothesline but a problem with pigeons. And also, the woman below us, I don't believe she's changed her grease since we've been here, and she likes tripe. She cooks lunch at 2:30 and dinner at 10:00. The tides of the Spanish day ebb and flow around these hours. If you have anything on the line then, it has to come down.

There's a pull chain on the toilet, which is in the water closet off the kitchen. I never knew what a water closet was before, but it is just as the name implies, a closet with a toilet in it. The toilet never quite stops running. To get hot water, you must first light the hot water heater, which is above the kitchen sink, with a match. I've already explained our gimcrack heating arrangements. Our oven doesn't work, and we must fry or boil food on top of the stove. Now we have a mouse. He made his way four stories and chose to take up residence in my suit pocket. I only have one suit, which I retrieved from a dumpster and have not as yet worn. I guess he noticed there was a vacancy. Except for having mice, it's all different from any place I've resided before.

But I dislike these times when little things go to hell on you all at once, it doesn't matter what country I'm in. To take my mind off this, I am attempting to compose my last words. I don't want to go out muttering about ass and cunt. I want to say something for the ages. Thoreau, on his deathbed, had two last words, one of which was *Moose*. I am going for something along the lines of this eloquence.

Megan tells me I'll soon have to give Aunt Sylvia a call, as we are running out of money. She is really my great aunt, my grandmother's little sister. She's in her 90's but old now for so long she no longer seems to age. There appears to be some witchery in all this, and no one gives her any chance of actually dying. Because of her financial acumen, the family money has filtered down to her, and she is very tight with it. Parsimonious hardly covers it. And giving her a call asking for cash is an unpleasant and humbling experience.

Sylvia's two husbands passed long ago. I never met the first, and the second I barely remember, but she's had a boyfriend for decades. He has his own money and, for many years, liked to take her on cruises. The Mediterranean, Panama Canal, Alaska. He's gone daft, however, and the cruises are off. Aunt Sylvia is slowing down a bit, too, her right hip shot, and she gets about in a wheelchair or else uses a cane. There's little left of her but bone and angles, but she keeps her mind sharp playing bridge. She plays bridge every day, and when she's not playing, she's on the phone talking about the game to one of her cronies, or long distance to my mother. Sylvia lives down in Key Largo in a two-story condo.

She has a chauffeur named Garret. He's been with her a long time; he's getting on toward retirement age himself. He answers the phone for her, possibly, I think, to see if it is me calling. I only call her when I need money, it seems, and sometimes, when she knows it's me, she'll take the phone but say nothing. Her silence says much and states it quite emphatically, and I feel as though I'm talking into the void on these occasions. I decide to postpone this call as long as possible. Though it must be noted, as much as she hates my phone calls and begging, she has a true fondness for me, even a soft spot I think. I'm not sure why.

I have given in too much lately to the charms of introspection. I thought of getting a pet. The mouse offers scant companionship. A bird of prey, perhaps. Something that I could relate to. I notice there are a lot of people on the streets here who talk to themselves. It is a big city phenomenon. I've been doing this myself. I thought about getting a dog to give the appearance I'm talking to it. I favor pitbulls. They generally like people but hate all other animals, including other dogs, of which there are many in the neighborhood. At any rate, I stopped at a pet store during my walk several days ago. As I stood outside the store window, a green parrot I had been considering turned its head, caught sight of me and started laughing. It was a very loud, ratchety laugh that had several customers and the shop help looking around uncertainly. I was wearing my watchcap, which I usually, at Megan's request, only wear at home. It's not that funny a hat, really. It doesn't have earflaps or anything like that.

15 November

I'm waiting on the bombona truck at the moment, as we are down to one canister again, which I must shift between the stove and heater, wherever it is most needed. Around 1 o'clock I went out to get a paper. It was so nice out—I mean it was cold, you could see your breath, but the sun was bright and the sky that deep, robin egg blue—I just continued on down the street to Montaña. There was a real clarity about, the mountains in sharp relief. They seemed much closer. Snow on the peaks and in the folds of them. The leaves are starting to fall now.

I sat on a bench in the sun and read the sporting news. A Spaniard approached me. Dígame Pepe, he said. Then he asked a question. He ran it by me in high-speed Castellano. As is the way of some Madrileños, he barely moved his lips, and there was an air of ventriloquism to the speech. No sé, I replied. No conoces o no entiendes? he asked. But I was still on Pepe and did not answer.

On the way back to the apartment, waiting at a light, I heard moaning to my left and glanced over, whereupon I received a close-up of a young couple tonguing each other. There is much of this going on among the young, social intimacy displayed in public. Sometimes I think, God bless 'em—for the joy of it, for their pure hot blood. Other times I'm not so sure. Just depends what mood I'm in. These two seemed a little theatrical. Walking by a hotel on Princesa then, I was stopped by a young woman who asked in Spanish if I would like to discover her. She had a large blond dog on a chain. What a cute way of saying that I thought. I said Qué? And she repeated it. I tapped my ear several times to let her know that perhaps I am deaf and walked on.

Sixty-four years ago on this day there was a tremendous Civil War battle taking place in the neighborhood. The block I'm walking on, some of Franco's Moroccan troops had made it this far through Republican lines, only to be shot down one by one as they ran toward Plaza España. The Morocs had uniforms that were very colorful—crimson-lined cloaks and red turbans. Their cloaks would rise and flow around them when they ran, as if they were strange wings, and to emphasize the illusion they screamed like hawks. I was trying to picture this scene when the young woman stopped me. It all happened so fast, I can't now recall exactly what she looked like. For some reason I remember the dog better.

That November, as the first winter of the war set in, it was cold, a winter that would turn out to be one of the worst ever recorded, and foggy. German planes came in the night. The soot caused by fires settled on everything, including the faces and clothes of the population, who walked around ashen and shadowy. There were one million people in town, it was much smaller than now, in area too, and apparently all concerned had a feeling of being easy prey.

Megan has a cold. She could hardly sleep for coughing last night, and I wasn't much better off listening to it. It is a bad cough, aggravated by her cigarette habit. She fires up her Dunhills no matter what. She's not alone. The entire town is hacking and sneezing. It's especially so in the mornings when the air is very cold and smells like gasoline.

I woke to rain tapping the windows, heavy dripping sounds from the building well. I didn't find it oppressive, as I sometimes do the rain, but rather pleasant instead. I had a notion that I might stay in bed all day and listen to it. But soon enough it stopped. Now it's raw and windy outside. The sun comes and goes, not too sure about things. It's snowing in the mountains. Winter's coming to town, perhaps on the afternoon train. Many people are wearing long, black coats and, heads bowed, walk along like crows hugging themselves.

I saw a fat woman on the street wielding a cane. You don't see many fat people here, and this one stood out, shook like jelly. She seemed to think she was a sailor, slowly tilting to one side, then the other, as she made her way. For some reason the men in green haven't been around for several days to clean the sidewalks and they are completely trashed, as if the circus had pulled up stakes recently. She waded through it, occasionally flicking a plastic bag or wine bottle aside with her cane. She wore a beautiful ring on her little finger, gold filigree and amethyst. I wanted to rip it off her hand, take it home to Megan as a gift. I often have such primitive desires and entertain thoughts which perhaps made more sense in the rain forest and savanna, or the Neander Valley. I know my dreams at night are not connected to the street I live on during the day. When I was younger, I often as not acted on these impulses and, conversely, it seemed important to me then to not do what I was told to. I could never, at the time, imagine why I was being accused of erratic behavior.

Tuesday, Megan has a night class, so I went walking, down into the briar patches along Gran Vía. The whores you see there at noon are some of the most ghastly in Europe. But the quality, at least that evening, had picked up sharply. I developed a thirst passing one of these damsels. I was looking for a drink and came upon a bar just then, not difficult to do in Madrid, a town seemingly built to an alcoholic's blueprint.

The bar had a show. A young couple making love on what resembled a large revolving dinner plate. They were very athletic. I'd never really viewed so much as that in public and thought momentarily to be in ancient Rome or Gomorrah. They had an admirable endurance, too. Watching them, it crossed my mind that I am certainly not the man I used to be—but then, who is. The woman had some large equipment all around. I've seen her on the street before. There is so much to contend with, she can barely walk right. The fella wore a black ball cap, inscribed with the name Real Madrid, and yawned a number of times during the performance. He must have lacked sleep, as the work did not seem to be of the boring variety. When the show was over, he tipped his cap to the crowd like a sports idol. What a great way to make a living I thought. If I were younger, I might try for an apprenticeship in the trade.

18 November Thursday—A bright, cold, windy day, the sky cobalt blue.

I asked Megan, How'd we happen to run out of money?

You don't remember the party?

What party?

The one this summer that lasted 55 days.

Oh, I said. That.

We had visitors from the 19th of May until the end of Pamplona in mid-July.

You know how I feel about calling Aunt Sylvia, I said.

You'll need to start drinking that pig wine if you don't, she said.

She's referring to wine from a bodega a couple streets over. You take your empty bottles in, and they refill them. The wine is from Toledo, not exactly famous wine country. 125 pesetas a liter. The dollar is at 161 pesetas today, so it's quite inexpensive. They keep the wine in pigskins, a whole pig turned inside out with a tap where the snout used to be. There are three of these. At the beginning of the week, they resemble pig balloons. By Saturday afternoon, they look like roadkill. The hairy side within is covered with pitch, and the wine carries a taste of it.

That makes my stomach hurt, I said.

I know it, she said. So why don't you just go ahead call and get it over with?

I noticed then that she had narrowed her eyes, squinting at me. This is Megan's idea of a hard look.

Would you stop that, please, I said. You're frightening me.

She was about to leave for school. She's wearing thermal underwear plus a sweatshirt under her clothes, heavy wool socks. She puts on her black leather jacket, scarf around her neck, gloves. She never wears a hat. Her hair is caught up carelessly on one side with a turtle shell barrette.

At the door she says, By the way … what are we having for dinner?

I thought we'd go organic, I said. Some nice lentils and bulgar wheat.

She raised her eyebrows an eighth of an inch, duly impressed.

Call, she says. Or that's the kinda shit we'll be eating. Our fall from luxury to hardship won't take long … stop laughing, Lucas. I'm not jokin'. Then she kissed my cheek, went out the door and closed it.

Luxury? I glance around the apartment but quickly exhaust its delights.

The Spanish have a custom of kissing on both cheeks when they greet or depart from one another. I think it kind of the beauties in Madrid to let this mug of mine that close. And there are many beauties here. Yet I feel funny at times kissing women I've never seen before, don't know in the least. I come from a society that shakes hands and from a family in particular where no one touched.

The old man especially. I have no memory of him ever having touched me, in anger or love. Dad's gone now, and I don't want to talk about him in a bad way, but still, I never saw him kiss my mother. Never once caught them holding hands, nothing. They had me, and he was married before and I have a half-brother ten years older from that union; so he was doing something when no one was looking. Members of my family hug each other about once a decade, at weddings or funerals, usually accompanied by an involuntary shudder. So though I find this Spanish custom charming, it's not something that I'm used to.

This is all leading up to an incident that happened last evening. Kevin Ray came over to the apartment. He's looking to buy a new laptop, and there's a computer store near us that has decent prices. Megan is computer savvy, and he just wanted a little help. It's easier to do things here when you have someone with you. His full name is Kevin Ray, and when addressing him, you tend to do so with both names.

Kevin Ray, I asked him, what were you up to this weekend?

I got besotted.

But you maintained your dignity?

Not in the least, he answered.

Anyway, I went with them, and we looked at laptops. They're much more expensive than I had it. I can't use them; my hands seem too big for the keyboard. The machine I use isn't hooked up to the net, no email; it's just an extremely functional typewriter to me.

It was dark when we came back out on the street. We started

walking but only made it to the next building, a shop where they sell and work on motorcycles. Kevin Ray and Megan stopped, talking about computers on the sidewalk near the curb. And I got to looking in the showroom window at a Harley.

I guess a couple, three minutes went by when I heard some fella behind me in a loud, jovial greeting, and saw in the window that he's hugging and kissing Megan. Seems like he's had some drinks. He's overdoing it certainly to my way of looking at it. He's probably mid-40's, too much Brylcreem, slick clothes, one of those Madrileños looks like his mother still dresses him. I take all this in in a matter of seconds and have a scientific question come to mind I think maybe he can help me with. It went like this: If I slap my two hands together just brutally as I can on his ears, will an eardrum blow, or will it just stun the fuck? And I turned toward him to try and solve it.

Just then, Kevin Ray saw me getting set to put on a rush, divines that something nasty is coming—he said later the look on my face was one like that I had been talking to animals—catches my eye and shakes his head in the negative, slight as can be. As if to say, You don't want to do that. And I turned at a right angle, walked up the way some. Perhaps 25 seconds had gone by, from the beginning to the end of it, when I turned away, but I took many things into consideration and thought with some precision, even gave myself a little advice—stay cool—which I rejected, so that it seemed as if some real time had elapsed. I carry a knife in my back pocket, good Toledo steel that sharpens well. But I didn't consider using it. I wanted to hurt the asshole in the most ancient manner; I wanted to get my hands on him.

Afterwards, Megan mentioned in passing the guy is the Jefe de Estudios of her department at school. He's sort of like a dean, she explained. I'm not real sure what a dean is either.

19 November Friday

I feel out of sorts today. I'm thinking about the call to my aunt, about the dentist. I'm trying to comprehend the vagaries of house dust. It's cold now, the windows are closed, and against all logic the dust has increased. We have little tumbleweeds of it rolling about. I set a trap for the mouse but somehow only managed to catch his tail. This was four, five days ago, and I hadn't seen him since. Today as I'm reading the paper, he comes over and sits close by me. He has a bobtail now. By the way he looks at me, I take it he's none too pleased. I go to the kitchen and make a big production of throwing away the trap. Then I gave him a piece of cheese, which he scurried away with. I'll tell you … I lose my way with this kind of shit on my mind. The only mail I received this week was a professionally done Nazi propaganda tract from Brazil. It was printed in Spanish and sent to our address, to one Tomás el Bueno, who lived here sometime in the past, one of our landlady's relatives. It told me all I wanted to know about Rudolph Hess, some glossy photos included.

20 November

Megan and I go to the big market every Saturday. It's a couple blocks away.

I thought we were out of money, I said.

I have money for the market.

Where'd you get it?

I pulled it out of my ass, she says. Now come on, 'fore it gets too crowded.

We buy our meat from a butcher named Maximo Suárez. He does his work on an antique chopping block, a large segment of log stood upright. He has the best salchichas. To Vincent Fosi's Mariscos y Pescados for some trout. To another shop, Huevos y Cava to buy chicken and eggs. Two people work this shop, a mother and son. Watching them, I begin to wonder if there are any psychic consequences to chopping off chicken heads and throwing them over your shoulder every Saturday morning of your life. I enjoy looking at all the fruit and vegetables, the mass of color. I like watching men cleaning fish for some reason, perhaps because I am good at it myself. There are two stories to this market, 50-60 tiny shops. There are cheese shops, sausage, ham, olive. Many bakery goods, sweets. Neruda:

All
was loud voices, salt of the marketplaces,
heaps of throbbing bread,
markets of my Argüelles quarter with its statue
like a pale inkwell among the merluza:
the olive oil reached the ladles,
a deep beat
of feet and hands filled the streets,
meters, liters, sharp
essence of life,
           fished stacked up,
the nature of cold sunny rooftops
upon which the weathervane
exhausts itself,
fine ivory of the potatoes
and row upon row of tomatoes
reaching to the sea ...

Sunday morning I woke thinking about my father. I'd been dreaming of him and lost the dream and the exact memory of it when I opened my eyes. I am at a certain age where I'm getting to be haunted by those I've lost. Mainly, I believe, because there are just so many of them. Those who loved me since the very day I was born. They're irreplaceable. A good part of this population has moved away, and the past decade took a big share. I'm good at disguising my emotions, at setting them aside, but they go on nonetheless down below like a negative charge. Those who are gone now remain close by, sometimes more so than when they were alive.

I worked at my father's liquor store off and on through the years I was in high school, and after that I just sort of parked it there awhile for the comfort it gave me. When he saw that I'd be staying on, he began teaching me how to run the place—to order and inventory and handle the salesmen and help and do the books and how to cook them to take the bite from his taxes. And then he more or less started taking it easy.

He'd come by every afternoon to take the deposit bag to the bank. He liked to flirt with the young tellers at the bank, and the money was the only thing that ever interested him about the liquor business. He didn't even drink. He didn't much care for dealing with customers. He knew every drunk in the area on a first name basis, but it was a fact they bragged on, not him. He didn't really like people in general. He was not comfortable in their society, and it's one trait he seems to have passed along to me.

I'd never thought of him as having an artistic side, except that he was creative in generating cash. He was very good at that, and it's not something necessarily communicated in genes; at least it did not come down my way. But what he did after he stopped working surprised everyone in the family.

Dad took up sewing.

He bought a Singer sewing machine, and he got my Aunt Jim to show him how to work it. Then he redid all the furniture in the house. He recovered everything in sight. When you'd go over there, you'd see all this had been done and comment on it and he'd comment on it, but he never once said who did the work. Aunt Jim and Uncle Harlen knew what was going on, but it was one of those times when I didn't see them much; and Mom knew, obviously, but she kept quiet, probably not knowing what to make of it herself. You would have had to know him to understand this. Because he was hard around the edges, a gruff old Florida cracker. He carried a Beretta .25 in his pocket, and he didn't need to. Just by looking at him, if you had any sense at all you'd know he was not someone to be crossed. But to get back to what I was saying, after he mastered sewing large items, he began doing what he was heading for. First off, he practiced building dollhouses. He was a good carpenter, and he made some fine little houses for the neighborhood kids. But then he made one for himself.

It was a masterpiece. It had two stories. It was clearly a replica of grandma's house in miniature. And he made little furniture for it. And he bought some little people at the dollar store in Dade City. And he started sewing tiny dresses and suits for them. It was at this time that he owned up to what he was doing, he was proud of what he had learned and accomplished really, and suddenly started showing these little dresses and shirts and pants to anyone who visited the house. To see him seated before a sewing machine smoking a cigar and at work on this tiny wardrobe and all, his sleeves rolled up and forearms sculpted like driftwood … it was more than hard to believe. It was a shock.

The clothes he made were not modern. They were styles from the turn of the century and on up through the 1920s and 30s. There were eventually quite a number of small people in the dollhouse, and I got to wondering if they weren't significant in some way. He was not the sort of man, however, you would ask that question. But after awhile I began recognizing some of them, the young Mexican kid mowing the lawn for example, and to understand that they represented actual people he'd known when he was young and, by the sheer number of them, perhaps everyone who populated his life back then.

Over a period of two years, the house filled up completely, and the little people had to start sitting on the front porch and the like, because inside they were getting in each other's way. The only room that wasn't packed was the kitchen. There were only three figures in the kitchen, a woman and two young boys sitting at the table, and an empty chair, which I took to be my grandfather's.

20 November
from the *International Herald Tribune*
Court Is Asked to Rule on Felipe Gonzalez

MADRID—A Spanish judge asked the Supreme Court on Friday to decide whether there was sufficient evidence to charge former Prime Minister Felipe Gonzalez with involvement in a 'dirty war' against Basque separatists in the 1980's.

Judge Baltasar Garzon, who has gained international fame for seeking the prosecution of the former Chilean dictator, Augusto Pinochet, asked the court to determine whether declassified security documents implicated Mr.

Gonzalez in the covert campaign.

Mr. Gonzalez has maintained his innocence and has never faced formal charges, but allegations of state-run death squads helped bring down his Socialist government in 1996.

Judge Garzon's move stems from his investigation of the 1983 murder of a Basque waiter in Bayonne, France. It has been linked to a wave of killings alleged to have been orchestrated by senior members of the Gonzalez government. Former security officials have accused Mr. Gonzalez of being the mastermind behind the Anti-Terrorist Liberation Groups, which opposed Basque separatism.

Sunday afternoon, Chelo came up from Lavapiés, Kevin Ray from the Toledo Glorieta, where he's rooming with a gay couple, Emilie from her apartment in Cuatro Caminos, which she shares with another American girl, a lunatic named June, Megan and I from our quarter, and we all met around 2 for lunch at La Taberna del Principe in Plaza Santa Ana. It's one of the few places in town that has good salads. We split three smoked chicken salads, as they are large portions, and three bottles of house wine, a rioja with no label. We sat at a table by a window and watched the crowd all bundled up and shivering moving along the streets. People with scarves covering their noses and mouths, like the town was full of bandits. It was cold as I recall it being in Madrid during the day. This was the first time Chelo had met Emilie, and he was quite struck by her beauty. She seems little conscious of existing in the eyes of men, however, and paid him no mind.

23 November Tuesday
from the *International Herald Tribune*
Europe Surprised by Early Winter
Some 240 Spanish villages were cut off Monday after freak snowfalls over the weekend, with mountainous central

and northern areas hit worst. Rare snow fell in Barcelona on the Mediterranean coast and normally arid southern region of Almeria.

Since my calendar says it is full moon, I go to the balcony several times throughout the night to take a look, but cannot find it. The sky is an unusual dark violet. Now I don't want you to think I'm a peeping tom or anything, but at midnight I went to the window and looked across the street, being a creature of habit, and was caught by the bright lights there once again. I'd hardly noticed my neighbor this past month. I think she was away a good part of it. But now she and her boyfriend are on the couch in the living room. Her boyfriend is lying on his back and she riding on top of him. The couch is navy blue, and it strikes me that she is on a small boat tossed about by violent water. I can barely see the boyfriend. He is somewhat lost in the cushions. He raises and lowers one arm occasionally like a drowning victim.

Someone answers the phone.
Sylvia Bowles, please, I say.
Luke … is that you?
Hey, Garret. How's it going?
Very well. Extremely well.
How's Sylvie?
She, at the moment, has a mud pack on her face. Very exotic looking. It appears to be green clay and renders her somewhat alien in appearance. And she's not supposed to talk or it will crack. She has just handed me a note, informing me I should say that.
She's there, I say. I take it Garret can sense my disappointment. It's the first time I've had to call her since we've been in Madrid. I was hoping to just leave a message.
She's right across the card table from me. We're working through a bridge problem.
I guess I need to talk to her, Garret.
How unfortunate for you …

Hi, Honey, Aunt Sylvia says.

Hey, Sylvie. How are you?

Dreadful, I'm afraid. I have purchased a bridge computer. I am moving into the modern age, you see. This program is supposed to be easy to use. However, I have found it vexatious, to say the least. Also, if you don't play perfectly, you lose to the damn thing. We have resorted to working by hand at the moment. Are you calling from Madrid?

Yes, I answer.

Do you like it there? Is it quaint?

I wouldn't call it quaint, no.

I somehow picture it quaint and labyrinthine.

She'll go on like this all night if I let her. Before I can get in another word, however—

What about the natives? Are they white?

She stopped smoking awhile back, but sixty-five years of cigarettes have turned her voice masculine.

How are the saloons, dear? she continues. I know you favor saloons.

The saloons are quite good, I say.

Are you working? she asks. You're … in the diplomatic service? No. No, of course not. You are a member of the leisure class, as I recall.

I note your sarcasm is still intact, Sylvie.

She laughs.

Where would I be without that? I must say I need it around here. Garret is about to retire and has become insufferable. Whenever I cross his shadow now, he wants to charge me for the shade.

I start to speak but—

What *are* you doing there? I hope nothing illegal. You aren't are you—like before? I kept having visions of you going to prison then, and … I don't think you would do well incarcerated, dear … the way you drink … having to steal sugar from the prison pantry and concocting some horrid fruit-based wine in the toilet bowl … what do they call that? Jailhouse juleps, or … raisin bounce, Garret says

… and you would then have to share it with God knows what sort of vicious and enormously fat cell mates with those appalling tattoos.

I'm working on a book, I say.

You don't want to sell it to me I hope. I still own the rights to your poetry, don't forget. The collection you immediately ceased work on the moment I bought it?

Look, Sylvie, I say, I need to cut to the chase here.

I had fears of that.

A grave pause follows.

Luke … do you remember when you used to read aloud to me? Those were pleasant times. You had such good manners then.

This was when I was ten or eleven.

I would give you a 50 cent piece, and you'd be quite pleased.

I need a bit more now, I said.

No response. It's like the phone went dead. I hand it to Megan, and the two of them talked for half an hour.

A repairman came to the apartment today and fixed our washing machine. Apparently it was fouled by toothpicks I had left in my shirt pockets. The repairman spoke no English, I my wretched Spanish. These encounters are slightly hilarious. Many hand signals. The hands knowing an older language. But things get accomplished. He knew what he was doing, more or less, and I had cash, the main ingredient. At one point the guy left to get a part. It's not going to be too expensive he said. Turned out to be about 90 bucks, which I know I could find better use for. He had on a sweater and tie, looked very civil, and smelled like a goat. He told me several times the plumbing under the sink was bad. I'm not sure why he's telling me this, but after he departs I turn on the water, and, of course, now there's a leak. I solved this with a green bucket.

This narration I note is at 60-some pages. It is certainly progressing at a leisurely pace. As usual, in whatever I write, I have no idea what's going on exactly. This doesn't concern me. I would surrender it altogether to reverie and musing. There are now some characters, however, wishing to enter who are coming on their own.

I don't know them personally, that is to say. They are arriving like uninvited guests. I politely introduce myself.

25 November Thursday

I am in Café of Our Virgin of the Stars. I like to come here whenever I get some money together and spend the afternoon. I order shrimp al ajillo. I have that and bread and a bottle of rioja.

There are tiny red peppers in the garlic sauce and they heat you up, needed on this cold, rainy day. I always sit at the same place, on the second story by a window. There's a table and a single chair, and I can see the street below. The lighting is dim away from the windows. The waiter who takes care of the second floor has a gold tooth and a voice like a bull gator. He worked in Mallorca when he was young and knows some English. There are four old guys who play cards by another window—the same ones every time I'm here, as if they never leave the premises. Cigar smoke and odor of spilt wine about them, and sometimes, say one of them has to use the bathroom, the waiter will sit in a hand for him. Other people come and go, but not many, as most of the business takes place on the first floor, where there's a tapas bar. So these are my surroundings, and this how I write sometimes—I start with a little celebration in the solitude of a good afternoon bar, a celebration without purpose or explanation exactly, and I wait to see what happens.

This is Thanksgiving Day, an ordinary Thursday in Madrid. By my grandfather's watch, it's 3:00. Earlier I had walked in the park, the gingko trees in full, butter-yellow display, through fallen leaves, the streambed yellow and red with them.

It is the same pocket watch my grandfather was carrying on a day in 1917 when he was killed in an industrial accident at the Tampa shipyards. He was a pipe fitter. A hot water main exploded on him in a small room—a man I never met but think about every time I am burned by water. My father was two years old then, and my uncle Harlen was one. My grandmother Tillie was 23, and the news of his death all but killed her, too. But she lived 60 more years, never remarried.

Harlen, who had no children of his own, gave me the watch. He's gone now, too, not so long ago. He was a truck driver. He lived 87 years, most of this bloody century, stayed a gentle man. He was the last link to the old people of my father's clan. The watch is gold and engraved on the back, a beautiful design I can't describe exactly. Say it is the wind, if you could see the wind, on a turbulent day. I must hand-wind it every day. It never loses time. I will have it in my pocket when I go away.

A decade ago now, in this decade when my old people left, my father had a heart attack in his car on the outskirts of Tampa on I-75. His given name was Melrose, which was also my grandfather's, but I never heard anyone call him that. He went by Junior his entire life. I suspect he was in the slow lane and observing the speed limit. He had time to hit the brakes, saving my mother in the process, as she was with him. But that was his last act. The car floundered off the highway, and he was gone forever.

He grew up in our town when the town still had wooden sidewalks and horse-drawn wagons on the streets. That he died on a super highway in a machine he never thought too much of in an age that was always a bit foreign to him, he would take ironically I know. He passed on April Fool's Day. The men in my family make a habit of dying in the spring. They never do so during football season. He was a good man, by any standard, though we did not always see eye to eye. He knew how to make money. He lived frugally. He did nothing in excess.

When I turned 30, at noon I threw up at work into a wastebasket, left, and went to the nearest bar. Soon afterwards, I started thinking about death in my spare time. Some reckoning of my time here was taking place; I knew something irreparable had occurred. It bothered me for a good long while. Now all that too has passed. It was just I had discovered that time is quicker than I thought.

I never went back to work, not the nine-to-five variety. It had never gotten me anywhere. And I've been in one bar or another ever since but, truly, I don't think any the less of myself for it. I am an atavism in my family, harking back to the railroad men and hell-raisers in the early part of this century that is almost gone now. And in many respects, I can never be my father, or close to the man that he was.

Walking here today from the park I regarded myself in the store windows as if I were someone else. They say a man can tell he's getting old when he starts to look like his father. I see him now in the window of Café of Our Virgin of the Stars.

By this oddity of light and reflection, he is sitting near by me again. He is not saying anything, as was his way. There is the sadness of the rain in this, the demolition from son to father, in the last days of the fall.

26 November

If you walk on the sunny side of the street now it is still autumn. In the shade it is winter. I went down past Montaña to a small park just north of the palace called Jardines de Sabatini. It is laid out in hedgerows with fountains and statues here and there. On one of the statues, I notice a horse has a broken leg. And a spray-paint artist had turned its hooves baby blue, and another brushed in an eye patch and fancy black mustache on its rider.

There are cats living in the park. I'll have to save my meat scraps for them. I need to work on my saintliness, having neglected it lately. I crossed underneath the bridge to Plaza España. I saw a decent looking, at least from afar, winter coat lying on the steps. I went over to check out its size. Somebody had taken a dump on it, however. I strolled through the plaza observing the olive trees around the Cervantes Monument, the statues of Don Quixote and Sancho Panza. Several teenagers were sitting under Panza's ass smoking hashish. I saw, taking the sun, the bag lady that recently has been sleeping in our stairwell at night. She was nodding on a bench, her face as heavily painted as a clown's. She must have found some cosmetics in the trash. She had her hair in a ponytail and looked sorry in the light of day, like a sullen and broken-down show girl from a production that had closed decades past.

She was a gift from Chelo. When he moved to the flat in Lavapiés, she was already established in his building. He would find her asleep in the mornings on the stairwell, on the landing where the stairs turned, surrounded by various ratty belongings scavenged from dumpsters. She is partial to calimocho, a mix of red box wine and Coca Cola, and tends to throw empty boxes and cans down the stairs when she's done with them. Chelo made her angry one night because he wouldn't give her a light for her cigarette when she knocked at 4 a.m. Fuego! she screamed for a good while afterwards and in retribution started pissing in front of his door. He wrote down our address and told her our building was much warmer, that we were expecting her, ask for Luke, he said, and gave her a five hundred peseta coin to move on, which, for some reason, she actually did. Chelo found humor in all this. She opened her eyes as I walked by but, of course, did not recognize me. I have disconnected our buzzer so she can no longer pretend that I am the desk clerk at her chosen hotel.

Don Quixote was a mad but saintly fictional character who roamed 15th century Spain, turning inns to castles, windmills into giants. As he passed by, he tried to let people believe momentarily that their lives were something more than that which was strewn so roughly about them. He was rewarded with ridicule and, almost nightly, a good beating, but it didn't stop him. He was looking for adventure, a thing you must go far out of your way to find, it seems, and often out of your mind. I am curious to know if, somehow brought to life from the book and even wearing his outrageous costume around Madrid today, anyone would bother to notice him.

Last night, I set about to fix my walking shoes. The soles were peeling off at the front. I had purchased some Superglue. I glued the soles and propped the shoes against a large book, so that the glued part would get some pressure against the wood flooring. This morning I went to take a look at them, and they are stuck to the floor. I removed the book and now have two black shoes, toes down, as if some loutish invisible ballerina was holding at point there, free-standing in the living room. Shortly thereafter I attempted to make some soup for Megan, who now seems to be hovering near death with cold and flu. I stood close by the stove to keep warm. As I added ingredients, I began to detect a strange odor. I kept wondering what it could be and noticed at last that my shirttail was smoldering. I mean to leave the shoes awhile, just to recall the folly of which I am capable.

29 November

There was much news on TV today about the Basque separatist group ETA, which announced an end to their self-imposed cease-fire, which lasted 14 months. They cited several reasons, not the least among them the Spanish government's arrest of Belen Gonzalez, a negotiator at the May peace conference between the two sides. ETA warned that armed attacks could resume after December 3rd. It has been a thirty-year, low-grade war, some 800 dead, but persistent— this cease-fire the longest period of calm during the conflict.

ETA, whose initials stand for Basque Homeland and Liberty, insists on self-rule for the region, where 2.1 million people live. But Prime Minister Aznar seems to have little but contempt for the rebels. You can see it on his face when he speaks of them. It is a contempt hard learned. They tried to take him out with a car-bomb five years ago.

I received in the mail a note from Owen Wolf, a biker friend from San Ann. He promises a long letter soon. This will not happen until after hunting season I suspect. I'd asked him to check in on my mother from time to time. She's not doing well, he says. She has a housekeeper, but when she comes, Mom has the girl out driving her around doing errands, going to the bars for lunch. No cleaning gets done, Wolf says, and my mother is living in filth. In the note he mentioned that he was the one who gave the young lady my address—the young lady, you may recall, whose curious letter began this narrative. She came into Red Fred's bar one night asking if anyone knew Luke Gatins. Everyone there knew me, but nobody said a thing, as they were all too busy looking at her body. About what

Goya's Head

might this concern? Wolf asked her finally. The Wolf was slightly distressed that she gave him nothing in return for his information. I left the note on my desk where Megan happened upon it.

Who's Owen talking about? she said. What letter?

I forgot I hadn't shown her that. So I had to go find the letter, as Megan knows I never throw anything away, and then she read it carefully.

I don't understand why she wrote to you, she said. She's not coming for a visit I hope.

I don't … I barely remember her …

I feel my nose elongating a bit.

The girl wants to rub her face on a bunch of cocks? Where do you find these people?

I can't even remember what she looks like, I said. The memory of her breasts, which were quite spectacular, is poking me in the arm as I speak. But there is truth in my comment. I really can't recall her features well. She had blonde hair …

She comes to Madrid, the bitch is *not* staying here, Megan said.

She's just watching out for me, I know, as I do her, but after this conversation we don't have much to say to each other for several days. There's a chill factor in it, this coldness between us. Since it happens so seldom, it feels worse.

Just hearing from Wolf, I have a sudden urge to scrap Madrid and go home to my dogs, hunting season, football, America. Wolf is taking care of my two dogs, simply added them to his pack. After a number of bloodbaths they've sorted it out. Later, when Megan starts talking to me again, she'll remind me that what I'm feeling is simply culture shock, which we experience from time to time. That's one way of looking at it. As the week goes on, I continue to feel somewhat goofy, nonetheless, and can't seem to shake it. The last few days, once again, I've had to force myself to go outside. Perhaps some of it has to do with the dental appointment she has made for me. I go in Friday at 6 to a place called the Anglo-American Medical Unit. I've not been to this dentist before. The last one apparently left town.

And this … I fancied naming it *The Diary of a Nobody* but recall that title had already been used, about a hundred years ago. I'm a bit late as usual. But it has dawned on me that there is really not much to it, at least so far. I simply throw everything into the yaw. There is no design. No complication, climax, denouement. Nor do I really have much to say, nothing that one might want to read, unless perhaps, any number of years down the road, a curious scholar with say a drug problem might want to know of one man's raving at the turn of the century. Is that its purpose? If you are that person, reading this in what I would call the future, especially if in doing so you appear to be staring down some dark tunnel, mark my words: As I once was, you are today. Otherwise, believe me, I don't know that I'm saying anything here.

I make a vow to myself. What I don't say from now on, I at least want to put it well.

It is right now a quarter till two in the afternoon, the last day of November. The sky outside is a beautiful dark blue and a rare slant of sunlight has made its way to my hands as I type. It is not direct sun but a reflection off a window across the street. I have already consumed a bottle of wine, Vega de la Reina, '94, from Valladolid. It's a good table wine, though I'd forgotten to set the table with anything to eat. And I must now make myself leave the apartment. I need cigars. Cigarettes. More wine. Some milk for coffee.

I wait until the last minute, then hustle down to the tabac shop before it closes. I go to the market around the corner that stays open all afternoon and find some cheap wine. I select a big bottle. My brand of coffee is on sale. A bag of that. A box of milk. Some Manchego cheese. Fat green olives. By this time I'm getting a little jangled. I ought to get back to the apartment I think. Maybe close the blinds, get under the covers. There are three checkout lines. I pick one that seems to be moving the fastest. However, just to have something to occupy my thoughts, I mark the spot where I would have been in each line. I note the person in front of me had I chosen that line. The line I'm in immediately turns to stone. I'm in with a group of statues. Those people I had marked, of course, depart the store in rapid order.

I have been slightly deranged all my life. I have two personalities, which at times cross with bewildering celerity. I myself am no more than an observer in the dressing room on these occasions. At odd moments they actually square off. One is a hermit and the other cannot be reined in. Of the hermit I will say this: If there was ever a person you might like to stay in for awhile to hide from the world, he makes for good lodging. Of the other, I don't want to mention a thing—it might rile him. Either can be tipped toward immoderation as though a large ninepin; it is the only trait they have in common. I think my soul is shaped queerly, out of plumb.

I went to a shrink years ago in Tampa. I'd go see him once a week, and we would talk for an hour. He was very stiff. He seemed almost starched. His tie knotted tightly about his neck. He was more off than myself, I thought, literally freezing up. I feared he might go catatonic on me some day during a visit, so I tried to keep the conversation lively.

He was very keen on my sexual escapades. Let's go back over _____, he'd say, and your relationship with her. The one with the tattoo on her ... well, do you recall the one I'm speaking of? Usually when he spoke, he'd only give me a profile. When he asked such a question as this, I'd be looking at the back of his head. If nothing interesting had happened since the last visit, I'd just make shit up. He gave me a script for blue Valium. This colored all my responses. There were times that I imagined myself in bad shape, but mostly it was a ruse. You can get hooked on Valium pretty hard. It becomes one of the necessities in life. There was a guy always had the meeting after mine. When I was signing in one day I happened to glance at his folder, which was open on the desk. I recognized the doctor's writing on a note: *Patient thinks he has a radio up his nose*. And I understood then I was just light entertainment before the loons arrived.

2 December Thursday

A day can make a difference. This morning I took the Metro to Atocha to a health store, Herbolario, at Santa María de la Cabeza 3, to purchase St. John's Wort for my winter numbness. An American woman named Nancy and her Spanish husband run the place, and I enjoy talking with her. I pay no attention at all to my health during the summer, but in the winter I turn into a hypochondriac. The only wort they had in stock was a large bottle, 8 thousand pesetas. The dollar is at 165 pesetas today, the highest it has ever been during our stay here. Still, I'm put off by the price … but have little choice. I've spent the past two days in a brain cloud. Tuesday I wrote three new sentences. Sometime later I noticed that one of these was simply moronic, the kind of horse shit that makes you want to do yourself in as soon as possible. Then yesterday, nothing at all. I lost all purpose and only sat in my chair throwing an occasional blank look to the walls or, for a change of pace, I would eat. Between trips to decimate the icebox I returned to the chair and my repose. I don't run the heater when Megan is at school, and I sat in the chair dressed as if riding a ski lift. I ate an entire baguette. I scooped out the soft bread inside and filled the crust with mashed black olives. I would, from time to time, run through the TV channels to see what was on. Spanish TV is dreadful, all three channels of it, the afternoon programming especially so. The commercials, though, can be of interest. They don't have anything against nudity here.

There's a holiday sweet called turrón the markets are stocking now. They are from the Middle Ages, brought by Arab invaders. They are made of sugar, wild honey, eggs, almonds. The most popular are the classic duro and soft blando, but there are many varieties, including chocolate. They come in slabs. Megan had purchased a Turrón Tarta de Limon, sort of a compressed lemon pie. Since there was nothing else left, I ate the entire thing and washed it down with a quart of beer. The quart was all I drank that day, but for some reason it turned me into a stumble bum. I was reeling around the apartment. In this condition I put out a little end piece of bread on the balcony for the sparrows to eat. However, a pigeon soon found it. I ran the pigeon off. I wrote on a small piece of paper For Sparrows Only! And set it by the bread. Back in my chair, I thought—You're scaring me here, Luke.

Anyway, I bought the St. John's Wort and walked over to the Atocha train station and took in the rainforest there. It's aerated overhead with fine steam, the only place in town with any humidity, and warm, though the palms looked ragged, too cold for them at the moment or not enough sun.

Then I wandered over to the corner of the Botanical Garden to get a paper and headed up Calle Claudio Moyano, the street on the hill with little outdoor book stalls, called bouquinistas. Usually there's not much in English, romances with the front covers torn off and the like, but this day there was a whole load at one stall of old Signet and Penguin classics from the 40s and 50s. I didn't have much money left but bought one, *Gulf Coast Stories*, by Erskine Caldwell, published by PAN books, and another called *Memoirs of a Midget* by Walter de la Mare. These books don't look to have been read before or even touched too much. So that was a find, I started to feel better, and then the sun came out.

I walked up the street to Retiro and entered the park at the southwest corner. The horse chestnuts are most prevalent here, their leaves rust-yellow now, some with a bit of green still in them, and half fallen already. A nice little breeze at work. I went to the big waterfall on the hill that has a feeling of North Carolina to it, surrounded by laurel, listened to the sound of it. I walked north, the dirt paths covered in leaves, my feet shuffling through them. Then the breeze picked up, the leaves rustling along the path creating a descant to the sigh of the wind in the branches. The air smells better in the park, cleaner. Buckeyes on the path. A girl jogged by with purple hair. The voices of birds and children. The white, black-and-brown spotted feral cat that lives in this part had upset a magpie. I went to the sculptured garden at the Puerto de Felipe IV entrance, across from the Cason del Buen Retiro. The laurel trees had been trimmed there recently and the smell of bay leaf in the air. I sat on a bench in the sun near the old cypress tree that was planted in 1633 and read the paper, and after awhile I had to take off my coat and cap.

This area, usually full of people, today was quiet, all but like a painting in its stillness. The guy on the bench near me was sleeping, and sparrows hopped up beside him playing a game among themselves—see how close we can get to the wino. My eyes felt weak; they hadn't been in that much light for so long. A green woodpecker on the lawn, its body just green as a parrot and a red head. Ornamental cabbage planted in the flower beds. Earlier, I'd spotted one of the big red squirrels that inhabit the park, down by the Crystal Palace. There is a purple cast to their undercoat. They're fairly psychedelic, as squirrels go. There does not seem to be many of them left. To see one is rare.

I left finally and crossed the six-lane street and headed downhill between the Army Museum and the very old two-spired church, down to the Prado on my left and the Hotel Ritz on my right. I went down the steps to the Prado and lit a cigarette beneath Goya's statue and had a few words with the old boy. A pregnant woman stopped nearby and adjusted her clothes for comfort. I think of Goya's wife, Josefa, nicknamed Pepa, who became pregnant 20 times. She bore seven children. Only one, Javier, made it to adulthood. Otherwise, little is known of her. She and Goya were teenage friends in Zaragosa. In his letters, Goya speaks of her with affection, but he did not write many letters and doesn't mention her often. They were married 39 years until her death in 1812. He did two portraits of her, which are now in the Prado. In the 1801 likeness, she has golden-red hair and fine, large eyes. You get the sense that she might have been pretty when she was young. There is the hint of a smile on her thin lips. In the 1805 portrait, she looks coarse and used up. She spent the last twenty years of her life with a husband stone deaf, who was a close friend to several of the wealthiest beauties of the age, obviously in love with one of these, the Duchess of Alba, and who spent a good amount of time with the prostitutes he used as models. There is no record of what Pepa thought of all this. She may not have been able to read or write.

I crossed the street and went up Calle Cervantes, to the Basílica de Jesús de Medinaceli, where every Friday a crowd queues up to the kiss the feet of a statue inside the church, the line stretching around the block and back down toward the Prado paseo. Across the street at Cervecería Cervantes I stop and have a shrimp tostada, which are very good there. Go down to the corner of Calle Lope de Vega to Taberna de la Dolores, have a caña, then up to Calle León and hang a left and on into Antón Martín and then downhill to Lavapiés looking for Chelo. On the way, I several times encountered Madrileños being kind to one another. What a fine, unusual day.

4 December
from the *Independent* (London)
Spanish hold vigils urging ETA not to break terror ceasefire
By Elisabeth Nash in Madrid

Thousands of Spaniards protested yesterday against the decision of the separatist organization ETA to end its 14-month ceasefire. Crowds gathered in town centers throughout the country to mark the end of the truce with five minutes of silence.

On the eve of a public holiday marking Spain's 1978 democratic constitution—which many Basques have never accepted—Spaniards waited, in fear and sadness, for the first new attack.

Those close to ETA's thinking are pessimistic. Julen de Madariaga is a founder of ETA who served long prison sentences and years of exile before becoming disenchanted with the means—though not the aims—of the organization.

'It claims to speak for the Basque people, but really it's cut off from Basque reality. Their leaders are clandestine, living abroad; it's hard enough for security reasons to meet their own comrades, let alone keep in touch with what ordinary Basques are thinking and feeling,' Mr. Madariaga said yesterday.

Madrid sees ETA as an enemy to be vanquished, not an opponent with whom eventually to reach a settlement.

Two ETA leaders arrested in recent months—Belen Gonzalez and Jokim Etxevarria—were the organization's contacts with government representatives. Mr. Gonzalez attended the one meeting held between the two sides. 'That was like shooting the soldier who emerges from the trench waving the white flag,' said Mr. Madariaga bitterly. 'It was a provocation.'

6 December

Spanish newspapers yesterday called for Lorenzo Sanz, the Real Madrid president, to resign after the team lost 5-1 to Zaragoza in Madrid Saturday night.

Sanz left at halftime with Madrid losing 3-0. The club said the president had to leave the stadium because of a stomachache.

Fans jeered their team, waved white handkerchiefs and, not politely, called for Sanz to step down. 500 fans surrounded the team bus after the match and pelted it with beer bottles. It was Real Madrid's worst home defeat in 25 years. The club has won only one of its last 12 league matches.

Soccer, which they call futball here, is to the Spanish the only game in town. They're sort of crazed about it. The Real Madrid stadium has over a hundred thousand seats, and it's always packed. Everyone else watches the matches on TV. When the hometeam scores a goal, the buildings along my street erupt in joy. That has not been happening so much of late.

9 December Thursday

We've just had another long puente holiday, and Megan got a five-day vacation. Monday celebrated Constitution Day and Wednesday the Immaculate Conception. That the entire country gets off for this fable I find amusing, but I don't guess it matters what you get free time for. It seemed also one of the very coldest days of the winter, 28 degrees when I awoke, and it didn't warm up much as the day progressed—blowing smoke out on the streets, walking fast like you've got somewhere to be, not even warm in the sun.

Megan and I went for lunch to a place called Parrilla Matador on Calle de la Cruz, between Santa Ana and Sol. The restaurant is on a second floor. We sat by a window and watched the crowds go shivering by. The Matador specializes in Cocido Madrileño. It's a rich soup broth, and when you finish with that, they bring you the items it was made with—cabbage, potato, blood sausage, a chunk of pot roast, chicken, a piece of salt pork, chorizo, and a whole lot of garbanzo beans. You get bread also, and we had a bottle of Coto rioja, one of the heavier riojas, and it was more food than I eat in a week.

I finished nearly half of mine, and it took me awhile, the plate about a foot around. And Megan kept sliding me portions of hers. Everyone there had the same dish. I watched in fascination as the Spanish downed the garbanzos as if attacking a rare delicacy and soon after were mopping their plates clean with bread, and then ordered desserts. There was not one fat person among them, none even remotely heavy as I, but these people can really eat and, of course, do so shouting at one another. As for garbanzos, I can eat one or two of this fine legume, but that's the limit, and I had visions of the rest of these diners perhaps exploding on the way home. One skinny old guy with a hard little pot belly walking about collecting empty plates had stenciled on the back of his T-shirt: SOY MATADOR. I'm the matador. We had coffee and then waddled home.

10 December Friday

Much too cold. Toast and a pint of Pedigree Bitter for breakfast. I've also had four cups of coffee already this morning and feel somewhat rattled. It's said that Balzac consumed forty cups a day. I don't guess you needed to ask him what was shakin'.

Kevin Ray just called. He has found a restaurant he wants to try this Sunday, but we're taking our landlady out to lunch, so we'll put that off till the week after. This is Kevin Ray's third year in Madrid. He'd worked for several years in Japan, where he made good money, banked twenty grand. Megan found him in a department store on

Gran Vía one day while she was shopping for cosmetics, heard him speaking English to himself and struck up a conversation. The first talk I had with him when he came to the apartment, he said out of the blue, I'm queer, you know. And that he didn't much care for the term gay. During the week I'm mild-mannered Kevin Ray, he told us. On the weekends, someone entirely different ... I'm Queerboy!

I don't know. You just had to smile.

He's 30 years old but looks 19, tall, thin, with straw-colored hair and a sense of humor, a sign of intelligence to me. He's a gentle soul, and I've gotten quite fond of him. He and Chelo are working together, but Chelo shies away from him, not comfortable with his orientation. I have two outlooks on homosexuals. One is my redneck way of looking at things, the one I grew up with. The other tells me that if you can find affection in this hardshell world, no matter what direction it comes from, you should take it and count yourself lucky.

I mailed a letter to Owen Wolf. The Wolf was our first visitor this past spring. He's tall and wiry, his body elongated as an El Greco model, hair down to the middle of his back he keeps in a ponytail, beard gone gray-threaded now—dark glasses, jeans, motorcycle boots. Always a cigarette in his mouth. He stayed three weeks. The two of us went down to Gilbralter and Tarifa for awhile. We took the night train south to Algeciras. There were six bunks in our sleeper car, two tiers of three with a narrow aisle between them. Wolf and I had the two bottom bunks. The beds were like shallow coffins. Wolf said he felt like he was practicing his death.

The best area we found on The Rock was Land's End, Point Europa. It was the quietest place we encountered. We were surrounded by wildflowers there. You can see Africa across the straits. It was windy, almost chilly, but quiet there. I can't say that for the rest of Gilbralter. We went to Tarifa for a day, where the wind blows sideways. Put clothes out on a line there, they can get torn to shreds. Then back home by that brutal night train. Both ways it was Wolf and myself and four Morocs to a car. We got up early and left the sleeper and went to the club car to wait for the cook to show up and make coffee. We were looking at some Quixotic windmills on the meseta that morning, drinking coffee and smoking when three railroad undercover police, two men and a woman, introduced themselves, checked our passports and searched our bags. The cops like to stop Wolf. He looks always like he's out on parole.

I love the Wolf like a brother, but three weeks is a bit long to spend with him. He's mad, he never sleeps. He went through 80 thousand pesetas worth of hashish in that period and left town coughing like he had black lung. The railroad bulls looked through our things thoroughly that morning. Wolf told me later he had his hash in a boot. They missed it. He's dealt with cops for so long, he's calm around them.

He thought Madrid a loudass place, and rude. Out on the streets one day he said:

People look at me funny here.

They look at you like that at home, I said.

Letters are posted in a large, yellow mailbox on the street called a buzón. As I dropped Wolf's letter in the buzón, I suddenly realized that, over time, I have sent away my very best work in this way, in cards and letters, spread it over the world … that a work exists already in time and space like a textual hologram among the private minds that have read these. It would be nice to recover this, either physically—all but impossible—or imaginatively. Or, it has struck me, one device I might consider is that, as I wander around Madrid, I could write cards and letters and send them to myself. I would get more mail this way certainly.

A fascinating bit of information has come my way. If an ant gets so drunk as to pass out, it always falls to the right. This has occupied my thoughts for several hours and raises many questions—not about ants exactly that I can think of but rather about the folks who collect such data. But, getting back to the mail, we received a note from Daryl and Emma, friends from San Ann:

We have booked our flight to Amsterdam. MartinAir from

Orlando, a direct flight. Flight 632 to arrive in Amsterdam on Friday, March 24, 7:10 a.m. Depart on Saturday, April 1, 10:25 a.m. Hope you all can join us. Did you get our Christmas package?

Daryl and Emma were our last visitors this summer. We went to Pamplona with them. And let me interject, that's one hell of a party up there. Some people have so much fun there they die on the spot. Others wait till they get home to find out. From Pamplona we went to San Sebastián and Hondarribia in Basque country, St. Jean de Luz, Biarritz in France. The Amsterdam trip should be interesting. That last time there, I all but left on a gurney. We got the Christmas package last weekend. The presents were wrapped in the October 2nd, Sunday edition of the *Tampa Tribune*, which I read through. Only one item caught my interest, a 30-year-old unsolved abduction case. Two young women, 20 and 21 at the time, disappeared without a trace while on a scuba outing in the Ocala National Forest. A kid reported seeing them on a trail at Alexander Springs with *a man who parted his hair low on the side.*

I read my horoscope for that day, not this particular day, but so what. It said: Find something to believe in. It will give you an anchor to hold on to when changes blow through your life.

I thought about that a good while. What do I believe in? But did not get anywhere on it.

Recently I came across a black and white photo, taken soon after the Civil War, of our apartment building. The building has several large holes in it, on the second and third stories, though our apartment, other than being pockmarked by bullet holes near one window, seems to be unaffected. There are a dozen soldiers in the street in front gathered around and staring at an object which is so blurred in the photograph I can't distinguish what it is. I take it to be some sort of small field kitchen. They are so intent on this, it must have something to do either with food or mail I'd think. The soldiers are wearing winter coats and stocking caps and have their hands in the pockets.

To the left, and separate, a man is leaning against a storefront.

His face is gaunt and unshaven. He has on a beret pulled far down on his head. He has a blanket over his shoulders. He is looking at the camera with a haunted and angry expression. There are three children, none of whom is more than waist high, huddled against him and the blanket. Beside him, not many feet away, a woman under an umbrella stares into a store, apparently window-shopping.

Closest to the camera, and the most striking image in the photograph, is the back of a huge Guardia Civil. He is wearing a trench coat with a high, Napoleonic collar, his tri-cornered, patent leather hat. He is totally black in the image and looks like a large shadow, or dark symbol, observing the scene.

Sunday, the 12ᵗʰ of December

We took our landlady, Ana Dolores Blásquez, to lunch at Las Cuevas del Duque. The restaurant is located in an ancient cave, at 16 Princesa, about a block west of Plaza España. I had roast leg of suckling lamb. I'd never had suckling lamb until we came to Spain, mutton not being a big item on the menu in Florida, but it is one of my favorites now. We consumed two bottles of 15 year old rioja, Rincón Baroja. Some bellota after. This is an acorn liqueur, which I have found to my liking. While Ana Dolores and Megan had coffee and dessert, I ordered instead a glass of beer. I think the waiter called me a barbarian for this. I put together a clever comeback after awhile but, short of hitting him with a mallet, it was difficult to get his attention. The meal took three hours.

Ana Dolores does not usually drink much. I'm okay with one glass of wine, she explained. With two, I'm touched. Then she commenced to drink her ass off and got a bit lively for it. She is a stewardess for Iberia, though over 60, stocky, and bowlegged, not what usually comes to mind when you think of a stewardess. She speaks English fluently. Her husband passed a few years ago, he was connected to the military in some way she won't get into, and only one of her three sons, Graziano, is still at home. She is, at all times, sad that Franco is gone, and much of the conversation centered on this while she reminisced about her youth.

I'd never in my life heard anyone speak well of Franco. Since I'd always considered him, at best, no more than a sociopath, the conversation threw me.

I see some of the old Falange around on my walks along the Rosales Paseo, little rich guys with Errol Flynn mustaches. Listening to Ana Dolores, I began to wonder how far under the surface the war is here. In the northern states of my country, our own Civil War is a dead issue, but not always so in the South. There is still resentment there. I remember an older woman in Turkey Creek, Florida, a person I thought much of and who was, otherwise, completely rational, saying to me once that she did not like to be in the same room with Yankees, that they made her feel dirty.

Ana Dolores does not remember the fighting, she was only a baby during the war. But she remembers the aftermath, as a child in the rubble of Madrid. She wouldn't talk about atrocities, saying only that bad things were done on both sides. Her half-brother was arrested after the war and jailed for seven years. He hadn't done anything criminal she said, but he was a Republican.

One of the reasons she thought well of Franco was that he had given her a job. It wasn't much of a job, as she told it, and the pay not so good, but it was important to her to have work. She is such a very nice person. If you ever hear there is no such thing as a good Falange, don't believe it. Still … I came away from this saddened. While she was talking about Franco riding a white stallion, I recalled an eerie passage from a poem by Garcia Lorca, *Fable and Round of the Three Friends*:

When the pure forms collapsed
below the *cri-cri* of the daisies,
it came to me that I had been murdered.
They ransacked the cafés and the graveyards and the churches,
they opened the wine casks and wardrobes,
they ravaged three skeletons to gouge out the gold from their teeth.
Now me, they never found.

Goya's Head

They never found me?

No. They never found me …

In 1936, at the outbreak of the Civil War, Lorca was taken from a friend's house in Granada by a group of Falange thugs. Two days later, very early in the morning, he was driven to the countryside and shot. He was, to my way of thinking, the finest poet to walk this earth, and his death the most senseless of the millions lost in that war. His grave has still not been located. He wrote the poem in which he predicted his disappearance several years before he was executed.

The churro maker below us told me once that Ana Dolores was pretty in her youth. She and her husband had lived in our apartment when first married. Sunday at the restaurant, I noticed for the first time she has a lovely ironic smile and a sharp sense of humor she usually keeps folded up like a pocket knife. And when she smiled I saw her in the past, and that she is still beautiful beneath her rough exterior; it's all still there; it's hidden in the raw disguise time has thrown across her. You almost didn't know what to make of that smile, whether it was given in simple kindness or that she was letting you in on a joke, but it brought back her beauty. And maybe the wine had something to do with all this, too. The Spanish say that old wine has a memory.

We took her out to eat to inform her in person that we needed to break our lease, that we'd be moving when we found another place. But she was having such a good time, I failed to mention it.

I even dressed up for the occasion. My winter sports coat and duncher cap, a blue V neck sweater, light gray shirt buttoned at the top, no tie, as I don't own one, my brown Oxfords made in England. Since this happens so rarely, Megan took some pictures. Dressing up makes you dream a little. I started to imagine myself in a bowler and silk bow tie, some two-tone shoes, kid gloves. Add a swagger stick to it, why not. Portrait of a nicely got up lout.

A letter from Wolf came in the mail this morning:

File this under—if it was not for irony there would be no humor in my life at all. One of my co-workers has decided to test my morality. One of those Sicilian girls from Ybor City. A secretary in the office. She is 20 or so and stone fucking beautiful. One of them you just hum along to the way they walk. I am flattered by it, I will not lie to you.

At first I figured it was a trick. Thought she was either kidding or practicing her female wiles on an old burnout. Counting coup maybe. But that was not it. So I told her I had boots and saddles older than her. That I have a horse nearly her age. She just smiled.

So then I am up to flattered and confused. I explained to her that I did not even have fantasies about those her age no more. And she looked me right in the eye just like a grown woman and told me that I would now.

Next I told her that while I might be lame and funny looking I was a sincere and honorable man and had not yet taken to robbing cradles. She said that did not surprise her one bit. And she winked at me and turned and swanked away.

Something is rockin, you see it? That is no cradle though, she said.

Good Lord. She is also the daughter of one of the bosses, which means there is gravity to the situation. It will be my ass in a sling if he gets wind of it. So now I am up to real flattered, confused, and paranoid. And I been around too long to be any of them things. I mean one of the advantages of living out here like I am is that I have little drama in my life. I have about got it down to the essentials. Food, shelter, gas. Damn few rules too. Do not break nothin you cannot fix. Keep your head down and your mouth shut. Do not do nothin stupid, you done used all that up.

But you know how I admire tenacity and man she has

got that. For the most part I only go to the office on Fridays to get my paycheck. I do not think I could handle seeing her more than once a week. She is way too open about what she is up to.

So I am really on edge and wondering what the hell did I do to be tested like this. I am much better as Cosmic Witness than I am at The Guy Doin Time. I mean this has to be illegal. Ought to be if it is not. And I keep thinking her old man is eyeing me.

In other news, I went out with dogs and gun yesterday. Old Dog is about done. Puts me in mind of when my Granpaw went down. He has been mostly blind for a long time. Now he is deaf and gets confused as to what he is doin. I would have lost him several times but the other dogs kept track of him. Had to slow down and stop and wait for him a lot. But when I hit a passing dove he got the retrieve. I don't know how. He cannot even hear the gun go off. After the hunt I had to pick him up to get him into the bed of the truck. I'm pretty sure he was embarrassed by that.

Megan and I and Chelo went to Sol last night to see the Christmas lights. An unbelievable crowd. The entire area strangled with people and cars. This is normal with traffic at Sol, but I've never seen that many people around, and you were simply locked in at some places by the sheer number of pedestrians, no movement, just pinned there. I did not get the Christmas spirit. I experienced a sense of claustrophobia and panic instead and came away with the thought that there are far too many people in the world.

From my reading—I have always read a great deal; it has been a big part of my education as I learned little in school; I'm a bookworm, that is to say, an autodidact, and I'm not selective; I read whatever comes my way—some clues on handling sexuality from the French photographer Serge Lutens: There is an immobility in Japanese art that I admire. Form exists but expression does not.

This creates a certain tension and energy, which is as powerful as the more suggestive western art. The Japanese do not now depict nude women. The hair and make-up are very important and can be intensely erotic. The Japanese use a specific method of coding, a sort of eroticism in chains …

14 December Tuesday
Rain last night and early this morning. A large forest-green truck parked out front, and a load of oak firewood delivered to the Carbones below got away from them and spilled all the way up against the apartment building door. We are, for the time being, trapped in the building by this. Looking across the street, I see a woman shaking out a rug on her second floor balcony, dust and dirt falling. Directly under her on the sidewalk are three nicely dressed pensioners chatting. Neither party has any idea of the other's existence. The Carbones are hustling about below me. Nacho, I notice, is quite busy these cold days but seems no more the pleasant for it. While I am watching his wife and assorted relatives trying to clear a path through the wood as he directs them, he catches sight of me and stares back momentarily like a rat on a leash.

Sometime later in the morning, Chelo came over to use the computer to type a test. He took off his coat and scarf, retrieved an enormous amount of paper and books from his briefcase and distributed this around the machine, got an ashtray. He occasionally mutters to a cigarette when he lights one. References to Lucifer mostly I take it. I only heard him clearly once. Beelzebub re-ups, he said.

There are times such as this when it is difficult to tell if Chelo has dressed for the day yet or has simply rolled out of bed in what he wore last night when he passed out. I remember in Tampa a fashion statement he touted for awhile, sort of Guatemalan-colored bermuda shorts with a mis-buttoned shirt. He's obviously not keen on doing this test. After coffee and another cigarette, he looked through his papers and discovered that he had left the material he wished to type at home. He had to return to Lavapiés to get this.

My machine was all but buried under his belongings. I left after awhile to find a newspaper. The *Herald Tribune* was sold out at the kiosk. I bought a *Guardian* instead. I like the English papers quite a lot, but their sports pages are foreign to me, much horse racing news, soccer. I glanced through it in line. The fella in front of me was short and bald. He had a large knot in the middle of his head like a horn was trying to break through. I returned to the apartment after walking around a bit. I opened a bottle of wine and started drinking. Chelo came back about the time I'd finished reading the paper.

Where you been?

He says, I went home to get what I needed. I stopped at a bakery to get some doughnuts to bring. They're actual doughnuts, not churros. Sort of like Krispy Kremes. I go to pay for them and discover I'd forgotten my wallet. When I go back to the apartment to get my wallet, I notice some letters on the kitchen table I needed to mail. I went back to the bakery, paid them. Go to the tabac shop for some stamps. I get on the metro. Two stops later, I notice I have the stamps, but I'd left the fucking letters at the tabac shop. So I had to turn around and go back. I've been hanging around the metro a bunch this morning. When I get to the Argüelles stop finally, just as I'm walking out into daylight, I feel something. I'm wondering, Is it raining? No. A pigeon nailed me. Look …The back of his coat is speckled.

Where's the doughnuts?

Aw hell, he says.

I have what I think of as a shadow story going on adjacent to this one. Items I have written but rejected I put into a file designated #2. It's not a fourth as long as this, maybe not even that, much rougher—and yet with a certain vitality to it. There is a purity in mistakes. And I have trouble throwing things away. They might have meaning that, at the moment, I can't fathom. Maybe they'll add to the mosaic of detail along the way. Some of it is inappropriate to this, other parts simply fragmentary. Also, for reasons I don't quite understand, my persona has a mind of his own and seems about afraid that if he looked over his shoulder there might be another, and another, that he is an echo touching down in a given pattern. To counter this he gets out of line occasionally.

Megan informs me that she has been stricken with culture shock. She has lost her bearings, she says, her back up against it, bent out of true, a sense of dislocation about, a certain disgust with the people we're in with. This happens from time to time. She calls it The High Lonesome, with all due respect, she adds, to Bill Monroe. Stacked against this, as counter-balance, she says, is the fact she loves the city itself. She lost me there a bit. She holds that I'm in a state of permanent culture shock but too stubborn to admit it. What she describes, however, sounds very much like my normal condition no matter where I am.

I do know I'd rather live where I understand what folks are saying, even though I realize they're probably saying no more nor less than people anywhere. I'm gaining little on the language. There are a lot of words to remember, and my memory doesn't seem up to par any more. I am just now, at this stage in life, getting a good feel for English. But I'm not cut out for big city life. The Madrileños are high decibel people. They even wear loud shoes. And I'm starting to believe they are happiest when putting all their strength against a car horn. It is the mantra of the neighborhood, and I cannot convey on a quiet page the clamor of it. They love to be elbow to elbow in tiny restaurants and bars all talking so fast and loud at once. It is simply a different concept of space and sound than I'm used to. And far as time goes, the odd way they break up their day and don't seem to sleep at night … it's all beyond me.

Last night at 3 a.m. a dozen singers gathered on the corner. By coincidence, they arrived at the same time as the garbage men. The truck used to hoist the garbage cans and empty them is much larger than it needs to be and yet groans and strains as if to soon explode. This combined with the drunken songs woke me. Our bedrooms are right against the street. You need an interior bedroom here; it's a necessity. Noise travels up our building like over open water. When I got back to sleep finally, I dreamt of yellow crime scene tape, the outline of my body traced in chalk on the sidewalk.

The machine just advised me I'm traveling at Mouse Speed Factor 5. I somehow suspected this all along.

Our neighborhood is puzzling, and a big part of the problem, the accidental and awkward combination of pensioners and college students. It helps to be either deaf or young. There are three bars across the street in which some of the students who attend the university seem to actually reside. There's been talk about skinheads invading the neighborhood. I would welcome the skinheads, a little nihilism from the margins of society to shake things up. Then too, there's an egocentricity to the Madrileños. The old city walls are long gone, somehow broken into three million people. It is this sense of *I am it*, and no one else exists. This translates into rudeness much of the time. Though I've all but begun to think of it as some strange reach for privacy in this great mass of people.

16 December Thursday

Sometimes I go to bed but then wake after awhile and spend the night in the living room where it is quieter. I watch TV or read and fall asleep at 4 or 5 a.m. Whenever I do this, it takes me several days to realign my waking and sleeping. I had eight hours shut-eye last night, slept in until 7:30. This is luxury. I usually take a nap in the afternoons, around 2. Today I had a small salad and a couple glasses of bodega wine for lunch and immediately started nodding. The hell with the nap I decided, I need to be outside; so I took the metro to Atocha and walked up the hill behind the Botanical Garden, past the outdoor bookstores and on into the south end of Retiro.

It's been much too cold the last few days and now a wind to blow the cold around. Normally, two glasses of wine don't do much for me, but for some reason I felt drunk in a real heavy sort of way. I'm dragging. I walk to the waterfall and pool below and take it in awhile, then on to the apple orchard. Mentally I'm fine, but I can't shake the leaden feeling of my body. Finally I come across a

Quaker parrot. He's sitting on a fence squawking. There's a wooden bench nearby, so I sit down and watch the parrot. He seems to be a young one. Though there is a colony of Quakers over at the lake, I'm thinking this one either escaped or his owner kicked him out for being loud and obnoxious.

It's a sunny day, very cool when the wind comes up, but it's not steady. It comes and goes, and the sun is warm on my face. I've been crazy for getting sun lately. I can't stay in when it's shining. We had an exceptional autumn and only a few bad days now and then, but in those I saw what's in store for me. I can't seem to keep my eyes open at all. Two cops go by on white Arabians, the clopping hooves about put me out. The parrot flies closer to the brick wall at the back end of the park. It strikes me that he's bouncing his voice off the wall for the illusion of companionship. I don't think they like being alone. They're flock birds. I'm hearing the echo of his voice now. The horse chestnuts are dropping the last of their leaves, the wind taking them.

My bench is between the apple orchard and one of the broad avenues behind me. Four of them come together here and in the middle a statue of Satan, apparently the only one in the world—the fallen angel looking to the heavens, a thick snake around his waist. You could have parades on these streets they're so wide, but there's no auto traffic. People walk their senile dogs, push baby carriages. Many joggers, bicycles.

The leaves are tumbling along the ground. There's a nice smell to them, of things on their way back to earth. I stand and begin to shuffle homeward. I'm glad it's downhill. I've not yet gotten over this drunken feeling. Maybe I'm intoxicated by the day. The leaves are five inches deep and overtaking my boots. The flat winter light in the trees seems dense, almost solid, and the wind is against me now … I'm in slow motion … I make my way out of the park the best I can. If I'd stayed there any longer, I think I would have become a very old man.

Friday afternoon

I'm walking along Gran Vía and run into Kevin Ray, Megan, Chelo. Kevin Ray wished us well and went his own way as usual, and the rest of us headed down to Chicote's at Gran Vía 12. The gays, out of necessity or simply because they like each other's company more than most, know how to connect with one another. Kevin Ray goes to the Madrid Gay Dining Group get-together every Thursday night. He didn't get in till 11 this morning and had to be at work at 1. He was a bit punchy as we said goodbye, but otherwise in good spirits; he had to catch a train to Seville with a new friend from Wales.

Hemingway set two short stories in Chicote's, 'The Denunciation' and probably his most humorous, 'The Butterfly and the Tank.' His instinct for finding good taverns is inarguable. Chicote's seems not to have changed since he wrote about it. You enter by a revolving door. It does not have the heavy sturdiness of the bars that have been around for over a century or longer. It is more art nouveaux. The waiters are attentive and load you down with tapas. There's a 1938 photo of E.H. on the wall. He's drinking wine, appears to be nibbling on the glass. The camera angle shows off the sort of incredible bump he had on his forehead. He's wearing wire-rimmed glasses, a coat and tie, overcoat, quite rumpled. He's obviously thinking about something, a distant look in his eyes. I went back to *The Sun Also Rises* not long ago. He hit on something in that book that matters I think: That we aren't meant to have what we want, and that's the tragedy.

It was early at Chicote's, only a few tables occupied. Chelo started talking about his Spanish girlfriend, who lives up in Oviedo in Asturias. She's twenty-one and is embarrassed to be seen with him in public, though she certainly likes something about him. They stay in bed most of the time when he visits. But when they go out, she walks ten feet in front of him. She doesn't want her family or friends to see them together. She made him agree to this, plus a few other minor conditions, one of which is that he has to pay for everything.

And you slavishly acquiesced to this arrangement?

Yep, he said. I promised her up one side and down the other. He grinned like a dog.

Megan's rolling her head around on her shoulders like she has a stiff neck.

He met her family once. Her parents thought him just an American friend, he had been her English teacher when she went to school in Madrid, took him for a casual acquaintance, an avuncular type, and treated him kindly. The girl's sister wasn't so sure though. Then she happened to find a letter Chelo had sent recently. The sister didn't know English, but she was skeptical enough of Chelo to have it translated by a friend. The letter contained some explicit sexual language—Your cunt is like a little sparrow, and so on. Chelo quotes this to us as if he takes it to be very close to literature. The sister gave the translation to her parents, however, so now the relationship has hit the skids. His young lady is equivocating on their next meeting. She's supposed to call tomorrow night, but Chelo has little hope. Looking ahead, he is working in a replacement, a woman in the Spanish class he's taking. He already knows Spanish. His family spoke it at home. The class is for social contacts. This girl is Japanese.

After Chicote's we stopped at several cafés on the way home. There are fifty thousand bars in Madrid proper, many of them nondescript, and we found some of these. I was stumbling around. It was different from the ponderous feeling I experienced in Retiro. I was just so drunk I lost coordination. When we got back to the apartment, Megan soon fell out. It was still early, not even 8 o'clock. I didn't want to stop even though it was way past where I should have.

We don't want to squander the slight edge we have on the night, I said to no one.

Then I staggered back out into the crowded streets and wandered aimlessly until I came to a liquor store and bought two bottles of wine. Some ratty-haired fellas offered me hash as I walked by them, and I stopped and took a couple hits. One would have probably sufficed. Soon afterwards, I noticed some potato chips in a window. They looked awfully good. In that store also were jars of penny candy. I purchased licorice strips, fried eggs, pink and blue teeth, loops. Then I came across a little place that sold only olives. I bought a quarter kilo each of five different kinds. I stopped several more times. I had sacks of food before I was done. I had some beers at a little stand-up bar. I was actually talking to people, though I don't have the faintest notion what I might have said.

A pretty winter day—

0 degrees centigrade when I awoke this morning. The sky is clear and hard blue. The air very dry. The aridity here makes certain things necessary in order to maintain oneself. A bath every day, or every other day, for instance, wouldn't hurt. Some kind of grease on your face, or your skin starts to mummify. My Florida tan is a distant memory. I'm very white and my face red blotched. When I come in from outside my cheeks are like crabapples. I don't nearly keep up with the bathing schedule, of course, as our apartment is so cold. I have to talk myself into it, and often I'm not very convincing. I stink at the moment but have so many clothes on, you wouldn't notice. After a bath the other day I was looking at myself in the mirror like Narcissus. In spite of the beauty tips mentioned above, I seem to have aged all at once.

There's a commotion out front, and I go to the balcony. The grúa, a city tow truck, has appeared to take away a car. I've noticed this car; it has been double-parked for several days now and at a bad angle. The Madrileños dislike the grúa intensely. They stop what they're doing, gather around on the street and balconies, and stare at the grúa driver in hatred like it's unwritten law.

I bundled up and went out. Here in the many of the crowd and each intent on his own inner map, I have had to relearn how to walk. Defensively, let's say. And now I do so without thinking too much on it. If you don't do this, you get bowled into. I've always liked to walk, but in San Ann there are only 500 people and it's unusual to encounter more than one or two others on foot. Even though we live within the city limits, the house is surrounded by grove land and woods, and my nearest neighbor is a block away. His name is Seth Cowart. He was 80 when we moved to Madrid. He's some sort of relative. My mother explained it once. She was his second cousin twice removed is how she put it, which meant nothing to me.

Seth always kept a fine winter garden, which took up most of his back yard, that and a very old orange tree, one of my Grandmother Tillie's, the only one still alive and bearing sweet oranges, planted in a corner very close to his house and protected by it. When I'd see him on the road, as he was a walker too, or more of an ambler say, we'd walk together and later, often as not, inspect his garden and tree, check on the progress of the oranges, which the tree made hundreds of, and if they were ripe, we would share one.

His wife advertised herself as a teetotaler though everyone in town knew her to be a lush. She was just as odd as Seth was nice. When she was loaded, she'd masquerade as a bag lady and wander along our street. If I ran into her, we'd speak, though sometimes she wouldn't exactly get who I was, and a talk with her could not be confused with anything even slightly meaningful. I seemed always several minutes late to those conversations, no way to catch up.

I might also pass Buddy Stortch, who didn't own a car and walked to the bar each morning down Curly Road; this is the main street. There is only one bar in town, Red Fred's. Or I might see him in the afternoon when he had finished his eight hour shift. Buddy retired several years ago and now drinks full time. He'd turn expansive in the afternoons. He's a home-made philosopher of sorts and, also, usually had a squirrel recipe to share. I enjoyed listening to him. But most everyone else drove in our little town, no matter how short a distance they were going, and my walks were solitary, where I could blunder about at will. In Madrid I try to make myself smaller.

The leaves remaining on the olmo trees in the neighborhood are yellow-orange and seem that they might fall all at once. I took the metro to Sol, walked to the statue of the bear and the madroño tree, cut in one block and turned left. At number 12 Tetuán is Café Labra where they have the best croquets. I purchase four of these and take them with me to eat on the way. The terrazas are long gone, and the town is much the less for it. It is stark, and there is no sense of relaxation now at all. The crowd is on the prowl.

Back at Sol I bought a paper at a kiosk. Going by the headlines, I take it the world is coming apart at the seams. I went up Calle Montera then, one of my favorite streets—body-piercing and tattoo parlors, junkies, sex shops, pickpockets and whores. The whores on display here at noon are all but hilarious. I notice one blonde with a butch haircut. She looks like an antique punk rocker. She wears a studded dog collar and a short, chrome yellow dress some twenty years too young for her. The legs shown between the hem of the dress and her high boots resemble cauliflower. I can only wonder what desperation a man would have to be in to pay her money. All of them, truly—I've never seen prostitutes so in need of darkness and the night.

Montera leads into Gran Vía, and I turn left toward Plaza España. Gran Vía is Madrid's fairest street. You really get the flavor there. The heavy crowds, the most distinctive buildings in town, blind dwarfs selling lotto tickets. I pass an older Spanish woman whose face is yellow. That jaundice yellow announcing a bad liver. I feel my side. A man walks by with a false nose. Here goes a fella wearing a sandwich-board advertising lunch at Miravia's, Menú del Día 875 pesetas, 1st plato: paella valenciana, judías verdes con jamón …the crowd swallows him.

At Plaza España there are often Japanese tourists taking photos. This plaza seems to be starred on their map. Sometimes I'm asked to snap a shot or two. They carefully show you how the camera works, like you're Goofy the cartoon or something. I take a picture of their feet.

I find a bench in the sun and read the paper. The strike is still on in France. Public workers in Spain will soon follow. There's a holiday next Friday. Emilie has relatives in Toulouse. We were thinking of going there, but the strike will alter that plan. After awhile two old ladies take a bench across the sidewalk, shoot me a couple ancient beavers. Is one of them winking at me? I bury my face in the sports pages.

My ears are getting cold. I finish the paper, cross under the street to the Rosales Paseo and walk to Montaña. Just before the abrupt steps up to it, there are always some old guys playing cards on picnic tables under big plane trees. The card game is called Tute. I don't know the rules. The cards are not even familiar; they resemble Tarot cards. The players at the tables wager Spanish nickels. The interest shown by those standing around is deeper than any news the world could offer.

Montaña is covered with fallen leaves. There are many school kids about. Some boys kicking a soccer ball. I check out several 14-year-old girls in mini skirts and combat boots. What a combination. It does something for you.

I write in my notebook: Cold silver light. Goya sky. Seven cranes flying east against the backdrop of the mountains, which today are blue. The red-orange of firethorn berries. An old man with a black cane. A white-faced bulldog at the reflecting pool, looks at himself in the water, then discreetly averts his gaze from the creature in it. A small yellow whirlwind of leaves twists around my boots. On the most beautiful days I am stricken with sadness. It's in the blood, it's older than I am, some sense of loss I can't begin to understand. I should like to be a dignified loser, such as Cyrano de Bergerac …

I head back toward the apartment. It's lunch time and people walk by eating sandwiches—a long hard roll and, inside, thin slices of Serrano ham. It tastes somewhat waxy when you first try it. No mayonnaise, no mustard. I don't know how they swallow these without something to drink. This reminds me … and I stop at Lafuente Liquor Store on Quintana just before they close, purchase wine. Soon after, I see a woman watering her geraniums on a balcony. Some overflow catches the light, blinks down through it. A young boy on the sidewalk below tries to catch the drops in his mouth.

I hold to the sunny side of the street the rest of the way home.

As I type this there are 20 million unemployed in the European Union. Nearly a quarter of the labor force in Spain is out of work.

Even more than that in our neighborhood I'd think. There are any number of them across the street right now drinking beer and watching soccer on TV. In my icebox there's nothing to eat but Maille Dijon mustard, horseradish and bread. I make a sandwich of these ingredients and try to fathom the world. In my country nearly everyone is employed, but not many I know seem very happy about what they do. And you have to be careful there. If you get good at something you hate, they'll make you do it for the rest of your life. Money grows on trees there, they say; you just can't pick it every week. But I don't know about that. I've never found it to be quite that way. I've lived through a portion of the last half of this century and have not found it especially easy; and I was not born until the hard part was over.

There was a loud noise outside our building last night, like a car crash. Nacho the Carbone and his family live in the apartment above their shop. One of their balconies collapsed it turned out. The largest piece is still on the sidewalk where it landed. I don't celebrate this exactly, but I declare the rest of the afternoon a holiday. I listen to Stephane Grappelli. A pleasant lassitude overtakes my body … I am bone idle.

A sadsack morning.
Sunday is family day in Argüelles. The most boring day of the week. You can all but see clock parts floating in the air. Everybody dusts off grandma and takes her to lunch. I'm working through a hangover. It is the same one I build every night and attempt to tear down during the day. I'm having sinus trouble. My right ear sounds like it has the gulf in it. Voices issue to a mucked well on that side of my head. Bits of conversation, disconnected, seemingly from nowhere, get caught in my good ear or else hit it at an odd angle, the words glancing off. It makes me nostalgic for the old days when I'd crack a beer and have that and a pain pill for breakfast; health wasn't something I thought about much then.

I'm tired of this also, the constant mulling over of things.

I've got to break through. I need a road trip, even a good book to read, something to take me away. I'm thinking this on a bench on a sidestreet to us. A morose youth strolls by with a black-toothed comb in his hand, gives me the once over, the razor boy look. He clicks his tongue and goes on by. I probably look like I feel. I didn't exactly dress to go out. I'm wearing the clothes I slept in, and I didn't sleep well. That and two flannel shirts and winter coat and my watchcap pulled down over my ears. I'm freezing. I sit hunched up like the shoulders of a heart.

I woke once last night gritting my teeth to the point of snapping several of them off. I woke twice after that, each time with the odd feeling that Billy Jenks was near about. That maybe he was in the living room. But the living room seemed very far away, maybe in another dimension. I thought if I opened my bedroom door, he would have just closed the one to the bathroom. That no matter where I went in the apartment, he would just that instant turn a corner and be somewhere else. And I was too sleepy to get up and check anyway. I keep wondering what the hell's going on with all that. I don't even know why I'm sitting here on this bench, except that I prefer to bitch in private, to mire in it on my own. Even the sky seems a reflection of my mood, the palest gray. I want the sun like a searchlight on me. But it is behind a veil today. Some beauties pass by all dressed to the nines, on their way to church. My eyes go with them. To be ugly and out of contention for them is something you never get used to. I feel so pathetic just then I start laughing. I sit there snorting and slapping my knees.

Then along came one of the old Madrileña birds, dressed in black, iron hair, heavy shoes. She sounds like a horse clomping down the sidewalk, even though she is so very small she appeared to be in the distance even when quite close. She gave me the stare. The Spanish look at you sometimes like they are dead fish. Usually I'd give it back, but just then I didn't feel like continuing the fight. I dropped my eyes. She stopped a moment, cracked her knuckles. Then she went on. I lit a cigarette. My ear has a constant high piping tone in it, as though someone had struck a tuning fork. I slap my

Goya's Head

head a couple times. I'm mumbling to myself, staring at the ground. After awhile I hear the horse clomping my way again. She stops in front of me, holding out a cien coin she wants to give me.

Chelo showed up at the apartment Tuesday after his workout. He didn't seem to have any clear idea why he was here. As though he happened to wander up to our door and since he recognized it thought, What the hell, I'll go ahead in. He took a seat in my chair, the only one in the place you don't get a backache from, and stared straight ahead like he was dazed.

You okay? I said.

Yeah … sure.

Did your girl call … what was her name?

I don't want a talk about it, he said.

I'm not wearing a hat, and his attention is drawn momentarily to the scar on my forehead, maybe the light emphasized it, but he doesn't say anything.

What happened? I said.

She called Friday night. I went up there on the train Saturday … He looked at his left hand, noticed that it was empty. You got any beer? he said

I have some wine, I said. I went to the kitchen and poured us each a glass.

I happen to sit by this cabbie in the bar at the train station, he continued, and we strike up a conversation. He tells me he knows just what I'm looking for. He took me to a motel outside of Oviedo, about three miles north of town.

I check my cash after paying him. I've got enough for the train ride back to Madrid, that's about it. I called Belen and arranged everything. I had to call at a certain time we'd set before-hand, see … so she would pick up the phone and not anyone else. I'm beginning to feel like a secret agent. She'll meet me at the motel after she has dinner with her family. At 11, she says. But she's always late. It's not psychologically possible for her to be on time. It'll be midnight at the earliest. She's gonna drive her car out there. She can drive me back to the train station I figure.

How'd you pay for the motel? I thought you were broke.

VISA card. Not sure how I'm gonna cover that.

Anyway ... I got this nice room. A big long motel, but my place was to the back of it. There's some little duplexes back there. Three, four of them, sort of rustic. Like cabins. I think maybe they started out with these, then built the motel part later. The place is small. It's one room with a bed and a bathroom and closet. And really clean. It's spotless. Oak furniture that smells of polish. The whole place is oak. It backs up onto some woods and there's plants landscaped all around. A real doll house setting. Very romantic to my way of looking. Got a mini-bar in the icebox. There's an older couple on the other side of my duplex, but the others don't seem to be occupied.

I unpack and then I fell asleep for awhile. When I woke up, I felt great. I didn't even think I'd get to see her, and now this ... things were fallin' my way. I drank a couple little whiskeys from the mini-bar. It's only about 9:30 maybe. Time for a shower ...

Any of that wine left? he said.

When I carry the bottle into the living room he sees it's cheap shit.

Could you find a brown paper bag for that ... I have my standards, he says. You got some cheese or something? I've not had any ornate cuisine lately. Actually, I've not had anything lately. I'm on the verge of penury once again.

I brought out some cheese and mustard and olives.

Okay, I said. Go on.

Where exactly in the debacle did I leave off?

The shower.

Oh, yes, he said. How do you botch a shower?

I wasn't included in this question. He was asking himself and seemed genuinely bewildered by it.

A little electric heater in the bathroom ... I let it run for a long time, get the place nice and warm. Lay out on the bed what I'm gonna wear. Though, why bother, I'm thinking. When she knocks, just answer the door with a hard-on, and to hell with clothes. It's all she's interested in. I coulda sent my cock up there, and she wouldn't notice the rest of me ain't around.

Anyway, I strip and throw my dirty clothes in a corner. I deadbolt the front door. Go into the bathroom and close the door. I guess I locked it, too … though I don't remember doing that. Maybe it locked on its own. I just don't know what happened there. I take a nice long shower. Get it like a steam bath in there. I'm feelin' on top of things. I'd brought a couple bottles of good wine along. I'm thinking about how the night's gonna be, dreaming like.

I get out the shower. The towels are on a shelf right outside the door. But I go to open the door, and I'm locked in. The door won't open at all. I kept workin' on it to get it open, but it don't give. There's something you should be able to do with the door knob to unlock it, but I'm at it like a fucking demented squirrel got a nut he can't crack … nothin' happens. And it's solid oak. I ram it with my shoulder and just bounce off. An' this goes on for awhile that I'm fightin' this door.

Finally I start bangin' on the walls. The couple next door went out to dinner or something. An' nobody's walkin' by that hears me. No one comes. It's goin' on 40 minutes or so I'm stuck in this goddamn bathroom.

I'm beyond pissed at that point. I'm startin' to get desperate. I notice there's a sprinkler head in the ceiling. You know how they have … for in case there's a fire? I'm thinkin' I set that off, somebody from the office has got to come, right? I try holding the heater up next to it, but the cord's not long enough. So I get it real hot, unplug it, hold it up next to the sprinkler head. I try this about five times, and it don't do a thing.

Then I got mad and slammed the hell out of it, and the head broke. An' it don't start sprinkling. The water pours out instead, and it's black and foul. It smells like shit, and it's gushing out. An' it don't have anywhere to go. Some is getting out under the door, I guess, but the whole place is carpeted, and it ain't leaving exactly. It just builds up.

I'm banging on the walls. Yelling. I'm still hoarse. I started to panic. 'Cause the water's getting up to my knees eventually. It crosses my mind I'm likely to drown in there. What a way to go. It's a couple hours have passed by already that I've been in there, and I'm startin' to wonder how it feels to die by drowning. I can picture the headlines. The word *moron* prominent in them.

I hear a bunch of commotion out front finally. The management's trying to get in, but I'd dead bolted the front door. They hear me yelling in there and break a window to get in. Then they can't get the bathroom door open either. The water's up to like here. Stop laughing, Luke, goddamn it.

They finally have to break the door down. I'm in there naked all this time. I grab the shower curtain an' wrap it around me. It's got pink flamingos on it. They break the door down and all the water rushes out. The carpet's fucked in that room now, too. An' I'm a wreck. I've damn near come unhinged. The motel people are going mental on me. Just bright red in the face. They look like tomatoes. The wife's holding her nose ... and for good reason. I'm rank.

I'm trying to explain to them what happened, standing out in front of the place, freezing my ass off in this shower curtain. There's a workman taking furniture out of the room, setting it on the sidewalk to dry. The manager and his wife are both talking to me at the same time. Shouting, rather.

I turn my head and just by chance see my date come around the corner. She takes one look at the scene, does an about face and is out of there. Peels rubber about twenty feet getting gone down the road.

That's it for young cunts, he said.

They look nice, though, I said.

That they do ... you have to give them that. But they're not the same person from day to day. You can't keep up with who they are. An' somethin' goes wrong, there's no way they can handle it. I get into any more young shit, I'm just gonna fuck their brains out before they come to their senses ... then dump their ass. No involvement allowed.

Uh huh, I said. You weren't in love with that girl, was you?

Love? You got to be kidding. I don't even know what that is anymore. I ain't been in love since I was married … and a lot of good that did me.

They give you another room then?

No. They kicked my ass out. And I don't have so much as cab fare. I hitch-hike and walk, mostly walked, back into Oviedo to the train station. It was a long ride home.

We bought a small electric stove that sits on top of the kitchen counter and Sunday had a pre-Christmas dinner before all take off in their own directions. Turkey, jalapeno corn, marshmallowed yams, smothered green beans with almond slivers, dirty rice, cranberry sauce, chapata bread, wines from Navarra and Rioja. Coffee with Tia María, roasted pecans and pear pie for dessert. It was a feast. Megan spent all day Saturday cooking, then Sunday morning, too. Chelo and Emilie and Kevin Ray, Megan and I, and Emilie's roommate, June, who she invited just because there was no way around it. I've not said anything about June Bug yet as I don't like to advertise sorriness. But it was such a good day, even she seemed bearable. Afterwards we went to an Arab bar down on Mesón de Paredes in Chelo's neighborhood, across the street from the ruins of a church. He insisted it would be a perfect place to end the day, and it turned out that he was right.

An icy rain.

You can see your breath in the apartment. As Megan dresses, she complains about having to go to school.

I thought you liked school, I said.

I used to, she answered.

Turns out she thought she'd found a boyfriend in one of her classes, then discovered that he was married.

He doesn't wear a ring, she said. How are you supposed to know? She might like to cry but won't. She was such a tomboy when she was a kid, and even now, as a young lady, crying won't do.

No use fussin' about it, I said. It'll just run you crazy. Move on.

She came over and hugged me then and held on a long time.

Later that day I heard her on the phone talking to Emilie about back home.

They ate a lot of rattlesnake in the old days there, she was saying. In my grandma's time. You barbecue it. Ten pounders were common then …Tastes like quail to me … Rattlers are bad on dogs. Some say a rattler smells like cucumber when you come upon them, but I can't smell them. Now a cottonmouth, that's different. They smell like skunkweed.

Gator? You have to fix it right … but even then … I just never cared for gator meat. Cooter's my favorite … It's a soft-shell turtle. They're in the lakes around San Ann … You know what? Me, too. I'm sick of it already. I just flat ass hate the winter …

Though I noted she was speaking quite a lot about reptiles, I heard no direct mention of boyfriend made.

I am now receiving a subscription to *Guideposts* magazine. It contains little religious stories, which I have found uniformly unreadable. From my mother I'd guess. I don't know anyone else who would do such a thing. The holy-rollers must have knocked on her door. Somebody knocks, she'll go talk to them, especially if she's been drinking. Even the Lord liked his wine, she'll tell them, if they happen to take a step back from the alcoholic fumes enveloping her. This in sharp contrast to Grandma Tillie. You knocked on Tillie's door it would be answered by a pitbull with a very large head that held a bad opinion of you.

Mom prays for me I know. She goes to mass every Sunday and Wednesday. She takes a cab to the church and back. Other than those two time periods, however, I'm not sure faith much enters her thoughts. Still, she thinks I'm a heathen. It became clear to me at an early age that churches would mean little to me but that those who did not believe in God must live in cities, or least not sleep alone in the woods at night as I often did then.

Last night I watched *L'age d'or* by Luis Buñuel. Then I woke in the morning with the TV still on, just in time to see any number of people on the European news getting their heads smashed by nightsticks. Always comforting. Whenever I see a nightstick employed, I'm reminded once again that a word such as *modern* is no more than a concept from the fashion world.

I had the curious feeling when I went out on the balcony that I could conjure up another age. That I could look into the long ago, at old Madrid, carriages throughout the street and Goya in his landau pulled by a matching pair of smoke-colored mules, their manes plaited, and with fancy brands all over them, harnesses jingling music. But it was not so.

Winter coats and scarves instead and everybody walking with their heads tucked down in them like turtles. My right ear is now completely mucked up. I refuse to go to a doctor. I've had enough of doctors and hospitals to last me awhile. I've prescribed a treatment of hot olive oil. Megan says stuff some tomatoes and onions in too, what the hell. But I can't hear shit out of that ear. Being deaf is not so romantic as I had it. People talk to you from vast distances. You are somewhat at a remove. You have to keep saying, What? And this eventually annoys the hell out of everyone, including yourself.

At the end of 1792, or early in '93, Goya was stricken with a mysterious illness while on a trip in Andalucía that temporarily paralyzed his hands and ruined his hearing. He spent two months in bed hallucinating. No one is quite sure what the illness was. It may have been polio. It may have been meningitis or a rare syndrome known as Vogt-Koyangi. Or maybe he was poisoned by food he ate on the road. You can imagine a good many people at court thought it a side effect of syphilis, a prevalent disease of the time. To have his hands fail must have frightened him beyond measure, but that passed, and he was back to his painting within a year. For the next 36 years of his life, however, he was stone deaf.

Even when the sun is out now, you have to work at getting to it. I've lately been taking the Metro to the sun. Down to Puerto del

Sol where it's open and bright. There are long lines at the betting parlors. Lotería para hoy! The entire community buying tickets for El Gordo, the fat one, said to be the world's richest for the total sum dished out, last year over $3 billion in prize money. The city has put up a giant Christmas tree, and lights are strung all about the streets. As usual I have not the least idea what to get Megan for a present. Our last year in the States I gave her that pearl-handled .32 Walther which fits nicely into her purse. That was as good as it ever got I'm afraid.

Then on to Plaza Mayor. I follow the black cobblerstone pattern, north to south and back again, taking in the sun and the tourists. Often I make my way over to Plaza Santa Ana and have a beer at Cervecería Alemana or take a bench in the plaza with the winos and pigeons. If some asshole comes in there with so much as a crust of bread your life is on the line. A riot of low flying birds. Pigeons three deep on the ground trying to shoulder each other out of the way for crumbs. You'll spot one now and then at a balcony dining on a potted plant as if it were salad, but otherwise they survive on handouts of stale bread. If you were to eat one of these, it would not have that nice, faintly liver taste of wild dove.

The other night I dreamed that Megan and I moved to Tampa. We took a trailer at the Kum Back Motel on Nebraska Avenue and set up residence, only slightly miffed that we had to pay by the hour. The big problem was in that we had a full-sized bear, stuffed and mounted and a blonde grizzly to boot, which stood nine foot tall and that we couldn't get into the trailer because the ceilings were too low. We left it outside a yard away from, and facing, the front door. I was quite attached to this trophy, for reasons I could not clear up, and spent nights on guard duty looking out the window every couple minutes so nobody would steal it. Megan kept asking, Who would take the damn thing? But I wasn't having any of that. A neighbor offered to watch it one night so I could get some sleep. He was the most amicable of our neighbors but had, when he smiled, large snaggled teeth stained by blueberries. I said, Sure, right-o …

and woke.

This afternoon I will be huddled over the machine in winter coat and watch cap. Megan has gone off to lunch with Emilie. I will look across to the sunny side of the street, where the exhibitionists lounge on their balcony in the glaring light wearing dark glasses.

I have volunteered to help Megan make chocolate chip cookies. She purchased the chocolate chips at a place called Taste of America. Appropriately the store carries mostly junk food. I tell her about Chelo's motel experience.

He's an idiot, is all she has to say on it.

According to Kevin Ray, Megan says, Chelo is being difficult at work. He does things his own way. Though Kevin has no official title, he is generally thought to be in charge, but Chelo pays no attention to any of that. He is not part of the generality.

She's had the cookie ingredients sitting on the kitchen counter for two days. I volunteer my help to get her moving on it. I feel like eating some cookies. I seem to be here mainly to keep her company though. She has me put flour in a bowl and then add salt and baking soda.

What do I do now?

Mix it together, she says.

This takes about three seconds.

Will you find the gilhooly. It's in that drawer.

Gilhooly? I said.

That's what mama always called it. That thing you use to help get the lid off a jar.

I found it.

There's a jar of bread and butter pickles in the icebox. Would you open it, please. I just feel like some pickles.

She in the meantime has been hard at an electric beater mixing together butter and sugar. The butter is cold and the sugar dry. It takes a long time and looks like work. After she mixes it thoroughly she adds two eggs.

I would probably have put the eggs in first, I say.

That's because you don't know what you're doing, she says. You have to mix the first two to make sugar cream.

Oh, I say.

She's adding flour to the mixture now a little at a time.

You know that asshole, she says, is vaguely trying to hit on Emilie. It's not playing well with her. He is out of order.

I assume the asshole you're speaking of is Che, I said.

Not well at all, she said. She's wearing an engagement ring. I guess he can't see that.

I guess not.

Hold this bowl for me … Anyway, Emilie's starting to get pissed. She doesn't like him, period. It's another thing he doesn't see.

He sees things the way he wants to I think.

That's a problem, she said. He is one of those Grandma Tillie used to call a scantling.

I never quite understood what Tillie meant by that.

A no-count, she said.

She's finished the cookie mixture finally and has it all over her fingers.

I don't like that part, I say.

What part?

Having that shit all over you.

God … Put some tinfoil on that pan, will you? I wonder how they did this in the old days … before electricity and all. They must have had strong arms … and time on their hands.

She puts seven cookies in our little oven finally. The first of many batches.

Lucas, you haven't been loaning money to Chelo have you?

Yeah, some, I say. Seems like he's always broke.

Don't do that, okay? First of all, we don't have it at the moment. An' I just love you somethin' awful, but you don't have a grain of sense about money. You know that. You just don't seem to give a shit—

I lag behind in that regard, I said.

Goya's Head

And he's broke because he's a nightcrawler, she went on. Have you taken a good, hard look at him lately? He took a wrong turn somewhere. He's broke down by the side of the road.

How long do they take? I asked.

Eight minutes … Look, I meant to tell you … the other day at lunch, Emilie showed me a photo of her boyfriend. I think he's a black guy. It wasn't a good picture, and it's hard to tell, because he's … lightskinned … but I think he's black. Emilie says he's a really nice guy, but he's got a jealous streak. And he's very large.

Maybe I ought to mention that part to Che, I said.

I feel now always somewhat out of touch. I can't seem to catch up with myself. I drink many beers, smoke too many cigarettes—the 20-mule team into Death Valley. Besides this my suicide appears to be taking a gastronomical direction. I like to eat recreationally. I have a big dinner and then snack until I fall asleep. Fat and sugar are highly thought of in this diet. Last night I caught myself literally slamming food into my mouth. It's almost sport. I'm on the lookout for a competitive edge in dining.

A man some fifteen feet away on the crowded sidewalk this morning hailed me as if I were a long lost friend and started running wildly my way, his eyes unstrung. I calmly took in the scene, as it slowed down for some reason. I noted that he'd shaved his head and beard about the same time, maybe 48 hours ago, and didn't do such a great job of it. He must have worked in the dark. Then all of a sudden it speeds up. He's coming so rudely, it crossed my mind that he's going to throw a punch. I'm ready to drop him if that's the case. But then he shoots right past me. I step to the curb and follow his run. He comes to a stop about ten feet away, spots another old pal up ahead and repeats the entire process. Nothing to do but shake your head and continue on into the city of loons.

Emilie came over in the afternoon with fresh dates. They were still on their stem and seemed far better than any I remember. We played bouré awhile until Megan had to go school, and Emilie left then with her. It rained for an hour and a half. Then the rain stopped, and I went out. The sun was shining already. A good many people kept walking with their umbrellas up. For reasons that are beyond me, I felt like getting into a fight. I had a hard edge. It's laughable, I know. The shape I'm in, some of the old ladies could take me.

I don't own an umbrella. I carried one several times, but it made me feel that I should curtsy to everyone I passed. I have instead a raincoat with a hood. As I was standing at a crosswalk, the light turned green. When this happens, you get a bird noise, a chirping, that tells the blind that it's time to move. There was a lady close beside me … a puddle in front of where she's standing, so she cut in front of me to avoid it. She had her umbrella up, which whacked me in the face. Following her across the street, I had an all but irresistible urge to knock the living hell out of her. At the next crosswalk, as I'm almost to the curb, a car jumped at me. Time for me, he's saying, get out of my way. I start screaming, Fuck you motherfucker! I'm very articulate on these occasions. Gave him the up yours. It's encoded in the DNA. Ten thousand years ago, I guarantee you, my ancestors felt the same about this sort of bullshit.

At the southwest corner of Plaza Mayor, past the booths selling joke gifts—Artículos de Broma—and belenes, the gypsies' Christmas trees and the pine smell, and the deep green moss and cork bark and mistletoe they have also, if you go down the steep steps through the Arco de Cuchilleros, stay to the left past Restaurante Botín, and follow the street around to Calle Latoneros, you'll come upon Casa Antonio, a little stand-up bar that has good wine by the glass. It is run by a Basque, who in Madrid goes by the name Dos Santos. He told me his Basque name once, Iriarte. He's from a place called Durango, a town outside Bilbao, and a guy who kisses his fingertips maybe a little too often, being passionate about things, but having realized early on that I knew about wine, or at least how to drink it well, he likes to talk to me about it.

Dos can speak English. He spent two years in New Mexico with relatives when he was a boy. I didn't know this for awhile, a couple visits anyway. He was jabbering on in Spanish about a wine from Vitoria. I must have looked perplexed. He stopped mid-sentence and stared at me. He said in English, You don't know what I'm saying, do you? Part of it, I said. That's good enough, he said and continued on in Spanish. Since then he'll rarely speak English to me but keeps the Spanish simple and slow, and I can understand him better than anyone else here.

The best wine he has at the moment is Viña Diezmo. It's from Rioja, and I can remember the name easy enough. I translate it as 'ten mo.' You drink a glass, you feel like saying, Give me ten mo. It's delicious. He tells me that up till some twenty years ago, before the government put a halt to it, the vintners in Rioja would throw a dead cat into wine vats to get the fermentation process started. It gave the wine just the right ... (he kissed his fingertips). Diezmo, he says, for reasons which he can't guess at, still has that dead cat tang.

Half way down the steps yesterday on my way to Casa Antonio's, I came out of the kind of zen stupor I sometimes attain while walking to notice a pigeon hopping down the steps with me. When I stopped once, the pigeon stopped, too. We looked at each other. When I started down again, he did the same, all the way to the bottom. It was quite curious.

It led me to thinking about a job Billy Jenks had driving a delivery truck for Hartz-Mountain one summer. He delivered tropical birds and fish all over south Georgia and down to Jacksonville in Florida. It was a decent paying job, the only one of that type he ever held, and when he started it Billy had the idea that he was stepping up in the world. He was thinking career. But the driver who broke him in cleared that up early. He was a summer replacement. The fella explaining this to him was going on vacation. When his vacation was over, Billy would fill in for another driver who was going on vacation, and that's how it would go until early September, when he'd get canned. This took some of the romance out of the job, but still, the money was good.

Billy didn't care much one way or the other about fish, but he had a soft spot for his birds. They were in little cages in the back part of the truck, which was climate controlled. Billy had spent time in jail, mostly in drunk tanks. He knew how it felt to be cooped up, and when he'd stop for the night, sometimes he'd open the cages and let the birds stretch their wings. He'd sit there in the back of the truck in a lawn chair and talk to them.

He kept this job a long time for him, nearly three months. He was always on the road, and I didn't see him then until he got fired. Here's how it happened: A ten hour day was a short one but mostly they were fourteen, and every couple weeks he had to learn a new route, new faces. The peculiar cross-grained, contrariness, don't know exactly what you'd call it, that would in later years become his madness started to kick in. He began to note that the pet store people he delivered to just in general didn't seem to like him. They looked at him, he said, like he reminded them of someone else but not particularly someone they cared for much. Just something about him that they divined. Something not him exactly but something near enough to him that was way different than they were themselves. So he started drinking in his motel rooms at night after work to relieve what he called job-related stress. Then he started drinking late in the afternoons on his way to the motel rooms. And pretty soon he began at noon. He'd have a couple tall boys with his lunch and just keep on.

He rented a motel room outside Thomasville, Georgia, one evening. The gas pedal on his truck had been sticking all day. He worked on that a little. He didn't know jackshit about machinery, but he liked to think he did. He studied his map to see where he was going the next day. He checked the fish tanks and threw out what dead fish there were, and then he opened the bird cages. The birds didn't seem inclined to do much; they were about to roost. Billy spoke to them for awhile until he ran out of beer.

It struck him that another six-pack to round off the evening would be just right. Actually, he thought, three cans would be perfect, maybe four; he'd have what was left over for breakfast, start the new day on a good note. He drove several blocks until he found a convenience store. He put the truck in park, left the motor running, and went inside. It was a rural area but a busy highway. Across the road there was a ditch and beyond that a cotton field. Not by this time paying such close attention to details, Billy had failed to engage the transmission properly. He only came to this realization later of course. As he was purchasing the beer, he heard honking, and screeching of brakes outside.

Lookit that! the clerk said.

When Billy turned, he noticed that his truck was no longer where he'd left it. Had someone stolen it? he wondered. He ran outside. The truck had backed out of the parking lot and across the road on its own, knocked the hell out of itself clearing the ditch by the looks of it, and was just then careening in a mad slow way around the cotton field in reverse, flattening the crop there. He saw a turtledove fly away, no others escaped.

There were two fellas standing by their car nearby.

Who's at the wheel a that? the driver said. The car door was open, he was leaning on it. They were ready to leave.

Seems to be on its own, his buddy said. He asked Billy, What d'you think?

Billy opened a beer and took a sip. He said, Y'all goin' by the motel?

I was observing the exhibitionist last night when she did something out of the ordinary. She was looking right at me, though there was no way she could have seen me. I was in the dark, with just my nose showing around the curtain. She had on a gray sweatsuit. She doesn't look particularly good in clothes, so I don't know why I was watching her exactly, except that there wasn't anything on TV. She stood in front of her picture window and put on lipstick. She made a big production of this. Put it on thick. Then she gave the window a kiss, laughed and turned out the lights. Her windows look not to have been washed in years. Everything is a little blurry, so I didn't get the significance of it. But this morning, in the morning light, there's a blood red kiss on the windowpane.

The Madrileña women are sporting their fur coats as winter sets in. I find these exotic on the avenues of the dusk. Christmas lights are strung in designs around our neighborhood now and all of old town. It's pretty at night. It looks clean and bright and like a different place than in the day. During the nights I can't sleep, I've taken to walking through them. It always surprises me how many people there are on the streets and in the bars then. They brag that they get by here on less sleep than any other city in Europe, and I think this must be true.

Rain again this morning and an oddity—thunder.
It's not the kind of rolling thunder I'm used to but explodes like artillery. When the rain stopped, the air turned cold. Out on the street I observe the city at its finest. People walking so fast they would, at times, simply have to start running. A guy alongside me for awhile with a whole side of beef on his shoulder. A fish monger freshening up his items with a blue, garden watering can. The open-air fish markets with the produce on ice are a cold business now. A city clean-up man in a green jumpsuit singing opera over his rake. Madrileños in a lotto queue joking and stamping their feet. I pass a barbershop window, a man inside on the chair with a hot towel over his face. That looked enticing.

I took the Metro to Sol at lunchtime, around 2:30, and the car was packed. It was claustophobic. Standing room only. A woman in front of me—I couldn't tell you if she was pretty or what—had her ass pressed up against me. She had long black hair with a streak of white through it like a skunk, wore a black leather jacket cut like a matador's. A big ass. This is all I know of her. The movement of the car, and I right against her, gave me a hard-on. When she felt it, she jammed backward. This went on for a couple stops, her pushing against my pipe. When the train arrived at Sol, everyone piled out. She disappeared into the crowd. I never once saw her face.

I received a letter this morning from Jack Putz in Ireland, who is going to school at a place called Port Muck, up near Belfast. Outside of the weather there, it sounded ideal—lodging in an old farm house by the sea, only 11 students, he's working on his masters in poetry, and so on. Knowing Putz, however, I have an abiding suspicion there's something shady to it. He is purchasing a degree, say. He might be dropping by for the holidays, he tells me, if he can work it out. No return address. Signs his name Big Jack.

I'm curious how he got my address. I'm pretty sure I didn't want him to have it. Emilie's boyfriend is coming for Christmas also. He's black she finally tells Megan. This doesn't bother me. I don't get along with blacks anymore than I don't get along with whites. *Big Jack* has me a bit stumped though. I don't recall him being so big. He was always writing poems about Vikings and Druids. He was lost in time like that, but neither was he working with any precise historical knowledge. His Vikings were perpetually landing on a shore in some unidentifiable country. They came at night in their longboats. Sometimes though, if I remember right, in one poem especially, I think they came in cars.

Megan has rented us a room at the parador, or state-run hotel, in the village of Sigüenza from the 24th to the 26th of December. It will be, I imagine, the only time we'll ever spend Christmas in a castle.

Wednesday—rain. The scene outside grainy as an early 1920's movie. When it stops finally, a cloud descends into the streets. Old women move through this like black scarves in smoke.

I receive two post cards from Big Jack Putz. The first one says: Arrive the 23rd. Jack never was one for specific detail. The second contained a short poem—I'll spare you that—about a Viking washing up on the shores of Madrid.

Then, as advertised, on the 23rd, just before noon, Big Jack arrived.

Lucas, Megan called to me. She was picking yellow leaves off the geraniums on the balcony.

There's a very large drunk boy with a red nose cursing at the buzzer.

Our intercom has been intermittent lately. Sometimes it works, sometimes not.

It was Jack, sure enough. Looked like him in the face anyway. He has big teeth, with a gap between the two front ones. But he'd gained at least a hundred pounds since I'd last seen him. A wide 280 now, maybe more, and he's not but 5'9" in his boots. He was having a brief exchange with Nacho the Carbone about something. Jack had a flask he was nipping on.

I yell down to him, go down to meet him.

We shake hands; then he goes to pay the taxi fare. He says to the cabby: How many piñatas you need there, Ace?

It takes a while to get him up the three flights of stairs. He's sweating his ass off, puffing and blowing. I'm wondering why he has so much baggage. He's staying two weeks it turns out.

Wha'd you say to Nacho?

I said Fuck you too, ya goddamn ferret.

What happened?

I flipped a cigar butt into his shop there. I wasn't lookin'. I thought it was an alley. He come out an' got in my face.

I introduce him to Megan. She takes an immediate dislike to him.

We install him in my bedroom. I'll sleep with Megan. Within half an hour he turns it into a shambles. He unpacks, throws his clothes around. The room looks like a debris area left by high water along a creek. He chews cigars until they resemble wet rats and then leaves them lying about for Megan to jump at. He's diabetic, and you come upon him at odd moments shooting up insulin. This recalls other times, other friends, some of them no longer with us. And he will simply fall asleep while you're talking to him. There are any number of people I felt might like to sleep during a conversation with me, but he's the first one who actually did it. The diabetes doesn't stop him from eating pastry, however, and he will soon be frequenting the churro shop below. Or from drinking. He quickly downed every beer in the house—it wasn't even cold, a six of Aguila we had in the cupboard. No matter. He put some clothes in the washer. Later, Megan hangs these up to dry in the building well. She calls me to the kitchen on some pretext, points out his drawers. She observes them in disbelief. They resemble a one-man camping tent.

Emilie phoned just then. Her fiance's here, and after awhile they come over. He's this giant spade. He's six and half feet tall and can barely get his shoulders through the doorway. His name is Erik Giles. Emilie told us he was an All-American swimmer at Boston College a decade ago. Now he works for a health club in the Back Bay area. In the apartment all at once, there's no room left.

They, along with Emilie's lunatic roommate June, have rented a place for New Year's Eve at the American Hostal, which overlooks Puerta del Sol. They invite us to come.

They'd brought five bottles of wine with them, and we sit around and bullshit the rest of the afternoon. Erik can put it away. He drinks with the best of them. Putz recharges his glass often enough but doesn't handle it well. He gets a little maudlin. He needs to call his girlfriend back in Tampa he says. Talks with her awhile. I take it things aren't going so well between them. After Emilie and Erik leave, Putz starts throwing up. He'd eaten everything we had in the icebox. It goes for naught.

A short time later he asked if I'd look over some of his poems.

You're my mentor, Luke. This is said in a baying slur. Are you working on anything?

A story, I say. Maybe I'll put you in it.

What's it called?

Excerpts from the Book of Thieves.

What a title! That's terrific, Luke. I wish I could come up with a title like that.

He went into the bedroom to get his poems and, luckily, didn't return. He passed out.

Megan levels those oversized hazel eyes on me. She is noticeably pissed.

How old is he? she said.

Twenty-two.

When he drinks, she said, he's only 13.

This rings true. His old man is a preacher. At least on Sundays. The rest of the week he trades in baseball cards. Both parents sheltered him, especially his mother, who is a friend of mine and a fine woman. But Ireland is the first time he's lived away from their influence. He was a teetotaler at home. I have the terrible feeling that, in upcoming days, he's going to share some scenes with us that should have been worked out with his buddies when he was a kid.

He needs to learn how to drink, Megan said. She'd just finished cleaning the bathroom. Look at this. She's pointing to one of Putz' cigars. He's laid this one to rest on her crossword puzzle. It sits there like some ravaged lizard.

We're leaving for Sigüenza in the morning, I remind her.

Thankfully, she says. I can't take much more of this asshole.

I look at the clock. Putz has been in Madrid all of seven hours.

Sigüenza is northeast of Madrid, two hours by train. In medieval times the town was a powerful outpost, controlling the nearby salt mines, and it hasn't, in appearance, changed much since those times. The weather was cold there, a hard wind blowing, a sparse dry snow. There are 5000 inhabitants, but we didn't find many of them. Those we did come in contact with had a certain mineral quality, somewhat flinty I thought, a little salty, too. It was the most tranquil Spanish town I've ever been in, but it was Christmas and everything shut down.

The castle is built over Roman structures, on the high, defensible ground they favored, the Henares River curling around the base of the hill. Visigoth, Moor, Castilian followed. In the 14th century it was transformed into a residence for the Queen of Castile, Doña Blanca de Borbón, who was banished there by her husband, called Peter the Cruel. While she was en route to her wedding, the king fell in love with another woman. It was too late to call off the ceremony, so he went through with it, then imprisoned his new wife in the

Sigüenza castle. From our room overlooking the courtyard, you could all but picture her on the walkway atop the castle wall, facing west each evening toward the sunset and Madrid, and cursing him till the day she died.

The village spills downward from the castle. The houses are stone, the streets cobblestone, an occasional tiny courtyard with a fig tree behind granite walls. Here and there an arm-thick grapevine, growing directly out of the road, reached up to a balcony. Everything hemmed into small space. You walk straight up or down mostly, the streets only wide enough for an ox cart. And the countryside is pretty all around in that high desert, lonesome beauty way.

They had decent food in the old dining hall, which was a huge room. Most everyone dressed up to eat. The very strangest diner sat several tables from us the first night, a man with a three-day beard and paisley shirt who looked like a shrimper just out of Chokoloskee. He was the only one there I thought I might like to talk to, but the occasion never arose.

I'm afraid that I've hurried through Sigüenza. I've not mentioned that the full moon rested on a castle parapet Christmas Eve or how very luxurious those days were. But since the story isn't further concerned with this place, it must be enough to say that we went there for some peace and quiet, so that worked out well; and we were pretty sure it would be the last of that for awhile.

When we returned to Madrid, both the apartment and Putz were a complete mess. His girlfriend had called Christmas day and given the Dear John news. He's devastated. He's in ruins. He drank every bit of liquor in the house and then spent the rest of his money buying more. He's broke. He had mentioned several times being on a tight budget. Come to find out, he only brought a hundred bucks with him. And he can't go back to Ireland until the 5th of January. Megan's ready to throw him out on the street. She can barely stand the sight of him. He'd eaten all the food in the house. Now there's not even any sugar left, nothing. He ate the flour somehow. The place looks like it's been tossed by the cops.

Megan starts withdrawing money from the bank, giving it to me, telling me to go drink. Anything to get Putz out of the apartment. So Putz and I and Erik end up touring the bars. We call it touching up the day. We make up strange plans to amuse ourselves, like doing some caroling in the neighborhood. Go around to the balconies, sing *We Three Kings* or something. Day after day of this. I'm getting worn down. Putz is drinking his troubles away. He gets stumbling drunk. He's a load to steer around in this condition.

He seems to have grown even larger since he arrived. He really gets into the tapas. Olives, albondigas, cheese, shrimp, calamares, chorizo, ham, morcilla, clams. He shovels it down. He even likes callos, which is tripe. At one place they give him a plate of barbequed pig ears. Hey, Luke, he says, look—there's hair on this shit. What is it? I'm not interested in telling him. You don't know how he'll react. He'd already decorated several taverns in the neighborhood. We have to keep track of those we shouldn't return to.

One day, Megan and I and Putz go for lunch at a little restaurant down the street from our apartment. Platos combinados are 750-900 pesetas, the Menú, or daily special, 950. The food is cheap, they have a good waiter, nice checkered tablecloths, and it's a greasy spoon. As if to emphasize the point, whatever you ordered, the cook threw a fried egg on top of it. Megan had a meatball dish, I had roast pork, and Putz had fried fish. In an oddity of presentation I'd never quite seen before, they all appeared to be the same item.

Even stranger was the entertainment.

Putz took two bites of his food and had to go to the bathroom. I'm sitting there watching my plate coagulate, when in come six, seven deaf and mute folks. They were that and also acted somewhat goofy. They're all dressed alike, hospital greens. It took awhile to discover who their attendant was. At the moment, he's out trying to find a parking spot for the van. Three of them, three ladies, had to go to the bathroom, and pretty bad apparently.

Lucky like that how we are, our table is located right next to the toilets.

The women's toilet is out of order. It's closed up, there's a sawhorse in front of it. And the men's is locked from the inside, as Putz is now in there taking a dump.

The three signers seemed to utterly flip over this locked door. Perhaps it was the sawhorse, too, that inspired some ancient terror—I just couldn't understand it. But suddenly they're demented. One of them grabs the doorknob and starts yanking hell out of it. The second beats on the wall with her little fists. The third, the biggest of the lot, stands behind these two, admiring their work I took it, and from time to time, hopped up and down wildly, although, bless her, she's kind of hefty and never quite got off the ground.

From inside there I hear Putz say, Hey, Luke … is that you? Quit horsin' around now … But the ladies are nearly routing the door, and it finally dawns on him that it's not me. He starts yelling— Hey motherfucker I'm takin' a shit here goddamn it! The ladies, of course, can't hear this. Now from behind here comes the big one, rams the door with her shoulder …

Putz is a weird looking character. He appears to be dressed in prison garb. His clothes fit him like sackcloth. His pants land in a puddle over his boots. No neck. Bristly head. I give him my watch cap to wear, and he pulls it down over his ears. He has a long winter coat he calls his Viking coat, claims it's made of musk ox hide. He walks hunched over, headlong, but somehow as if he's in deep mud, gravity tugging heavily on him. He snorts and moans. It's like walking around town with a short bear.

All the time now he's crying in his beer over this girlfriend who dropped him. Her name is Pattie. A couple times he actually starts bawling in public about her. She works at a fast food joint in Tampa. She went sweet on one of her fellow hamburger flippers. I've met this girl. A big blonde. A big body anyway, her head's kind of little. As far as I'm concerned, even Putz could do better. I finally tell him, Look, Jack … you mention Pattie's name in front of me one more time, I'm not going to speak to you again in my life.

The next morning he starts off, Luke … you know that person

I'm not supposed to mention no more? And starts carrying on about her again. He just doesn't say her name.

One day he asked me to take a look at a poem he'd started. I'm expecting more Vikings, maybe some Druids. But it's even more appalling. The first three lines read like so: *I remember the apartment we had/ it was over the fire department/ where you cooked me noodles*

What do you think? he said.

A thing I really started to find troubling was that he never strayed more than a foot or two away from me. Try that sometime. After awhile it got so I'd push him away, keep him at arm's length at least. Tell him, Stay the fuck over there. What's the matter with you? And it never occurred to him to go anywhere on his own. He'd just sit around in the evenings with us.

I started sending him to the market for wine. It allowed me a small measure of solitude. The old ladies there, however, are a hardened lot in the check-out lines—you just can't let them share their madness with you—and they soon got the best of him. He returned one night empty-handed. He gave a short but impassioned speech: It's brutal in lines, he said. I'm tired of being bullied by tiny, 80-year-old women. I've had it. I'm at the end of my rope. I'm starting to push back. They're stronger than they look. They're savage. I can't match them there. And stupid. I could use wit against them, but they wouldn't get it. And besides, they don't understand a goddamn thing I say. I'm thinking about dropping one with a right cross. Maybe the word will get around. They'd better watch their P's and Q's from now on, if you know what I mean ... It was like some nutter addressing the public at large. Noting that he had stunned his immediate audience, he went to bed.

Do you have any idea, I asked Megan, what that was about? Try not to be uncharitable.

Where's the wine? she said.

I found out from him later on that the old ladies had so unnerved him, he'd bolted from the store.

Finally Megan tells him point blank one night, You need to go out on your own tomorrow. I want to spend some time with Lucas.

He slaps himself in the temple.

That's what I was thinking, he said, taking another handful of pretzels. That was just the thought I had in my mind.

Megan about rolls her eyes out of her head.

I gave him 20 bucks in pesetas the next day, and he went off by himself. He's gone all day and into the evening, and when he returns he doesn't say where he's been but is much happier than he's been of late. A big goofy smile. He's manic.

Finally I asked him, Wha'd you do today?

The three of us were sitting in the living room.

I went to a convent, he says.

A convent?

It was really interesting. They have … like a trophy room.

Relics, I said.

That's it. I saw St. Thomas of Padua's skull. He was the first one who read books without moving his lips. He sort of invented that … Putz glances at Megan, who is ignoring him, looks back and gives me a wink.

He takes me aside at some point later.

Luke, he says. I think I fell in love.

He looks at me like I'm supposed to say something to that.

I want you to meet her.

When?

How 'bout now? It's early.

I figure he's out of money again and could use a drink. Anyway, we go downtown. As it turns out, he hasn't actually met the woman either. Would I introduce them? We end up on Calle Valverde. Whores and cops in equal number tonight. They stand around chatting with each other. There's live sex acts. Putz guides me along like I'm new in town, pointing out those parts of the street where was the most sport. He stops in front of a sex parlor.

I'm gonna put you next to something good, he says.

He pretends like he's holding me back.

Don't you run in there like a blind dog in a meat market now! he says. He's laughing, getting a kick out of it. I remember that in Tampa he had this weakness for local color.

I went into a stall. Putz took the one next to me. He has some trouble with the lock on his door. He's banging it. The set-up is like a peep show, only when the windows open, there's live people there, young, sexual athletes presumably, sometimes not. At the moment there's a woman lying on her stomach not even moving. She's talking to her partner, who's behind the curtains. We're looking at the back of her head. A straw-haired blonde. Her ass looks like it's been deflated.

Is that her?

I'm not sure, he says. I can't see her face.

I hear him flopping around over there.

Watch it, Luke, he says, the floor's slippery.

There's a pane of glass between me and the woman. Somebody in there before seems to have pressed his whole face to the window. It's so smudged I can barely see. The pervert. She turns her body a little so I can see her cunt, shaved of course; it seems to be in vogue—all but for a little patch at the top that looks very much like Hitler's mustache. It must call to mind some strange thoughts dining there. She slaps it a couple times, maybe trying to wake it up. Putz starts yelling, Hey, damn, let's get with it! Finally she notices that customers have arrived. She turns her face toward us and licks her shoulder—she's got the same little brush under her nose. It looks real. It's no five o'clock shadow. Maybe it's pasted on. That's got to be it. A stage prop. It's theatrical. All this runs through my mind quickly. But I'll tell you, it made you feel like a goosestep or two right there, only there's not enough room.

Definitely not the one, I hear Putz say.

I come out of the stall. Putz can't get the door open on his. He's locked in. He starts bellowing. I went outside the shop and had a smoke. He's done the same thing at the apartment. Everything he touched broke. The hot water heater. The floor lamp. At the moment they're useless because he handled them. By the time I'm done with the cigarette, they've gotten him free.

He says not a word about being detained inside. He muses: Nothing quite like a mustachio'd woman ...

We're walking aimlessly and soon come across a tall transvestite in our way. As we pass by, Putz gooses her. She starts following us shouting in English, That'll be five bucks, asshole ... you owe me five bucks for that!

We escape into the nearest bar. There are dancers on a catwalk here. Others working the crowd. I moved around trying to find one that was acceptable to look at. They were all very large and bottle blonde, their hair in various stages of distress and electricity. The place was big, and I managed to lose Putz somehow. All of sudden he wasn't beside me, and I didn't look very hard to find him. I got a beer and wandered into the backroom, where the music wasn't so loud, and a sex show was just beginning—a fat lady and a midget.

The midget was this little old bald guy. He sported a handlebar mustache, had on combat boots, and that was it. He stood around doing muscle poses—which, he didn't exactly have any muscles to speak of, so it was pretty funny. He had to get up on a chair to reach the fat lady. She was enormous, her breasts like water balloons that hung down below her waist.

It seemed more a comedy routine than anything. She was so fat, he couldn't get to it. Finally he's trying to stick it in her arm, her ear, etc. And I guess it was part of the act, but they didn't seem to be on the best of terms. It looked to me that there was some truth in it—the fat lady wasn't pleased with this little guy for some reason. He was sort of stealing the show with his muscle poses, too. He was bringing down the house with that. Whenever he'd start this, she'd give him a homicidal look, which he totally ignored, though, honestly, she didn't appear to be one you should cross. At this point, he pinched her or something. I missed exactly what happened. But she took one of her tits in her hand like a club and smashed him upside the head with it. He'd been into a muscle pose just then and didn't see it coming. He dropped off the chair like he'd been shot.

Freaks have always interested me. They are what a good many people look like, I suspect, if somehow a picture could be taken on the inside. They were just unlucky enough to be born without camouflage.

I was thinking this when Putz reappeared at my side.

You think he's hurt? he said.

The backroom crowd that had taken in the show are in stitches, but I'm keeping an eye on the midget. He hit the floor awkwardly and looks coldcocked to me, but then again I'm not sure if it's part of the act or what. Before I can answer Putz, he takes me by the arm.

Come on, he says. We return to the front room. He escorts me to one side. In the darkest corner, a man in a wheelchair was parked next to a dancer with ash blonde hair. He had on a 1930s hat tilted back on his head and held up a burned-out cigar as if making some point with it, but what struck me was the madcap expression on his face. He looked completely daft, like he was in a trance. Then I noticed one of the woman's hands was missing, buried inside his fly.

That's her, Putz says.

Every morning now, Big Jack fries a half dozen eggs in a pool of butter. The apartment is rancid with it. He can't bother with a plate. The frying pan is more direct. He doesn't eat food exactly; he inhales it. The toilet's on its last legs. It rocks back and forth when you sit on it. The washing machine has learned how to walk. It apparently wants to escape. At night in bed, he snores loudly and has a varied repertoire of sleeping sounds. Bear snuffles. Seal barks. A duck gagging. We've got a zoo in there. Megan has taken to crossing off days on the calendar. The 5th of January has a big star by it.

New Year's Eve Day.

Erik is here and our endless houseguest, who woke at noon, shot up insulin, then had some churros and a beer. We stay around the apartment all afternoon while Megan and Emilie are out shopping.

Everyone is tired. The drinking excursions have taken their toll. Putz is completely strung out. The previous night, the three of us went down to the Lavapiés barrio looking for Chelo, who wasn't around. We ended up at Café Barbieri. At midnight Putz says he has to go home. He's bouncing from this to that, customers, tables jostled in the process. He'd learned how to drink in Ireland he said, but not well we thought. He plows through the crowd finally. He gets to an area near the door where there are couples dancing, stops and does some movements, like he's setting the hook on a fish—combined with this he appeared to be stamping out a cigarette with his left foot.

I guess it was a dance step. Then he continued on. The metro's visible from the front door. Hard to miss. It's going to take him three hours to get back to the apartment, but we don't know this at the time. We don't even say goodbye. We just watch him leave. Erik said, There's goes Cinderella.

Erik calls his brother in the States. He puts down some bets on the bowl games that have yet to be played. He's interesting to talk to. He's bright, irreverent. His hair is cut close to his big cat head. As large as he is, I notice that he treats Emilie gently, his hands on her like touching an item breakable. There are not many blacks in Madrid and certainly very few as tall and wide as he is. He's an attraction around the neighborhood. The entire Carbone crew appear petrified as he walks past. And nobody else, it seems, knows quite what to make of him. In my shirt pocket I find a napkin I'd written on last night at Barbieri's. It says: All looked have did badly, but the truth is knowing ever.

Megan rented a room in the Reina Victoria Hotel at Plaza Santa Ana for New Year's Eve. We go there around six. Our windows look out on the Plaza del Ángel side. Across the street is Café Central. Bullfighters used to stay at this hotel in the old days. It wasn't so fancy back then, but neither were they. The most skillful now are no less than movie stars. At the same time, it's the only profession that requires you to wear pink socks, a sherbert-colored suit, and get covered in bull snot and blood when you work.

There are elegant people around the hotel lobby. I hear English, Spanish, German, French, Portuguese … each group looks upon the others as if they're from a developing country. There's much gold in the room. There are dark tans—these stand out in the Madrid winter, as everyone has gone pasty by now. Most of the fellas are in tailored suits yet retain somehow the look of traveling salesmen. But the women are looking smart, no doubt about it. Some of their handbags must go for a grand. Galliano is big with them. Stella McCartney. How do I know this? a man who buys exclusively from thrift shops. I overheard a conversation between two Brit ladies. They were quite critical of the room—*Check out the bitch in that muddy plum sort of thing. What would you call that look … chronic malaise?* And there are a few in lingerie-inspired silk dresses; these women appear to be wearing their slips. The old Spanish men from the neighborhood who drink at the bar observe them with a mixture of amusement and interest.

There's something deeply superficial about the rich, but they always *look* so good. The men could dress all in white if they wanted to and get away with it, whereas I would have such an outfit trashed within hours. I know a few ranchers from San Ann who probably have as much money, but you'd never know it. They always look like they're going fishing.

The hotel room we're staying in is larger than our entire apartment. We brought two bottles of rioja with us, Castillo Ygay 1987, black olives, Manchego cheese. We finished one bottle and went out for dinner. There's a little working class restaurant around the corner we eat at sometimes. The food is good and inexpensive. It was closed, however, and we ended up at a paella place on Echegaray. They had already run out of paella, but I wasn't so hungry anyway. I had a bowl of fish soup. It was neither bad nor good; it was of no consequence. I didn't pay attention to the price when I ordered. Mcgan had roast veal, which resembled jerky. When the bill came, my soup was 2300 pesetas. A place like that, you feel like they just stuck a hand in your pocket. Why bother to eat? I'm thinking. Just go to the door and throw cash at them. In my usual sage manner, I commented to Megan as we were leaving, It should, at least, be the last indignity this particular year can hand us …

Around 10:30, in a pouring rain, we walked over to Puerto del Sol and the American Hostal. At Sol, ten streets meet and 'debouch' as one old writer had it. The room is on the third floor. It's not a room for any of us to stay the night in; it's just to take in the scene. There's a balcony, all but too narrow to stand on. The room is small to begin with, and a bed takes up a good half of it. A bathroom with a tub and shower. If you sit on the toilet, your head is lodged in the sink. There's Megan and I, Emilie and Erik, June Bug, Putz, and a Brazilian couple, Guillerme and Virginia, who take a Spanish class with Emilie. Virginia came to Madrid to learn the language. She's a real sweetheart, and her body just sort of knocks you backward. Guillerme is a lawyer in Rio, but he soon followed her. How come? I asked. He speaks some English. He said, Because of the way men look at her. I laugh awkwardly, I start looking around for something. Putz' theme for the night is to get mortal drunk. He's going to yodel in the thundermug, he says. We don't know what that means exactly, but we're to find out.

I'd given him some money the day before. With the last of that, he'd purchased three bottles of very questionable wine, the cheapest he could find at the market. It's little more than swill. He drinks it out of the bottle, and he's not wasting time. He's doing some trying-to-forget kind of drinking. The bed is stacked with coats, beer, wine, cider, food. Not everyone can fit in the room at once. June Bug is saying how she had to pull strings to get it. We need to be on our best behavior she keeps reminding us.

June Bug always strikes me as a grown-up majorette. She threw her baton into the air one game, and it never came down. Life's been a little off since. Something missing. The big baton I take it. And *since* is getting on to ten years now. She and Emilie became roommates by circumstance and necessity, and it's been a mistake. You just have to like Emilie, even putting aside her beauty. To her looks she adds vitality and good humor.

Emilie is many things, in other words, that June Bug is not. The latter is wearing a black and white pantsuit that calls to mind a disheveled magpie or penguin. The pattern seems to make her hips even larger I notice, though they are hardly in need of exaggeration. She keeps close tabs on her possessions in their flat. She's told Emilie expressly not to let Erik use certain things. Especially don't use her soap she warned. Erik tells me he soaped up his ass good with it.

June Bug talks in a whine that drives me nuts. She needs someone to hand her a laugh certainly. Both she and Putz are so lame, I'm thinking something might shape up between them. I see them sitting together once. Before long, Putz says, Well … S C E U S E me, and shortly thereafter takes a nap while she's speaking to him. Down the hall, there's a bar with a dance floor and a big long balcony that faces Sol; and out in the street there are 10,000 bedlamites in the downpour partying away.

Somewhere during the night I overheard Putz ask Megan, How come in Tampa they call him St. Luke?

Who calls him that? Megan said.

Well … Putz had to think on it and doesn't come up with an answer. Like maybe he's the only one said it.

Megan says, The only thing saintly about Lucas is that he used to be so much worse.

As things play out, this is to be the last complete sentence she ever speaks to him.

Close to midnight we're all out in the bar area, 15-20 people besides us, a good many of them American, the rest Spanish, just having a great time, but then June Bug comes over to me, I'm close to the balcony watching the crowd below, the incredible number of umbrellas. At each chime of the big clock bell across the street, the Spanish girl beside me has eaten a grape. She will eat twelve of them, for luck, she has just explained. One for each month of the year. June Bug says, J a c k n e e d s h e l p. I had an all but irresistible urge to knock the shit out of her. But outside they're counting down: *seis ... cinco ... cuatro ...* I look behind me. Putz is on a couch turning green. He's pickled. Just then the New Year hit, but through the commotion I hear a familiar gagging sound. Putz starts projectile vomiting. People around him are going, Oh, for Christ's sake! A nice older couple from Iowa, who were visiting their granddaughter in Madrid and that I'd had a pleasant conversation with earlier, are standing there with hands limply outstretched, looking down at themselves in revulsion. He's doused them.

It took Guillerme, who doesn't even know the ass, the next hour to get him sober enough to put to bed. Holding his head under the cold water shower and all. He was flopping around in the tub like a fish. Finally he went comatose. We thought he might be dead, but nobody seemed overly concerned about it. We had to carry him from the bathroom; this was very much like trying to move a large pudding. We left him at the hostal to sleep it off. Megan says she has some cautionary advice for future visitors. Bring money, don't plan on staying long. And no children allowed.

But let me return to the street scene a moment. It was what I'd call flat out crazy there and just kept getting rowdier. At midnight thousands of people uncork cava or champagne, make a toast, drink, then take the bottle by the throat, shake it and spray those standing around them. I see an area down to the left starts clearing. There's an empty circle of cobblestones. I couldn't figure out why. Then all of a sudden the first bottle came flying out of the crowd and broke there. There's fireworks, bells tolling, everyone screaming and laughing, much thrashing around in the fountains, the statues covered with riders, all kind of noise-makers going, but here comes a hundred bottles breaking, now a thousand, and suddenly the scene turned into a cross between a celebration and riot. This went on until the entire plaza emptied of people. Nothing left but broken glass and police and the rain.

We returned to our hotel by 1 a.m. The next day at noon, back in our neighborhood, there were revelers still wandering around in tuxedos and evening dresses, champagne glasses in hand.

Putz showed up at the apartment soon after us. They'd found him in bed at the hostal and quickly gave him the boot. His clothes are soaked. He's got hangover eyes like I've never seen before. They are orange and totally uninhabited. Somewhere into the third bottle of wine he lost track of the night. He's curious why Megan refuses to speak to him.

Megan tells me, I don't know who I'd rather have visit than Jack … though, any of the major root crops would have been fine. An artichoke even, a nice leek.

There was snow in Madrid on New Year's afternoon, and it really came down—the Madrileños walking the streets under snow-covered umbrellas, the tree branches like Japanese prints. The snow covered everything, and I'd never seen the town prettier.

Some days later, coming back on the bus from the airport after seeing off Putz, I remember a dream I had in the night. I had shaved my beard and looked like someone else. Now and then, when I took a step, the earth moved underfoot, something like stepping on dog tails. I noted, as in all my dreams lately, that I carried a loaded .38.

I'm not sure what it is about me—why the lame and bedeviled and those on a fool's errand gather to me like some mad constellation. Or why it is that I grow all but fond of them. Big Jack is just the latest in the cast. Maybe the bus was full of them even as I thought this. I didn't want to look around or notice it too clearly, as they stretch away from here and back through time.

I've never determined my own motivation for dealing with them. They have a certain entertainment value. They show me what I have fallen away from, perhaps. But it's something more that I don't understand.

Our last bit of conversation, just before he boarded the plane, Putz tells me:

I came up with a good title for my poem.

I nodded vaguely.

I'm gonna call it 'The Noodle Eaters,' he said. It's sort of like Van Gogh's 'The Potato Eaters,' see … only this is noodles.

He'd been working hard on the poem the last couple nights. It's at 35 lines, few of which made the least bit of sense or seemed in any way connected to the rest.

You don't think it gives it away too much, though? he said.

6 January
from *The New York Times*
Spain: 5th Terror Suspect Held

The police arrested the fifth suspected member of a cell of the Basque armed separatist group ETA. said to have been planning a bomb attack on a Civil Guard convoy in the Basque region. Francisco Javier Cano Arce was detained in Bilbao after four other suspected bomb-making members of the cell were arrested and explosives, bomb-making equipment and firearms were found. Still at large is the cell's reputed leader, Francisco Rementeria, who eluded the police after the plot to attack the convoy was foiled, officials said.

The millennium didn't do much for me. I think I should feel differently, more aware of time slipping away possibly, but it's not happening. When I notice the year 2000 on the calendar, however, it does throw me a bit.

Before Erik left for Boston he mentioned, You know … I was watching Putz … and I was aware of the clock. I think he puked across that space … from the old millennium to the new.

A bad sign?

Not good, he said.

8 January Saturday
Ana Dolores invited us out to her chalet located in the town of Aldea del Fresco, about an hour road trip from Madrid. Few people live there year round. It's a town of summer homes for Madrileños. She'd brought back some steaks from Argentina and made soup and green beans. Her son, Graziano, drove us there. He's a ballroom

dancer. He spoke English well. On the way through Madrid I asked him several questions about what we were passing, but he seemed to know little. I don't like to watch monuments, he explained.

Basically we went to the chalet to feed Ana Dolores' cat that lives there alone in the basement. There's a little swinging door the cat can go in and out of, and that area truly reeked. She takes the cat food every couple weeks, a bag of it. The chalet was large. Standing by the swimming pool, I got ticked off that this huge place housed only a cat. I was comparing it to our hovel in Argüelles. I had asked to stop on the way in to town so that I could buy some wine. I felt like drinking. I have wine, she said.

We eat lunch. The bottle of wine Ana Dolores brought along went quickly. The Argentine steaks were quite good. The soup, I don't know. It was cocido, just the watery part. But the green beans were very good also. She has another bottle, 2 litre, about half full of wine from a local bodega. I'll try that, I said. I pour it down. Megan tells me later it was a horrible little wine, that it'd been around who knows how long, but it tasted fine to me. A bit sour, but what the hell. Seeing that I'm still thirsty, her son finally digs out of a cabinet a really good bottle from Navarre. Fifteen years old. I detect that perhaps his mother is not too happy to let this go. Only Graziano and I want any. He takes a sip or two from his glass. Otherwise, it's just setting there. I was about to say, I'll polish that off for you if you run out of patience with it, but then he left for Madrid. The rest of us will take a bus back. Graziano's glass is across the table from me. This Navarre wine, soon it's done, and no one had drunk of it but me. It was good old wine.

I kept my eye on her son's glass. It was nearly full. I was maybe a little skunked at this point, slurring my words. I watched hopefully for Ana Dolores to turn her back, but she never did. Finally, cleaning up the table, she took the glass and was about to dump the wine into the sink. I rushed out of my chair and grabbed it from her. No use wasting good wine! I shout and throw it back in a ludicrous theatrical way.

She looked at me funny after that, perhaps like she'd seen me for the very first time. I don't think we'll have any trouble breaking the lease now. She didn't like what she saw.

I walked through Plaza Santa Ana this afternoon. I stopped on the corner and bought chestnuts, mainly to stand by the roaster's grill for a few moments, the air trembling with heat above it like a living thing. Those he gives me are charred black. I eat a chestnut and look around. There are no terrazas now, no tourists. It's all rather dismal, given over to winos and the unconscionable number of pigeons that moan in the trees, having taken over for the leaves, long fallen.

One fella with a shopping cart for a closet was warming his hands over a little fire he'd made on the ground, mostly smoke, orange peels for kindling. Other street dwellers, men and women, I'm not sure if they're winos or addicts or if they are in any way preferential in their habits, sit on the wooden benches in the sun, engaged in argumentative conversation. They like to make their point. They have gone primitive in their looks, ancient mankind camping here awhile. Their faces this time of year are bronzed from all day exposure to the winter sun. Another who stood somewhat separate was pretending to feed the pigeons. He didn't have any bread to throw to them, he just pretended that he did. Great sport there, as you can imagine, and he had a good crowd of birds around him. One pigeon sat on his shoulder, as if studying his actions and trying to decipher the trick.

The area has been transmuted from the garden spot of the summer and fall when the bars that line the streets have tables and chairs crowding the sidewalk under the old trees there and the square in the middle too is full of tables, and waiters sweep by distractedly avoiding eye contact. That's all gone like it was erased.

But I find the plaza somewhat more amusing now in its bleakness.

At the east end stands a dark statue of Garcia Lorca, a dove in his hands. Perhaps it has a kind of scarecrow effect, as I don't often see pigeons on it. There is a wino now who likes to stand next to Lorca and assume the same pose, holding a tall can of San Miguel beer or a box of wine. He has a twisted-wire beard, any number of layers of clothing, and often as not a cooking pot on his head. He fancies himself I think the oracle of the plaza. He's fond of overlong speeches to the public, which universally ignores him.

The people of this neighborhood are the owners of some of the largest dogs in Madrid. Afghans, Great Danes, Wolfhounds, beasts that alone must take up most of a room in the little apartments around here. Who can make anything of that?

As usual I record this but can find no significance to any of it at all. Recently I read an article in the paper about writing. Write what you know, it said. They always tell you that like it's big news. This is all I know today. I make a note to myself, I jot it down on a bar napkin: These are the chronicles of a very small life.

Due to administrative problems at Kevin and Chelo's school, the crew does not go back to work until Monday, January 11th. They will work until the 21st and then have three weeks off. Until the 10th of the month, up to about 11:30 in the morning, however, no one had any idea where Chelo might be. Then he showed up at our place. Megan had just left to have coffee with Emilie.

Chelo sat down in my chair.

You got any tuna fish? he said. I've been thinking all morning about tuna fish.

He'd brought a bench and a hundred and sixty pounds of weights with him on a little dolly. He'd bought them off a guy in the neighborhood. They'd been advertised in *Segundomano*. He can't afford the gym anymore.

It's freezing in here, he says. You want I should light the bombona?

It broke.

I bring out the electric heater from the bathroom. It's 43 degrees outside, the high for the day. With the electric heater, I can't get the temperature in the living room above 52. At the moment, I'm wearing jeans, a t-shirt, two sweatshirts, flannel shirt, a heavy wool vest that makes me look like a sheep, and my watch cap.

You tell Ana Dolores about it?

She's not returning our calls. I think I insulted her.

That's hard to do, he said.

It's a long story, I said.

We started lifting weights. After awhile I took off my cap. I see him once again looking at the scar on my forehead, acquired from a glass shard when my truck window shattered.

I asked Megan about it, he says.

About what?

The scar.

Wha'd she say?

That you got in an accident.

She say anything else?

She says after the accident, you lost your bite.

Sure.

Says all of a sudden you became a nice guy.

I thought I was that way before.

No, he says … you weren't. I remember … He's doing some bench presses. You were different then … kinda sulled up. Hostile … like you was always pissed. You were hard to get along with.

I don't know, I said.

No, really, he says. You were an asshole.

I really don't know how to answer that. He hands me the dumbbells. I do some curls.

What happened anyway? He nods at my face. The accident …

I'm only planning on doing 10 reps but end up doing 30. The accident takes some thought.

You remember Earl Boss? I said.

The big guy?

Yeah …

Earl claimed to be a bastard grandchild of Babe Ruth. Ruth had spent time in the bars of St. Petersburg and Tampa during many a spring training. Earl was not always trustworthy in his comments, however; as a matter of fact, he hardly ever was. He was prone to outrageous yarns, but he did resemble Ruth, large head, beefy face, big stomach, only a larger version, 6'4", 300 pounds, and not so much of it in his legs. They were spindly. He liked to wear a pinstripe t-shirt with the number 3 on the back, Ruth's number, and he ate a lot of hot dogs. He was in a perpetual beer-drinking contest—Earl against the icebox. But Ruth's career batting average was .342. His was .000. He wasn't an athlete. He could do the 7th inning stretch pretty good. That was about it.

That's one guy, Chelo said, I guess I knew him ten years, I mean I didn't really know him that well, just to say hello, how the hell are ya, but I never once saw him straight.

Me either, I said.

The first time I met him, Chelo said, he was sleeping on the sidewalk outside a party up in the north end. It was early in the afternoon. He'd fallen out already. A friend I was with woke him up and introduced us. He got into a sitting position there on the sidewalk. He mumbled something. I think he was trying to say, Hey, nice to meet ya, something … I don't know, it was unintelligible. Then he turned his head to the side and threw up.

Earl was the neighborhood pharmacist, unlicensed but quite knowledgeable. He'd decided on the profession early in life, though to complete any schooling meant that he would have to leave his apartment for long periods of time without a beer in his hand, long for him being a half hour or so, and getting a diploma wasn't an option. So he studied on his own. He was a pharmaceutical hobbyist.

He was married to a nurse, a stocky, pleasant woman, obviously very understanding, who seemed to work 60-70 hours a week. I rarely encountered her. Earl augmented their income by selling marijuana, though he smoked so much I don't believe profit came of it, and he didn't, for as long I knew him, do much more than sit around his duplex apartment and get high, read history books or popular magazines, watch porno or sporting events, drink whatever beer happened to be on sale, and talk continuously in a drawly, over-loud, out the side of his mouth way about this and that and whatever had caught his interest at the moment. He bought his food exclusively at convenience stores. He, at one time, seemed very serious about doing a sort of dining guide for such establishments. He had plenty of time to think in these directions.

Earl was knowledgeable about a good many things—politics, for example, law, even the tax code—but he knew best of all how to con doctors. It didn't always work, but often enough doctors would write him a prescription just to get him the hell out of their waiting rooms. He dressed most days like he lived in a van down by the river. But when he went for a script, he wore a suit and tie, which was somehow much more disturbing. He'd park his big ass in a waiting room and start commenting loudly about politics or religion. His hulking presence made people uncomfortable to begin with, and doctors weren't immune to this. So he'd get a script or not and almost always the admonition to not return. But he had one steady who wrote him scripts. This doctor was an out and out crook. Earl was always on the lookout for more of this type physician. The end result of his efforts, however, was that he had quite an array of drugs on hand. The one that interested me most at the time was Ritalin.

What's Boss got to do with it? Chelo said.

He was the one caused the accident, I said. I was hangin' around with Earl then because I had a lot of free time that summer. I was in Tampa, staying with Billy Jenks. I got into following baseball. If there was a day game on, I'd go over to Earl's, get loaded, and we'd watch whoever was playing, mostly the Cubs. He always had the air cranked down to 65 degrees. It was comfortable there.

But he had this bad habit, say if someone come over to his place and he didn't want them around just then, or maybe you interrupted him too many times or some such, he'd slip you a mickey.

I saw him do it a couple times. He had this downer called Soma. You'd have to be in a state of panic to need this drug in real life. Any normal person, it'd just put you to sleep and wouldn't take long doing so. And if Earl didn't feel like listening to you, he'd put some in your drink and knock you stupid with it. Then that one day he did it to me. I'd warned him not to do that, but …

I was talking too much for him, I guess that was it. We watched a game and drank a case of cheap beer. I'd brought a pint of Evan Williams that day. He didn't have any Ritalin on hand. Nothing to keep me ahead of the drinking. I get to talkin' on whiskey sometimes, which is better than when it, like it usually does, just makes me angry. It was hard to get a word in edgewise with Earl, but I'd done it. He was one of those guys, you had something to say, you had to be quick. But I'd got on his nerves, and he put that shit in my drink.

Only thing was, I was leavin' just about then anyway. I take what's left of the bourbon with me in a plastic glass along with some Coke in it. He mixed that last drink. I thought it tasted funny, but I wasn't exactly thinking clear. And the Soma don't hit me till I'm on the road. I finished off the drink, and I remember this big downward rush and toward the end there going about seven miles an hour and having a difficult time of it.

Then I just drove off the side into a culvert and rolled my truck. Though I don't recall that, being as how I was asleep at the time. Totaled my pickup. And I liked that truck, a good little Ford Ranger, only had 50,000 miles on it, just getting broke in.

Did your life flash before your eyes? Chelo said.

Yeah. What I noticed was that it was pretty short. But ... no, that didn't happen. Nothin' like that. I was probably dreaming when it happened.

I woke up in the emergency room. They'd shot me with speed so I'd come around. I mean I was awake just like that. The airbag had knocked the hell out of my face. It burned like crazy. That's what concerned me at first. That and the blood all over me from the cut. I felt disoriented. I wasn't hearing well. Some of the things I thought I heard didn't make good sense. I heard a nurse say, I can't get a pulse. I guess it was a nurse. I can't see who's talking 'cause my eyes are swollen shut.

A little while later, and I don't know if this was even real or not, I hear a voice ask, Is he going to die? And someone else answered, No ... worse than that. That had to be the drugs talking, right?

Then a voice I took to be the doctor's says, We need to scan his head. See if there's anything in there.

I'm a source of amusement to medical people.

I was in the hospital four days. After I could open my eyes, I was seeing double for a good long while. I had this cut on my forehead, the doctor wondering aloud how the glass had made such a straight line. I was black and blue all over. I couldn't have looked any prettier. But the real damage was inside—my brain had been jarred, good and proper. And it was six weeks before I got back on my feet, got somewhat normal again.

Megan took me home from the hospital, home to San Ann. I'd been staying with Billy, like I said. He had a trailer on Nebraska Ave. The highlight of the view was a dumpster. So it was nice to get to familiar ground. Megan just stayed on then and took care of me. I couldn't remember how to do the simplest things. One day I went for a walk around the block. I was on the lookout for my old self, which tells you something, and locked myself out of the house. Megan was inside taking a nap. But I couldn't recall how you would get someone's attention inside. To knock on the door, ring the doorbell … didn't occur to me. So I started throwing my body at the door. I did cross-body blocks on the door until she opened it.

They never did pin down exactly what was wrong. I had a big headache, and it wouldn't go away, and this feelin' of being underwater. Gave me pills for this and that. One thing they put me on was lithium carbide for the manic behavior I was experiencing. I'd get way under water for awhile and kind of insubstantial. Then a day would come where I'd have this unaccountable feeling that good things were about to happen. And my head would float up to the ceiling and stay there.

But I lost track and took a extra lithium one day, then every half hour or so I'd stamp hell out of my right foot. I mean, that'll make you feel like a peckerwood. I threw that shit away then and there and never took another. When I come out the other end of all this is when Megan started telling me, You know, you're different. You're much more pleasant to be around. You're a better person.

It musta been quite a relief to her that you weren't a prick anymore, Chelo said.

13 January Thursday—Very cold.

Chelo left his weights at our apartment, which I suspect will now become his new gym.

I asked him that day, Where you been anyway? I tried to get hold of you a couple times over Christmas, but you weren't around.

I met someone, he said, and left it at that.

I received a letter from Wolf:

> *I've been wondering what you were up to. Nothing great going on here. Work is slow right now and I am spending a lot of time at the house. Yesterday I got so drunk the woman went crazy on me and poured down the kitchen sink the following—one half bottle of vodka, a good bottle of single malt Scotch, some cheap gin, the last of the Spanish brandy I brought home from my visit with you all, and four cans of cold Miller. I got pissed off and went to the bar.*

He's talking here about his ex, Lorene, who stays at his house occasionally, sometimes for a few days, sometimes a week or so, until the arguments start again. She's a dog trainer. If it happens there aren't any dogs in the immediate area, she'll try a little work on the humans that are around. As much as she tried, she'd not been able to train the Wolf. He stays true to his own wilderness.

> *I'm sitting here a few miles from sun, he goes on. January and it is hot and still. Same shit this morning. The woman yelling about this and that and the hell I have made. Goin on and on about who knows what. Then she is out the door. Says something like—That is what you never do. Always!*
>
> *Thoughts together hard to piece. But that is usually the case any more.*
>
> *Put on some music. Full throttle guitar shooting out the box. Two tenor sax. Trumpets join in. Riffs running sideways and fast. Spiders, fiddler crabs pouring out the speakers.*

Goya's Head

Just finished a bowl of collard greens I bought from this dusty old guy on the side of the road. Looked like he was made of tobacco leaf. He moved in slow motion. He was in another century before the clocks took over. I wish I could get back to the time before this one. I am out of place here. I do not fit.

What was I saying? My thoughts are vibrating a little from the beauty.

There I am reflected in the window glass—a case of who gives a shit visible on my face I can not lately seem to get shed of.

Should have known beforehand there is nothin in the cards for me with this woman and her redheaded temper. I realize you have heard all this before.

The long season drags on. Winter did not make it this year. Sometimes I think about shouting black words out on the corner. But there is no corner nearby.

That little Ybor angel came up to the house twiced. Lord I wish she would a come a third time. Though believe me when I tell you, those were two bright stars on my calendar.

14 January

I'm sitting with the balcony doors open to air out the place after Megan had her half pack for breakfast and left for school, and a pigeon lands on the railing. Sits there looking at me, doing his head-bob. He jumps down to the balcony tiles and walks around in a circle. He seems tame, like he was raised by humans. He has a nice, fluorescent-green neck but otherwise looks your standard, run-of-the-mill pigeon. I went to the kitchen for a piece of bread. When he sees it, he flies in, sits on top of the ladder-back chair at the computer table. I find that I can feed him by hand. I get a bowl of water. He hops down on the table. He's a messy drinker. He looked directly at me, seemed to mutter something, which, it was in bird language so I didn't quite catch the meaning, then nodded a couple times and flew off.

I now have a bird and a dead friend that visit me in Madrid. I feel like a social gadfly. I somehow think this will not improve. I will never break through here unless I change, and that would involve my whole way of being. It is not viable. I'd go haywire.

There were several incidents that led to Billy's demise. One had to do with drugs, and the second that he couldn't ever make enough money to live on and then money came his way; and that was his real undoing.

He had a nice looking beater for awhile, a '67 Sedan de Ville. It was 19 foot long and lemon yellow. He'd bought it cheap from an old lady whose husband had passed away. This husband apparently spent time keeping the exterior of the car looking fine. The paint job was spotless and waxed, the interior like riding around in your living room. The windshield wipers operated on their own volition occassionally, otherwise, everything but the engine was cherry. But the car sat in the garage for two years before the old lady sold it, and the gasoline had turned to shellac. It barely ran, 45 MPH downhill top speed. Billy'd spoken to a street acquaintance the previous afternoon, a skinny black guy with dreadlocks who went by the name Dirty L. Billy had no idea what the L signified. Billy referred to him as Dirt. He sold rock cocaine. He gave Billy a cellphone number, said call him tomorrow night around 10 or thereafter. He told it that by midnight he'd be throwing the phone away. So Billy called and Dirt gave him a North Hubert address down in Drew Park. He had the goods, he needed a ride out of there.

Drew Park is a mostly industrial neighborhood east of Tampa International Airport and south of Hillsborough Avenue. Billy didn't know the streets there and had to drive by map. He liked maps, liked them more than the actual streets they named—the streets were an annoyance—and it could take him awhile to find an address. He'd get lost in the grid, trying to see where things led. He was drinking vodka from an orange soda can. He wasn't such a great driver when he drank. He drove fast and careless then, but with the de Ville, fast wasn't in the equation. And he had to be watchful. He'd failed his last roadside drunk test in a spectacular manner when he couldn't stop laughing at the cop's instructions.

He made it to the address finally, which turned out to be a whorehouse. Dirty L. had a friend with him, large and agitated and named Curtis. Curtis was wearing a shower cap on his head. They'd been at it for three days and nights. Dirt rode shotgun, Curtis sat in the back. The back was a mess. Look like a recycle bin, Curtis said. Every time Billy braked for a light or stop sign, Curtis exploded. What the fuck you stoppin' for? he wanted to know. In between these outbursts, Dirt kept going on about how he'd always wanted to drive a de Ville. It was apparently one of his dreams in life. Then he said something, but Billy didn't catch it.

Leave I ax you a question, Curtis said. That's what Billy heard anyway.

Leave I? Billy said. They'd fired up a pipe and weren't passing it to him, and he was starting to get agitated himself. It wasn't in Billy's makeup to take shit. And it didn't matter how the odds were stacked against him.

Levy, Curtis said. Levy his name.

Oh, Billy said. I thought maybe you was reinventin' the language again. Like, Fuck you 2 … use the number there. That's deep … So what's the question?

Can we stay at your place tonight? Dirt said.

No, Billy answered.

I don't like yer tone, man, Curtis said.

It must be tough bein' a smudge, Billy said. Nice hat, by the way. You gonna pass me that goddamn pipe or what?

They hadn't yet said where they wanted to go. That was left up in the air. They had a couple spots in mind and couldn't decide. Then they decided on a bar, but when they arrived there the building was boarded up and condemned. The three of them sat there looking at it.

They shoulda been closed it down long ago, Dirt said. Them girls workin' there was scary lookin'.

Curtis was perplexed by the comment.

I didn't find dem so, he said.

They moved on.

Billy said, My impression is that we're on an excursion. I'm gonna need some gas money this goes on much longer.

Just then Billy stopped at a red light.

The fuck you stoppin' for, cracker? Curtis howled. And he put a little stubnose pistol to Billy's ear.

Billy looked quickly to get his bearings. He recognized where he was, not far from Blake High School, on a street he'd always thought of as Dodge City.

They forced him into the trunk of the de Ville and then drove around town for half an hour or so, 45 minutes. Billy could hear them talking. They were having a big time.

The two finally stopped and parked. Billy figured they were going to kill him. Instead, Curtis spoke through the trunk lid.

We at a Big Macs, he said. You be wantin' anyting.

I'm wantin' the fuck out a here, Billy said.

I'm talkin' food items, Curtis said. You want a burger?

Billy could hear the drive-thru speaker in the background, sounded a good ways off.

Tap twice you want a burger.

Billy tapped.

How 'bout some fries wit it. Come on now, I axin' you nice.

Billy tapped again.

Then one of them snorted, and he heard them walking away, cracking up.

Billy wasn't discovered until 5 in the morning, when the police stopped them. Being in the trunk didn't do his mental health any good. He was claustrophobic to begin with. Then the law started on him. No valid Florida driver's license. No proof of liability insurance. Stolen tag. Open container violations, though most of the beer cans were close to antiques. So that was a disaster. And he spent months afterwards in half-way houses and abandoned buildings.

Goya's Head

Then his luck changed. He got a roofing job.

It was a week into December. The heat hadn't broken yet. It was one of those endless Tampa summers that come along now and then. The job was putting a tin roof on a house on 12th Street. The second day of work, Billy stepped on some pigeon shit and skated off the roof like it was ice. He sprained his ankle bad, maybe broken by the feel of it. The bossman let him stay in the house, where he drank whiskey against the pain. But when the leg kept swelling up, he gave Billy two hundred bucks and told him it was time to leave, and also to forget his name.

The next day, when things were at their darkest, money came to him from an old claim he'd lodged against Robbins Lumber, where he'd worked and hurt his back. This had happened several years previous. But a check came to his parents' house for two thousand dollars, and his father drove down from San Ann with it. He gave a grand to his father to hold on to and, afterwards, had a thousand dollars cash to contend with.

And that was the end of him really, money in his pocket. Billy took a room at the Royal Palms Motel off Hillsborough, close to the interstate there. The motel had been a nice place once, back in the '50s. There weren't any palms left now. The swimming pool had no water unless it rained. When I went there afterwards to look at the place, the pool was full of tadpoles. He bought a pistol at some point from a street budro. I've never learned what sort of pistol that was exactly. A Saturday Night Special I'd imagine, and stolen. The cops kept it. Billy purchased a whole bunch of Mad Dog wine and meth, and he holed up while he composed his suicide note. The cops kept that, too. Billy's father used the grand to bury him.

There's a strange truth about the Spanish. Put three of them together with a bottle, and they start singing. I'm listening to a song from the street just as I finish this piece about Billy.

At the moment we're right next to broke Megan tells me. We won't have any more coming in until the 1st of the month. In the meantime, whenever she goes for groceries lately, I notice she comes back with flowers. The apartment has an abundance of cut flowers. She just came in with yellow freesias. Finally she explains that there's a gypsy woman selling them in front of the market. She's afraid if she doesn't buy any, the gypsy's going to put a hex on her. There's something about her, Megan says, makes me give her money. An' if I don't buy anything, she gives me the stinkeye.

I'm drinking 129 peseta wine. It's from Badajoz, over by Portugal, and not bad really, a bit watered down. Badajoz—what a great name. I prefer rioja, the resiny, earthbound taste of it. Or Ribera del Duero. But I'll be having cheap Scotch tonight. Something called Queen's Choice. I'll have mine neat. I'll drink it slow like a gentleman should. I'm pretty sure the Queen would not touch this swill.

I cut back to one bottle of wine daily. I do not drink for pleasure but strictlty to counter melancholy. I'm melancholic perhaps because I realize I can't drink two. Several liters of mineral water from Barcelona. A clove of raw garlic shaved into a small glass of La Guita manzanilla when I awake. It's good for the heart. At least a two hour walk each day, checking out Madrid street oddities. A short nap; I must attend to that momentarily. A good dose of pumpkin seeds for the prostate. I put them in my noon salad, plenty of olive oil on that and a dash of apple cider vinegar. Vitamins E and C. They are supposed to do something or other. Several Echinacea a day to keep up the immune system. St. John's Wort for the depression existence hands me. The old name for depression was melancholy. See one of Goya's black paintings, *Saturn Devouring His Son*. Saturn was the God of Melancholy. I'm the son. Melancholy has eaten my head. Goya painted this particularly gruesome item on his dining room wall. In spite of the above mentioned precautions, however, I can't quite get a handle on the void.

Truth be owned, my inner life is going primitive. Going winter. An eclipse of the mind is on the way. It's below freezing when I wake in the mornings, and getting out of bed I feel reptilian. I begin to wonder what it would be like to have scales on my hands. To touch the one I love that way. Perhaps if I had a nice reticulated pattern to the scales … And always now I feel the city edging in on me. I retrieve a flannel shirt from the line in the building well; it smells like fried sardines. I remember I dreamed last night I had misplaced my hat and couldn't find it. And this terrible notion I can't shake that the bad news has just begun. In my reading I come across a quote by Cyril Connolly: *No town should be too large for a man to walk out of it in the morning.*

To add to my unease, several days ago a tooth lit up on me. I think to get it fixed, but then I think not. Perhaps tonight Ill speak with the tooth fairy. The sensitivity has not gone away. I just bear with it. I take it that tooth is the little house where the sadness of the world has found its place in me.

15 January
from the *International Herald Tribune*
Spain Hit by Heavy Snow

  MADRID—Traffic in and out of several Spanish towns was chaotic Friday because of heavy snowfall in many central and northern regions, including Madrid.

  Traffic department officials in Spain urged drivers to use snow chains in rural areas of 11 of the nation's 17 regions. Traffic was snarled on three of the seven main roads into Madrid.

What we had in our neighborhood was a hailstorm. It only lasted about five minutes but came down like heavy rain, and afterwards the streets were white.

17 January Monday
I had a bottle of wine with lunch just now. Felix Salas, a vintner in Valladolid, 350 pesetas and uncommonly good for the price. I took a walk to Sol earlier, around noon, then to Plaza Mayor, and down to Latina where the Rastro starts, walking toward the sun. It's cold but the sun is bright, and as long as you can stay in it, you're fine. When you turn off on the alley-like side streets, you emerge

from them thinking about icicles. Coming around the corner from one of these into the light again, the sun is an alien goodness.

It was one of those days all the beauties were out. I don't know what occasions this. But I was passing beauty, one after another. It's not unusual here to see beautiful girls next to their boyfriends, who don't measure up. It's hard not to notice the discrepancy. A good many of these are lame and at the same time puffed up about themselves, and for what reason? you wonder.

But Megan says it has to do with how they're raised. That mothers here dote on their sons. Girls start going with a steady by age 14 and stay with him forever, come what may.

Then I think of Megan and I walking these same streets and the abiding question it must pose: Why is that pretty girl holding hands with a beast?

Just outside Corte Inglés I saw a tall blonde chatting with two midgets. They were all three dressed like sports. The blond had a shiner. The midgets looked like very small body builders. I followed them momentarily, curious as to what they might be discussing but could make no sense of it. Then I was almost run down by a delivery truck. It came right up on the sidewalk after me. Can't let such things bother you. I laughed maniacally and kept walking.

Back in the neighborhood, I spotted the exhibitionist out strolling with her boyfriend. Up close she's a rough cob. A hardass Madrid barrio girl, looks like she'd know her way around a bar fight.

Kevin Ray called. He wanted to get a recipe from Megan, but she's at school. We talked awhile. Thursday night he went out with his Gay Dining Group, he said, and didn't get home till nine this morning.

How was it?

I think I kept my clothes on, he said.

Where'd you eat?

We haven't, he said, actually had a meal in weeks. And I should have had something. Around 2 a.m. I tried to lean on a light pole that wasn't there. But … gawd, you wouldn't believe it. I ended up in a cocaine speakeasy with some Russian mafia, Spanish royalty and a politician's daughter …

18 January
from the *International Herald Tribune*
The Rain in Spain? Comets, Not People
> *MADRID—At least 10 melon-sized ice balls that have slammed into Spain in the last week are probably debris from comets, not human excrement as first suspected, a Spanish scientist said Monday.*
>
> *Enrique Martinez, head of a team at the Higher Council of Scientific Investigation studying the phenomenon, said it was thought at first that the ice balls were human excrement ejected from high-flying aircraft.*
>
> *"But they lack the typical coloring and texture we find in those cases," he said.*
>
> *A man escaped injury last week when an ice ball 20 centimeters (8 inches) across hit his car.*
>
> *Yesterday the southern outskirts of Madrid (Mosteles) was bombarded with pieces of ice.*

In a nationally televised address tonight, Prime Minister Jose Maria Aznar called a general election for March 12th.

Aznar said he had asked King Juan Carlos to dissolve Parliament and that he was seeking re-election to a second four-year term. This wasn't a surprise. He's been quoted in the papers for some days now that an election would serve as a referendum on his free-market policies and hard-line opposition to ETA.

I had the same thoughts I always do listening to Aznar: Phone the mortician. I'm not detecting any pulse. But he and his party will most likely win. The Socialists have little to offer. They ruled for 13 years before the last election, and apparently damn near everyone got tired of their antics. And Aznar's stand against the Basques is wildly popular. It strikes me what a good system they have here, where you can call for an election today and have it over with in two months.

Today in the mail I received a Christmas card from my brother and his wife, Gale. Megan received hers along with a check well before Christmas. Gale likes to withhold mine awhile. It's a form of protest. They were two of our visitors this past summer, stayed for several weeks in June. We rented a car and drove over to Nazaré on the Portugal coast, later to Sintra and Lisbon. From there we returned to Spain and went down to Sevilla. My brother paid for everything, and we stayed in paradors and expensive hotels along the way. When I drove, I took every back road I could find. My brother likes to travel on freeways. And that's a symbol of the difference between us. I don't want to say much about him, as he is blood, and benignly demented in his own way, just as everyone in the family.

I thought since they were visiting us, Gale would speak to me again, but it wasn't to be. If she had a comment, she would make it through Megan. This turned out cumbersome and absurd, as you can imagine. But here's the reason my sister-in-law no longer talks to me:

My nephew was getting married ... to a girl who was a real dreamboat, as Gale put it. Things were moving fast, she'd told me on the phone. Come over. She said this like I lived in the neighborhood. They have a house in south Tampa. Have you seen Megan? she asked. I can't seem to get hold of her. I wish I could recreate Gale's twang, but it is not transferrable to paper. She's a San Ann girl, from the Eller family, and Cracker to the bone. She's gone high toned down in Tampa, but she still talks San Ann. No, I said. I haven't seen her. Megan was living with me by then, had been for awhile. It was something we'd so far kept secret from them. I didn't want to go, and tried several excuses, but my brother got on the phone then and insisted. He wanted to show me his new invention.

So I drove down there from San Ann. And then I was seated at the dinner table with them—Gale, my brother, nephew and his bride-to-be.

Long ago, my brother had a devil of a time getting Gale pregnant. Finally they adopted Megan. Ten months later my clown nephew was born.

The young lady was pretty, I'll own to that. Her mouth, too, the way it turned up on one side, told you things that she might not. She had her hair yanked back severely in a ponytail. Her fingernails were painted blue. Still in all, she was not from among the usual entourage of trash my nephew called his friends. There was something charmingly fresh about her. His last girlfriend, Gale told me, had turned unpleasant. A painfully thin girl, as I recall, with multiple tattoos.

Megan avoided these get-togethers as a general rule and particularly this table. There are unspoken table manners that go along with it. No one started to dine until all were seated. No one got up until everyone else was done eating. This sounds decent enough, though it seldom turned out that way. But the main thing was, in my mind at least, this young lady had no business at all with my nephew, who is little more than a vagrant.

My sister-in-law had, at the time, been on diet pills for the past year. She'd lost 30 pounds in that year and scattered her wits along with them.

She had a lot of energy, however. She'd moved the dinner table into the living room. It was pretty much all that was there, besides her collection of dolls that sat around on little chairs. They have button eyes, yarn hair. Some of these resided in my brother's gun case. She made these dolls herself, many years previous; it seemed for a long time, when she couldn't have a child, these dolls made do. I studied Gale just then. I observed what could only be described as a beatific smile on her face. She couldn't seem to make it stop. She must have taken pills just before I arrived. She had gotten her hair done for the occasion, a windswept look, and appeared to be riding in a fast convertible.

We finished the gumbo. I started to get up to take my bowl to the kitchen.

No! Sit still!

I forgot myself … you're not to move. She's the only one allowed to do anything. It's one of the rituals.

As I uncorked my second bottle of wine, Are you supposed to be drinking? she asked.

Well, no, actually I'm not. It's one of the reasons why I'm here, though. I'd brought two bottles of good California wine and another bottle of homemade Tampa Italian, called Dago Red. One of the Cali wines went well with the gumbo. I'd been living for several months on bananas, mineral water, yellow split pea soup and the like. They were to counter some problems due, mainly, to excess. I was here to take down some good food and drink away from Megan, who keeps a careful eye on my health.

Next came the corned beef, which I don't, however, particularly care for. Cabbage. Baked beans. My portion seemed enough for several men. I nibbled on a cabbage leaf and took in the scene.

Although the table is quite large, all the food and drink is confined to place mats. Glasses make water rings on the wood, and so on. There was much cherry wood showing, like a dark red river swirling away from me, and little islands of food. There was also a round mirror lying flat in the middle of the table. In it I could see the disembodied head of my nephew, who sat opposite me. His betrothed stared at him from time to time like he was a rock and roll idol. He had apparently satisfied some appetite of hers. He in return barely acknowledged her existence.

I looked around at the dolls. I noticed, by their facial expressions, they appeared to be suffering from depression or possibly heartburn. There was a large painting on one wall, a still life of lemons and quince in a wicker basket. The bride-to-be was seated nearest me. A lovely girl, I thought. What was she doing with my dolt nephew? I was baffled by this.

The wine had made me expansive. I started talking to her. To marry my nephew, it struck me, she must possess such low self-esteem she had to be parked next to something offensive in order to feel good about herself. But, as we spoke, I came to realize that wasn't it at all. From what I could gather, she was marrying him because he was a good Catholic, for one, and secondly, she had been hit by lightning recently.

Gale, noting how little I was eating, slowed down. It was her notion that she should be last done. Something to do with being a good hostess. Also, whoever finished last, everyone else got to watch that person eat. She would then become the center of attention. When she had consumed her last bite of food and you think it's over finally, she'd bring out some crystallized fruit for dessert.

She was, just then, observing me peck at the corned beef. The cut had a lurid scarlet color. She started moving her food from one side of her plate to the other. Rearranging it like she'd done the furniture. She had just this weekend put her bed up on cement blocks. She showed it to me earlier.

You'll need a ladder to get into it, I said.

We studied the bed.

Where was I? she asked, like she'd been telling me something, though she hadn't. I've had her down as a saint for years now, just for dealing with my brother so long.

I love you, I said, but … god dang it, you're drug addled. You're mad.

What are you talking about? I never felt better.

You're under a spell, I said.

Nonsense.

She looked at me closely, evaluating my tramp wardrobe. No argument there. I'm dressed like I might want to do some yard work later on.

Do you have a job? she said.

Not at the moment, I said.

How does one get by on fuck all? I've never understood that.

I looked at her.

Her eyes were star-bright and glittering.

I looked at the bed again.

Maybe you could levitate into it, I said.

My nephew got up from the table to make a phone call. An

important call, he said. To his bookie I suspected. He glanced at his wrist as though he had a watch on it. If you asked how he made his money, he'd tell you that he's an entrepreneur and won't go into details. He ran his tongue around his mouth several times, made a face and said to his mother, What sorta barbs did you put in that cabbage? Then he walked away. Gale spoke to his back. *Herbs*! They are called *herbs*!

I studied the bride-to-be once again. I dismissed the good Catholic part as a romantic notion and began to question her about the lightning.

I was interrupted by the dog. He was nudging me under the table with his snout, wanting a handout. It is said all dogs descended from wolves, but this one looks to have passed down from the common pig. I kicked him away. I don't much like the baked beans on my plate ... a thought occurred to me, but I put it aside momentarily.

Tell me about the lightning, I said.

My boyfriend ... his name was Rod ... an unfortunate name as it turned out, but ... we were on the golf course. I wasn't even playing. I just walked along with him chatting. It was hot out, and I was sweating. There wasn't a cloud in the sky. The bolt came out of nowhere. Rod lit up like a bulb. It was over just like that (she snapped her fingers). He fell into a sand trap, his eyes still open. His golf shoes were melted to his feet.

Not that I recall any of that. It's just what people have told me ... people who were there. The bolt went through him and struck me, too. It knocked me for a loop. I went flying I guess. The only thing I recall is this brief instant of being set on fire and my entire body flapping like a broken wing... I guess it's a memory. Otherwise, the day is gone ...what I did or didn't do—

I know the feeling, I said.

I woke up in the ambulance, she went on. I had a cross around my neck. Look.

She undid several buttons on her blouse, spread the material, which moved like silk. And there on her skin was a perfect keloid imprint of a cross and chain. A rather large cross at that. I saw a couple other things there, too … much larger than I'd thought.

Later, in the hospital, I had this strange dream or vision … that the lightning entered me through the cross, then escaped from my left eye. She pointed to that eye, which still seemed a bit startled. I know that doesn't make any sense, she said.

From the chair farthest away, at the head of the table, my brother suddenly piped up. He tends to get loud, though he doesn't realize it, when he drinks. The stock market had fallen somewhat dramatically that Friday. He'd been grousing about it since I arrived. He was on that again. I'd been with him for half an hour before dinner. He showed me his invention, which was a good one, a bobber that replicated a hyacinth bulb. I was impressed. But then he'd gotten into politics and economics, items that don't take up much of my time on a normal day. I had nodded inexorably whenever it seemed he desired a response. He likes to play the piano before he eats a big meal, but the piano was lost in what used to be the dining room, which was crammed to the doorway with furniture from the living room. It'd thrown him off some.

The Glenfiddich single malt had kicked in. He drinks it out of a tall glass with ice, pretends that it's English tea. No one paid the least attention to his outburst, except the bride-to-be, who smiled at him just then uncertainly. Almost as an afterthought, Gale turned toward him and said, Duval … just don't talk.

He didn't reply.

He got back at her instead by taking his plate to the kitchen and helping himself to seconds. He made a big production of it, moving about like a sleepwalker. He'd gained nearly as much weight in the past year as Gale had lost. He is getting stout and, in the face at least, has started to resemble a manatee, those doleful eyes, his nose like the crook of a cane. He's eleven years older than me, and I didn't grow up with him; he lived with his own mother. But we saw each other often enough. I don't remember him being anything but a stick.

He retired when he turned 50 and has lately begun to recall the bygone days in somewhat heroic terms. He was quite a Boy Scout when he was a kid. They gave him some sort of busy beaver patch, which he still has and will show you if you let him. Astonishingly, he retains this well-scrubbed Boy Scout look and appears at odd moments about to break into a chorus of "Kum Ba Ya." Now, and the time I'm talking about too, he has little to do but work on his inventions, maneuver his stocks, trim his mustache.

What happened to the cross? I said to the bride-to-be.

Vanished. At least no one ever found it. I think the Earth took it back, she said. I guess it saved my life. It diverted the lightning away from my heart.

You seem to have come out of all that okay, I said.

I was lucky, she said. I still can't exactly feel my toes. For awhile I had these red marks up and down my body looked just like lightning. They went away finally.

I asked her several questions about my nephew, being circumspect about it yet trying to figure out how he fit in.

He was at the golf course that day, she said. He saw everything. He came to the hospital—

He golfs? I said.

Yes.

Oh for Christ' sake.

The dog was chewing on my boot.

Excuse me, I said. I bowed to everyone in utter servitude. I'm going to get more gumbo gravy.

The dog followed me to the kitchen. I scooped the beans into the dog dish.

When I returned to the table, my nephew was back. Instead of making a phone call, it seems he had shot up instead. He was sitting there a bit stunned.

Seven years previous, in the summer after he graduated high school and in a similar condition, he was arrested for armed robbery and spent several of his formative years doing roadwork for the county. He had been out all night and, for reasons that remain obscure, found himself far from home in the morning, no cash left, not even a coin to call for a ride. As luck would have it, he stumbled across a toy gun in a yard. He stuck it in his belt. He had a tiny Barlow pocket knife he always carried. Thus accoutred, he swaggered into a convenience store and demanded cash.

The woman working the register refused to give him any money, however, and she was so polite it confused him. She owned guns herself, the newspaper reported, and knew the caliber of this one. Plus she'd been robbed a number of times already and was a little tired of it. Finally, my nephew asked, since she wasn't into the money part, would she at least call him a cab. She'd be more than happy to, she replied, and phoned the sheriff's office.

Since I was barely touching my food, the dinner had stalled. My brother and Gale were having a discussion. They were both talking at each other at any rate. They were not on the same subject. My brother was speaking of hedge funds, whatever they might be. Gale, for her part, spoke of re-doing the house. I'd like to have a bathroom large enough someday, she was saying, that I can have a fireplace in it.

It was mid-August in central Florida that day as we sat around the table. Outside the window, 8 o'clock was still smoldering at the edges. Gale had a rouge flower painted on each cheek, perhaps to give the illusion of health, but her face was drawn, emaciated, haunted looking. She was moving the various food groups around her plate counter-clock-wise. My brother, now in complete revolt, drew cartoons on the table with spilt drops of Glenfiddich. My nephew had gone catatonic. The dog was back under the table doing some tootle-ling. The bride-to-be sat there in her loveliness.

I looked out the front windows. There went one of the neighbors. She is the one who walks around the block for hours at a time reading a paperback novel held in front of her face all the while. She'll be back around momentarily.

There was a yellow butterfly lazily volplaning about the yard. A gray squirrel on a post of the white picket fence. The squirrel had a red rose bud in his little hands, brought it to his nose several times as if contemplating its perfume. Gale, then, left the table to consult her cookbook. She wasn't sure she had prepared the corned beef correctly.

I said to the bride-to-be, This life is hard fare. I don't even know why I said this. It just came to me.

She looked at me like she knew better than that, but she'd humor me on it. What I really wanted to tell her, diplomatically some way, was that she should flee from this lunacy as soon as possible.

Pointing to my nephew, who was nodding across the way, I said:

Did you know his grandaddy had three eyes?

I touched a finger to the middle of my forehead.

It would weep occasionally. We never knew why.

You're putting me on! she said. She turned wildly to my nephew. He was wired into another place. He laughed unaccountably, but it seemed to be directed at something else he was thinking on. She looked at my brother. He was drunk now to where he was amused by little things.

We don't like to talk about it, he said.

Oh, you guys, she said. Y'all are a couple cards. She laughed then as if in some sort of delirium.

A short while back, she'd asked for a taste of the Dago Red. The alcohol content of this homemade was much higher than it was supposed to be. Sixteen percent at least I'd imagine. I had polished off the two bottles of store-bought with pleasant results. A third of the way into the Red, I was turning to stone.

How 'bout a kiss for your new uncle? Uncle-in-law ... whatever. My eyes were drawn suddenly to her blue nails. I guess I had mumbled.

What? she said.

A little peck on the cheek ... I presented my cheek.

When she went to kiss my cheek, I turned my face and tongued her. I'll tell you, that kiss was full of sparks.

Even my nephew took note and, subsequently, the marriage idea began to unravel. But I stopped then, as I felt someone behind me, turned, and Gale was standing there with her hands on her hips. She wasn't concerned with the kiss, however. She had other things on her mind.

You know, she said, I just called Megan's place. I've been doing that for a good while now. No answer. Nothing. Then this time, her roommate's boyfriend answered. No, he said, Megan doesn't live here anymore. And he gave me her new number. It's your number, Luke.

Back at my place in San Ann, when I told Megan about all this, she cocked her head.

That's why the phone's been ringing then, she said. Don't worry about it. When Mama gets like this, she goes from apeshit to crazy and back again. No other stopping points. But I'm not into dealing with her right now. She thought for awhile.

You ought to've told Mama to mind her own business.

I was out of there too quick to give any speeches, I said.

Lordy lord, she said. I kint … get my thoughts in order.

You kint?

No. An' stop makin' fun.

Well, shoot, she said finally. Do you feel like a road trip?

Where to?

Cape San Blas?

Sure.

Call Owen, she said. See if he can take the dogs.

Grandma Tillie and Aunt Sylvia paid $750 for the San Blas land in the mid-1930s. Tillie borrowed her share from Sylvia. She didn't have any money of her own then to speak of. Tillie thought the price outlandish for an acre of dune with nothing on it but sand oak thicket and dwarf pine, even though it sat on the Gulf. That was her lament, but you could tell she was fond of the land. What it's worth now is anyone's guess.

At the end of WWII, frozen orange juice took off, and she got near well to do. She had what she called a cottage built on the land then, two small bedrooms, big kitchen, living room, the house set up on telephone poles, a wraparound porch, but it wasn't much more than a fish camp really, the floor and walls rough plank. There's running water now. There's still no electricity. A small wood stove for the winter. The place smells of burnt wood or kerosene smoke from hurricane lamps. The stove and refrigerator are propane. These are recent additions, only thirty years old. A barbecue pit and smoker. Everyone in the family has a key to the place, including some I wish didn't. The Cape is up above Appalachicola. They call this the Forgotten Coast. People forgot to come here, and it's all the better for it.

They bought the property from an oyster man in Appalachicola who had developed a bad back and fallen on hard times. If you've ever seen the long wooden tongs they use to harvest oysters, you'd understand how a bad back in that line of work could hinder you. They're nine foot long and not light, especially with a load of oysters in them. How Tillie and Sylvia came to know this man I'm not sure of, though they used to stay at the Gibson Inn hotel in Appalach in the old days. They vacationed there for years. For four dollars a day, they'd each get their own room and three all-you-could-eat meals. Traveling salesmen set up their wares in the hotel lobby, and I guess it was an old-time version of a shopping mall to the sisters. They always spoke highly of that inn.

Both Megan and I had been coming to Cape San Blas since we were little. We went flounder gigging one night with miners' lamps on our heads. Walked across the road one day to the cove and went scalloping. Caught some whiting out front of the cottage. The old-timers there call them ground mullet for some reason.

We were having a time, as we always did here. The place brings back good memories, and makes more. Then the fourth night Megan said:

I have a feeling we should move on.

Why?

Daddy comes up here every summer about now. He'd be alone, but still … Mama wouldn't consider coming. She speaks of it as camping out. But, I don't even know if that's it. I just have a feelin'.

Just about then this black Ford pickup, a 250 Super Duty, jacked up, big tires, mud-splattered, pulled into the driveway and peeled up to the cottage and honked. I recognized the truck and driver. It was Ty Hill, a cousin on my mother's side and not one of my favorites. Ty was 19, maybe 20, then but kind of a throwback Cracker, the old slouchy ways about him. He had on his arm a high school beauty. They had brought along a croaker sack of oysters on ice. That night we built a driftwood fire on the beach and shucked oysters and ate them with Ed's Red hotsauce and drank beer. Ty's friend was named Kate, and she was from Blanton, a hamlet not far from San Ann. She was a sweetheart. I was tempted to stay around a bit just for the scenery she provided, but the next morning we moved on.

We ended up at Amelia Island and stayed there three weeks. We rented a furnished condo at a place called The Captain's House. Nine units, three floors. We were at the top far right apartment. People came and went, usually on Friday and Saturday. We pretty much had the place to ourselves the rest of the week. We'd take long walks on the beach at sunrise, nice sea oat dunes there. In the afternoon we'd go to Fernandina Beach and walk that old town. We'd have lunch, then end up at the Palace Saloon for a couple. I guess it's the only actual saloon I've ever drank in. It's been around since the 1870s. On our balcony, the cool breeze never stopped. We'd watch the sunset, play cribbage in the evenings, listen to the shuffling of the sea. Those were good, simple times, and we took soundings of each other there.

Megan had brought along a manila envelope with paperwork in it, Spanish stamps on the envelope. She was looking over the contents one night.

What is that? I said.

It's from a school in Madrid, Spain. It's called Complutense University. I can go there as an exchange student. I'd take classes. I'd have to do some tutoring. I'd get some money for it, though.

What would you study?

Spanish, she said.

She'd learned Spanish from the Mex farmworker kids she played with in Tillie's orange groves. She was fluent by the time she was four.

You already know it, I said.

That's not the point.

That settled for awhile.

Will you come with me? she said. We'd have to do it in a timely manner. Classes will start before long.

Her face was taken over by her eyes just then.

I nodded. Sure, I said ... What about the family?

That matters, she said. But it matters in a way that doesn't change anything.

20 January

from the *International Herald Tribune*

Famed Goya Portrait Will Stay in Madrid

MADRID—Spain has intervened to block the sale of a famous portrait by the 18th century Spanish master Francisco de Goya and will itself acquire the painting for about $24 million.

The education and culture minister, Mariano Rajoy, said the government was exercising its rights under a law on art works that have been classified as part of Spain's national heritage. The painting in question, "The Countess of Chinchon," was so declared in 1983. Under the law, when such a work is owned by a private collector in Spain and offered for sale to another private party, the government can step in and buy the piece if it matches the agreed sale price.

In this case the painting belonged to the heirs of the Dutchess of Sueca, who had found a buyer after a four-year search with help from the British auction house Sotheby's. The sale price was 4 billion pesetas.

The painting is considered a masterpiece among Goya's portraits. Its subject was a niece of King Carlos III and the wife of his successor's prime minister, Manuel Gudoy.

This painting is one of my favorite Goya portraits. The countess rendered in it was a beauty, and he captures her beauty and sadness. Gudoy was having an affair with the Queen and completely neglected his wife, seemed to forget she existed. And the Queen was a dog.

In Goya's day, his portraits hung in royal apartments or private collections. Only the wealthy or the connected saw them. Many of the works on which his fame now rests could not be seen at all. The many drawings, tapestry cartoons, the Black Paintings from the walls of his country house, and Los Desastres de la Guerra, were not published in his lifetime. The etchings of his Caprichos series made it to local bookstores, but in four years only 27 sets were sold. He was all but unknown outside of Madrid.

On my walks lately I've noticed a lot of shell games. Not actually shells but rather bottle caps. Three bottlecaps and a pea set up on a cardboard box on the sidewalk. They're popular around the Atocha train station, Gran Vía, the Rastro, anywhere people are moving in quantity. When you see the same hawker twice, you realize the three or four fellas standing closest to him, those who seem so absorbed in the game, who win money and make a show of it, are the same ones who were there last time and that they bear a remarkable likeness to each other and to the hawker himself.

Returning home today, a block from the apartment, once again I came across the exhibitionist on the street. She's leaning against the pole of a street lamp. She looks me dead on and, as I'm passing, says something.

Te veo.

Qué? I said.

Te veo mirándome, she says. Try to remember that, this a note to myself. I don't stop, I'm nearly by her.

Claro, I mutter, and then I'm past her and on my way through the crowd. Claro is one of my standard replies when I don't know what the hell's been said to me. But I translated her quite clearly by the time I'd reached the apartment. She said: I see you watching me.

It's snowing a little today. It appears to snow in the city only enough that when it happens people get to smiling. Chelo came over, and we lifted weights. Our place is now his gym, as foretold. After working out, we went to Kiko's for a beer, then took the metro to Lavapiés. We go to his place and pick up some money he owes me, which I have insisted on. He lives on Zurita, off Calle de La Fe. His apartment was someone's attic once, the ceiling slanting down. A half window facing the street, a tiny balcony which is not for standing on. The bedroom is a 45 degree angle that ends in a corner, a trundle bed there, a chest of drawers. The whole place is angles. He's painted the living room light blue, and the odor of fresh paint lingers. Two people won't fit in the kitchen. The icebox doesn't fit in the kitchen either but resides in the living room.

He seems to think of the place as cozy rather than claustrophobic, but he doesn't stay in it much. Whenever I call him lately, there's a message to one woman or another to meet him at a certain time, a certain café. We're not there long and go to a bar nearby at 13 Esquinita de La Fe.

Why'd you come to Spain? he said at one point.

I came along for the ride.

It don't bother you not working?

I'm not cut out for it, I said.

Wha'd you work at when you worked? I don't remember you doin' jack.

Back when I'd see you at Morgan's Pub, I worked construction.

That's right, he said. I remember that.

I did some shrimping. Mostly I worked in the old man's liquor store.

How was that? the shrimp boat.

I liked it all right. I did it for a summer. We worked out of John's Pass in St. Pete. The crew ... they were criminals but good guys. We called each other *chum.* You stay near shore, less than 5 miles out.

That's a job where you'd get a little fragrant I'd think, Chelo said.

Yeah, a bit. Then I went longlining one time. We were out eight days before we reached our quota, fishing for red and gag grouper in the middle grounds. I baited hooks, shoveled ice, whatever needed done. And that was the end of it. The walls of the cabin closed in on me. The longer you're out, the smaller the boat gets. I haven't even been to the beach since that trip.

I sold marijuana, I said. I did a good job of that. It was close as I ever got to driving ambition …

I have this cousin, Pogey, down in Grand Isle, Louisiana, grows reef hydroponically. He was one of the first to do that that I know of. He went to Amsterdam years ago and brought good seed back. He calls his product Lou'sana Skunk. An' he's not the least bit interested in selling it, only in growing it. He thinks of himself as a gentleman farmer.

He'd give me a call, whenever he harvested, usually twice a year, and I'd drive down there, pick up a couple pounds of bud. We'd go into New Orleans and have dinner down in Bucktown, say … go to the Quarter afterwards. A good time for both of us. Otherwise, he'd just sit there amongst his crop listening to jazz and breathe in the skunk smell, read up on horticulture, eat crawdad creampuffs, drink Dixie beer. He don't do much. He hardly leaves the property except to go to the liquor store.

All the houses are up on stilts in Grand Isle. The whole town a fish camp. He's got one house he lives in, and he owns the shack next door, too, where he's got his setup … which, he calls the Lower 40. One big room where he's got the latest in hydroponic equipment. A clockwork irrigation system. High sodium vapor lights. Silver tarps covering the walls and windows and ceiling. It's like a tanning bed in there. I'd stay with him a couple days. Do some fishing off his dock. Then I'd take the reef back home and make some phone calls. It'd take me a week, ten days to go down there and back and then unload it in Tampa. On two pounds, after expenses and what I'd send back to Pogey, I'd make eight, ten grand. It was always the best shit in town, by far, and if I happened to bring it in when supply was tight, I'd make a killin'. I sold exclusively to lawyers. I kept raisin' the price. They didn't care.

You were working yourself to the bone there, Chelo said.

I'm telling you. Plus I got some family money comes in now and then, whenever I can coax it out of my aunt.

There some legal basis for that on her part?

I'm not about to aim a lawyer at her, I said. It's a trust from my grandma. The money is funneled through Aunt Sylvia. She's sole executor of the thing. An' it's for the best really. It'd be gone by now if she'd just handed it over. It didn't start out as so much, but she's invested it. She's a magician with money. But … you know, there's enough people like to work. They enjoy it, and there's millions of them. That's honorable, and I think they should be encouraged … but I never cared for it. It cuts into your day somethin' fierce.

I tried selling weed one time, Chelo said. I managed to lose my shirt.

How'd you do that?

First of all, I was in it with this other guy, who was an idiot. Pete Logadice, you remember him? We bought a pound and broke it into bags and sold it. It wasn't that good. Mexican brown. Industrial. But we got it cheap and made a few bucks, and he got some free smoke out of it. I never cared much for reef. I'll smoke occasionally, but I never really got into it. It just generally makes me stupid. An' kind of nervous or something.

Anyway, then we buy three pounds. We stop at the Cadillac Lounge that night. The reef's in the trunk of Logadice's car. When the band breaks we come out and roll one. We're leaning against the car, joking. The bouncer there, that friend of yours—

Wade Bonner.

Yeah. He stops by to see what we're up to. Takes a couple tokes, moves on. What a great bar. And we decide to stay for another set. The band's actually decent for once. The next time the band takes a break, we come out and are gonna have another smoke. We're thinking at this point, Let's jus' stay on till we get laid. Having a good time, pretty drunk and all. Then we go to lean on the car again, only it's not there.

Thought was, it'd been stolen. Logadice can't call the cops though, because of the reef in the trunk. But we learn the next day, no … that wasn't it. The car had been repossessed. He hadn't kept up with his payments. An' this wasn't no expensive car. It was a beater. The guys that repossessed it got a nice bonus. But that was the end of my drug dealing. I'm probably one of the very few people in the history of Tampa who managed to lose money at sellin' drugs in that town.

We order another round. The bartender is an old guy and somewhat of an asshole. We're the only two customers, but we're made to understand it's a bit too much to ask for another round so soon. It's inconsiderate. The old guy's face is a circle, and his face and head are covered in white stubble, and he has a little beak for a nose.

Lavapiés, Chelo says, is the old judería, the Jewish Quarter of Madrid. And I guess there were moriscos here too, the Muslims that converted … you know, a while back. 1492. This street we're on is named Street of Faith. Man, he says … this waiter looks like a barn owl.

He'd just brought the drinks. We had switched to red wine, a mistake.

I'd call this wine cynical, I said. It has an attitude.

It doesn't have good manners, does it? Chelo said. I detect notes of tobacco—

Tobacco?

I think he put his cigarette out in mine, he said.

Pick up Chelo in the middle of a conversation two drinks down the line:

The other night I watched *Lolita* on TV. It came out in '62. I kept wondering what people in America made of Peter Sellers back then. His humor was ahead of them.

I don't think I attained a sense of humor till after high school,

I said. At 18 I hadn't evolved that far. I played football on Friday nights in the fall. It was a release for my violence. After the season ended I was in trouble. On weekends then I'd get into fights out of a sense of nostalgia.

How'd you ever get from there to writing poetry?

It came about on its own somehow. I can't explain it exactly. Billy Jenks turned me on to reading. That's where it started.

You don't look like a poet, Chelo said. You look like a longshoreman.

Say, whatever happened to that oriental girl? I said. You've not spoken of her lately.

She got tired of me being broke. Or maybe not even that. It was just the bitchin' about my finances got to her. But she was fun. An' no hard feelings. She's with this older guy now. A businessman here in Madrid … he's Jap. They like their own kind. The kind with money.

What about this new one?

She's something. But … I don't know. I've lost track of her at the moment. She's Scottish, and a beauty. She's a masterpiece, he said.

Just before we finished the last drink Chelo said:

You workin' on anything now?

I'm writing down what happens to me every day. Like us sitting here. I remember it later, I'll put down what was said.

So I'm like a character in it?

Something like that.

He slicked back his hair.

Put me in a good light.

Hey, Hoot, he said to the waiter. La cuenta, por favor.

22 January

Army officer killed as car bombs rock Madrid

from the *Independent* (London)

By Elizabeth Nash

In Madrid

In an attack bearing all the hallmarks of ETA Basque separatists, two car bombs exploded in central Madrid early yesterday morning, killing an army officer, gutting vehicles and blasting windows of surrounding buildings in a massive shockwave.

The attack was carefully planned and the killers deliberately targeted their victim, Lt-Col Pedro Antonio Blanca Garcia, 47. They detonated a Renault Clio packed with explosives at 8 a.m., just as Lt-Col Blanca Garcia had left home and was waiting, as was his custom, for an official vehicle to take him to his place of work as a Defence Ministry economics supervisor. In the second blast half an hour later, two blocks away, the killers destroyed their getaway car.

Lt-Col Blanca Garcia's body was hurled 12 meters from the blast by the impact that shattered windows and wooden slatted blinds on all seven floors of the neat red-brick apartment blocks, in a chaotic scene of burning cars and terrified locals fleeing the immediate area.

"I tell you my building shook," said Isabel Pertejo, 50, who went to buy bread shortly after the blast. "Those of us who live around here are used to the sound of explosions and I knew instantly what it was. My husband is a military doctor, and ran out from the house. I know the family. I feel sorry for his wife and two children."

This modest area of flats for military officers and their families lies in the shadow of the Vicente Calderon stadium, home of Atletico Madrid football team.

"A lot of generals live around here and we've suffered terrorist attacks before," continued Mrs. Pertejo. "It used to be well guarded, with security jeeps constantly circulating, but security has fallen off during the ceasefire and we thought we'd put this horror behind us. And look what happens. It's heartbreaking."

Police towed away the burning and twisted hulks of several cars and showered streets with broken glass as they pushed scores of perilously shattered windows to the pavement below.

Chus's bar, where locals were taking everything in, was just out of range. Pepe, a pensioner with a tumbler of wine before him, had been awoken by the blast. "It was the biggest, most terrifying thunderclap I've ever heard and then a huge mushroom of thick black smoke rose into the sky. It's a tragedy and a disgrace. God protect us from these devils."

Spanish TV does not edit out uncomfortable scenes, and often a news crew is on the street before police arrive. They've been showing clips of Colonel Blanca Garcia when he was alive—at military ceremonies, sharing time with his family. It is hard to reconcile the living man with the piece of raw hamburger he ended up as.

23 January Sunday

A million people marched in Madrid today in protest against ETA. I saw the march on TV as it started in Colón Plaza. From there they went to Sol, a good long walk. I made my way to Sol and took my place in the multitude. José María Anzar stood next to the Socialist opposition leader Joaquín Almunia. It seemed a strain on both. I don't think they're fond of one another. They each gave a speech condemning ETA under a banner that said in Spanish: For Peace and Liberty. No to Terrorism.

Neither of them is very exciting, but the crowd cheered. They spoke and then left. Marchers were still entering Sol an hour later. There were many young people about with their palms painted chalk white. They held their hands in the air, palms out, and chanted Basta Ya. Enough Already. Their ghostly hands were much more effective and eloquent than the politicians talking. I think it's something I'll remember the rest of my life.

The crowd was well dressed. They were having refreshments and seemed happy. A kind of outing I took it. A Madrid-style picnic. There's a saying here—There are no eccentrics in Madrid. Looking around I noticed, except for the young, most were dressed in black or muted colors. Wanted poster photographs of two rebel suspects were passed through the crowd, thin young men with boot camp haircuts, spotted at the bombing site. I pictured them already sitting on a mountaintop in Basque France drinking txakoli.

To me the government all but begged the violence by detaining the ETA leader who had contact with them. But then, who am I to say? Seeing Joaquín Almunia up close, I realized I'd run across him before, just last week in a big alley close to Sol. I recognized him at the time as somebody from TV is about all, he is otherwise nondescript, shopworn, but he noticed that I recognized him in some manner at least and we passed and exchanged greetings and continued on our own way, he toward Sol and I away from it. I left the rally finally and meant to stop at Casa Antonio's on the way home but came upon a hat shop down the steps from Plaza Mayor and opposite Botín's. I stopped in and purchased a boina to keep my head warm in the house and then had no money left for wine. The old guy who made the hats and ran the shop was worth the visit. A neat old Madrileño gent. One of those you couldn't even imagine when he was born. He had one of the wanted posters on his counter. He tapped it with a finger. Mala leche, he said. Bad milk. A term used here to register disgust.

I've been keeping an eye on my character lately, the persona I put down on paper. In the short distance from my brain, as I see what's to happen, and then to my hands when I type it, I perceive that he changes from me to him. Often the change is greater than expected.

At certain times, he seems more articulate than I am. I might have to look up words he uses to be certain of their meaning. Other times say, he'll talk in slang I'm not familiar with, as if he's been around places I have not.

I get the sense that he is changing on me, changing from me; sometimes, already he don't know me. When I'm out walking in the city, it's almost like I see him in the distance ahead of me. He's not looking back wondering if I'm keeping up. It strikes me now and then that it might not even be me in fact. You get that in another country, that sometimes it feels like it's not you anymore. You can't possibly be this far from home.

When I look at him closely, his face seems dissolute; there's an odd pigmentation under his eyes as though he drinks too much, never sleeps. And he does not hesitate, he jumps in, does not suffer from awkwardness the first time doing things. It is not the way I am, and I like him for it. He can be erased, I do that often enough, or the occurrences when he goes strange are delegated to the shadow file. He seems to have an existence a bit separate from mine, however, or one that has gone somewhat differently. And I wonder if he is not that part of me which has always gone astray.

Lately, every day, I have walked through Lavapiés looking for signs that read Se Alquila. For Rent. I like that barrio. There is one street especially, Olivar, a narrow cobblestone street on a big hill with new street lamps and young trees planted that seems just right. Today I saw a few places for rent on Olivar and jotted down numbers to call.

I've been checking out the bars there also. Many of them down at the bottom near the metro are small, smoke-filled, elbow to elbow with standup, serious drinkers and talkers. And all men. No women. No air conditioning, no fans even. In the summer they must be unbearably hot. But, no matter to this rough crowd I suspect.

I found a guitar in a dumpster and took it with me. At one point a man came out a front door, stopped, and crossed himself before going on his way. You need all the help you can get out here I guess. Later on I turned down a stark, industrial-looking street—it appeared as if natural life had never existed there—and came upon a white-haired lady pacing back and forth in a small area as though she were enclosed in a cage. It was only a seven, eight foot area she walked, holding close to a building, her nose almost against the bricks, saying things, a stricken look on her face. She took one terribly deep breath. It was a heart sob. It was the soul of mankind coming up for air. She was interested only in her lunacy and did not notice me pass. Then I walked to Plaza Santa Ana and encountered a young British couple having an argument. The fella stomped away from the young woman, saying, That's the end of it— She spoke at the same time, Please, Ian … no… Oh, Ian, please … Something inutterably sad about it. Perhaps I felt myself walking away from her, and for no other reason but that I was angry at life.

The guitar has no strings. I've been working at my poetry like a dog trying to bury a bone, and getting nowhere on it. That well, for the time being, has dried up on me. So it seemed a perfect symbol at the moment, this guitar without strings. It has a nice shape, but it don't say a thing. I like finding symbols on the street as much as the next guy, but I wish they'd hand me some good news occasionally. I put the guitar in the closet. It looks like a nice place for the mouse to nest.

At home, I pace around the apartment. I observe the outside from within as if from a bird cage. Part of a recent conversation with Chelo comes back:

Were you kidding about not finishing a poem since '89?

No, I'd answered. Actually, I started that poem then. It just took me awhile. I was busy then.

Doin' what?

Coke.

Oh … right, he said. I remember that … somewhat. There was more damn drugs in Tampa then … I came out of it much older than when I went in. There was a dealer lived in my building. I got to know him. He had any left over from Saturday night, he'd come by Sunday. Say, Take this eight-ball, pay me later. I was so in debt to him after awhile, it got serious …

He didn't go on. He changed the subject.

I look out through the bird cage. The bars are not so that you can see them exactly. It's a cage full of mirrors, and few toys. I consider my character some more. He looks back at me, and I perceive the thinnest possible smile of repressed irony. Sometimes it strikes me that everything here is in place simply to make me feel ignorant. I believe winter gets into the soul, and mine is not dressed for it.

31 January
from the *International Herald Tribune*
8 Basques Arrested in Sweep on ETA

BILBAO, Spain—The police have arrested eight suspected members of the Basque separatist group ETA, state media reported.

The arrests, which included at least two leading members of ETA's political wing Euskal Herritarrok, were part of an investigation by Judge Baltasar Garzon into the guerrilla group and its former mouthpiece, the newspaper Egin, reports said Saturday.

The clampdown in the northern Basque region occurs a week after an army officer was killed in a car bombing in Madrid.

Chelo and I talked on the phone several times lately, have to drink a few beers some night we agree, but it doesn't happen. Kevin Ray tells me Chelo's having trouble getting to work on time. He has a new girlfriend I should think. Or he's hooked back up with the Scottish girl. Megan as she dresses sings, Sick of school … sickathis … shit … sick … of … it. She drank wine last night. She doesn't drink very much or often but gets contemplative when she does. Starts saying things like, Let's get the fuck out of here. Go home and start replanting Tillie's grove, at least the five acres by the house. We can put in kumquats, satsumas. The cold won't hurt them. We can harvest the pines. It'll give us start-up money …

I was listening.

It seems like it has been winter for a very long time now and that it will always be winter.

The last rain we had caused the wooden doors and windows on the streetside to go swollen so that they won't close all the way. The cold comes in as it pleases. Friday I finished a bottle of wine by 9 a.m. I was working on the computer and managed to hit two or three keys all at once, which made the machine do several oddities. Best to shut it off at that point, wait till Megan gets home to figure it out. I scraped together all the money I could find in the apartment and bought a quart of Jack Daniels. It took till midnight to finish the bottle, and it didn't do a thing for me. The hangover will last two days.

Looking out the window a bit past midnight, I observed the exhibitionist at work. She's a brute. She doesn't have a whole lot going for her, a big ass and a great tangle of black hair she likes to shake about and run her fingers through as she rides her mount. She's always on top. A wild west fantasy it seemed this night. A cowgirl. Or maybe a jockey. Giving her horse the whip … pounding home … it was a long race. They had turned off the table lamp next to them but it had a short, which resulted in a strobe effect. This, to me at least, heightened the show. I wonder how many others on my side of the street are taking this in … or do I have some unique angle by which to see it all? My response to her out on the street that day, Claro, was not exactly appropriate to the situation. Or maybe it was. It means *sure*.

What's amazing to me is how a thing can so quickly become routine. Just the other evening, as Megan and I were eating dinner, she happened to notice the exhibitionist giving her boyfriend head. I could see nothing of the boyfriend but the ole flagpole, which appeared and disappeared, but it was really nothing new; a fork full of green beans paused momentarily on its way to my mouth, then I went on eating. I'm beginning to feel quite jaded. I know without her though I would have no view whatsoever. I am left with the thought that she waved to me once last night as she made the turn to the wire.

1 February
from the *International Herald Tribune*
  Pedro Almodóvar received the prizes for best director and best movie for Todo Sobre Mi Madre (All About My Mother) at the Goya film awards in Madrid. One of the

movie's stars, Cecilia Roth, won the award for best actress.
Almodóvar recently won a Golden Globe for the movie and
it is also a candidate in the foreign-language category of
the Academy Awards. The Goya awards are organized by
the Spanish Cinema Academy.

There's a whole lot more happening here in the industry than
Almodóvar. The Spanish are passionate about movies. The other
night Megan and I watched an old film, *The Spirit of the Beehive*.
It's by Victor Erice, released in '73. It's been called the best Spanish
movie ever filmed. The action takes place in 1940, just after the
Civil War. One of its stars is Fernando Fernán Gómez, another Ana
Torrent. Both of them are still around. Erice makes a film every ten
years or so. Its setting is a little village in the Castile meseta. There's
beauty in the slow way the story develops. Image and symbol carry
it. Two young sisters see the film *Frankenstein* and afterwards
imagine that the monster is nearby. Isn't it always?

Almodóvar has caught America's eye, but I'm not so sure. I
know he's got nothing on Victor Erice.

Just as I finished the paper, Chelo showed up to lift weights. He'd
hooked up again with the Scot. She's been showing him the night,
he says. She's 23, and he's having a hard time keeping pace. He'd
gotten in at 4 a.m. He looks pasty. Some pretty severe bloodlines in
his eyes. His nose is red. He has on a sports coat and over that a kind
of hunting jacket. They don't match, but he overcomes it by wearing
sweatpants. You have to love the guy for his effrontery. He notices
me looking over this ensemble.

Nothing else clean, he says. I had classes this morning, both of
which I taught before I woke up.

You doin' any good with her? I said.

Not yet. I'm working on it. You never know what a Brit's
thinking, though. So far we're just pals.

What happened to your resolution about the young?

This is different, he says. What the hell stinks in here?

See those purple flowers. Megan's gypsy got into hyacinth bulbs this week.

Smells like a funeral parlor.

Yeah. Look, I said. When you get done, let's go down to your barrio. I've got cabin fever.

We're in Bodegas Alfaro on the corner of Olmo and Ave María, sitting at a corner table. The doors are open and sun comes in bright this time of day. There's an empty lot across the street on Olmo, a couple holes covered by bars in the concrete wall, and I see four kittens playing. I think to get something to feed them, as they look starved.

Alfaro is a simple neighborhood bar. It's open at the front and the side that turns the corner. People come and go. Drinks are cheap here, and we start throwing them down. This barrio, Lavapiés, is all but serene compared to mine. I'm going to move here I say to myself like I'm into telling fortunes. Chelo starts coming to life finally. He's reminiscing about being a kid in Tampa.

This patch of woods along the Hillsborough River where we used to play, when they cut the trees down and started building, he said, me and my buddies thought it was the end of the world. There was three of us hung out together all the time. The River Club is what it was called. A big apartment complex. But when they were done and occupied finally, it brought something that'd been missing in our lives—girls. We hit the complex on our bikes every day that first summer looking for action at the swimming pools. And it wasn't long till we found this one daring girl named Penny. Man. She was one of the whores of old.

She was 16, tall legs and tight shorts. She was built. She looked after her 12-year-old sister and two girls from next door, about the same age. We made it our mission to pop their cherries … though, none of us had done much yet but personally abuse ourselves.

We were just learning how to spit good. We weren't that far removed from considering a hard-on an act of magic. But Penny was already into sex. She had a boyfriend that worked at a pizza place.

During the day, we had her to ourselves, and she had what I'd learn to call a sadistic nature. Before we'd get a chance to diddle the other girls, first we had to be put through her tests, and they took a while. Just as an aside, I don't believe she ever had any thought of letting us at the younger ones. She used them for bait.

But these tests, like … one day she made each of us spread open her ass and stick our tongue up her bunghole. But no sex! Then another time, she shaved her pussy to surprise her boyfriend on his 19th birthday, and we had to watch her foam up and use the razor. We sat cross-legged before her like worshipers at a miracle.

Or the time she played this game where I had to close my eyes and point to the cunt on an invisible woman, some movie star, say, I had in my mind … at which time Penny took my finger into her mouth, sucked on it a little, then bit down hard. That hurt, believe me. Look. I still got a scar. I damn near cried. And this kinda shit went on for weeks. We were all in a frenzy. I'd ride my bike home, head to the bathroom and jack off like a zoo monkey.

Anyway, my cousin Gate Suazo came up from 7th Avenue one day to visit, and we took him over to Penny's. His first name is Gaitano, a good Tampa Cuban boy. That got shortened early on. He's currently serving time for narcotics possession and won't be getting out soon. I'm not sure what happened. His family's not eager to talk about it. Though I know he had a sweet tooth for Dilaudid. But Gate was two years older than any of us and knew the score already. He was one of them kids you figured knew everything.

Now on the way over to the apartments, I told Gate what to expect if she pulled the invisible movie star routine. He says, We'll see about that.

Penny found something in him right off the bat. She couldn't sit still. You want to play a game? she asked him. When she started doing her point to the cunt bit, Gate feigned to stick out his finger, but as Penny's mouth opened, he yanked down his shorts. And there was his cock dangling inches from her face.

A look of indecision crossed her. She seemed momentarily lost in thought. Then she leaned forward and took him into her mouth.

Gasps all around, from the girls and from us. She let go of Gate then and stood up. She told the girls to stay there and took us into the bedroom, much protestation on the girls' part. But she kept them out and locked the door ... which didn't work out so good in the long run. Her little sister tattled on her, and the whole thing fell apart. But in the bedroom then, Penny stripped off her clothes, was naked on the bed crazy with laughter, and all of us jumped her. I'll tell you ... she had her hands full that day.

An experience like that, Chelo said, your first one, too ... you never forget it. Somehow I think it's affected all that's gone after.

As he was finishing his story, five men came into the bar and ordered cañas. They were different ages but all still fairly young, and looked remarkably alike. They were in good spirits. Chelo got to talking to the one standing next to him. They are five brothers. They're taking their father on a last run of his favorite bars. He's outside in a casket. Chelo explains to me what's going on.

The hell you say.

I stepped outside. There's a young boy, maybe four years old, all bundled up against the cold, sitting on one end of the casket, watching over his grandfather. The brothers finished their drinks. They come outside. There are handles on the sides of the casket. Four grab handles, and they start off to the next bar, commenting that the old man was getting heavier as the day progressed, sharing a laugh about it. The fifth put his arm around the boy's shoulders, and they followed.

We made our way slowly up from Lavapiés toward the Antón Martín area, heading to the Scottish girl's apartment, stopping now and then for beverages. Chelo and Emilie had gotten into an argument the day before. He tells me about it at a bar called Miñas, on Calle Ave María . The bar has a ración of gambas a la plancha, 6 grilled shrimp, for 160 pesetas. And we're eating shrimp as he speaks.

Two of Kevin's students were in the office yesterday afternoon when I come in, a guy, and this girl that was really cute, Chelo said. They hadn't made it to class the day before and wanted to know what they'd missed. Emilie was there. She had business with Kevin. I think he'd scored some hash for her. The guy didn't stay long. He got the assignment and was about to leave. Before doing so he asked, When is this curse over? Meaning *course*. That started it. Okay, he says. I have to go to spitch class now.

Both are second-level. Their English skills ... they sort of have it, and sometimes not. They seemed like good kids, nicely turned out and all. But when the guy left, I'm chatting with the girl at the time and she says of him, I don't care for that one. Kevin had already gone to class, and Emilie was standing in the doorway. I don't know why she was hanging around. I don't know. My mind tells me she's there because she wants to fuck me, but—

It's a gift, I said.

What? Chelo said.

The way your mind sees things.

Oh. Yeah. Right.

Anyway, I ask the girl, Why is that ... why don't you like him?

He's always coming on me, she says.

I said, Say again ... And she repeated it.

He's always coming on me.

And you don't like that? I said. I was just playing with her a little.

No, she said. I don't like guys coming on me all the time.

Then Emilie started in.

Coming on *to* you, she said. *To* you!

She's upset about it, giving me dirty looks and all, like I'm contaminating the students.

That's it?

Yeah ... well ... So I says ... well, it don't matter what I said. No wait. I didn't say nothin'. I started laughing. Which really set her off.

An' she slapped at me, and I restrained her. Maybe I held on too long. I'm not sure. Then she called me an asshole, and a few other things in French, and left.

Emilie is one of the coolest customers I've ever known. And she has a great sense of humor. Chelo's explanation doesn't quite cut it. I get the idea he left something out, he's holding back, but I'm too lit at the moment to worry about much. From Lavapiés to Antón Martín, which isn't very far, we'd stopped at five bars. I'm drunk to where I feel that I've got the palsy, which, at the time, I'm thinking is alright, nothing wrong with that, and I'm ready to stand up and be counted, though for what exactly is not clear.

We arrived at the apartment finally. It's in a building at the corner of Ave María and Magdalena and located over a flamenco bar and a furniture store. The bar stays open till 5 each morning and might explain why this girl isn't crazy about getting home too early.

Calle Magdalena is a bad street. It's a main bus route, the noise rumbles by, many Chinese wholesale stores, goods forever being unloaded from white vans, horns honking up and down it all day and into the night, gridlock and petrol fumes.

Darlen is a little ditzy sometimes, Chelo says and hits the intercom. Maybe just stoned.

That's her name? I said.

Yeah, he said. He spelled out the first name. Then said it all: Darlen McKenna.

A voice comes on. Diga …

It's me, he says.

Che … where are you? the voice asks.

He looks at me.

Like so, he said.

The door unlocks. The wooden stairs are worn down in the center almost like the curve of a horseshoe from the centuries of people traversing them. I don't know why, but I count the steps. Thirteen. I think—13 steps to the hangman's rope. The door to the apartment is open. The door is solid mahogany; it must be several hundred years old. Just as we're about to enter, Chelo stops. He says, One thing I haven't told you. She's extremely well put together …

What are you tryin' to say?

He looks me up and down.

Oh. I see. You think I'm gonna act a fool.

You don't get out much, he said.

A faint odor of perfume as we enter the apartment. I think of the German iris at Retiro. Odor of hash. The apartment is nice and warm. She must have central heating. And it would be the only new thing in the place. Otherwise we have entered a museum, something frozen in time, and all grandeur gone to seed.

We go down a hallway. The three doors on the left have padlocks on them. The apartment is cut in half. She only uses the one side of it, though it's plenty big enough at that.

We enter the parlor, which faces Ave María, a high-ceilinged room, fluted wainscoting, the plaster on the ceiling and walls covered with peeling ocherish-white paint, tea-veined cracks running through, ending in french doors and threadbare silk damask curtains, balcony. Bookshelves, coffee table, mantlepiece, every flat surface covered with wine bottles, most of them empty. Expensive wine to the worst sort of swill. I notice a bottle of txakoli, the cider-like backyard wine of the Basques. It's pronoucned *chakolee*. You can't buy it in the stores here. They say it doesn't travel well, that it doesn't like to leave Basque country. All the furniture is red mahogany, claw-footed, 19th century or further back, carved, upholstered in tattered, persimmon-colored velvet, scarred and in various stages of disrepair, and very large, as if meant for castle rooms or a giant. Everything taken together is sort of weirdly beautiful and somewhat amusing at the same time.

Darlen in an easy chair in long-sleeved, white cotton blouse, black pedal pushers. She and Chelo kiss and fool around a bit, and then he introduces us. She looks at me just slightly amazed, like she knows me from somewhere. She says a few things, which go by me completely. She has a smokey voice—a cigarette rasp, or maybe she drinks a lot of whiskey. Something's going on there. She's looking me over, taking my caliber, smiling. It's a smile that undermines all seriousness. I'm staring at her badly I realize finally as Chelo gives me an elbow. He wasn't kidding. She's a knockout. I mumble, Pleased to meet you. She's drinking albariño from a bottle and goes to get some glasses. Beside the bottle is a knife and a green apple that looks like she'd just peeled and cut in half.

When she returns, I sit down slightly apart from her and Chelo. The chair dwarfs me. I feel like a little kid in it. A black marble fireplace to the left of me. There's not been a fire built in it for awhile. They're talking in front of it.

Darlen's eyes are mauve, like wisteria flowers, a broad forehead, strong nose and chin, her teeth slightly uneven, a dimple in her right cheek when she smiles. Her oak-blond hair is wet and cut straight at the shoulders. No make-up. Her face is very expressive, a smile playing there, and lovely in an odd way. She is not beautiful exactly, as Chelo had it. Or maybe it is just an unusual sort of beauty. But whenever you look at her, her eyes take you back before long, the kindness in them. And I'm thinking maybe she's one of those that get prettier the more you know her.

When she notices me staring at her, she focuses on me slightly puzzled again, the same look—she can't quite place me—but then goes back to her conversation with Chelo.

I listen to pigeons cooing on the ledge. A man coughs on Ave María. He's hacking away. Two dogs get into an argument. Footsteps running. A radio singing in Arabic.

What do you say, Luke? Darlen asks.

I look at her. She has put on her head a black pillbox hat. She switches on a lamp. She models the hat. I hardly notice it. Her breasts are like two large evenly matched drops of oil that move beneath her blouse when she moves. She's barefoot. A tattoo of a scorpion circles her right calf, dusty, light brick in color like a Paleolithic cave painting or a fossil in stone, the hair slight blonde down on her ankles.

Very nice, I said.

She turned in a circle.

I concentrate on the hat finally.

It throws everything into a different time, I said.

Quite, she said.

There is something so utterly sylish and sensual about her I cannot take my eyes away.

Chelo is looking at me like, You're just a natural born son of a bitch, aren't ya.

It has begun to rain outside, the windows mizzled with it. I hear the buses, just out of sight, lumbering by on Magdalena, the hiss of tires, motorbikes droning like large flying insects, curses, horns, all the mad commotion. The tides of the Spanish day changing. I begin to wonder what could there be in the padlocked rooms. Does she keep the bodies of old lovers there, like in fairy tales? Or maybe just their hearts? Chelo had to use the bathroom. I'm staring at Darlen's body again. This has got to stop. I hear myself asking her:

How much do you weigh?

The words tumbled out before I could stop them. My God, I think … who is this talking in my stead?

I'm bang on nine stone. She laughed. I say … what are you on about? She took a cigarette from her purse, asked if I had a match. I lit her cigarette. She touched my hand as I did so, and I held the match there a little long.

Do I look old, she asked, in the light?

No, I said. You are looking quite good.

I'm 29, she said. I tell everyone I'm 23. I make more money that way.

Right then Chelo returned. I went to the window and looked out, wondering vaguely what she meant by that.

They're making plans to go out. Darlen went to a bedroom to change. I walked out to the kitchen. Different here. Plainer. A long, solidly built wooden table of the simplest design. It looks well used and cared for. Whitewashed walls. A big chopping block, cooking utensils, knives, wineskins, garlic bulbs strung on twine. An antique violin hanging from one of the rafters. It looks homemade. A fireplace here also, smaller, this one for cooking and a stew pot hanging from its bail, but the pot is clean and the fireplace, just as in the front room, does not look to have been used for some time, the hearthstones swept. It strikes me as a man's kitchen.

When Darlen came back she's wearing a pale yellow sweater, a black leather skirt with a slit way up one thigh, black boots. I was headed home at that point, but she sat opposite me, just the very tip of her tongue protruding between her lips. She crossed her legs.

We're going on a carousal, Luke. Are you not going with us? she said. We're going to drink plonk, create havoc. Or at least have half a shandy at the pub down the street.

There were legs all over the place.

I remember Chelo acting funny around her that evening, not himself, distracted, inward. Acted like he just had it so bad for her it was making him sick.

He nearly got into a fight with a Spaniard. I'm not sure what this fella did or said. I missed that part. I asked Chelo what happened.

Just some hambone, he said.

She drew attention from the boys, though, their eyes cutting things in half to get to her sooner. I thought then and think it now, looks like that could scar a man.

I seem to have lost several bar napkins of notes I jotted down then. I've got so much junk in this room. The room I'm speaking of is my mind perhaps. What a shame, really. But as I look around, finding anything at all here would be an immense project, one I'm not capable of at the moment.

My recall is fragmented. The night didn't last so very long for me. I remember being at Casa Asturias on Argumosa in Lavapiés. I knocked over an empty wine bottle. It hit the floor but didn't break. I took it as a sign that luck was my date. But soon afterward I started nodding.

You might need to go lie down, Luke, Darlen said. You're falling out.

She was right. I just couldn't keep my eyes open. Chelo gave me his key, and I went to his place, which was close by. They were to meet me there shortly. I thought I'd rest awhile, wait for them, though I doubted they would show, then go home before Megan started worrying. But I ended up sleeping the night.

Toward morning I dreamed I was at a red, barn-like house where Billy was staying with some of his family. Billy had four brothers and two sisters. None of them were present. But there were members of his dream family around. I've come across them before, though when I wake they are indistinct. It was good seeing Billy again as his old self, in a time frame before the paranoia and lunacy began. His dream mother nudged me once with her elbow and said, Don't you think he's coming in clearly?

Then I heard a phone ring, and I woke up on Chelo's floor.

The phone rang a number of times. Then it stopped.

I rubbed my eyes and tried to think if I had insulted anyone the previous night. It's one of the things I do when I wake with a hangover, an adaptation to the vagaries of my conduct. And too, I try to think of anything rather than the sadness of my physical state. But I felt rattled, neural misfirings in my head. My tongue felt like a salt lick. I went to the bathroom to take a leak. I went to the kitchen and took a long drink from the faucet. The phone rang again. Chelo answered it this time.

I listened off and on to him talking, his voice hoarse. He was in the bedroom. I sat on a chair in the living room. I heard him saying:

I'm thinking of this one 4th of July, when he decided, for unknown reasons, to walk home from a party we were at. I remember wondering, Where the hell is he goin'? It was a long walk home. He only made it to the side gate, where he fell down face first, no hands out front to break the fall. That was impressive, especially in that he started right off laughing. It'd been me, I'd just have gone to sleep there, but he popped back up immediately and somewhat magically I thought. Almost a rebound of sorts—that seemed at the time to defy the laws of physics. I've studied that move in my thoughts many years now without once coming to any resolution as to how he did it. It's a mystery …

At this point, through the fog, I realized he was talking about me.

He's pottered off somewhere, he said. I don't know, he said. Pottered. It means what it means. A pause as he listens. Then—I don't know as I'd go that far. And finally he bleats, The same to ya! and slams the phone down.

He comes out of the bedroom, sits on the floor and lets his head loll back.

I look at my watch. It's 7:05 in the morning.

Who was that?

Megan, he said. She's looking for you.

For Christ' sake. What are you doin'?

I just … have no fucking idea, he said.

I called Megan and explained the situation, told her I'd be home soon.

Turns out Darlen had given him Ecstasy.

It was curious, he said. I just felt like touching. I was touching everyone. Like my hands had some new dimension. And I danced my ass off. I was thrashing around out there. That music in the clubs, I hate that shit, an' just this violent light show going on, but … it's all different when you're loaded.

He's about to lose his voice entirely.

You gotta shout in there, he explains.

How you feelin' now?

Like a very slow roller, he said.

He was once into bowling.

Why'd you hang up on Megan?

She called me a scantling. What the hell's a scantling?

It's not good.

I got that, he said.

Thursday

Much like a spring day, 60 degrees by noon, and Megan and I went to the lake, sat at a café with a clear view of the Madrid city skyline to the east. She hadn't particularly talked to me for awhile after my night away, but she forgave me soon enough. She's used to me finding the wrong crowd. It's one of my talents.

Chelo is another matter.

Why do you reckon he did that? Was he just fuckin' with me? she wanted to know. I'm near worried sick about you, and he starts telling me bullshit stories.

I can't account for him, I said.

And as I thought, he hadn't exactly spoken true on what happened between him and Emilie. This is more serious. Emilie is talking about going home. She specified that she didn't care to be handled. If Megan knows what happened exactly, she's not telling, but my thought is that he grabbed her ass, maybe grabbed whatever came his way. He had his hands on her, Megan said, and took his own sweet time taking them off. That's as far as she'll go with it.

He's apologized over the phone to Emilie's answering machine. She is not picking up. He's backpeddlin', Megan says. But it won't work. She is beyond persuasion.

Since Christmas, Erik's been serious in wanting her to come home. He's had enough of distance. And living with June Bug has become open warfare. She's telling Megan it looks like it's time to go, and Megan is heartbroken by the prospect. She thinks much the less of Chelo for all this of course.

6 February
from the *International Herald Tribune*
Socialists in Spain Back Leftist Alliance

MADRID—Socialist leaders on Friday formally approved their first alliance with the Communists since the Spanish civil war in a bid to oust Prime Minister Jose Maria Aznar in a March 12 election.

The Socialist candidate, Joaquin Almunia, hailed it as the "start of an unforgettable campaign," but Josep Pique, chief spokesman for Spain's center-right government, dismissed it as a "pact between losers."

The alliance poses a new threat to Aznar's Popular

Party, which holds an opinion poll lead of 4 to 7 percentage points over the Socialists.

On this day also, Emilie Dessommes left Madrid.

At the airport, they'd had a hard time letting go of each other. Megan says of her feelings at the moment, Hecho polvo. I am dust.

In the afternoon, Kevin Ray came over, and we decided to go out to eat. And something small happened that, in the long run, turned things around for us.

I save my coffee grounds and feed them to the trees on our street. I did this as we were on our way to the restaurant, and an old bird came flying out of her apartment and protested. She was really squawking. She didn't feel like looking at that shit outside her windows, she said. The city workers hadn't been around to clean up yet. I glanced down the street. It's a derelict's dream. There's a blasting wind. The street moves like a river of garbage. These coffee grounds aren't going to spoil the esthetics. I wondered how she got on me so quick and notice that there's an apartment on the ground floor here. She must be the only one in a ten-block area who lives at eye level with the weekend street party. No wonder she's nuts. She probably hadn't slept since Thursday night.

I rolled my eyes and moseyed on. Kevin, however, took up the fray. He started screaming back at her. He really let her have it. He knows Spanish well and can say it loud. It was both ugly and comic. Finally, it looked like he was winding up to deck the old lady, so I pulled him away.

There's something about this neighborhood, he said, brings out the meanness in you. Damn, he said, shaking out his shoulders and laughing. I haven't been in a good scrap in ages.

As far as the old people of Madrid, I try to keep in mind that nobody really started learning anything here until the 1960s and, consequently, there's a bunch of old farts around that are just ignorant. But this was so out of the blue. And senseless. Then I thought, Aw, fuck her. We went down to Casa Mingo and had roast chicken and a couple bottles of sidra. By the end of the meal I'd pretty much forgotten the incident. But it weighed on Megan, though I didn't know it at the time.

There was a group of young people near us drinking Sidra Natural. You hold the bottle high overhead and the sidra pours in a thin stream to a glass held below one hip. It is called descant. Then you drink it quickly. Your aim is skewed after awhile. The floor got pretty wet. They didn't care. They were having fun.

There's more trouble at work Kevin tells us. Chelo has gotten on the wrong side of their boss in Tampa. There are things they need to know from her, but she's stopped returning calls. He says of Chelo, He spends so much time and effort to avoid what he's supposed to be doing, it's almost like a perverse sort of ambition.

Also, we'd had it in mind to meet up with Daryl and Emma in Amsterdam next month, and Megan spent several hours on the phone yesterday trying to find lodging for us. But it turns out there's a big flower show going on then, and the city is booked.

That night, the wind whistling a lively tune through the apartment, Megan told me:

We need to move. I'm tired of being cold. The neighbors hate us … She had a list.

Then she couldn't get to sleep. I woke once and heard her pacing around. I'd just fallen asleep again when she called me.

Lucas. Would you come here a minute?

I threw a blanket around my shoulders, went into the computer room. She was standing by the french doors.

That awful woman across the street … she's fucking her boyfriend and waving to me.

I looked out the window. Sure enough.

Really, she said. It's just too much. We need to get out of here.

Late that night, Billy Jenks dropped by.

I finally found a bona fide job, Billy said. It lasted a month.

I had scraped myself off the couch to proceed with a diligence I haven't seen in myself since … At any rate, I was offered two jobs the same day. Whoever claimed my creative juices were sapped was somewhat mistaken. What a dilemma! One job, an apartment-maintenance gig, offered me the princely sum of six dollars an hour. I could see the Town Car pull up to take me to the gardens. What gardens I didn't have time to figure out because the catch was about to spring. I'd have to wait a month for my first paycheck. But it would be for three days! No problems there. The landlord and the electric company would certainly understand another month of delinquency. Meanwhile, I'd just forgo the noodles and eat steam.

You have to get a job where you're at? I said.

Yeah, sure. But let me finish … The next offer was slightly less lucrative, $4.50 an hour, but definitely tinged with nostalgia. That's right. Another factory job. And I bowed down and grabbed my ankles and took it. You would have loved it, Luke, what with the way you cherish noise. After two, three hours of tidal machines pounding their insane rap into your skull, you could sit outside for ten minutes and hear the jets landing at the airport, while you rolled a Bugler, complacent in such a variegated change of rhythm.

But I'm getting' too old for this shit. I quit, and I wasn't even all that hung over, like the last thirty or forty jobs. I always get there whether I have to walk or not, but it's something about staying there that does me in. When the boss man asked why I left, all I could tell him was, I must have got out the wrong side of the bed. Just consider—I blew a chance to make five dollars an hour if I'd only stayed another two months. Where is my thinking?

What I was doing wasn't so bad. I was culling doors. It was a door factory. Someone asked, What do you make there? I didn't make shit. I culled doors. It's a beautiful word—cull. I'd never heard it before, or it hadn't registered. I was the first one appointed to the task who actually did what he was supposed to—that is, examine the doors returned, decide which ones should be credited and which ones to say fat chance to.

I was fair at all times in my judgment. An' these doors were heavy.

I spent most of the day shuffling them around to make room. Here it is, a huge factory, and the scarcest commodity, outside a decent wage, is room. And that's another thing—the place is crammed with spades, and one of the white boys there pisses me off, intentionally, mind you, filling up my fucking space with his doors. I tried to be nice about it, but he wouldn't have anything to do with pleasantries. When I walked off, I shoved a finger in his face and scolded him with words, something like, You no good shiftless motherfucker … I'm walkin' behind you … don't you dare make a move or I'll kick your ass. He weighed in with, What? And it's a good thing that's all he said …

I looked around the room as Billy talked. I was sitting up in bed, and Billy was on the straightback chair that acted as a catch-all in the bedroom. He was wearing a blue T-shirt and jeans and didn't seem affected by the cold.

I'm not alone, he went on, in this impetuous disregard for jobs. This character I know came back to the neighborhood recently. He goes by A.J. He'd just abandoned a half-way house for ex-cons on receiving his first pay check. He got the notion to return to the Hindu Hotel across the street from me, where he'd stayed six months previous, entertaining the fantasy that his long-leg AA gal might overlook his drinking this time, especially if he took her back to the place of magic lights and exotic odors. The exotic odors wafted from Baba Ram's office, a proprietor with a taste for roadkill, judging by the smell. The lights were neon, but let's not quibble. She would have none of it, this time around. She'd burned that bridge. Neither would Ram. A.J. gets drunk twice and quits his job. One hour late on the rent and the Hindu with a picture of Jesus on his wall confiscated his belongings.

A.J. takes it quietly. Others besides the law are after him, he says. He doesn't want to trumpet his whereabouts. All three of his belongings I might add—his granddaughter's photo, his spectacles, and a small stash of heroin. The Hindu tells him it's gonna cost 25 bucks a day to get his possessions out of hock. A.J. can't believe the guy is so heartless. Here's a guy who's been to Nam and in the joint, and he still ain't grown up. He's naïve. I said, That's Hindu for you, be they Christian or not. A few more beers and he asks, Do you think that fella owns the little store will run me a tab? Again I play the sage. He's the one charged five cents extra for nuking your apple turnover!

We played chess and got drunk for three weeks and had some laughs. He's now recovering from his alcoholism at … a basement place, he calls it. I'm fast on his heels. Fare thee well, Luke—

Wait a minute, Billy … damn it. Hold on a bit, will you?

He looks around nervously. He frets with his cigarette pack.

Make it quick, Luke, he says. Hey, you got a beer?

Suddenly there's a Cinco Estrellas in his hand, and it seems to calm him. He takes a drink and looks at the label.

Good beer, he said.

Billy … I don't know what's goin' on, but … you remember when I saw you last time, at the red barn house? You were different there. You … I'm trying to think of some nice way of saying he wasn't paranoid and delusional—

That was a dream, though, Billy said.

This isn't?

He held his hands in front of him, palms out.

There's things I'm not allowed to tell you, he says. I just thought I'd come visit while I could. I need some levity what with my guardian angel, Jimmy, always cracking the whip. He's got me on a scaffold, scraping paint off an old house. It's what I'm supposed to be doing right now. But I'm daydreaming. Before he dropped down, exactly in the nick of time, I was eyeing the streets, or rather the alleys. I'm actually three or four days ahead on my rent now. Things are looking up. Even though the job's only part-time. He's just doing me a favor I think. He said if I fell from the scaffolding, though, he doesn't know me.

His name is Jimmy?

You were lookin' for something more Biblical?

I said, It's good to hear your voice again, Billy … but, you're—

Let's not get into that, he says. And it ain't so bad now. Let me take you back half a year, when things were truly sorry. I actually got my ass up at four in the morning and drove to the labor pool. They were advertising for cars.

You have a car?

I had one then.

What was it?

It was a beater. But … let me tell this, okay. I ain't got so much time. I have to get back.

So anyway, he says, I go to the labor pool. I was greeted by three mohawk punks in fatigues, a dozen derelicts, one with a deep-purple nose, and a coupla handsful of browns. Jam-packed. No communication. Two hours later I finally got out. They all look at me, the ones still there, like, Fuck you. They're thinking, Come back tomorrow and we slice your tires. Jealousy, I suppose.

I had to speak up to my employers, being the social security number that I am. Look, I said. I've got a car and I'm willing to suck ass, just so long as you don't get too bothered about a quart or two along the way.

Next thing I know, I'm out on the highway with a Texan, whose wife waits all day for him at the labor pool apparently, and two spades—one dumb as dirt and one who thinks he's not. I felt like auditioning for *Little House on the Prairie*, just to know some good would come of it.

Our mission was to spruce up a dump. I'm not kidding, that was it. All of us praised the Lord and considered our blessings. But you know how it goes, when things appear so smooth.

In the first place, the spade riding shotgun wouldn't let me get a word in edgewise. An' it's not like I've taken a vow of silence lately. I'm thinking, The Texan probably considers me a nigger lover … the niggers are sayin' to each other, Easy prey. I was eyeing down the perimeter of the dump, exploring a little, checking if my car would fit through these two shrubs, just in case, when the shotgun groid starts prodding me about my lunchtime habits.

You like beer? he goes.

How'd you guess? I answer.

Then he starts warning me about all the sneaky motherfuckers who'd slice you up for a dime. They're everywhere, he said. I said, Mmm ... go on ... but make it quick, I'm nodding. I said, I don't know about you, but I'm damn sure getting a beer for lunch, and I know exactly where I'm going.

Him and the dumb one did their mumbo-jumbo ... meaning, White boy don't know shit.

These are strict rockheads we're talking about. I made sure they bought an extra quart, their taxi fare, and I had to give that quart the evil eye to make it pull. The one ridin' shotgun, seemed he didn't want to share it after all. His eyes dead in the windshield lookin' at me. I'd insulted him somehow. This broke my heart as you can imagine. I'm crushed.

Then, after regaining his composure, he starts up again ... all about the back stabbing ass kissers at the labor pool. You ain't been on the streets, have you? he adds. An' I say, You gonna drink that beer, or court it? Mine's done.

All the joys of downward mobility.

Vgh ... ehgg? he quips. Nothing like a rock monster for conversation.

Billy, I said, you're gone, right?

I'm in a different arena of time, he said.

What is it like ... tell me ... to die ...

Nothin' to it, he said.

Hard to know what to make of this, Billy carrying on about his old obsessions, in Madrid no less.

Megan was holding me then.

You were talkin', Lucas, she said. You were talkin' to someone in your sleep. I could hear you in the other room.

I put my arms around her and held tight.

8 February
from the *International Herald Tribune*
3d Day Of Violence In Spanish Town
EL EJIDO, Spain—With a Moroccan man charged with

murdering a Spanish woman, anti-immigration protesters clashed with riot police officers Monday in the southern Spanish town of El Ejido on a third day of ethnic unrest.

Police officers charged at about 400 demonstrators wielding sticks and iron bars who were trying to get to a neighborhood heavily populated with Moroccan immigrants, Spanish National Radio reported. Four people were arrested and one policeman was reported to have been slightly injured. A small fire caused minor damage to three homes belonging to Moroccans.

Residents of El Ejido, a prosperous farming town of 52,000 where thousands of immigrants work in greenhouses, went on a rampage Saturday after the death of the woman, Encarnacion Lopez, 26. Rioters burned cars and shops belonging to Moroccans. The violence continued Sunday as demonstrators used sticks and bars to attack immigrants.

Megan has started buying *Segundomano* to check the want ads. It comes out Monday, Wednesday and Friday. She brought boxes home and started packing up. She's jumping the gun I'm thinking, but then Wednesday afternoon she called from school. I found a flat on Olivar, she said. This is the one we're going to move to. I just know it.

I went down to Lavapiés to take a look at it from the street, a pretty, light yellow building, number 18, on the second block up on the hill. The apartment is on the second floor, three balconies full of plants.

The next day we met the owner, Mercedes Gaspar. She's in her early 30s, long hair in a ponytail, a good looking Iberian woman who wore black-rimmed glasses and talked extremely fast. She makes animated films, also does scriptwriting she tells us. She showed us the apartment. Twelve foot ceilings. Wooden floors. An ancient place well taken care of through the centuries. There's a large streetside bedroom and a smaller interior one, which I'll gladly take. A big living room and a much larger and better-equipped kitchen than the one we have, bathroom with a clawfoot tub. Once again, there's no heat.

I'm getting rid of the furniture, she said in Spanish. She waved it away with her hand, said—It's shit. We agreed on the spot to take the apartment. We liked her, and we liked the place.

The next evening we went there again, and she cooked a pasta dish for us. The sauce had in it chorizo and salt cod. The Madrileños seem fond of this item. To me it has the texture of gum. She also made what she called limonada, and it was very good. She put together in a big glass pitcher lemon peel, lemon juice, lemon slices and sugar, a bottle of red wine, a bottle of white. After dinner she and Megan talked over the rental agreement in Spanish, and I finished off the lemonade. Mercedes is going to Hollywood. She's never been to America before. Hollywood is probably one of the last destinations in our country that I would consider, but I kept my mouth shut about that.

I went to see Kevin Ray the next afternoon. He's been living with two of the sisters, as he calls them, at an apartment just off the Toledo Glorieta. Sisters being a generic term he favors. I want him to sublet our apartment if it's possible. His roommates, who are sometimes a couple, though, even when they are, cheat on each other horribly Kevin Ray tells me, have taken to arguing lately and like to make scenes in front of him. He is no longer pleased with the arrangements, thinks he might be cause for the drama.

He answers the door with his hair covered in mayonnaise and a plastic shower cap. Head lice—that he'd caught from the flat. He's ready to move, but I have to dicker with him. He'll spend any amount of cash in bars over a weekend and think nothing of it, but in other ways he's careful with his money. We leave all the deposits in place, plus he's getting what's left of February rent-free. Ana Dolores knows and likes him, having not the least idea of his orientation. And as I thought, our leaving doesn't strike her adversely. She seems rather relieved. All Kevin Ray has to do is move in, and I agree to help him with that, whatever help he needs.

We need money to finance this. Amersterdam is out for sure now. Daryl and Emma will have to go on without us. I give Aunt Sylvia a call. I tell her I need a loan. Just a minute, she says. She drops the phone loudly, gets a dictionary, looks up the word loan, and reads me the definition which, she says, has little to do with the meaning I have historically assigned to it. I ignore all that and tell her how much we need. Dead-air time follows. She only agrees after Megan talks to her.

My first piece of mail in the new place will be from her, a receipt showing the transferred amount and a note that reads:

Luke, you have to make money mind you.

Before I give you any more, I would like to have an accounting, some idea of your spending habits. What, for example, does your monthly bar tab come to?

I will ignore this as well.

It takes a week to finalize everything with Ana Dolores and Kevin, and with Mercedes—the rental agreement, where to send the rent money to in the States. She and Megan go to Telefónica and she helps us to get a phone, which is an all day affair. In short order she gets her belongings out of there. She has friends to help her with this. Then she's off to Hollywood for a year. We started moving in.

The apartment is unfurnished now. There's nothing in the place but a table and two chairs in the kitchen. The rest of it's all down on the sidewalk in a heap. She left her plants for me to take care of, some fifty of them. This pleases me, and I start right away fertilizing and watering them.

I get Chelo to help me move. We spend a morning doing this by way of the Metro. But the Lavapiés station lets you out at the bottom of the hill, it's a good truck up Calle Olivar, and we're worn out. Chelo suggests that we take a taxi from then on, which worked out a whole lot better.

Chelo and I are sitting on the floor at the Olivar apartment the second day of moving. I'd already made one trip alone. He'd just showed up. We're drinking cheap wine out of the bottle he brought along. He's wearing faded blue jeans, a porkpie hat and a gray sweatshirt that has S C I T E S printed on the back like maybe it's some kind of prison issue. The half circles under his eyes have darkened appreciably of late. He's getting a raccoon look. Our new place is only blocks from Darlen's apartment, and she is on his mind. He even keeps looking over that way, staring off in her direction like he stares at her, spellbound.

You doin' okay?

He looked at me in a somnambulant way.

Splendid, he said.

His eyes didn't seem focused.

I just ask, I said, 'cause you look like shit.

Thank you so much, he said.

You know, he said. She's got money. I keep wonderin' where it comes from. Most of her clothes, she designs herself. They look like hippie rags to me, but … I'm there the other day, and this grocer comes to collect a bill. She gets all her groceries delivered. I see the bill. Not so much food, it's mostly for wine. Darlen's in bed under the covers. She's naked under there, and she don't want to get up, give me a view of it. She says, Look in the second drawer of the dresser. The money's there. Would you pay him? I open the drawer and, I mean, it's full of cash. The equivalent of a couple grand American, or more. She's flush.

The weekends, she just tells me she's busy. I'm not to come around. Don't come around! But then she ain't there anyway.

You're not checking up on her?

Sometimes.

You're in trouble.

May be, he said.

He went on:

She don't tell me busy at what, where she goes, nothin'. It's none of my business.

What d'you think she's up to?

Just off hand, I'd say she's turnin' tricks … but I can't think about that, because it tears me apart. I mean, I guess it's good somebody's getting it. I'm sure as hell not.

You're kidding, I said.

No. All kidding aside. I feel like I'm back in 9th grade. We're dating or some shit … feel like pretty soon I should ask her if it's okay can we go steady.

How do you keep your hands off her? No disrespect but, those tits—

They're not real. I've had my hands on 'em. They're store bought. Just off the rack.

No.

My wife had large breasts … they were natural. These are different. Which is not to say they aren't fine.

But you're not getting laid.

Not even close. But I'm fucked, buddy, I'll admit to that. I fell in love. And nothin' broke the fall. It's like I been pole-axed. I don't get it. I think she cares for me. An' it's not like she's cold.

No, I said. She doesn't strike me that way at all. But … hell, who knows? Maybe she don't like cock.

Or maybe she wants one she can tie in a knot.

Hard to imagine her not having a boyfriend already, I said.

She's got one. He's in prison.

For what?

She didn't say. Only that he won't be getting out for a long while. I don't know … I can't figure it. I play with her … but that pussy's off limits … an' it's turning me into a fool. The other day I kissed her fucking hand. Can you believe it? Did you ever kiss a girl's hand?

Can't say that I have.

Her fingers smelled like ceviche …

A lot of moving parts there. And that ass, I said. You can trip over a heartbeat lookin' at that.

Hey, he said and gave me the mad-eye.

It's hard not to notice.

It's a little big, he said.

No, it's just right.

Damn it, Luke. You ain't supposed to be lookin' like that. And he added, Sorry ... pay me no mind ... I, when I see her, it's like she just came down from Huckleberry Mountain or some shit. But there's something else about her ... just I can't put my finger on. Something out of reach.

She's got style, I said. A touch of class.

Yeah. She's got that for sure. But ... so I'm over my head. That don't matter to me. Never has. Somebody's got to make love to beautiful women. Might as well be me as the next asshole.

I thought you was in love with that little Spanish girl from Oviedo—

Don't mix that up, he said.

I'll tell you what bothers me, he went on. What you know about Darlen is about all I know, too. She won't talk much about herself. An' when she does, it's only to let you in on what she wants you to know.

You think that's her real name?

Doubtful. She told me once her clan made a name for themselves in the old days stealin' horses. That was probably true.

But she can make up shit, he said. I know that. A guy asks her a question in a bar, she just takes off. Says whatever bullshit comes into her head. I find it charming then, and funny, but ... when she tells me something, I wonder if I'm not gettin' the same run-around.

She talks pretty, I said. That Scottish lilt, or burr ...

He paid no attention to that, said, She grew up on a farm. Says she lived in London for years. I can believe all that. The rest of what she says about herself, it seems out of plumb. Or sometimes she just shuts up when I ask a question. Acts like I hadn't spoken. It's startin' to drive me a little nuts, he said. Just too much emotional noise in my head.

You're lucky, though.

How do you mean?

At least you found her.

Right, he said. I'm just swingin' in a horseshoe.

Wine often helps, I said.

This is true, he said.

We finished the bottle, called a taxi then, went to the old place and moved more boxes.

That was the last of it. We're sitting around again, the apartment full of boxes and little else. Mercedes left the lamps. We're going to have to buy some furniture. Of what was in here, three chairs and a sofa now reside on the sidewalk. You couldn't sit on any of it without getting covered in cat hair. Two mattresses down there also. Mercedes chucked it all over the balcony. Not sure what she did with the cats.

Che starts telling me about his wife and daughter. He speaks lovingly of his daughter, who is a teenager now, just turned 13, and lives in Jacksonville with her mother and stepfather.

I met your wife once, I said. She seemed a good woman.

She is. I just … made a mistake, is all.

Wha'd you do?

He sat there and thought about it awhile. He said:

My wife's mother came up from South America one time to visit. We were living in Tampa then. It was after Barcelona. I'd gone back to driving cab. The baby two, three. Her grandma hadn't ever seen her. Her nana. The worst sort of loud, pushy bitch. A stocky, tough-looking old broad. She'd fit right in here. Never stopped giving her opinion. A high-speed talker in that Venezuelan singsong they got. I didn't like to be around her much, but then it turns out, after the visit, I have to drive her down to Miami. She's got a 1st cousin down in South Beach, some other relatives in Miami Beach. So I get to be her chauffeur. I got no transportation then but the cab, which I bring home two days out of three. I shared it with this other guy, this part-timer.

I worked that night and in the morning we took off for Miami. I'd gotten a couple hours of sleep, off and on, at the airport. I was feelin' rough, and the trip down seemed to take forever. She hadn't seen her people there in years. By the time all the visiting is done, it's night again. I'd polished off a couple pints of blackberry brandy on the road. I'd been drinking whenever we stopped, too. I didn't know what the relatives were going on about. Talkin' about the old days and all. Didn't give a shit really. I'd just hung around like a dumbass, knocking down beers or whatever they handed me. When we leave both places, she jumps in the back seat of the cab, like she's my fare. I thought she'd stay with this 1st cousin of hers, but somewhere along the line she explained to me that they really couldn't stand each other. I'm thinkin', Then why the hell'd you come see her?

She has a flight out at noon the next day to Caracas. I'm way too fucked up and tired to drive back to Tampa at this point. Stay in my room at the hotel, she says. Sleep on the couch. We're in a hotel called The Shelley down in South Beach. Lot of pastel purple to it. Puke stains on the stairs up to the third floor. So that's what I did, but then I can't get to sleep she's snoring so loud.

I duck out and go to the little hotel bar. This Cuban chick sidles up next to me, says she knows me. Where you from? Tampa, I say. I remember you from Tampa, she says. Complete bullshit of course, but … from where in Tampa I'm wondering—maybe she's a lap dancer. She's looking okay to me, her body anyway. Sort of got a mug like an old shoe. But dressed nicely. She's in office supplies, she says. She's flying to New York City in the morning. And she buys me a drink, so I start listening to her line.

She's complimenting my shirt. This Hawaiian shirt, blue and gold parrots on it. It's nothin' but lame. Then pretty soon she's all over me, she's begging for it, and I know it, the bartender knows it. She acts like she just came down with a case of nymphomania, but I'm wasted. Time for bed, I say, meaning I have to leave now. She didn't take it that way. I go to give her a little kiss goodnight, and she opened her mouth to receive it. And that kind of set me off.

So we go up to her room, that, just my luck, is two doors down from my mother-in-law. Which, I just tell her—That's my room. I point it out, because I'm drunk and that's the sort of thing you do when you're not thinking. I don't say nothing about no mother-in-law. But the next morning, the Cuban comes knocking on the door. My mother-in-law answers it. The Cuban girl seems to think she's the maid. I'm in the bathroom shaving. I hear her say, Oh, pardone … the gentleman left this in my room last night. I just wanted to return his nice shirt.

My mother-in-law pauses before she speaks. I take it she's studying the shirt.

What was the gentleman's name? she says finally, real loud, obviously for my benefit.

And that was the beginning of the end … of a good thing.

He sat there for awhile and didn't say anything, then he didn't say anything some more, and I said:

Go on. What happened next?

Ah, well … I hauled ass back to Tampa fast as I could, the whole time trying to think up any kind of excuse, but none came to me. And I'd had the cab out too long and that'll be the end of the job, too. No excuse for that made good sense either. Then somewhere on Alligator Alley, I try to adjust the seat, and thing flies forward and stays locked in that position, and the rest of the way back to Tampa I got my nose jammed to the steering wheel. It was the worst day of my life.

She had cleared out. Her and the baby and … she took some of their clothes but not all of them. No note. She just erased herself from my life. And I didn't realize it at first. We lived on Central Avenue, south of Sligh. She took the baby to that little park there most every day. I figured maybe she was down there.

She'd gone up to her aunt's in Kentucky, but it was months before I knew that, when I was served with divorce papers. I didn't know where she was, except gone.

I started drinking and didn't stop for a year. That wasn't a good time, to say the least. I'm in a tailspin. I quit driving the cab after awhile. I couldn't concentrate. I got into a couple little wrecks … not paying attention. I moved in with my brother. You've met him, Eloy. He's, you know … a hapless sort. He had a night watchman's job then.

I watched TV and drank, and that was my life. I was watching shit like *Mr. Ed*, the talking horse. It didn't matter. I was just staring at it.

It got so I could only last four hours between drinks before I got the shakes. I was on unemployment for awhile. About when that ran out, my mother died. She had Alzheimer's and she'd already been gone several years, just hadn't got around to the dyin' part. Me and Eloy got a small inheritance. Eloy bought a used Corvette with his and took up meth. The motor wasn't in very good shape, but the car looked good. Candy apple red. He started smelling like mayonnaise from the crank. I just kept drinking.

He went back to talking about his mother:

I'd go sit with her sometimes. She called up her childhood often. In some sense, I thought she received a gift of sorts, that in her mind at least, she was able to replay her life in reverse and see things a second time. It was hard on us, but I had the idea she was not in too much discomfort, not for a long time anyway. She became toward the end what the doctor called a sundowner. She'd be okay during the day, but at night she was nuts. She forgot how to sleep during that stage. She'd roam the house. Then finally she forgot how to breathe.

Then picked up on his own case again:

You can almost live on beer, he said. For awhile. And coffee and cigarettes. An occasional Twinkie. But then I started on cheap vodka. It wasn't even made from potatoes, it was made from grapefruit, and always on sale. I'd get stumbling drunk, throw up, drink coffee to get back on keel, and start again. That was my routine. I was strictly a nonfunctional member of society.

Anyway, I went into a detox program finally. I kept feeling dizzy. I'd gone thin. They did some blood tests. My platelet count was 40. It measures red blood cells that are responsible for clotting. The normal count is 180. If it drops below 50, you can bleed to death. My doctor said I had the blood work of a car radiator. Pure antifreeze.

I was seeing an aura around him when he said that. Everything jagged-edged and intense—noise, motion. The night before at home, the overhead lights kept firing off like flashbulbs.

I stayed in detox three weeks, which used up the rest of my money, and then some. Eloy had run his Corvette into the ground by then. He put it up on blocks in the yard, and we were back to where we'd started …

We'd bought a six pack of Voll Damm and were waiting for it to cool in the fridge. When Chelo finished that last statement, he said, Let's go ahead and try one of them. It's my understanding that you have to drink beer, or it'll go bad.

So we got a beer each, which were about half cold, sat down at the kitchen table, and he went on:

I wanted to get back into life again. But it was like it always is with me. I think the main trouble with connecting to the world is the fact I can't afford to do anything in it. So I addressed that problem. I took out a school loan and went back to college. Got into ESL, which you can make some money at. You could get work.

While I was going to school, I got a job on the weekends. He started smiling just as soon as he said this.

What? I said.

Well … it was probably the strangest job I ever had. I answered this ad in the paper. It was just a blind ad, but it caught my eye— Parade Work. And you only worked on the weekends and holidays, 'cause that's when parades take place. And I got the job. I was the only one applied had a sense of humor I guess.

What you did was wear a big muppet suit and make people laugh. The characters were about seven foot tall and supposed to be Florida animals. They had a bear, and a gator. A squirrel. A bullfrog. I was a possum supposedly, but they were like cartoons. My possum suit was made outa blue shag carpet. Red leggings. It was a real garish lookin' goggle-eyed possum. Big smile on its face. You know, a possum when he shows teeth, he ain't smiling, but … I looked out through a hole in the neck.

It wasn't easy work. I mean physically it was tiring, but it was kind of fun, and the job paid good. The suit weighed 35 pounds. A big, rotund body. Bubble-toed size 20 sneakers. It had a pouch, and you kept the pouch full of tootsie rolls to throw to the kids.

Anyway … I was this big goof possum.

I'd started drinking again at some point. I limited myself to once a week for awhile, usually Sunday night. I'd drink beer till I fell asleep. No hard stuff … until I could drink normally again, like everybody else. It wasn't my life anymore, is the point.

Wearin' this costume and bopping along a parade route, four, five miles, eight miles, whatever it was … in the Florida heat, you'd be soaked at the end of it. Just sweating your ass off. I had to put stick-on air fresheners all over the inside of it. Spray it with Lysol every time after I used it. Still, it had a stench all its own.

It had an 85-inch waist, so I started rigging it up to carry a six pack. Sewed these beer huggies onto the inside. It'd keep the beer cool for awhile at least. You get a little jag on, it's easier to act like an idiot, which is what the job called for.

It was all slapstick. I'd walk along doing Curly Howard routines, or pretend I was Harpo Marx. Leer at the pretty women. Smooch a blonde. Pantomime her stiff boyfriend, or spill his popcorn, say. You can get away with most anything you wear a possum suit.

Then we did the Gasparilla parade in Tampa. I'd never done that long a route before. And it's hot as hell. It's February. You know Gasparilla week it's always cold and rainy, but that day it's 88 degrees. Inside the suit it's over a hundred. I take a 6 pack and a quart of Bud this time. I take bottled water. I got a Cuban sandwich. I'm loaded down with shit, but a good third of the way through the route I'm done with the liquids, 'cause the parade kept stoppin' all the time.

I start stealing cokes from little kids. Takin' beers from old ladies. Just grab their paper cup and run. The beers I kept in my suit, I'd drink them with a straw. One of them hospital straws with a crook in it. I'd have to bring my real arm inside and leave my possum arm out there dangling around like he's a crip or something, but who's studying this? The beers I'm stealing from the old ladies, I throw down the hole in my neck. Crush the cup and chuck it away, and I see little kids looking at me and wincing.

Then all of a sudden I'm feelin' funny again. Straight lines are zigzagging on me. What's happening is I'm about to have a heat stroke, but that don't dawn on me at the time. I'm starting to panic, 'cause I think it's that other thing come back again.

Plus I've really got to pee. I work through the panic bullshit, talk myself down ... but, I gotta take a leak, there's no way around it, and we're still in Ybor City. It's a good long way to Bayshore and the end of the route.

I drop out of the parade and go stand in the shade under an awning that runs along this shop front, but the kids won't leave me alone. I empty out my pouch, give all my tootsie rolls away. But this one fat kid says he don't want tootsie rolls. He wants lollipops. He starts pelting me with the tootsie rolls I'd given him. So I get up close and backhand him with my paw. I drop the little shit and try to blend quickly into the parade once more.

The kid's mother starts screaming, Stop that kangaroo!

I shout back, I'm a possum, you fucking moron! But I don't stop.

I take a side street and stop at a little bar. Take a leak finally, which turns out to be a big part of the anxiety problem. Then I sit at the bar and shoot down a couple cold ones. I'm a big hit at that bar, but I have to catch the parade before it passes. The boss is stationed at the end of the route to collect the suits and so forth. I empty all the cans out of my suit and purchase another six. My money's no good there. The people around me pay for everything.

And I think at that bar, something changed around for me, something bigger than I knew just then, even though, I'll tell ya, I left there feelin' good ... everybody cheered when I walked out the door.

But back in the parade I have this horrible mood swing. I'm thinking, I don't belong in no parade. And also, I mean, I don't have to tell you of all people but, by this time, I'm tanked.

I start to assume the personality of a real possum. I'm hissing at the crowd. I'm giving them the finger. And for some reason, they think it's hilarious.

At the time I'm trapped between the Hillsborough High marching band that's playing 'Louie Louie' over and over and the Plant City Strawberry Festival float, which I'm staying near, to lean on when the parade stops, and also because there's a couple nice lookin' girls riding it who have started flirting with me.

I'm thinking, Well … this is different. I didn't mention that I hadn't gotten laid in God knows how long. The year I holed up, I just wasn't into it, and no self-respecting woman would look at me any damn way. And another half a year since I'd come out of that has passed, and up till now I'm invisible to women, far as I can tell. And it's starting to concern me really, 'cause this hasn't happened before, you know … since I was 12 or so. But now I'm bantering with these two Strawberry float beauties, who seem a bit high.

Anyway, I also notice that I'm starting to feel sick. I get the feeling I'm gonna throw up, which isn't a good thing to do inside the suit. I'm trying to hold on till the end of the parade, which is coming up pretty soon. But I'm right behind the bass drum, and my head's pounding from that. And then I feel myself reeling …

I go head first into a tuba player, and it's all I remember till I woke up on top the Strawberry float, laying out length-wise, and the band's playing a funeral dirge, and the two beauties are fanning me with pieces of cardboard. One of the beauties is saying, Damn, but he is gamey!

They tell me … when I hit the tuba player, he went down big and caused a chain reaction. I took out eight or nine of the band.

I hope they're not mad at me, I said. I couldn't help it.

The one who was talking said, No. They went into hysterics. And the other beauty just looked at me with her kind face.

I took them out to eat the next night, sported them to a good steak dinner at Pepe's, and later we went to the motel where they were staying. I asked them what they wanted to do next. The one with the kind face said, I want to fuck you. Spoke it like that in no uncertain terms. And the other said, I want to watch. And I thought to myself just then, with some satisfaction, You are back, Jack.

I called my mother yesterday. She's been declared legally blind. It's high time I'm thinking. She's not supposed to drive anymore but still does occasionally, she tells me. She gets one of her neighbors, who no longer drives because of advanced age, to go along with her and give directions as he can still see well enough. His name is Lloyd Aftergood. They just go to the little store, which isn't far, about five blocks, but she says Lloyd has gone off a bit lately and they sometimes get lost.

He's so far out of it, she said, he doesn't know any better than to get in a car with me driving. Can you imagine?

She tells me Lloyd's latest stunt was that he baked a melon in his oven at 450 degrees for an hour.

That was a mess, she said. He's turned peculiar.

I'm working on your daddy's tribute, she went on. I'm going to change it up this year.

Every April 1st she posts one of those obituary page tributes in the paper. It says this:

Gone, but not forgotten. Time has pass, but my heart will never mend. The years may wipe out many things, but this they wipe out never—the memory of the old days, when we were together.

The first time she did that I told her, You know, Ma … I don't believe that the departed read the newspaper.

You don't know it for sure, she said. Your daddy liked the paper an awful lot.

And what's this—Time *has pass* … That's not correct.

She read it aloud.

It sounds good to me, she said. She only gets stubborn when she's wrong.

I told her on the phone yesterday, It's kinda early on for that, isn't it?

I didn't have anything to do today, she said.

I don't know about tinkerin' with that too much, I said. You shouldn't fool around with perfection.

Hey Luke, she said, up yours. And she laughed.

Mom lives in the same house that she and Dad lived in together for a quarter century. She took his clothes out of the bedroom closet and burned them when he died, but nothing much else has changed since then. The fire caused no loss to the world of fashion. His sartorial tastes were even lamer than mine. The house sits adjacent to a pond-swamp. My house, a small, white wooden structure with a rusted corrugated tin roof, is on the other side of the swamp, though I can't see Mom's house from mine. She has friends who come by now and then; they play bridge, talk about the bygone days, go out to eat. She has a girl that comes once a week and cleans the house supposedly. I think the two of them sit around and drink.

We got her a seeing-eye dog early on, but the two of them didn't get on well. Then the dog's eyes went milky. He couldn't see a thing after awhile and had to be put down. Now her one every-day friend is an old doe that lives in the woods behind the house. Years past, the doe jumped the fence into the yard one autumn to escape Grady Ault's deer dogs that were chasing her. He's a neighbor. Grady wasn't hunting. The dogs had gotten loose and were doing a little work on their own. The doe stayed inside the fence for days then, until it rained and washed away the scent of the pack; and she and my mother's friendship grew from that time.

The deer comes to the back door now around noon each day. My mother lets her in the house. Florida deer are not very big, and this one smaller than most. Mom fixes it a peanut butter sandwich. Then the deer hangs around for the soap operas during the afternoon. My mother has watched one of these soap operas in particular for some 30 years now, and the deer seems fascinated by TV, all the movement and color and sound in such a small place. Though I've also seen them taking a nap together during these programs.

Whenever I talk to my mother, she is sure to remind me that her condition is hereditary. She has the same disease that Georgia O'Keeffe had. O'Keeffe said there were little holes at the sides of her vision where she could see clearly. If I am standing in front of her, my mother turns her head toward her shoulder now to look at me.

Today Megan and I attended the Burial of the Sardine ceremony. We spent the morning cleaning the old apartment so Kevin Ray wouldn't have to move into a place looked like junkies lived there previously. Then we wandered around the neighborhood, just walking without destination, and ended up down by the river and Goya's tomb and ran into this celebration. It's Shrove Tuesday, the last day of Carnival before Ash Wednesday and the beginning of Lent, and the Madrileños celebrate with this masquerade.

The crowd seemed dressed up like it was Halloween. All in black. Top hats. Veils. Some burly men dressed as women. People carrying around large sardines with much wailing intermixed with laughter. In the old days it was the Tuesday for eating meat prior to forty days of fast and abstinence. For weeks to come, the population would have to live on sardines. This was the staple food for the lower classes all year long to begin with. So it's a joke of some kind, one I really didn't get, even as we stood in the middle of it all. Being as I'm at arm's length from things in Madrid to start with, a situation like this is way beyond me, but the crowd was having a good time. And I fit into celebrations well enough.

We were standing off to the side later, watching the procession cross the Manzanares River. Then I noticed this guy staring at me, caught him out the tail of my eye at first, about three feet away and to the rear of us a little. I guess he'd been staring awhile, giving me a hard look. He's wearing a top hat and dangling a sardine by the tail, and the look is incongruous. But he has these greyhound eyes, that wild goofiness. When he catches my attention fully, he rolls his head on his shoulders dramatically, makes a grimace and sucks air through his teeth. Then he stalks away with his nose pointed to the sky. I still haven't added that one up. As usual here, I feel everything and know nothing.

During his last Madrid years, Goya lived in a residence across the river here called Quinta del Sordo, The Deaf Man's Farmhouse. By coincidence, a deaf farmer had owned the property before Goya bought it. It was a two-story house made of brick and adobe and sat on 22 acres. It had a vegetable garden and two wells. He described it as in need of some repair.

Goya's wife had passed away in 1812, and at this residence he took up with a companion, Leocadia Weiss. She was some 40 years younger than Goya and good looking. She was not apparently easy to get along with, but then, neither was he. You can read that she was a woman of disputable qualities, few other details given. But though they did not live in harmony, she was with him until the end of his life.

Leocadia had a daughter, Rosario. Goya loved her like his own, and she may well have been. The model for one of his late paintings, *The Milkmaid of Bordeaux*, is most probably Rosario. It was the only thing deeded to Leocadia by Goya. The rest of his estate went to his son Javier and grandson Mariano. Javier didn't much care for his father's mistress it seems. As soon as he arrived in Bordeaux after Goya's death, he kicked her out of the house they had been renting there.

Across the Manzanares then was all meadow and woods. In this bucolic setting Goya did his Pinturas negras, the Black Paintings, brushing oil directly onto the plaster of the interior walls of the house.

Fifty years after Goya painted at the Quinta, long after his death in 1828, the property was purchased by a French baron by the name of d'Erlanger, who, though he did not understand the paintings and thought them disturbing, as most feel looking upon them, nonetheless set about having them restored. The paintings were lifted from the plaster and mounted on canvas, and in 1881 he donated them to the Prado.

With the Pinturas negras and a series of etchings done at the same time called the Diparates, a certain line of the art jumped into the next century. It would take a young Dali to catch up.

The Quinta del Sordo was demolished at some point later on, and no exact idea remains of its outward appearance, though photographs were taken of the paintings inside. If the house still stood, it would look back upon the little church of San Antonio de la Florida and a

Madrid skyline dramatically changed. There are twin churches now. The second-built, an exact replica of the original, is for religious services. The original is devoted to Goya. In it, the ceiling is covered by his frescoes of the miracle of St. Anthony of Padua, the patron saint of those who seek missing things. It is said to be Goya's Sistine Chapel. That the painting has a religious theme seems remote when you look at it, almost incidental. What you notice more are the adolescent, blonde angels—they've been described as kind of shady looking for angels—and the everyday, Madrileño neighborhood kids playing on the balastrade Goya painted for them there. Some of them are looking down at you looking up.

Built into the floor of the chapel is Goya's tomb. At least his body is there. His head is elsewhere.

Afterwards, as the crowd broke up and we were leaving, well … let me tell you something. There's a curious thing that happens with certain middle-aged Madrileña women. They get to walking so fast, they'll spontaneously break into a run. They'll run for awhile, then finally slow themselves down again. Twice now when this has happened in my vicinity—and only after I have been drinking a bit—I've felt compelled, as I did just then, to jog along beside them. I hear Megan behind me: J A C K A S S!

Chelo came over to the new place Friday afternoon. He is resplendent in parts of two suits. His jacket is the top half of a blue worsted suit, his trousers the bottom half of a gray pinstripe linen one. Black T-shirt, white socks.

Nothing else was clean, he said.

He brought laundry with him, puts it in the washing machine.

Wha'd you do last night?

Me and Darlen went out. Stayed out till five. We're buddies, you know. He raised his eyebrows, took a deep breath, let it out slow.

How're you handling work?

He waved a hand, swept it aside.

The kids aren't showing up. Which is fine with me. They've got tests now for their real classes. Today, nobody. I took a nap in the classroom.

The day is mild, and we go stand out on the long balcony. We're on the first floor here, which is, of course, actually the second. There's a long balcony and two smaller ones.

Why don't you go get some of that furniture down there? Before they pick it up.

It's junk, I said.

Megan has purchased two easy chairs and a couch, and a little writing table and a chair for it, just by coincidence, at the furniture store cattycorner under Darlen's apartment. It's all to be delivered tonight or tomorrow. She also bought two waterbeds. They can't deliver these for a week. I didn't say anything to Megan about who lived above the furniture store, and now, for no particular reason, I don't mention anything to Chelo either.

Just then three whores came swanking down the hill. Bottle blonde, mini-skirt, platform shoes. Now up close you can see their faces are beat, and the heavy make-up can't cover it. They're on the sidewalk across the narrow street. All of a sudden Chelo starts barking at them. I don't know how he means it—because they look hot to him or more probably because they're dogs—but the neighbors are staring.

Hey, I said. What're you doin'?

Woof! he says.

The whores are giggling.

I pull him inside.

Chelo sits down on the floor, leans his back against a wall, knees to his chest, hugging his legs with both arms. He seems barely awake.

Nothin' personal, I said, but you look like hell.

Thanks, he says. I had no idea. So kind of you to point that out. Toward the end of this he goes into a coughing fit. He fixes it by aiming his lighter at a cigarette.

Christ above, he says.

We're just sitting there not saying nothing. The sun is slanting in through the windows nicely. Che smokes the cigarette down to the filter, looks like maybe he smokes some of it, too.

I wake up, he says, feels like nails been driven into my lungs.

I just shake my head a little, smile. Maybe you can't even see the smile.

You got it bad, I say.

She wants us to be pals she tells me. She needs a friend. A guardian angel. That was a laugh. We have a good time, isn't that enough? We don't need to take it anywhere else. I'm trying to kiss on her, and she's talkin' this kinda shit.

How'd you respond to that?

I grabbed her ass.

And?

She got pissed. He nods for a couple seconds, then opens his eyes. It was a great night up till then, he said.

He looks around vaguely.

This is a nice place. Much better. I'm afraid … for you, though, it'll just be a better place to hide out. You know what I'm sayin'?

I'm thinking, Oh, no. He's gonna hand out some advice.

I mean … what do you do all day? You just set around, what?

I spend a lot of time in front of the mirror, I say.

No. Really. You write all the time? You watch TV? I can't figure out what you do with all the hours.

I go for a walk. I eat lunch. Read the paper. I do some work …

What you mean, work … that's your writing? You still doin' that thing I'm in?

Yeah.

Luke … put me in a good light, like I said, goddamn it … or I'll sue your ass. I'll take everything you got … which, is nothing, right … but … what d'you think about that?

I don't, as a rule, I said, comment on pending litigation.

I don't know. I don't know if I'm so crazy about bein' a character.

I'll put you in a spotlight. Relax. I'm not gonna put you in the damn dark, now.

Okay. All right, then, he says.

You want to read it? You're welcome to, anytime you want.

He has to think on this.

I should wait till it's finished, he says.

He's got this weird thoughtful expression going, but I take it as diversion. He has Darlen on his mind, his thoughts of her attracted like smoke from a campfire. The rest of the world is not always there now.

He focuses on my face. It doesn't come easy. I realize he's still drunk in some way, and gone with tiredness.

You gonna be an artist, he says, you need to celebrate life. You got to have that spark. This whole thing is so wanting in time. You can't be wastin' none of it.

Time is short, that what you're saying? I'll have to make a note.

Time is a midget, he says. He takes a deep breath, lets it out as he turns his face to the side.

Fucking heartburn, he says.

There's a calendar on the wall near him. He looks at it. I look at it, too.

When's your birthday? he said.

Next month. The 19th.

We're getting' old.

Feels that way, I said.

Not old exactly. Just headed in that direction.

Yeah, well … we're all on that road, I said. If I just wouldn't keep gettin' uglier … that bothers me.

That's not important, he said. You jus' need to *do* something. You can't spend your life hiding out. You know the Spanish workingmen around here have brandy for breakfast. Fundador. It's jet fuel! That's something. It's something to consider.

Something like what?

I mean … for example …wha'd you have this morning when you got up?

Coffee. A little hashish.

That's a start, he said. Then what?

I let the day fall into place, I said.

I listen to advice but so seldom take it that I might as well not. And I'm thinking, This is the first time I've ever gotten tips from a guy wearing two suits.

What time do you go to bed?

About the time my neighbors are cooking supper, I said.

See … that's a problem. That's major. You need to get with the program. Hit the night. Make a spectacle of yourself. It's good for the soul. They call the night people here gatos. Cats.

I thought, I like the idea of the night; I just happen to sleep then.

Who is this speaking, Our Lady of Good Counsel? I said.

Yes, he said. Take heed.

You gonna see Darlen tonight?

No, he said. He thought for a moment. Your birthday, he said. The 19th of March is St. Joseph's Day. The old women in my family, you had something wrong with you, they'd make cookies that day. Say you got arthritis in your elbow, they'd make cookies looked like an elbow. Then on St. Joseph's Day you eat the cookies and supposedly your arm gets better. That was the idea behind it anyway.

One year my uncle Chino had prostate trouble. My aunts weren't all too clear on what that meant, so they make these little doughnut-shaped cookies. My aunts, they're Cuban and Sicilian all mixed up, you know how it is in Tampa sometimes.

What's these? Chino wants to know.

My tia Gracela says, They're little assholes.

The buzzer sounded then. I went to the long balcony. Kevin Ray was down below, talking to the mailman. He held up a letter and a magazine. He came into the building with the mailman. Chelo had fallen asleep in the meantime. Kevin Ray studied him a moment, said:

Good to see you again, Che. Don't get up. Nice threads! Faboo.

Chelo was snoring.

He looks rather … tarnished, Kevin Ray said.

He's in love.

Ah, he said. Love's undertow. How do you explain away that ensemble, though?

He is not burdened by fashion, I said.

He hands me the letter. It's from Wolf. I'll read it later. Last night was Thursday, Gay Diners' night for Kevin Ray. I usually don't see him until Sunday, after he's been at it for three nights.

Wha'd you all have for dinner last night?

A bottle of absinthe.

What time'd you get in this morning?

Six.

You look in pretty good shape for all that.

Drugs keep you young, he said. Here … I brought you an *In-Madrid* …

How'd work go today? I said. This is the same thing I'd asked Chelo. I'm a conversationalist.

He looked down slightly, put his left hand to his face, thumb under his chin and his first two fingers to his cheek and the third resting on one of his lower teeth. Then he undid all that and scratched the left side of his face lightly while looking toward the ceiling, as if hieroglyphics concerning the ancient history of this question were inscribed there.

Hell, I don't know, Luke. I was there, but I don't think I can comment on it in depth … My students keep wantin' to know what bars I hang out. I can't tell them all the sleazy ones in Chueca. This one girl's driving me crazy. I honest to God think she wants a date. I wouldn't mind goin' shopping with her, but …

Thanks for the mail, I said.

I excused myself and went to take a leak.

I stopped in the kitchen first and put Chelo's clothes in the dryer. Then I walked down the hallway to the bathroom. When I came back out of the bathroom and looked down the hallway, I had a clear impression Billy Jenks had just stepped around the corner and gone into the living room. There's a tall mirror on the wall where I stood. I looked at it, my eyes somewhat astonished there.

When I returned to the living room, Kevin Ray noticed me looking behind the door.

You lose something?

Yeah, I did, I said. But I didn't go into details.

I ran into your neighbor out front.

Which one?

The American.

Did you notice anything about her?

She has a large bum?

No—

Tell her to haul ass, she'd have to leave twice?

Naw. What I mean is, did she treat you okay?

She was quite pleasant. We had a nice conversation.

I seem to have struck her wrong, I said.

You tend to grow on people, Luke. First impressions aren't your strong suit.

No?

'Fraid not, he said. I remember the first time I met you ... when Megan invited me over. I couldn't find the place and ended up in what seemed like a carny bar to ask directions. Me and some biker types and a bunch of freaks. It was ... different. I've never come across that bar since. Not that I've been lookin' for it. But anyway, Megan at some point mentioned that you'd been in a bad automobile accident. When you started talkin' that night, I thought, O Lord, he's brain damaged. Come to find out, you were just high as hell and mumbling.

That girl's not American, by the way, he said. She just learned English from an American. She's Swiss.

That explains it, I said.

Look ... the reason I'm here, he went on, I've moved everything but my plants. Could you help me with them? There's no hurry. Just give me a call ... some day next week.

Sure, I said.

He studied Chelo again.

I haven't seen much of him lately. He's been avoiding me. He owes me 10 thousand pesetas. You don't suppose he's, like, in a coma or something?

I think he just needs to catch his breath some.

He's such a rascal, Kevin Ray said. Who would fall in love with that … who could desire such trouble?

I don't know that it's reciprocated. There's some question about that, but … you can't help who you fall for I guess. That's all outside the realm of common sense.

Chelo woke up some time later.

Kevin Ray was here, I said.

How long I been out?

A while.

You know … I like Kevin. I just don't like to think about what him and his pals do to each other in their spare time is all.

He's a good guy, I said.

Some skinny-ass faggot gave me an elbow while I walking through Sol … couple mornings ago. I couldn't believe it. Guy's twinking along with his arms held away from his sides like he's muscle bound or some shit, but he weighs about a hundred and two, and the fuck gives me an elbow.

There's something about February, I said.

Tell me about it.

You know that friend of mine shot himself—

Billy, Chelo said.

Yeah. I could a swore … a little while ago, he was here.

Where?

I pointed to the hallway. I didn't see him exactly. I just sensed that he was around.

You got that metal plate in your head, Luke. I mean, maybe it's shifting on you.

I don't have a plate in my head.

No? You got a problem then.

He picked up the *In-Madrid*, turned to the classifieds, the Heart to Heart section, and started reading aloud.

Listen to this, Luke—*Round-headed German boy looking for date*. Christ. They'll be making a run on him for that one. Here's another—*Lively lady, 48+, would like to widen her circle of friends*. That + has to give you pause. *Curious eyes*, she adds. They're crossed, right? He read some more. This one's pretty good—*Spouse's sex drive in neutral due to medical problems, mine stuck in high gear. He agrees that my motor should be kept running and may occasionally watch or assist mechanic with oil change and lube jobs. Tired of shifting by myself. Please reply before I throw a rod.* That's a good one. Here you go—*Sperm Donors Needed. Limit 2 visits per week. Males 18-40 only*. He looked at me. Do they need to specify *males*?

He stood, walked to the kitchen to retrieve his laundry. He slewed from side to side in doing so.

I'll be by tomorrow, help you some more. I have to go to bed now, he said.

Tomorrow's Saturday, I said. Megan'll be home.

Oh. He rubbed his face with his hands. Monday then.

We'd already moved everything from the old place. He'll catch up to that at some point.

12 February Saturday

Sunny, warm, the sky glass and deep blue, and a white moon setting in it all afternoon. I walked down the street to the Lavapiés plaza on my way for groceries at Champion and came across a scene. Two young Moroccans sitting on a bench shot up and the dose too hot I guess. They fell off the bench like they'd been assassinated and just lay there on their backs on the sidewalk in front of the mattress store. The Spanish are standing around them trying to figure out what's going on. I could see the two Morocs were breathing but just barely. There's an actors' troupe that does street theatre around here sometimes. And it looked like that a bit. These two lying there like they were dead, their bodies twisted strange. But there's not many Morocs doing Shakespeare in the neighborhood. And some in the crowd are saying, Are they dead? And others answering, Who cares?

The cops and an ambulance came. The medics take one look at them and start slapping their faces to wake them. Just slapped the hell out of them really and brought them around some and took them away. That must have been some good shit, is my thought.

Valentine's Day

Around noon, I took the metro to the north end of Retiro and walked through the park to the southern exit. I wore a sweatshirt and heavy flannel shirt but take off the shirt after awhile. The trees are bare of leaves but, surprisingly, there are a few things in bloom— an almond tree, a wild plum, and many German iris, a pretty blue/ purple to them. They've gone wild in the south end of the park; they're all over the place. I had bought Megan a Valentine's card and a box of chocolate-covered cherries. I woke at 4:30, put these in the kitchen and went back to sleep. She found them when she went to make coffee. I hardly ever do this sort of thing and she liked it, somewhat taken aback by it I think.

St. Valentine lived in the Umbrian town of Terni in Italy, where he was decapitated on the 14th of February in AD 273 by Roman centurions, reportedly singing the praises of the Virgin Mary before he died. How he became the patron saint of love no one quite knows. Historical accounts speak of his skill at healing. Before Emperor Constantine granted freedom of religion in 313, Valentine was one of the rare few who sanctioned marriage between Christians and pagans, believing love would overcome all. He, legend has it at least, liked to hand out roses, when his roses were in bloom, to lovers who were passing by. He was a romantic, that's clear all the way down the years. He lost his head over love. How many times has that happened since?

Chelo came over for awhile after work. He looked rested. The furniture was delivered finally, the couch and two arm-chairs, green with little white diamond stitching, in appearance somewhat old-time, Victorian, say. They are comfortable. Plus the little, very simple writing desk and chair. Megan had put away our clothes. She set up the computer. The printer did not care for the trip. When I ran off a page, it screamed like a mad electrical hawk. Megan ditched the boxes also. I spotted them in a dumpster down the block. There's nothing left to do. Chelo and I have a couple beers.

I guess I'll go see Darlen tonight, he said. Since it's Valentine's. Good luck.

I've got a new approach in mind, he said. I'm just gonna take it, whether she likes it or not. Next time you hear from me, I might be up on charges.

When Megan came home from school later on, she brought me a six of Pilsner Urquell and one bottle of something called Delirium Tremens, a beer from Belgium, 18 proof, with little pink elephants on the label, what they call barley wine in New Orleans, and seven little candies I like, small cups of chocolate filled with cream and a slice of kiwi fruit like a hat on top.

Tuesday—Another pretty day.

These days of false spring in the middle of winter leave you mildly dazed and euphoric. I walked down to the Botanical Garden and wandered around. It costs 250 pesetas to enter. I saw my favorite elm. It has a name, El Pantalones. It is two trunks that have grown into one another. It is over a century old they say but looks much older to me. There were some camellias blooming, crocus. The Garden is a peaceful place, though with 10 lanes of traffic snarling outside its gates. On the way home I stopped on Calle Ave María at a little fruit and vegetable store there that carries the type of spring tomatoes I like very much. They're early tomatoes from Almería, look sort of wild, squat, striped, and you eat them when they're half-green. I saw the kittens on the corner lot and went back to the store and bought sardines for them.

Wednesday.

I called Kevin Ray and met him down at the Toledo Glorieta. We went to his old flat. His roommates weren't around. We take his plants off the balcony and carry them down to the front door. He has quite a few, all good Madrid balcony plants, geraniums, jade, spider plants, cactus, that seem not at all affected by the weather, no matter how hot or cold it gets. We call a taxi and when it comes, load the plants into the trunk and take them to Argüelles. You can't help but notice the frantic pace in that neighborhood. My new street is all but serene in comparison.

Ana Dolores made it clear to me, Kevin said, that she doesn't care for drinkers who *overdo* it. I think she referred to you a couple times. She was giving me examples of what she meant by drinking too much. She kept saying, Some people ... I took it you were the some people, Luke.

Wha'd you say to that?

Nothing. We were sampling some wine just then I'd brought along. I took several barely discernable tastes. She kept going on about chapuzeros. I've heard this applied to electricians, plumbers. People who do shoddy work. But she was talking about artists ... writers. I think she meant it like what we would call a hack.

I wonder who she coulda meant? I said.

We went to VIPS then and had breakfast. They have American-style breakfasts. Afterwards Kevin Ray commented:

That was the most sordid piece of bacon I've ever tasted.

We just got to wandering around then. Took the metro to Sol. Then walked over to Santa Ana.

They should rename this Dog Piss Plaza, he said. The place reeks.

He bought a thousand peseta chunk of hash from a Moroc that was sitting on one of the children's swings.

You come by here at night anymore, it's very dodgy, he said. Morocs eyeing the tourists for purses to snatch. They all live down by you I think. One night I saw an undercover cop catch a pickpocket. The cop held him while the victim spit on the guy.

We wandered some more, heading toward Lavapiés. On Magdalena we turned left. I needed cigars. We came out of the tabac shop. It's across the street from Darlen's apartment. She lives at 34 Magdelena. We were standing across the street from her building as I lit up. There's some wind now. You can feel the air getting cooler.

That's where we got our furniture, Juan Díaz Muebles, I said. And that's where Che's new girlfriend lives. On the 2d floor there.

Kevin Ray studied the building. It's black-stained, ancient, not much to look at.

Really? he said. I used to know somebody lived there.

Just then one of the curtains opened, and a moment later Darlen stepped out onto the balcony and waved. We both waved back. She held up her index finger—just a minute. Then she was at the front door of the building, and we went over.

Everybody kissed in the Spanish way. She knew Kevin Ray and bantered with him a bit. She's wearing a plaid skirt, red sweater, tartan scarf around her neck, heavy black socks to the top of her calves. Somewhat breathtaking. The time I saw her before, I thought her not exactly pretty. Now I find myself getting drunk on her beauty.

How's Chelo? I asked. I haven't seen him for a couple days.

Kevin Ray's head turned slowly toward me. He was gazing at me sidelong, but really seemed to be looking a long ways off, his eyes blinking.

I'm afraid we had a spat, she said.

She shivered.

I better go back up. Ta, she said. Kevin, give me a bell sometime. See you, Luke.

We went on our way. I was to Kevin's right. His shoulders were shaking, his head turned away from me so I couldn't see his face, and it struck me that perhaps he was weeping, which made no sense at all.

I stopped and looked at him. He stopped, too. A very large grin as he faced me. Now I realize he'd been trying to stifle laughter.

How do you know her? I said.

Him, he said.

What?

Well, he said, that's a very special case, but … Darlen is one of the sisters.

That afternoon, around 3:30, a cold wind came howling off the mountains.

18 February Friday

I've tried to contact Chelo, without success. I called, left messages. I walked down to his place once. He wasn't home. Then I decided to just stay out of it. I didn't say a thing to Megan about any of this business, but when she returned from school awhile ago, she came in grinning like a Cheshire cat. It turned out she and Kevin Ray had been gossiping over the phone. I was sitting at the kitchen table reading the paper. She sat down opposite me.

Guess what? she said. Then she crashed her forehead to the table and broke into helpless laughter.

Calle Olivar

I left my mark on the neighborhood soon enough. My Spanish isn't very good, as I've said. I've learned to compensate for my ignorance in various ways. Take groceries, for example. I go to Corte Inglés or Champion for groceries, the large chain stores. You don't have to talk at those places, or listen either. You can see on the machine what you owe. The other day, I was going out to do some shopping and asked Megan if she wanted anything.

A chicken, she said. A big one. Kevin might come for dinner Sunday.

Well, I go to Corte Inglés and get this and that but forget about the chicken till I'm almost home again. I'm right by a little butcher shop when I remember, so I think, What the hell. There's chickens hanging in the window. No customers. I go into the shop and tell the guy in Spanish:

Una polla grande, para tres gente.

I hold my hands apart to show the size I want. And he lifts his eyebrows and gets an impish smile on his face. He's amused for some reason I can't fathom. He repeats what I just said to his wife, who's sitting at the cash register, and she starts cracking up a bit. She says back to him:

Enséñale la tuya.

It means, show him yours. But while I'm attempting to translate this in my mind, he grabs one of those long-necked chickens, puts it on his block there, chops off the neck and shows it to her, head and all, and they both start laughing outright and can't quite stop, though after awhile it's obvious they're trying to. In the meantime, I'm standing around, looking at him, at her, I point to a chicken occasionally, make chopping motions with my hand—I want it cut up, see … but really what I'm wondering to myself is, What's with these lunatics?

And it's not until I talk to Kevin Ray again that I found out what it was all about. Una polla is slang for cock.

I've been trying to figure out exactly who all lives in our apartment building. Some Moroccan girls moved in just after us. I can't determine how many. They're all olive-skinned and slightly large, and I can't clearly tell the difference in them. Their apartment is on the floor below us. There's an empty storefront at street level, and they're to the back of that. The apartment is down below and opposite our kitchen window, that we keep closed most of the time as they haven't stopped talking since they got here.

They have an odd pitch to their voices, a shrill chirping sound that jumps up several notches whenever they get excited, which happens every three minutes or so. I keep wondering what they are so passionately discussing. Did the rice burn? The mutton a bit tough? One of them flipped out the other day, screaming down below in the hallway. The rest of them locked her out it seems. I at first wondered if somebody was dying. It sounded like she was saying, Breathe papi! She said it over and over. Then I realized she was probably speaking Magrebe, telling those inside to open the fucking door. She took the screaming fit out into the middle of the street a short time later. A large balcony crowd observed the drama. These girls have several truly shady looking Arab fellas hanging around them. I saw one in the hallway yesterday. He was leaning against a wall. He appeared to be waiting until a later time when he had an appointment to go knife someone.

There's a blind man lives here. I recognized him soon enough. He sells lotto tickets at Sol, on the corner of Calle de Preciados. I pass him most every day when I get my newspaper. He walks to work and back on his own, though I don't think he can see one thing. His eyes are the color of his cane.

There's an interesting old guy, named César, who acts as the unofficial portero for the building. He sits on a stool out front most days, weather permitting, with his little dog Suzy. César is 80, and Suzy is an antique. They know everyone in the neighborhood. He and his wife have lived in this building 50 years. He is prone to wearing a black leather outfit that you would rather expect to see on a rock star. I found out from another neighbor, the Swiss/American woman who I'll speak more of shortly, that César and his wife raised four kids here. They have an interior apartment upstairs called the attic, 35 square meters. Their children slept in the kitchen, on the roof ... Apparently César's wife, who is 83 now, has never forgiven him for this. She no longer speaks to him.

A tall fella was talking to César one day in the doorway when we first got here. I took him for a neighbor momentarily, but it turned out that he was a beggar. He needed some money, he told me, so he could buy a hat like mine.

As for the Swiss/American woman, I had, what I thought, a relatively nice conversation on the stairs with her once. Her name is Cecilia. We spoke for ten minutes or so. Mercedes told us she thought there was another American living in the building; she couldn't remember for sure and, as is the Madrid way, didn't particularly care. At the end of my conversation with Cecilia I said something like, Well, it's good to meet you finally—we've been hearing rumors about you ... Meaning absolutely nothing. It was just small talk. But she gave me a funny look, excused herself, and all but ran away. Now I've seen her any number of times since, passed her on the stairs and so on, and she acts like I just shit in her pocket. I have no idea what that's all about.

The only others I can identify with any regularity are the couple who live in the apartment behind us. I heard them a good many days before I spotted them in person. Their bed is obviously against the adjoining wall of my bedroom. I'm sleeping in the smaller, interior bedroom to escape the noise Megan gets from the big bedroom that is against the street, out front of which a drug club has recently formed and is nightly adding members. Megan is not so bothered by noise, and her bedroom is palatial compared to mine and has a walk-in closet. At any rate, our neighbors on the inside probably don't realize just how much I can hear.

Every morning around 6:30 they wake. I see by now that she is the one still working. He walks her down the hill to the metro station at Plaza Lavapiés at about 8, then walks back alone. But since we've been here, I, by sound at least, have become intimately acquainted with them. Their alarm goes off, and then they make love raucously. Their approach to the activity makes further sleep impossible on my side of the wall. She's a screamer and has a name for him, or a part of him, El Gigante. It's a name she mentions breathlessly and, I would say, in awe. The springs in their bed are the worse for wear. It sounds a bit like trampoline aerobics over there. For awhile, before it actually happened, I began to fear a sense of embarrassment at finally running into them. But then one Monday I was heading up the stairs at lunch time, and they came out their door, this very short, sweet, old couple. God bless them, is all I could think.

One of the attractions of this apartment is that there aren't any bars on the immediate block. Candela, a flamenco bar, on the corner at the top of the street is the closest. If you're up early enough on the weekends, 5 or 6 a.m. say, they're just winding down then. They dance in the basement, which is an old cave and very musty smelling. As you turn the corner, next to Candela there's a bodega where I buy wine now and then, 125 pesetas a liter. You take in your empty bottles and they fill them. We had one of these bodegas in Argüelles also, where they keep the wine in pigskins. Just as there, it's a harsh little wine that bites.

Two buildings to the north of ours, there's a flamenco school for young girls. It's located in the basement. At three in the afternoon, they start stamping their feet like ponies.

Down toward the end of the block, heading toward the plaza, there's a neighborhood bookstore. It's tiny. No electricity. It's like a narrow cave stuffed with old magazines. I've never personally seen any customers enter this place. The hag who runs it eats and sleeps there. I spoke nicely to her a couple times, not realizing right off that she was crazy. Buenos días, I'd say. Mañana, she'd answer. I stopped saying anything. I just walk by her now. I noticed, though, that she started sprucing up. This to a somewhat comic effect. Blazing red lipstick. She made an attempt at combing her hair. And she brought her reading table out closer to the doorway and set it with two chairs, put plastic flowers in a glass.

Whenever she sees me now, she's sort of looking around me like, Where's my boy, the one who said Good Day? She also completely revamped her magazine selection, threw out all the old ones, which were yellowed and faded and appeared to be from other decades. Now she has soft porn tastefully displayed for all to see. The schoolboys go by there eyes-right like they're in the military. As usual, however, no one is buying. She reads her magazines from morning till night. Occasionally, I don't know what prompts it, she'll crumple a magazine roughly and toss it over her shoulder, where it lands in the street similar to some large shot bird.

Yesterday when I went down to Plaza Lavapiés to buy some lemons, I came across this maybe five-minute series of events: I noticed two heavyset women walking down the metro steps backward. A man walked by me wearing a false nose. A woman came past the other way with a plastic grocery bag on her head. I looked at the sky for some hint of rain, but there was none. I heard a sound between parked cars, like a cow taking a piss. I had a look that way, greeted by the whitest, skinniest ass I ever want to see, a Madrid grandma taking a leak. Looking away from this quickly as I could, I came across a young addict at the traffic light. He'd apparently reached into the little green trash can attached to the light pole, to retrieve an item or just explore the contents, but somewhere in the process simply fell asleep at it. He had his arm into the can up to his elbow and was kind of wedged there hanging, his knees half bent. He was dressed in rags, broken shoes, so motionless I took him for a modern sculpture. A motorcycle cop stopped just then and tapped him on the shoulder. I walked past this scene and followed it a moment. When I turned to the front again, a hunchback crossed my path whose hump was so high that his head looked to have migrated south on his body. From the back, walking away from me, he appeared to be a headless man. I turned again and caught my own reflection in a café window—another fair-booth atrocity. I looked through myself to the inside where a fella sat at a table who had two silver hooks instead of hands. He was eating soup. He balanced one hook with the other for stability of his spoon. The soup was very dark. It looked like ink. This is not your normal type neighborhood, I was thinking.

19-20 February

The most perfect winter weekend I recall here. Around 65 degrees both days, sunny, the kind of sky Goya liked to paint when he was less troubled. Megan and I went to Retiro Saturday, sat at a bar by the pond there and drank beer all afternoon. The false spring has lasted a week now—not one leaf on a tree, but things blooming, especially the almond trees in the young orchard planted at the far south end of the park. They say you can tell it's spring in Madrid when the almonds bloom. We watched some old guys playing bocce ball. A fella doing tai chi underneath a flowering plum. All week I've been somewhat high. Saturday night I saw the man in the moon once again—a profile, in pumpkin light, addressing a vague circle of animals.

Sunday we went to the lake, to the restaurant Fuente La Piña. They had their outdoor tables going. We had a plate of ham, good

Gallego bread, Manchego cheese, many beers, the table top full of empties by the time we left. It was a very busy day there and took us 45 minutes to get the bill. Ahora mismo, our waiter kept saying. Right now. But the sun makes you feel like things are okay again.

We were at the same restaurant this past August 11th to watch a partial eclipse of the sun. I'd rigged up exposed film over my glasses. At 11:30 that morning the temperature started dropping, and the spray from the fountain in the middle of the lake shifted from south to north. I was also keeping an eye on this old fella fishing from the shore. He was intent on watching his bobber. This interested me. Like all bodies of water in Madrid, the lake has a cement bottom. I'd personally never noticed any fish life there, not so much as a minnow. By 11:45 the moon had taken a bite of the sun. 12:10 seemed to be the maximum eclipse, maybe a quarter of the sun blackened. It was cooler then, and like twilight. The waiters that day too were busy to the point of insanity, but they stopped a moment to look at the sky. Everything stopped a moment. The old fisherman turned his head.

Tuesday evening I happened to walk by Darlen's apartment, no lights on there, and it struck me that she is a symbol of this city and country, and that I must keep in mind that even the things which I think I know here are perhaps deceptive and that I don't really understand them at all.

I woke in the night once thinking about Billy. I'd been dreaming about something to do with him, this time when Megan came to visit one weekend. It was long before she moved in. Billy showed up, and the three of us spent a Saturday together at the house. After which she told me, I don't guess you can see it. Or don't want to. But Billy's nuts.

He was up in San Ann because his girlfriend at the time had insisted that he stop drinking, otherwise she'd walk. Billy tried sobriety now and again, but it never took. He compromised with her. He stopped drinking at home. And she so rarely saw him then that she dropped the idea.

23 February

from the *International Herald Tribune*

Car Bomb Kills Local Politician in Basque City

MADRID—A car bomb exploded in the Basque capital, Vitoria, on Tuesday, killing a Socialist politician who opposed Basque independence and a bodyguard in an attack blamed on the ETA separatist guerilla group

"This action has been taken by those who know no other language than killing," said Juan Manuel Eguiagaray, a Socialist Party spokesman.

The explosion rocked a Basque country university campus. It occurred within a few hundred meters of the Basque regional government headquarters and created panic among university students and staff. Several vehicles caught fire, spewing burning wreckage into the street and sending thick black clouds into the sky.

The attack comes four days before the start of the official election campaign.

I read this report in Plaza Santa Ana, just up the street from us now. The plaza is as bleak and forlorn as the news, but the sun pours in here, and I take in the weird afternoon crowd, old people and winos and big dogs. It seems a favorite of street couples. I'm watching one such pair at the moment, the woman in zebra stripe pants and a white shirt with large black dots and her old man who can't keep his eyes open. They share a box of wine. They like to kiss. They have a pile of clothes next to them.

I sat on the very far end of a bench facing the sun. There's a bag lady at the other end sewing a shoe. All too soon, two old ladies show up, one of whom is blind, and this old guy who knows them comes along greeting them loudly. He's talking to them like they're the whole world. The blind lady starts all but beating me with her cane, trying to discover where she could fit in on the bench. I got up and left, went to another bench. A Saint Bernard came and sat on the ground next to me, acted like he knew me.

It is now less than three weeks before the March 12th general election. There's clear timing to the violence.

On the TV news this night, Prime Minister Tony Blair of Britain will call the bombing "a terrorist outrage."

President Clinton, in a joint news conference in Washington with King Juan Carlos, will praise the Spanish monarch for taking "a stand against the forces of terror."

The King will express his "shock and utmost rejection" at the assasination.

Mr. Aznar's Popular Party will suspend all campaign rallies for 48 hours.

Mr. Aznar and his chief election rival, the Socialist Joaquin Almunia, will join in a show of unity amid thousands of black unbrellas in front of Vitoria's city hall. They will not, however, look at each other.

I don't know any of that at the moment. I'm still at Santa Ana. I'm watching the blind lady closely. She's on the move again, swinging her cane like a sword. A gypsy enters the plaza with his band, a music machine and goat. The goat hopped up on the machine. A big brown nanny goat, all four hooves on a circular piece of wood the size of a dinner plate. Some polka music in the plaza now. The gypsy puts his hat on the ground for tips. It sat there and in short order became invisible.

I must interject an item or two about the King and Queen. The King's bodyguards have to keep a close eye on him. He disappears from time to time. The most famous of these lasted a week. No one in Spain had any idea where he might be during that time, and the security forces were near panic. It came out later that he was in the Netherlands on a tryst. As for the Queen, she has stated in public several times that if she weren't the Queen, she would most likely be a hair stylist.

26 February

from the *Independent* (London)

Amateur exposes the 'jumble sale Goya' as fake

By Ian Herbert

THE ESTEEMED *opinions of several art historians have been all but confounded by the near-obsessive attention to detail of an amateur enthusiast who seems to have exposed as fake a painting believed to be a Goya.*

Until Joe Chesters, a retired council worker from Norhop Hall, North Wales, intervened, Italian Woman and Child *was thought to have depicted the Spanish artist's wife and child Xavier. It was in the ownership of an estate near Mold, in North Wales, before it was bestowed on an employee as a gift and subsequently pitched up unceremoniously on a jumble-sale table at a chapel in nearby Buckley in the 1930's, lending it the title of 'the Buckley Goya' in local parts.*

In 1968 Tom Dempster Jones, a collector from North Wales, bought the piece for 10 shillings, promising its vendor a cut of the 100,000 pounds he believed it might fetch. He called in the Canadian Goya expert Dr Rolph Z Medgessy, whose conclusions could barely have been clearer. The work, he said, was indeed from the hand of Francisco de Goya y Lucientes, and probably portrayed the artist's wife 'with their first child Xavier.' He also said the painting was covered in the artist's 'microsignatures' a couple of millimetres high.

Mr. Dempster Jones sought a second opinion and received the conclusions he had been hoping for. The German art historian Dr Herbert Paulus said, in 1969, that the picture 'agrees graphically' with a picture in a sketchbook of Goya's work from his time in Italy.

Mr. Chester's obsession with Goya dates from his school days. 'My schoolmates were enjoying people like Dan Dare and Zorro,' he said. 'But Goya was my hero because he could

Goya's Head

make you cry, make you laugh, show you beauty through a woman's flashing eyes.' He developed serious doubts about the microsignature theory. 'Everything told me it was a fiasco,' he said. 'Slowly, I worked through authorities on the subject and none tallied.' His interrogation also revealed contradictions. Xavier was Goya's seventh child, not his first as Dr. Medgessy had asserted. He was also born in 1784—years after the artist left Italy.

His quest to prove the 'Buckley Goya' a fake was further helped when the Italian sketchbook believed to have been Goya's was exposed as a fake and the original—held at a private library in Majorca since the 19th century—turned up in 1993. There was no hint of Italian Mother and Child *in it.*

Despite attempts to sell the painting abroad, the 'Buckley Goya' remains in private ownership in North Wales. Quite how much money it might have changed hands for is unclear.

27 February Sunday

Javier, Goya's son mentioned in the article, was the only child of his who survived birth, childhood, grew up and lived a normal life span. Despite having the blood of genius in his veins, and also that his mother Josefa was a Bayeu, a prominent artistic family from Zaragossa, by all accounts Javier possessed no talent whatsoever. It didn't matter to Goya. He doted on the boy his entire life.

Our computer was in the shop part of last week. We got it back Friday evening. The exhaust fan had stopped working; it was replaced. This stopped the printer from screaming. The machine is very quiet once again. It had much to say before and in a somewhat unforgivably raucous voice. I found that I'm dependent on this instrument. It is also a place to go. In its absence, there seemed a very large hole in the living room, which I would wander to off and on, and stand before, vaguely at odds as to what I was doing there.

In the afternoon we went to the Madrid Zoo. I figured it would keep us outside in the fine weather we've been having. I guess it really is spring.

It's a large zoo, with nice animals, and not in any way enlightened about how to keep them. The aquarium was the best of the lot. There were some fine saltwater tanks set up, very colorful healthy fish. I found the shark exhibit mesmerizing. There were, I noted, an uncommon number of young mothers watching the sharks, though I couldn't account for this. The acoustics inside that building, however, amplified sound badly. This is not something the Spanish need. As for the rest of it, the animals lived on cement or, if they were lucky, bare dirt. The gorillas weren't outside yet for some reason and were incarcerated in the worst sort of county jail tradition. Goya could have done some good work there. Dim, the odor of urine strong. All their cells lacked were calendars with the days X-d off. To the beasts' credit, they kept their backs to the crowd.

Giraffes under these conditions will do almost anything for a peanut. Bears act the fool for popcorn. There were some really fine Spanish bears. There is still a wild population in a small area of the Pyrennes above Barcelona. But there was little for the animals to do but beg. The worst part, however, was the untold thousands of wild Spanish children. They were uncaged. Still, it was another fine day—add it to a string of them lately.

29 February—Leap Year Day

As far as months go, I've never particularly cared for February, and this one had an extra day to trip over. I got into a wrangle with a couple of ladies in the checkout line at Corte Inglés at Sol. Two bandy-legged, stout, tough-looking old bangers with that improbable red hair the nutters favor. One was slightly larger than the other, but they may well have been sisters they looked and acted so alike. I was in the fast line behind them, the line barely moving, about seven deep back in a narrow aisle. They had way too many items, of course, stocking up on sherry by the looks of it, and were talking to each other both at once in the kind of rancorous voices that make even the most amicable conversations here seem like bits of leverage in a dispute.

Suddenly a cashier opened another register nearby. Several people hurried to it. Then another. The two ladies studied the new line totally baffled, as if some sort of mistake had occurred. What's the sense in that, they seemed to be wondering, when the line we're in is nearly perfect in its tedium?

I tried to make my way around them to the other register.

Discúlpame, I said, pardon me, trying to get by. Nothing. They snorted a little, looked down their noses. At the ceiling. Glanced here and there. Had they heard a voice?

One of them touched her baguettte for a clue.

They've got me penned in good. I'm blocked by other customers behind. This is a treat for them, obviously. I don't think they can stomach a man alone grocery shopping. It goes against the grain somehow; it's not Castilian. Finally I did a quick end-around to the right. The wider of the two took a step to block me, but I gave her a shoulder, spun her out of the way. I hear her behind me:

Oh … BUENO! MUY BIEN! She calls me in Spanish MR. IN A BIG HURRY!

The next day, March came in wagging its tail. Cold wind, warm sun, back and forth. In the early morning, I took the metro to a little place called Ciudad Jardín, up in the northeast of the city. It resembles an ancient country village set down as if by magic in Madrid. The streets are cobblestone and seven feet wide. One or two story doll houses, and each with a small yard with grapevines, roses. To enter there is a step back in time. I walked the narrow streets. My mood turned light and easy. I thought of home. Thought for some reason of the wisteria tree in Tillie's backyard. It would bloom around Easter. I hadn't seen its flowers in some years, and just then I very much wanted to.

Thursday around 1:30 in the afternoon I took the yellow metro line over to the old neighborhood. I had it in mind to talk to Kevin

Ray, see if he'd take me to Chueca some night. He knows the scene, says Darlen works in a show there. I've been fretting about it for days now. Curiosity and disbelief have gotten the better of me. I want a lot of things, and I don't know why exactly, except no one had turned my head like that for some time. And it wasn't just Chelo, and it wasn't just me. I saw it in the bars that night we went out. Young guys standing around her with hard-ons, not knowing quite what to do with themselves. To find out *it really was too good to be true* and, even worse, there was no sleight of hand involved, not much anyway—you had been tricked on a much deeper level, betrayed by the senses. Otherwise, the visit to Kevin Ray is not something I want to explain, even to myself.

I came up above ground across from the Corte Inglés store in Argüelles and already I'm in trouble. The sidewalk is torn up on that corner, about 15 feet of it. Nobody working at the moment. Maybe the crew had already knocked off for lunch.

It's slow going. I get tied up in the crowd behind a lady with a walker. She has problems with the sand, keeps getting stuck. She meets a guy in a wheelchair half way across. They stare at each other. Nobody is giving way. All of a sudden there's a serious pedestrian back-up. I'm trapped there in a school of barracuda. The cripples are eyeing one another. I take it they'd like to knock the shit out of each other but, for various physical considerations, can't. We're all in the same boat now. We're paralyzed. A fella jammed in beside me holds a plastic cup to my face, wants to know if I got any change. I go claustrophobic. I have a tremendous urge to bolt, start knocking these people aside, walk on their heads, *do something*!

Finally I got through it. I hate that feeling. Things were so close in there, if I had jumped up in the air my feet wouldn't have touched the ground again.

I walked over to the old apartment. There's scaffolding enclosing it. Workers have started to paint the building pink. Kevin Ray ought to appreciate that. He isn't home, and I feel relieved. My thoughts are interrupted as I spot my old neighbor, Nacho the Cribone. He looks his old shysti self, eyes darting around suspiciously, pushing a handcart load of kindling. He stops in the doorway of La Parrilla, a cell phone to his ear. Every ham-and-egger in town seems to have a cell phone the last couple days. Telefónica must be handing them out again. Nacho acts as though he's passing down some mighty executive decision. He speaks loudly, he wants the world to know he's with the in-crowd now. I see what you're telling me, I thought, I just don't know what to say about it.

It's a pleasant spring day, and I walk through Parque Oeste. I'd been missing it. I come across the first daffodils. The plum trees have bloomed already, their reddish leaves starting in. Then a yellow bush, called broom or gorse. The park is crowded. The young Madrid flowers have taken off their coats, for the first time since autumn, always a bit stunning in this town.

I ended up at Montaña. I sat there on a bench in the sun by the fountain and reflecting pool. A woman comes and sits beside me. She's either a bag lady or one of the rich eccentrics who live along the Rosales paseo. It's hard to tell the difference between them. She takes a box of pink tissues and stuffs three, four of them between her teeth. Puts her face to the sun. She don't want the sunlight to touch her lips is the only thing I can figure. This made it look like she had a pink carnation for a mouth.

Awhile later, this little guy tottered up to me. He was about two-foot tall and had on black knickerbockers. He offered me some of his bottle, but I declined. I'm trying to cut down, I told him. He had escaped his mother, who soon retrieved him. I took it as a good sign. Usually, kids look at me and start bawling.

On the way back to the metro, on the corner of Princesa and Alberto Aguilera, a waiter walked by me with a tray—some lamb chops, fried, two cold beers. It looked pretty good. He has a white cloth napkin over one shoulder. He crossed paths with the wizened dotard who works that corner hawking these somewhat surrealistic woodpecker-head balloons. He sits there most days squeezing these things to make them quack, annoying everyone. When you get stuck there at a red light, he's got you. Do woodpeckers quack? Not the ones in nature, but this is Madrid. The old man had just recently put away his goods or hadn't gotten them out yet. As the waiter passed by, the old man squeezed his empty hand a couple times.

Friday, the 3rd of March

I noticed in our neighborhood the first leaves coming out on the fresno trees on Calle Argumosa. Or just their flowers I guess, small, pastel green, flat, thousands of them. There's a plague of construction work around. Dumpsters everywhere, filled to twice their capacity, waiting to be towed away. The workers take breaks, take lunch, standing out in front of the buildings, drinking quart beers and harassing the neighborhood beauties, most of whom are fairly rough characters themselves but look good, being 16, 17. The girls seem to have a standard reply, which I take to be very Spanish in nature: Go back to Morocco ya cunts.

It was Friday, also, that Kevin Ray called to get a persimmon pudding recipe from Megan, who wasn't home just then. Sometimes he likes to chat. The conversation got around to Darlen and Chelo. Che goes to work, Kevin says, does his job, leaves, doesn't talk to anyone unless he's asked a direct question.

He's been dodging me for a month now, Kevin said, so it's nothing new to me. I loaned him that money awhile back. The last time I asked him about it, he gave me quite a sob story, which … knowing him, I suspect was also true. Said he'd had his wallet lifted in the metro. He lost two credit cards and 50 bucks in cash, just about what he owes me, right? When he went home to call the credit card companies, he discovered his phone service had been cut off. He's a worse fuck-up than I ever thought of being. It's good to have someone around like that for perspective. But I hate it when I loan people money, then they act funny about it. The debt gets to be secondary. It's how they handle it pisses me off.

He saw me coming toward him in the hallway yesterday. He turned around and went the other way. Acted like he'd forgotten something. Sort of snapped his fingers even. Like, Oh, damn … I better go back and get that. It's a good way to keep him at a distance, though. Just loan him some cash. Have you talked to him?

No, I said. He's disappeared on me.

He takes some putting-up with, I'll say that for him. His students are complaining. They usually make their complaints known by not coming to class. Now they're actually talking to the higher-ups. His classroom door was open the other day. I stopped and listened in for a minute. I was at an angle where he wouldn't notice me. He didn't seem to have the faintest notion what he was saying but presented it in this stentorian voice. It was like the dead giving up their secrets. It's supposed to be a class in conversation, mind you. I moved over a step and saw his students, all three of them, sitting there in a bleak vegetative state.

And he just looks awful. His face bleary. Pasty. I've seen that before … in my own mirror, unfortunately. He's drinking his ass off, a nightly bender, is my bet. He looks like the ghost of his former self. A ghost with a red nose.

Mmm, I said. You … the apartment … you haven't come across anything odd there?

I've been keeping an eye out in our new place for Billy. Except for that one incident, which was questionable, he doesn't seem to have made the move with us. Or maybe just speaking aloud about him ended it.

Odd? … Yes, I did, now that you mention it. A lot of scurrying about at night … turned out to be a mouse. It seems almost tame. Acts like I'm supposed to feed him or something. He doesn't have a tail. I don't think I've ever seen that before.

I'll be, I said.

Then I finally got some traction on what I wanted to ask.

The other day … you said the other day … you saw Darlen work.

Yeah, sure … that once, anyway.

She any good?

Breathtaking, I'd say. She sings her own songs. Doesn't lip-synch like most all of 'em. She has that smoky voice. She did a Mae West song. *My Old Flame* … a great old torch song. You know it?

No.

He started singing some of the words.

I'm not familiar with it, I said.

Where you been all your life?

Here and there, I said. I guess I wasn't payin' attention.

She wore a ... kind of meringue wig, spun a lace parasol. Of course, that body ... that goes without saying. Most of 'em in these shows, it's ... life on the hoof.

That was it? I mean, she didn't strip or nothin'?

Are you asking out of curiosity, Luke?

I moved along quickly. I said, You can make a living at that?

It pays the rent, I'd imagine.

A silence on the line.

Then Kevin Ray said, I should think Darlen makes most of her money *after* work, if that's what you're getting at.

Yeah, I said, she looks ... expensive.

Local legend has it, she is.

You take me to scc her sometime?

Another silence.

On the level?

Yes.

Would Megan be coming along?

I doubt it.

But ... she wouldn't mind?

Why should she?

Still, I'd have to talk with her first I think. This situation is complicated enough ... Megan's the last person I want to cross ... under any circumstances.

Sure. Go ahead, I said. Clear it with Megan. Christ.

Don't get angry. I just want to be careful is all. How about next Wednesday?

From what Chelo's told me, she don't work but on the weekends.

Saturday'd be good then. Not tomorrow. I have a date. Next week. The only trouble with the weekends, though ... there are so many of the devil's pilgrims about.

Yeah, but.

I'm not sure where she's working. I could give her a call.

What time?

Say again.

What time should we meet?

Can you stay awake till midnight?

Wiseacre, I said.

The shows don't start till then. And really … the later you go the more interesting they get.

What do they cost?

They're free. They get you back on the drinks pretty hard.

Where should we meet?

You know Ángel Sierra? That little zinc bar in Plaza Chueca, little shooter bar, been there forever?

Yeah, I know it.

If I can't get hold of Darlen, we'll just take a walk down Libertad. She works that street. I saw her at a place called Truck.

Just … a

What?

… don't introduce me to nobody.

Like my friends? you mean.

No. I'm just sayin'.

My friends don't particularly go to these things. Unless they're looking for a laugh.

The shows are funny?

It's all camp humor. Bitchy. A lot of *short* jokes. I don't know what you're expecting. We see Darlen, that'll be something fine. Otherwise, it's second-hand glamour, at best. A good many of them look like my mother on the way home from Saturday night Bingo.

Short jokes?

You've never been to one of these?

I never thought about them being humorous.

They are, but not intentionally. Next Saturday, then. I think I'll dress up. That'll be good for me. I have an appointment to get waxed at 10. Otherwise, I'm free.

Yeah, okay. I'll see you.

We hung up.

Waxed?

The next day, Megan felt like cooking. She's a great cook, but the inspiration doesn't often strike her. When she feels this way, she really goes at it and has fun, and a feast comes of it.

First she put together some homemade mayonnaise. Then she went to the market at Antón Martín and bought steaks and shrimp and avocado and big mushrooms and strawberries and baguettes. The meal consisted of avocado halves stuffed with shrimp remoulade and capers. Filet mignon. She gets this from a butcher who ages the meat; it's very tender, and she wraps it in bacon. Baked stuffed mushroom caps. She stuffed these with finely chopped stems, green onion, parsley, a little flour, cream, nutmeg, topped with buttered bread crumbs. Bread with mayonnaise spread thickly. Several bottles of fine rioja, Blasón de Esquide. All this followed by puff-pastry pie crust filled with real whipped cream, strawberries and dark chocolate.

The meal put me over the top. I ended up eating most of the pie. After this we began talking about diets. Megan is always ready for a diet, for reasons beyond me. She tends toward thinness. I was just sitting around later at the kitchen table, fattened for the kill, when she asked off-handedly:

Tell me why you want to see this … what is she? an exotic dancer. I don't understand.

Like I said, you're more than welcome to come along.

I know that.

Well … I'm just curious, I guess.

Is she pretty?

Yes, she is.

How old is she?

I'm not sure exactly. In her 20s somewhere.

Under normal circumstances, I should be jealous, but … that

notion doesn't seem to fit.

Not hardly.

She smiled, said, Might it have something to do with that you're a pervert?

That comes into play, I said.

She'd had some wine that day. Megan doesn't drink much as I've mentioned, but when she does, here of late she starts talking about home. She said right then, I'm thinkin' about chicken fried steak, watermelon pie.

She fell asleep around midnight, she told me, but got up an hour later absolutely starving, which made no sense after the meal we'd had. She went to the kitchen and consumed half a jar of cashews, a carrot, and a box of milk. She told me all this Sunday morning when I awoke. She told me she still had a craving.

There's bacon left, she said. I could put that in the microwave, make it nice and crisp and melt some butter on it. Does that sound good?

I had figured out what she was hungry for, but I didn't say it.

8 March

from the *International Herald Tribune*

Spain Leaders Urge Calm After Bombs

MADRID—Spanish political leaders Tuesday urged voters in the Basque region not to be intimidated by the separatist group ETA after a car bombing rocked campaigning for the general election Sunday.

The bomb injured seven people—two police officers and five civilians—in the city of San Sebastián on Monday night. It was the third attack blamed on ETA in two months.

9 March Thursday

We've had spring and near perfect weather for three weeks now. Today was the first short sleeve day. The geraniums on the balcony are starting to bloom. I go on a one-day diet. I take long walks. No bread, beer, chips. I lose a 16th of a pound.

That night I got a call from Mike Shaloo, an old Morgan Pub friend of mine from Tampa. He wanted to know about the toros. He's an aficionado. He was also looking to borrow some money to put on a horse at the Oldsmar track. He's got some inside dope on it. There's no way this horse can lose, he says. It'll go off 15-1 or better. Not only does he know this horse will win, he knows by how much.

I bite. How much? I ask. By a nose, he says. They'll have him written up in the program looks like he only has three legs or some shit. They don't want to act outlandish with the win, they just want to cash in. What's the name of the horse? I ask. *Trouble Ahead.* He hears me laughing. What's so hilarious? he wants to know. I take it as a measure of his desperation that he calls me. When I tell him I don't have any money, the conversation loses energy.

I'd been hearing a squeaking noise as we spoke.

What's that sound? I ask.

I'm chalking a cue, he said.

You in a bar?

No, he said. I bought a pool table.

Shaloo was in Spain last year for half of June, all of July, the early part of August, spent seven grand on the excursion. Most people would save up money for such a trip. Shaloo saved up the credit cards he'd been sent in the mail. He leads an amazing life. It's full of drama, a great deal of it self-inflicted. There are so many subplots you have to shake your head. Most have to do with going under. At work, his employers are forever positioning him on the cross. He quit one job to come to Spain, got another when he returned home. However, it's up in Tarpon Springs. He's on the road a good four hours a day, just getting there and back. He must find jobs farther and farther from his house, in places where people don't know him yet.

Since he got the job, he felt he owed it to himself to buy a new truck to drive to it. The bank has him by the numbles. The sharks are at the door, in suits and ties, Shaloo says, the ties tight as nooses in the Florida heat.

Shaloo takes none of this personally. His wife, on the other hand, is very emotional, always on the verge of happy tears, if you know what I mean. She's overcome at breakfast by the deep and inexplicable sadness of the toaster. He leaves her in Tampa when he comes to Spain. It's a tradition. It was all but unbelievable to him that she took a boyfriend when Shaloo was gone this last time, some sort of preacher no less, or preacher's son, he's not certain. He tells me this over the phone. It's not something I want to know, but I hear it anyway. He even tries to characterize the relationship the two had, bats around the word *platonic*; this cements in my mind the image of two people fucking like rabbits.

This last visit, he had a purpose, to write a novel he said. He wanted to do it the old fashioned way. He showed me some #9 pencils, yellow legal pads. The pencils were sharpened. In his time here the novel turned into a brief short story. Far as it went, from what I could tell, it was a story about Christmas and death. It goes on and on, this drama that revolves around him like a dust devil. If I were in his shoes, I'd be pistol shopping, but he's used to it by now, it seems normal to him, gets a laugh out of his own plight.

Toward the end of the summer, after Pamplona, he took to writing in the mornings at Café Comercial in the Bilbao district. Every couple days I'd go have coffee with him. There were a number of other writers at the café doing the same as he, and he got to know them. A lot of conversation between the tables. At this point he was running out of money. He came across an ad in one of the papers, a Spanish woman advertising for an American writer to complete her husband's memoirs and continue the magazine they did together, as the husband had died recently. He was American. She was apparently the illustrator for the publication. So Shaloo applied for the position, as it had come down to making some money or going home. Figures she's got some dough. He's writing down on one of his yellow pads what he wants an hour, adding up the hours, tells me he thinks he can make it in Madrid pretty good on what he's going to get, maybe a blow job or two thrown in—all this before he even meets the woman.

She tells him over the phone she's in her mid-40s, a petite blond. He doesn't buy that, has her down for an elderly bird of prey at best but, having money on his mind, he gets an appointment with her one Friday night and goes to her apartment, a nice place up in the north end. Turns out she's at least ten years older than advertised, plus she broke her hip awhile back and moves about like a granny. She's petite in a way, though Shaloo says he thought more in terms of the stringiness of an old runner bean. First thing she does is try to sell him a copy of the magazine she's supposed to be hiring him to work on. Shaloo says it's some bad poetry interspersed with environmental articles and health tips. Let me see your husband's manuscript he says. He reads it. It's the man's life story, but only 11 pages long. You just need to flesh it out, she says, fill in the gaps. Have you a nip to drink? Shaloo asks. You're a bohemian, aren't you? she says and offers up a quarter bottle of port she found under the sink after rummaging about endlessly. Shaloo passed. She brings out a sampling of her illustrations. Shaloo's thinking to himself, They are just a notch above stick figures. Where do you expect to sell any of this? he asks. Canada! she says. Then she tells him if all else fails, she has a backup, a secret recipe. The end result of which is better than chocolate, and it can be made from common household items.

I've been reading *The Plague* by Camus. There's one hilarious character in it named Grand. Grand is writing a book. He can't get past the first paragraph, however. It's a somewhat horrid paragraph. Every time the main character, Rieux, encounters him, Grand reads the paragraph aloud, asks Rieux what he thinks about the changes he's made. He changes a word here, a word there. Sometimes the changes make it even worse, and Rieux never knows quite how to respond. Grand's dream is to hand the finished product to a publisher some day and have the publisher say to him, Hats off! The routine adds up as it goes along. I can't come across Grand's name now without starting to laugh.

On the phone last night, I asked Shaloo how he was doing.

I'm grand, he said with a weary air. Just grand.

By the end of the conversation I had a change of heart and agreed to wire him 300 bucks.

Mikey, I said, we win, I get ... how much?

I'll split it with ya.

We lose?

Ah, we're fucked then, he said.

Much to my surprise, I received a money order a week later for $2500.

Friday

The street lights come on at 7:35 in the evening. Megan and I were out walking. We saw the terraza tables and chairs being delivered to Plaza Mayor. The leaves are coming out on the horse chestnut and plane trees. There is a sense of awakening.

11 March (Midnight) Café Truck

I went to Chueca. I stopped momentarily at Carmencita, at the corner of C/Univeridad and Libertad, Lorca's old bar. It's a small place, a restaurant now, and only a few tables. Megan and I have eaten there. Good food, fairly expensive. Lorca's presence is still around, however, and that's the main attraction for me. I tipped my hat to the old boy, then walked on to Ángel Sierra.

The bar's front is open. Customers spill onto the sidewalk. The crowd is sort of fantastic here at night. Chueca is totally different at night than during the day, when it has an industrial appearance. The lights change it. I was leaning against the building taking in the scene. Plaza Chueca looks like most of Madrid on a Saturday night, a lot of young people standing around talking and drinking and smoking, only here the crowd is thoroughly gay. Mostly fellas. And some girls around, here and there, attired in vampire cosmetics.

Awhile later, a young prostitute flounced up beside me, stood about a yard away, taking it all in, same as I was. I glanced at her out of the corner of my eye several times. Tall and thin. She's wearing a black silk dress, one of those that resemble a slip, black leather jacket, vertiginous stiletto heels, marled nylons. Her light blue hair is in a page boy, lipstick that looks like varnish. When she closes her eyes, the eyelids are painted black. What a goddamn floozy.

Next time I notice her she'd edged closer. I'm thinking, Kevin Ray don't show pretty quick, I'm outa here. How can anyone fuck a street whore in this day and age? You'd need to wear a wetsuit for protection. I asked a guy to my left what time it was. He held up a wrist so that I could read his watch. Just then I felt a hand squeeze my right biceps. My whole body jerked. I said JAYSUS! like a tent preacher. Nobody touches you in this town. It's the young prostitute, who's right up next to me. She's crowding me.

The fuck you doin'? I said.

Whereupon she asked me dead calm, You lookin' for some quiff, big boy?

I stared at her face. I squinted.

Kevin Ray?

Call me Jadine tonight, he said.

We were walking south on Calle Libertad, past a bar called Black and White.

I couldn't get hold of Darlen, Kevin Ray was saying. We'll go to Truck. It's right ahead of us. She's not there, maybe I can find out where she is.

We stop at number 28, go inside. Pay about seven bucks for a beer. Someone named Pasión was performing when we walked in. She had little birthday candles balanced on her nipples, stuck there on hot wax apparently. We just caught the last of her act. She, of course, was not female, though it was hard to tell that.

Then something close to Bette Davis in her declining years, perhaps just before her death, came tottering out in high heels and corset. Soon afterwards, three hags surrounded her. They had curious wing appendages attached and acted as if they were flying around the stage.

What's this all about?

See, Kevin Ray said, those are the Three Furies. She's gonna pick one of them out. You watch, she'll take the one with the bouffant hairdo, in the cocktail dress ... one with the thick arms. That's her boyfriend in everyday life, is how I know. Then he's gonna fuck her in the ear ...

I turned my head and looked at him. He was chortling.

Very funny, Kevin.

Pasión was standing around, and Kevin Ray asked her where Darlen was working. Pasión was a little surly, or maybe too stoned to field the question properly. No tengo ni puta idea, was all we got out of her. I got no fucking idea.

What a bitch, Kevin Ray said of her.

We were about to get up and leave when a thin black queen came up to the table and said in English, You have to stay for *our* show. I won't take no for an answer. She seemed on some kind of stumble-drug. She threw a violet boa over her shoulder dramatically and lurched away.

You should probably see this, Luke. They call these three *Amateur Night*.

It was a seedy spectacle. The 3rd string was in. I can best characterize them as bikers in dresses. They looked like thugs and certainly tougher than anyone in the audience. One imitated Dolly Parton, the black girl was supposed to be that singer from the Supremes I guess, and the third Liza Minnelli. They lip synched a couple songs, couldn't follow the words with their mouths. Did some dancing. This was so pathetic it was hilarious. Then Dolly started talking. She was talking in Spanish so I didn't get all of it. But what she did was pick out the prettiest straight woman in the crowd by the looks of it and insulted her relentlessly. Dolly was nasty. And she went on and on. She kept repeating several phrases.

Wha'd she say just then? I asked Kevin Ray.

She said—Just think of my dick as pussy on a stick.

Then another phrase came up. She'd say it every three, four minutes.

She's telling everyone they're only working for tips, Kevin Ray said. Wants to make sure you know that.

Like most bad things, the show seemed to go on forever. I was starting to yawn. Then Kevin Ray said, Okay … get ready.

For what? I said.

The last song and dance ended, and Dolly said, We're going to pass the hat now. She said it three times, in German, English and Spanish. The place emptied out like there'd been a bomb threat.

After that, I took a taxi home.

The Ides of March

Nothing to beware of that I noticed. Then at 9 in the evening one clap of thunder, and a steady rain started. I watch the streetlights on the wet street. A long rolling thunder followed, lightning. This is the first time it has rained since I don't remember when. By 9:30 it had nearly passed. I laid down on the couch listening to the last of the rain tapping on the balcony and fell asleep for a little while, had a quick dream: Che had gotten hold of Darlen's shadow, cut it up in little pieces and sold it on a street corner as licorice.

Aznar and his party won the election. I don't much understand Spanish politics, and don't care to. Aznar's people, before they came to power and varnished themselves into a modern political party, would, on the anniversary of Franco's death, go over to a spot by the Royal Palace at Plaza de Oriente where the caudillo said Viva España! in 1975 for the last time in his squeaky, little girl's voice, and they'd give the falange salute. Aznar seems to be a front man for the bankers and Telefónica management. I think he probably still has a fine collection of Franco memorabilia and takes it out occasionally to pet it.

I go stand on the long balcony. Across the street a graffiti artist has tagged the building in two-foot high red letters:
PADRE!
APARTA
DE MÍ ESTE CÁLIZ!

What the hell could that mean?

I've been having lunch every day this week at Restaurante Continental, just down the hill at number 5 Olivar. It's a small, very unassuming place with a good little waiter, and another waiter that is crazy. La Cocina de las Autonomias is stenciled on the window in small letters. That is, they serve dishes from the various provinces of Spain. We passed by it any number of times, just completely missed that it was a restaurant. When we noticed it finally, we went in one day, just because it was convenient really and we were curious. We weren't particularly hungry, thought we'd get something light. We'll get an egg dish we decided. They're usually small. Megan ordered an entrada, stuffed red peppers. I chose a rioja, the same Blasón de Esquide I mentioned. I picked it at random. At 1050 pesetas, it wasn't even the most expensive on their list. Our little waiter brought the wine and praised it. And then it lit us up. It's delicious and probably the best rioja I've ever had, which is saying a lot.

The food was another matter, as there is no light fare on the menu. Megan's red peppers were huge and stuffed with hamburger and rice. They weighed a good pound each. Megan had ordered an omelet with trout. I chose shrimp with mushrooms. Hers turned out to be a whole trout stuffed with chorizo and fried in egg batter. Mine about three pounds of oyster mushrooms and half a dozen scrambled eggs. I found a shrimp here and there, also. But the wine was the thing. We finished the first bottle and ordered another. And they allowed us to take one home with us.

I ran into our little waiter on the street Monday, and he warned me they were on their last case of the Blasón de Esquide. So that's what I've been doing all week. Heavy eating and drinking and bringing a bottle home before it's gone. I've picked up weight in the process, and my asshole's about to jump ship.

A curiosity from the Saturday *Independent* out of London:

Orange Hopeful Disappears

Jonathan Hall, 38, a front runner to win the 10,000

pound Orange Screenwriting prize for his first effort, The
Butterfly Effect, *has been 'lost' by the organisers. If he does
not turn up before Thursday he will be dropped.*

Man. That's great. I understand it exactly, and I feel for the guy.
Who knows what he'd accomplished to this point, but I suspect
his life had never quite gotten under way. Now he's done well for
himself, fame and cash are on the way, but to have to deal with all
the horseshit surrounding this has him laying low. He'd used up what
vision he had on the script, and it's not now possible to picture himself
in motion. I see him hiding out in a friend's basement, carefully
keeping track of how many ounces of Scotch he's consumed so as
to retain purpose, thinking if he had a shovel perhaps he could really
get down into it good; maybe the dark angel lies just below.

Yesterday was my birthday. Megan and I were in Plaza Mayor
and decided to have something to eat there. It's not such a great
place to eat, but the sun is hard to resist. The plaza was full of stamp
collectors and sellers. Sunday is their day. Plus some fella with a
microphone and sound system barking about … who knows what?
Justice, I think. To an audience of several, his wife and brother
maybe, the mike full of sea gulls. Napoleon walked here, under
these arcades, and an incredible number of lesser assholes since. We
found a table at one of the terrazas, were handed a menu, but then
the waiter perhaps quit the job and went home. We never spotted
him again. We sat there a half hour or so taking in the sun, which
was really okay, I wasn't hungry yet anyway, then moved on to Casa
Gallego, at Bordadores 11, behind the plaza a couple alleys. We had
grilled salmon, mashed potatoes, salad, a bottle of High River rioja,
the house wine.

Megan gave me CDs for a present, Coltrane's *Giant Steps*, Van
Morrison's *No Guru, No Method, No Teacher.* An appropriate lyric
in that one: "I've been living in another country/that operates along
entirely different lines."

Also two bottles of Lar de Lares wine. I got to thinking later what I was thankful for at this juncture in time. Megan, certainly, and that I'm still alive. That I've never spent a night in jail, an accomplishment in this day and age. My friends, all six, seven of them, both living and dead. After that it fell off.

The bullfights have started and already there's been a goring. Juan Antonio Ruiz, who fights under the name Espartaco, caught a horn in the thigh at Valencia last Thursday. It was thought at first the wound was grave, but he's recovering. He didn't return to the ring until last summer, out some four years from another wound. He's a class act, as an individual and in the ring, handsome, rich, has his own line of bulls which are quite decent, but his legs are too beat to be in there now. He moves stiffly. You need to be quick as a snake, with an electrical grace. And sometimes, even that is not enough.

I was crazy for the toros when we first came here, but anymore I'm ambivalent. It's just so seldom, especially in Madrid, that you see a good fight. Mainly because the bulls are poor. They've been bred for certain qualities that no longer afford them the symmetry or personality to fight well. Unless you're talking about Miura bulls, just generally, the mettle is gone. And many times, when the bulls are good, the fighters aren't. The fatsos smoking big cigars in charge of Ventas, the Madrid bullring, put me off worse. They care for nothing but the cash involved. Goya has a painting set at a ventas, in his day the very cheapest of inns, where the humans and animals bedded down together. The fights don't always translate well to TV either. I've seen this first hand. It's a whole 'nother thing when you're ringside. It's a blood sport, and when you're down there close, you get it on you. I saw good fights with Shaloo last year in San Sebastián de los Reyes. José Tomás, Rivera Ordoñez, Morante de la Puebla. Shaloo says that if you see a truly great fight, it can change your life.

The best one I ever saw happened around this time, a year ago, down in Chinchón, just south of Madrid—Oscar Higares, Paco Cervantes, Manuel Caballero and some terrific bulls. It's a dramatic color scheme: yellow sand, red ring, black bulls. These bulls were in shape, not always the case, and all but the last one game. They were the kind that turn fast after passing the cloth. They were right back on it again, over and over, and the fighters were fresh and into it. It is said that you see something new each fight—this time a bull was spared. This is called an indulto. It happened with Caballero's second bull, which came into the ring in a truculent mood. This bull was a different color—red, with black, partridge eyes, body solid muscle. The first thing he did was put a horn through the barrea. The horn went right through the wood. Then he lifted his head and shot several planks through the air. He snorted and looked about. He seemed delighted with his work. The picador nailed him hard a couple times; he didn't seem to notice. Then Caballero and the animal went at it.

Caballero is not a first-tier fighter. He's not Joselito or José Tomás by a long shot, but he's capable and honest with what he has to offer and, really, I think this bull brought out the very best in him. Near the end of the fight, the official draped a flag over the railing, the color of which I'd not seen before. These flags usually denote an ear being awarded, two ears, a tail. I was there by myself and couldn't figure out what was going on. Caballero sighted the bull without his sword, went in for the kill. Went through the motion that is, and touched the bull in the kill spot with his hand. Then he ran off smiling, everybody else left the ring, and the bull was standing there looking around. The crowd, in the meantime, went crazy. I understood why they pardoned him. He never once opened his mouth to show tiredness, nor even considered it. By the end of the fight, he was just getting loose. It looked to me that he was having fun out there. I saw him in the pens afterwards. They were hosing the blood off him. He stood there, flexing his shoulders, enjoying the water. He'd just won the fight of his life.

23 March

The third day of rain. It's snowing in the mountains outside town. In order to gain some purchase against the depression this brings on, I plan to drastically increase my liquid consumption today, maybe stuff some toes of garlic in my ears, and hope for the best.

Around 3 in the afternoon, the rain stopped and I went down to the Champion store to get a few items, then sat on a bench in the plaza awhile with my grocery sacks. The cobblestones are wet and muddy in places from roadwork in the area. Turn certain corners and the wind is about strong enough to lean on. I'm wearing a sweatshirt, my heavy blue vest, but even so it's cool. The sun is out but comes and goes behind cotton ball clouds that are moving fast, gray in their bellies.

I head up Calle Ave María, stop at a place called Bar Aeropuerto at the corner of Tres Peces and have a caña. The airport bar on the street of the three fish. I am amused by this, and the beer tastes good. I leave there and a block or so later sit down at a table at Bodegas Alfaro on the corner of Olmo and Ave María. There are a few fellas standing at the bar. I have the table to myself. Me and three chairs. The place is open at the front and side, the sun comes-and-goes on my face. I notice a kitten enter the vacant lot across the street, through one of the two holes in the ochre yellow wall. He's black and apparently the only one left there of the litter. He's a little wet, shakes one paw. He seems to want to play with it. He's three-quarters grown now and looks healthy. I fed the kittens here several times. It started out there were four, two grays, an orange, and this black.

Alfaro is an inexpensive bar, a cien a beer, and I have a number of them and observe my neighborhood going by all the while. I take in the old lady street corner debate, diesel engine, dog bark style of the place. Teenage girls going home in their school uniforms smoking cigarettes. One pushes another into a parked car, and the alarm goes off. The traffic snarls by. Pigeons get out of your way here as if they hold a grudge. Blank rectangular windows, wrought-iron balconies, clay pots, green shutters, lacquered storefronts, brown, red, the buildings hard on one another, and, multiplying in solid angularity, they march down the hill and out of town. A pavement Venus walks by, looks at me, looks away. There's an excitement to this barrio. I'm wondering just then how you can hold that feeling without the brute noise of it driving you slightly mad. Reading about Madrid is a nice way to experience it. You don't get the background commotion. I don't like earplugs. Music perhaps … one of my neighbors carries around a small radio that she holds to her ear wherever she goes.

The sun comes on again, and I close my eyes and take it. When I open them, Darlen is standing there with a glass of beer.

May I sit with you? she said.

Sure.

Even though I know her secret now, she is still quite something to behold, as when you look at psychedelic plants or poisonous lizards and they're beautiful in their strange way; and even though you may not know exactly what they are, you know there must be special properties to them. Don't touch, is what they're saying. She was all that but her smile disarming, and it made you want to forget, too.

She wore black leather pants, a plungeneck white blouse, a black sweater, unbuttoned, over it.

I knew I'd seen you somewhere before, she said. It was here … across the street. She pointed to the empty lot, the yellow wall. I was sitting at this same table. Me and a girlfriend. I couldn't figure out what you were doing. I asked my friend, What's thon wide fuck up to, do you think? We watched you. You were holding up sardines. Take one in your hand, wave it around, made a clicking sound with your tongue, then toss the sardine over the wall. And you'd move up the wall apiece and do it again. He's daft, my friend said. But then I saw the kittens come out of the holes there, and you fed them. A sorry lot of kittens … filthy all of them, their noses runnin'.

The black one made it. I just saw him, I said.

So then I see this tall man half a block up Olmo there. He spots you and starts running at you. But you didn't notice him at all till he was up close—

That guy … yeah … I'd forgotten about him. All of a sudden he's on me like he dropped from a balcony.

An' he comes running at you like he's gonna hug you or throw a punch, hard to say what he's up to … an' you seen him then, an' ye're waitin', ye're ready, for whitever. An' he stops and screams—

Mama! Mama!

I seem to be a draw for that sort of behavior, I said.

You jus' rolled your eyes. We were laughing … the whole crowd here who'd seen it … but you didn't hear or pay it any mind, no more than you'd paid the madman. You went back to feeding the kittens. And you did not look like someone who feeds kittens.

My rough veneer, I said.

She smiled and lit a cigarette. I picked up the pack and looked at it. A brand called Sobranie, pastel colored cigarettes.

So when you came to my place with Che that night, I knew I had seen ye, but I could no quite place it.

I haven't talked to him for a while, I said. What's goin' on?

Between us? Not so much. It's all a bit rum at the moment.

He says you got a boyfriend.

He does, does he?

That he's in jail.

His name is Iker Carbó …

That's a Basque name, I said.

… an' he's in prison. An' I don't even know where they have him.

Wha'd he do?

He … mends cars.

A mechanic, I said.

My mind made a connection.

I see.

Aye, she said. She looked at me steady on, shook her head yes just slightly. And just like that, without saying it, we came to an understanding on what Iker Carbó was about.

He's very good at that, she said. He can fix anything. A broken heart, even.

Then, a vacant stare in my direction. Something gone bone cold in her. She seemed to forget me entirely for a moment, forgot the immediate world. She said finally, I don't like to talk about any of that. I may never see Iker again. Or I'll be old with fat puddling around my ass. Or not even then. There's little chance of it, and I have to live with that. Something good happened between us, but it's in the past now. If I talk about it I start to include people who don't want to be spoken of. I made an agreement not to do that.

An agreement?

With myself, she said. Excuse me a minute. I have to go to the loo.

I went to the bar and ordered two more beers.

We were talking about Chelo later.

Darlen said, I can be truthful with you … because I saw from the first that you are in love, or that you are loved.

Is that so?

Che … it's different. I can have a great time with him, but I can't talk to him. He wants to know things. But it just makes him angry to find out. Or sad. That awful Cuban sorrow. Sadness is just an illusion I tell him. Tomorrow you'll be happy as shite … an' that's an illusion, too, but … what I am, who I was even, I have a hard time telling him … even though, personally, I do not think of my life as misshapen.

But you did, obviously, tell him, I said.

I didn't have any choice.

What happened?

That blank attitude again.

I'm sorry … it's none of my business.

No. I was just thinking. After he left that night, he forgot his sweater. It had a hole in it, and I darned it. I'm so fuckin' pathetic. She turned her face away.

After awhile I said:

Are you still going to see each other?

I doubt it. I would like to. But I think he just wants to forget me.

I don't believe that, I said.

If he would start behaving decently … She said it to herself. Then to me, We're at … variance. He made a bloody hash of it.

He told me once that he was in love with you. It is not something he says lightly.

I don't know how much love he has in him, she said. I don't think he has any extra.

It's always there … sometimes we just don't attend to it.

Do people, she asked, often talk to you like this?

More than I like, I thought.

I feel like I'm blatherin' on about myself, and I don't do that. I don't even think about myself.

We sat there.

The bar had gotten busy. A girl asked if she could take one of the chairs at our table.

Where are you from in Scotland? I said finally, just to say something.

From a wee border town called Galashiels.

You ever go back?

Not since I got these, she said and cupped her breasts with her hands.

It's just one of those towns up there … been in gentle decline since the woolen mills collapsed. Everyone scratchin' to make a living. Go to a pub, get trashed … dance Strip the Willow … there's naught else to do. They're all crazy about football. I couldn't wait to leave. I'd drive my parents' truck down country roads, drive fast as it would go. If you're from there, you're in a hurry to get somewhere else. I waited till I was 17 and ran off to London. I was nearly mad by then.

Strip the Willow?

Aye. There's a bunch of you on the dance floor an' you get to swingin' each other 'roond and start crashin' into one another. It's a lot of fun. It suits the Scottish way … I fancy some good food sometimes, though … some lashings of cabbage and mashed potatoes, smother it in onion gravy, she said. Venison sausage with red currant gravy. Some good oatcakes. Pickled red cabbage. Any of that. She laughed. I think I'm hungry.

I drank with some Scottish soldiers once, I said. A long time ago now, down in Belize, in Central America. Your particular brand of

English, something about it … seems the prettiest spoken I think. It's a sweet accent. But those boys, I couldn't understand a word they said.

A friend sent me to elocution class for awhile, she said. You don't ever get rid of the burr exactly, and why would you want to really … then I was in London seven years. Thrown in with the blokes and the punters. I got to talkin' like them some. Before all that, I probably talked like your soldiers.

I felt like I wanted to tell her things. She had that sort of presence, those kind eyes. Tell her things I had forgotten, perhaps didn't know to begin with. I wanted to ask her things, too. I had many questions but held them. When she saw me staring at her, she looked to her left at the empty chair like that's where all the answers lay.

She stood to leave.

Do you come here often? she said.

What day is this?

Thursday.

I drink here on Thursdays I guess.

She smiled.

Maybe I'll see you here then.

I would like that, I said.

She walked away. And every pair of eyes watched her go.

There was an old man hunched over the bar, pouched under the eyes, wizened, white hair, black beret. He was drinking beside a grown boy, not 20, say, his grandson maybe, some look familiar to them both. As Darlen passed by, the old man winked at the boy, smiled. I took it he was recalling the great gift of youth, how it is but a nick in time, something his grandson would not know yet. The young man smiled, too, and told the bartender he wanted whiskey now instead of wine.

27 March Monday

Pedro Almodóvar won an Oscar last night for the best foreign language film, *All About My Mother*, and had to be dragged from the stage by co-presenter, Antonio Banderas, when his speech rambled on too long.

28-29 March

I walked these days away. It seemed like I had somewhere I wanted to go, but I never came across it. When I came home Tuesday night, Megan was frying slices of garlic pork loin for supper and suddenly Grandma Tillie's kitchen returned after all these years, that fried ham she favored and which I couldn't get enough of when I was little.

Some things my grandmother told me long ago: Two young Gatins brothers left northern Alabama in 1913. Their father was a railroad man, he and his several cousins local hellions and Saturday night roadhouse warriors. But the railroad held no romance for his sons, the town no prospects and, by their account, the only decent looking girl around happened to be their own sister, Faynell, and she wasn't exactly a beauty. The brothers went to New Orleans first. One, Elton, never left that city. He wanted to be a riverboat captain. That never happened, but he did well there as a finish carpenter. The other, my grandfather, Melrose, stayed with his brother a year, then took a steamboat from New Orleans to Tampa. He wanted to get into citrus. He got work in the shipyards in Tampa instead and made good money there, especially during the war.

One Saturday in 1924 he met Tillie at the South Florida Fair. They met at a hot dog stand on the midway, a fact that forever after amused her in the telling of it. He said his name was Mel and that he was from Scottsboro, Alabama. He chewed tobacco. He kept his conversation to that which was pertinent. He was a short, funny looking man Tillie said, but there was just something about him. And he was definitely a man. She was only 18 at the time.

They took in the Live Stock show. They went on the Ferris wheel. That evening he took her to a café restaurant on 7th Avenue in Ybor City. She didn't go to Tampa often or to café restaurants either. She'd been to visit a girlfriend from San Ann who had moved to the city after high school. Tillie was from the Bramlett family of San Ann, one of the pioneer families to settle the area. They weren't wealthy, didn't have money to speak of, but they were land rich. She invited him home the next weekend, and he fell in love with Florida hill country. He already had it pretty bad for her.

Tillie wasn't crazy about leaving San Ann at any point in her life, and after she and my grandfather married, refused to live in Tampa. They built a little house in San Ann on six acres given to them by her family. This is my house now. My grandfather boarded down in Port Tampa during the week. He had a favorite speakeasy in south Tampa where he ate supper every night, a dollar a dinner, and thought of the fare at Tillie's, of wild hog, palmetto cabbage, pokeberry greens, thought of Tillie's biscuits. She made biscuits every day of her life. And he came home weekends, which wasn't as easy in those days. The roads outside of Tampa then were single-lane, unpaved. He drove a Model T Ford. He loved that car Tillie said. The skinny tires made it hard to get stuck. In cold weather he removed some of the floorboards so that the engine heat would flow inside. The trip home was difficult enough, according to my grandfather, that it took him a pint of sour mash to accomplish it. He was particular about his whiskey and would only purchase that which had been aged six months. It was $4 a gallon in those days. Because he was making good money in the shipyards, this journey went on for those years until his death. Tillie said she was a married woman on the weekends only, but made good of it, speaking of my father and uncle.

On the five acres to the north side of the house, Tillie planted seed oranges. When my grandfather was killed, she bought five acres adjacent to her property with settlement money, along with railroad shares her lawyer advised her to buy and that in time became worthless. She never forgot that. When she had money and opportunity from then on, she'd cuss lawyers and buy land. Tragedy and constant grove work and raising two sons alone made her a hard woman. There was only one way to do things; there was her way, no divergence tolerated. Even so, I loved her without qualification. I loved her in my bones. When I was little, the skyline was the hem in her dress.

Goya's Head

30 March Thursday

A note on Faynell Gatins. She visited from Alabama once when I was very young. I don't think I'd started kindergarten yet. I knew her as Aunt Toddy. She made hers with Scotch. She'd let me help. Squeeze a lemon wedge, lick the honey spoon. She lived to be 103. She outlasted her brothers, husband, two of her children and most everyone she knew. She wore very dark glasses, both outside and in. She wore them to the table when we ate, which I thought was extremely cool.

Rain today. I take the metro to Sol to get a paper in the morning. In Plaza Mayor I see one lone crane fly north to south high overhead. I take a nap in the early afternoon. I woke from that to the slightly rank odor that signifies lunch in Madrid. I went for a walk in the rain. On the way out I checked the mail, a letter from Wolf, some photos I take it: Handle With Care written on it. I stuck it in my pocket. Then walked and walked in the cold drizzle.

The next time I noticed, I was in the Malasaña district, not far from our old neighborhood, on Calle Cisnernos, a classic Madrid street, all the store fronts in shellacked brown or red or dark green. Just off Cisnernos at Calle De Albuquerque No. 13, I stopped at the little bar that I like called Oldenburg. I remember the last time I turned at this corner was after a snowstorm, and a blind dwarf stood there selling lotto tickets with snow on her shoulders.

There are only seven seats in the cerveceria. The owner calls it a museum to beer and has 150 varieties in stock. I had a Stella Artois and after that a Leffe Negra, both from Belgium. A big plate of good chips for tapas on the first round, and on the second, pistachios.

I've got some of Shaloo's money in my pocket. I gave a thousand of that to Megan and kept the rest. After Oldenburg I went to Mesón do Anxo and had costillas a la brasa, good ribs. Also a bottle of Ribera del Duero—Fuentespiña. The wine cost 1800 pesetas, but the food was next to nothing. And the wine was very good and the food also.

I'm feeling much better now. It's a hike to the metro station from here, but I walk along in fine spirits. I stop at pastry shops along the way and look in the windows. I like the way they smell. I stop at a butchershop window. There's a pig head in it wearing dark glasses. Turning away from this, I encounter two of Goya's models from his black period walking arm and arm.

From the metro station at Lavapiés I walk up Ave María to Bodegas Alfara. Darlen is sitting at a table alone. She's eating cuajada, a kind of thick yogurt, a bottle of water half full on the table. She's wearing a light brown peasant dress, denim jacket, black and silver-eyed Doc Martins.

Gritty weather, she said.

I order a glass of wine.

What's new?

I called my mum last night, she said. She answers the phone very proper, but when I say my name she slips into dialect. How ur ye, son? How's it gawn wi' ye? It's miserable here the noo. Bliddy ran an' sleet. An' no even a guid summer tae look furrit tae. The last two years, we've hud nae summer really. But whit can ye dae? Ye hiv tae pee wi' the cock yer given, as ma faither used tae say.

As she's talking, I picture her in the gloomy hall of our cottage back home. Soon she's discussin' the Scottish parliament. Scottish politicians. They don't have a clue, she says. They're a crowd o' left-fitters, Celtic supporters. Aye, they're a' Cath'lics. Let me see whit else. I wis at a Burns' Supper awhile back.

Scots argue on just about everything, Darlen said, but they all agree that whiskey is good, the English are shite, and Robert Burns was a genius. Every year, in January, we celebrate his birthday with a Burns' Supper, eat a meal of mashed potatoes, mashed turnips, and roasted haggis.

What is that? I said.

Haggis? You take a sheep's stomach and fill it with a disgustin' mixture of ground mutton, blood and suet. It's this sort of round, blood pudding. At a Burns' Supper, to begin the meal, the guest of honor addresses the haggis, reciting a poem by Burns that praises the qualities of it—which, to my way of thinkin', isn't the best eatin'

Goya's Head

unless you get it at one of the chip shops, where they deep fry it.

Then mum works her way through all the relatives, all the latest on marriages, illnesses, careers, births and deaths. On my nephew Alan: He's got a terrible temper, that yin. He's three now, Darlen said. I've not yet ever seen him. Of his father's new job, my brother Angus, she says, He's got him a jammy number now. No work, just gives orders like a big shot. Kevin Costner is on the telly in some movie, she says. I'm well annoyed. E's on the golf course at St. Andrews, dressed in all this St. Andrews woolen mill clobber. It's pear-fict shite. Well, ah've goat to clean the hoose. That's a' ma news, cheerio, and hangs up without further ado. She's really gone quite funny the older she's gotten. My dad's been gone now a decade and no more emotional stoning from him, and it's done her a world of good.

I discover the letter in my pocket and open it. Wolf was over to Mom's house, some two weeks back, he writes in a note. Some photos included. Three of them of Mom and Wolf sitting at the picnic table in her backyard. There's a little cypress pond swamp behind her house. There are prothonotary warblers around her pond. I've sat at this table many times listening to their song. Wolf is wearing leathers, a copper bracelet on one wrist he claims keeps away arthritis. Mom is in a blue housedress. She seems to be looking at Wolf, but because of the nature of her blindness is actually eyeing the camera. No clue as to who took the pictures. There's a bottle of Bombay gin setting between them, two glasses on the table, the swamp in the background, live oak, cypress, pignut hickory, sweet gum, cabbage palm. Her big, light purple azalea bushes are blooming.

Can I see? Darlen said.

I tell her who's in the pictures.

He's a biker? she says of Wolf.

Yes.

Is he your mum's boyfriend?

No. More like an old son. He works heavy equipment. He's a crane operator. It's good money. He only works in the winters now. In the summer he rides cross-country, out to California, up into

Canada …

What's your mum's name?

Adelle.

I'm trying to figure out how old she is.

Not as old as she looks, I said. In the photos, my mother looks like she's just in from hell.

She lives alone?

She has a deer for a pet.

Really?

The deer's more of an acquaintance. But she's not around. She can smell Wolf's dogs on him, and she doesn't like dogs. She's layin' low somewhere.

What are those white things on the table?

Marshmallows. There's a young gator lives in the pond. It's about four feet long now. She feeds it marshmallows. Gators love marshmallows. I'm not sure why.

What's this? she said. She was pointing to the moss hanging from the live oak. I can see catkins have formed on the oak, some new leaves greening out. This particular tree is probably two hundred years old.

It's called Spanish moss, I said.

It's like long gray beards. Does it take root on the tree?

I don't believe it has any roots. It just sort of drapes itself around the branches.

It doesn't hurt the tree?

I don't think it makes that much of an impression on it.

That is truly curious, she said.

In the old days, I said, they'd use it to stuff mattresses. I've seen a horse blanket wove of it, though I can't imagine how you'd go about doing that.

She seemed fascinated by this thing I'd been around all my life and never thought too much on.

We watched some people leaving the bar. Then she said:

Che dropped by late one night. Monday, I think. He's perfectin' the art of passing out. He was rattling on about nothing in particular, all dross far as I could tell, and when he stopped I looked over at him and he was sleeping. I just left him there on the couch and went to bed. I woke up once in the night, and he was gone. I didn't know what to make of that visit. I reckon I'll just keep my chin up and not worry on it. I don't want to get all cross. An' really, I feel alone again.

I was not looking for a lover, she went on, just a mate. He never got on to that. I guess I nicked his heart, but it was not my intention.

I asked her after awhile:

You'll have to excuse my curiosity, but … how did you ever get started on—

This odd life of mine?

Yes.

There was a tailor in our village. He gave me a job when I was 14, cleaning up his shop on Saturday mornings. He would teach me the trade, he said, if I was interested. I always had this great ass. It's why he hired me, far as I could figure out. It was the only thing I had to offer. And he was after it, I knew. A year earlier, in the summer, a tinker boy'd come across me down at the swimming hole on our farm. He sat down by my clothes till I came out. And then he took me.

But I liked it all right. I agreed to meet him there the next day. She laughed. What a slut, she said. He brought his brother along that time. Said it was his brother. Who knows? A gypsy'll lie to you as well as not. Then his whole bunch hit the road soon after. But the tailor, like I say, I knew what he wanted soon enough.

He'd have me try on things. He'd hem them, see how they looked. He liked to measure me. My hips especially. He wanted to get me used to his hands on my body. Then one morning he had me try on a kilt, and I showed him my backside a bit too long …

I think I could go for a drink, she said.

I ordered a bottle of the house wine, and she went on.

He had his own way of doin' things. I had to let my hair grow long. He wasn't interested in nothing but my cunt, as he called it.

He'd have me go to the loo and masturbate before he'd take me. There was an upstairs flat to his shop. He kept it empty … used it if visitors or family came from out of town.

We settled into a routine. Work in the early morning. He'd have me try on items. He'd alter them. Then I'd model them. Mostly kilts. They were his speciality. Those he made for me after awhile got to be more like mini-skirts. He bought me high heels whenever he went to Glasgow. At noon we'd head upstairs, and I'd be his young girlfriend for an hour or so. Then he'd go home to his wife and kids.

The waiter brought the wine, and I poured us each a glass.

I guess I fell in love with him, she said. He was young. He was only ten years older than me. He wasn't from our town. I think they'd run him out of where he came from.

At some point he started rubbing me down with lavendar oil. He had me take it home and do the same there, and in time my breasts enlarged. They weren't much to speak of, but he was right proud of them. He started taking photographs of me early on. After he'd broke me in good, one Saturday in the spring he invited a young farmer to the shop. He was from the next village over and had a notoriety 'round abouts. He was nicknamed Pony. The tailor took a photo that morning you can still buy in Amsterdam. It's famous, I guess, among the sick fucks. It's considered a classic.

I'm sittin' on Pony's lap facing the camera, on this huge cock of his that won't fit in. I'm wearing stilleto heels and a stocking cap, and I have this goofy wee grin on my face … the tailor'd given me drugs for the first time.

I stayed with him three years. When I left I had a trade. I could make money. It didn't have a thing to do with clothes, other'n how to take them off.

She got a call on her phone then. She talked in Spanish, her voice gone flat.

My landlady, she explained. I have to go see her.

Trouble?

I don't know. She's too hard to keep up with over the phone. She put pesetas on the table for her part of the bill.

I'll be here next Thursday if you will, she said. At half 3, say.

I'll be here, I said.

There is an ease between us. She smiled. I like that. Then she turned and was gone. That smile of hers, I'll tell you, it can lock you up.

I sat there alone and finished the bottle of wine. The rain, which had not fully stopped all day, picked up. They don't much play music in the bars here. There's no jukeboxes or anything like that. Normally you couldn't hear it anyway with the Madrileños talking loud as all get out the way they do. But the bar was nearly empty, and a waiter listened to the radio, some nice jazz playing. I notice there are three bar taps, all the same brand of beer—Mahou. I had a glass of that. Thunder was popping like anti-aircraft fire over the city. I walked home with my hands stuffed deep in my pockets and pictures in my head.

Saturday night Wolf called. He'd been to visit my mother again. He hadn't liked what he'd seen. Hadn't liked it for awhile, and now it was time to speak.

The place is filthy, Luke, he said, an' she don't know it. She can't see it that well. I got the number of that gal helps her out and gave her a call. She says your mom is miffed at her, and she feels likewise. I don't know what the hell that's all about. Adelle was drunk, empty gin bottles settin' around, and that doe friend of hers has all but moved into the house. She talks to that thing like maybe she hears it talkin' back. The deer smelled the dogs on me and wasn't pleased. Like I give a shit, but … anyway … things aren't good there. She got plastic roses from somebody and went on and on like they was real. How long they'd gone without wilting. Then she puts her hand to sort of the top part of her head on the left side there and says, I can't exactly feel my head right here no more. It is just gone dull.

That don't sound good, I said.

That's what I told her. An' the last two times I've gone over, there's been a crow on the roof.

A crow?

Yeah. Settin' there in the same spot, on the left-hand corner at the front of the house. It just studies me when I come to the door. A bad sign to my way of lookin'. Like the old poem by that drunk. Nevermore, and all that bullshit.

That was a raven.

Same difference, he said.

Wolf has known Mom a long time now. She took to him years ago as a second son. They got on well together from the start. It began I think having to do with Wolf's extreme politeness. He looks like an El Greco in biker boots and old blue jeans and leather vest, but he's a gentleman beneath it all, has a down-home courtliness. They both believe in Southern, small town manners and considerations. And as different as they seem outwardly, both he and my mother are simple in their rules and their philosophy, and therefore consistent. They came to find that out about each other without much delay.

After awhile I asked him about my dogs, Buddy and Maud. I haven't spoken much of them as it pains me to be away from them. Buddy is a Catahoula and Maud a pitbull mix.

They're fine, Wolf said. Maud's a sweetheart, and she's all grown up now. Buddy, he's just Buddy. You ever notice the only time he wags his tail is when he's contemplating mischief?

I've noticed that, I said.

He'll run off on you still. Come back in a couple days, all rolled in cow shit or roadkill. Now I see there's some puppies 'round the neighborhood look a whole lot like him. But, he said, forget the fucking dogs. You need to start worryin' about Adelle now. She's in trouble.

The next day I called her several times but got no answer. And that was okay by me. I've got to be the right kind of drunk to talk to her. I send her postcards, say little and write big on them, no more than a sentence usually, but I call infrequently. Often when I do, I don't know what to say. She's been crazy a long while now. When my father died, a good part of her held his hand and went off with him.

Megan got through later. Mom told her that Wolf's heart is in the right place, but that he's wrong about her. She's doing fine, she said, though Megan noted it was 10 a.m. central Florida time, and she was obviously loaded.

We started thinking in earnest about going home.

I spent a good part of Monday and Tuesday walking, at least three hours each day. I saw things taking place on the margins but couldn't focus on them. Looked over my shoulder at things that didn't fully register. That these things were perhaps my time here passing I found momentarily troubling, but then forgot about that, too. The weather changed from one block to the next. I had a sense that the streets of Madrid equated to the wilderness. Several times I ended up in the slaglands. I never find these when life is sane. My ears seem to have wax in them, the sound there like listening to the gulf in a shell—or maybe it's just the bloodsong. Oftentimes I only feel right when I'm walking. It is a kind of solitude and a way of working things out minus words. I walk and my mind wanders off.

I'd stop at little castizo bars and have a chato and then go on. Tuesday late afternoon on my way home I encountered a panhandler on Calle Argumosa and gave him some coins. Here, I said, sure. Why not, and emptied my pockets. He said to me in perfect English, I also accept illegal substances. I felt like talking by that point and started doing just that, but it turned out that sentence was the only English he knew.

Wednesday morning I was walking to the Corte Inglés at Sol to get wine and groceries. Up on the first corner, across from the flamenco bar, I noticed a young black girl sitting on a stoop. Something about her hit me wrong. Just that little subliminal jolt you get when Death is on the street. She was very thin, face sunken in. Banjo eyes. Her hair long and braided. She looked my way a moment, then went on the nod. I didn't think too much about it; you see that a lot, and

I walked on. By the time I returned to that spot on my way back, she was dead on the sidewalk. There were two cops standing by her, just looking at her, a couple neighbors gawking. The cops were waiting for an ambulance to come pick her up. You could hear the ambulance up on Magdalena, its weeAHH weeAHH klaxon getting closer. Then it shot by, missed Olivar. It would have to wend its way back around. That could take awhile, and I went on home. She was probably good looking once, couldn't have been more than 18, maybe not even that, but now her face was gray, her lips blue.

6 April Thursday

Darlen was standing outside the bar talking on her phone. It's a cool day. She's wearing black sweatpants and running shoes, a light gray sweatshirt with a hood, and a black leather jacket over this. She has the hood on her head and dark glasses with black frames and her hair has been dyed black. There's a newspaper folded, tucked under her arm. I'm sitting at a table looking at her. I'd walked right past her upon entering the bar and hadn't recognized her.

She sat down at the table, laid the Spanish newspaper on it, *El Pais*. An ETA headline.

You're in disguise today, I said.

I like to change up my appearance now and then. I'm in to theater.

Who were you talking to? I asked. I wasn't sure why I said that. It just came out.

You're too curious, she said.

I thought, Because you're a mystery to me.

It was Iker's sister. His family's from Durango.

Good news?

Hardly. They don't yet know where he is. They're thinking North Africa, Ceuta, maybe, but they're just on to that because it's as far away as they can think. The government doesn't make it easy to see them. They've even got them at a place called Salto del Negro in the Canaries. Those prisoners are 4000 kilometers from their homes. She started crying a little, not much, but I noticed.

What? I said.

I hate to think about it. I have this fear there's no air for him to breathe. Hate to think about him getting kicked in the balls. He's hurtin' … I can feel it.

She said it like—*hartin'*.

I understand the prison guards here are nearly human now, I said.

I'm sure they're doing a sterling job, she said.

We'd been planning a trip to Florida, she said. Did I tell you that already?

No.

Iker has a friend in Miami, a jai alai player. Ugarte. Do you know of him?

No.

What's Miami like?

I don't like to drive in that town. I tend to get lost. Tall hotels and condos on the beaches. The beaches are really something, though. A lot of Cubans. You hear Spanish more often than English. It's sort of like being in a foreign country. Those young Cuban girls, now, they'll turn your head.

She smiled.

Iker believes in what they believe, she was saying a bit later, but he's not violent. When he was younger, he wanted to become a priest. That is not unusual for Basque kids. But he was so good at tinkerin' with cars and motor bikes … anything that runs on petrol. He loves speed. He drives fast, even around the city. Out on the highway it's stone mad to ride with him. He does everything like that, somethin' headlong about him, and wild.

I had some puppies once, she said. There was one, when it came time to wean, couldn't make the switch to solid food. She wanted tit. She was completely happy up till then, happy with her pack, her brothers and her mum and father. She had wild blood. The wolf gene. She didn't want a thing to do with me or with other humans. When one of her family groomed her, she was in ecstasy. I even tried to force-feed her, but it made her sick and she just kept gettin' skinnier. It was heartbreaking. I thought after awhile that she wanted fresh kill. Only that would do. Then I found the puppies one morning all huddled together how they slept, and she was dead. But I believe she died happy just bein' with them like that. Iker is that way. He loves his home, his mum, his hills, and the fog on the hills, and his mates … there's a deepness to it that nothing can dent.

What's he look like? I said.

She grinned.

Like a farmer, she said. He's short. Big shoulders. Muscular. His nose is kind of long. He has a substantial kit, too, if you get what I mean.

I rolled my head on my shoulders.

Quite a tadger on him, she said.

I get it, I said. Now stop, please, before I get ill.

Very black hair he combs straight back. Always wears a boina, tilted back like a tough. He's got a bad scar on his forearm where a horse bit him.

How'd he get in trouble?

He stole cars.

She lit a cigarette.

He had a shop down in Vallecas, she said. They do anything here, they use two cars. They use the first one in the operation, drive off a ways, then blow it up as a distraction. Take the second to get away. So they need cars and need them operatin' well.

The Guardia Civil, she went on, backtracked one of the cars to his shop. I don't know how that happened exactly. When they raided the shop, in the boot of a lorry … they found it rigged.

She was staring at me.

You have the same eyes as him, that brown-black.

She called out for more beer.

After our drinks came she said, Che told me that you and Megan are what is known as kissin' cousins.

He says a lot of things.

I like that term. Do you make love with her?

Talk about curiosity, I said.

No, she said. I have told you things and not held back. Now it's your turn.

We're trying not to, is how I'd put it.

Why is that?

You'd have to know her. She's a beauty … in every way. She deserves better than me. I wanted her to look around.

So it's your decision, she said.

Mostly.

But you're still together … I take it that she loves ye.

Yes.

An' it's not something she can be talked out of.

It don't seem like.

I'm envious, she said. That's everything to me. To love and be loved. All the rest is chaff.

You lose your fella, she went on, you feel vulnerable. You hurt. You hurt right in half.

Are you still connected to them?

The Organization? If you don't speak Euskera, you're nothing to them. Iker was not really one of them either. There are few combatants, maybe 75, or less. But there are many sympathizers. He was not a gunman. He helped them. They use up people like him.

It seems to me they're carrying on a war that's over, I said. Or ought to be.

Just so, she said.

It was said so coldly I could feel her receding into the distance. Then she came back.

The Basques fought the Romans, she said. They've been at it awhile. The enemy changes. The Basque never change. She thought for a moment, said, They're a curious lot. Sometimes it's almost gentlemanly how they handle a bombing. Unless they're after Guardia Civil or army or prison personnel, if they're going to hit a civilian area, they'll phone in ahead of time, and give warning so it can be evacuated.

After awhile she said:

I think I've found a way to help him. I'll know more next week.

How so?

There's a politician in Durango. He and Iker's sister are close. He may be able to make it easier on Iker at least, but I've got to do something for him. An' if I decide to do that, it'll be my ass on the line then. I'll need to leave the country, if I can get out in time.

He's of their political arm?

No. I don't think he likes them at all. But he's sympathetic to Iker's sister, though, and to the family.

What is it you'll have to do?

I shan't be tellin' you that. When it happens, you'll know.

I went to the Prado Saturday and Sunday. It's free on Sunday afternoons, though it doesn't cost much to begin with, 350 pesetas. I stand before Goya's paintings. I study them. But it's something more about him, too. There are those who are so much themselves, they make it easier for you to become who you are.

There was an original copy of *Los Caprichos* on display, eighty engravings. While Goya painted the frescos at the chapel of San Antonio in 1798, he was at the same time preparing the copperplates for these etchings. They were published the next year. In 1803 Goya gave the etched plates and 240 sets of the edition to the crown. He hadn't been able to sell them. In exchange, his son Javier was granted a yearly annuity.

Plate 19 caught my eye, Todos caerán. Everyone Will Fall. He's referring to love I'd think. I found of interest there two birds sitting beside each other in a tree, one with the face of the Duchess of Alba, the other of Goya. The Goya bird has its wings spread, in triumph perhaps. There are unspeakable things going on below them on the ground. They are not looking that way.

In these 1st edition prints, details are striking. Goya's method of using aquatint in tandem with line etching produced an effect like watercolor wash. He was the only one in the world using this technique at the time. He would continue experimenting even as an old man. In his art, he did not like to repeat himself. You have to wonder if the tendency had to do with his deafness. How many times in his life must he have said—Say that again. Difficult for a proud man. Say it slow so that I can read your lips.

In exile in Bordeaux he took up lithography, a technique invented at the turn of that century. His five Bulls of Bordeaux lithographs had to be created with the use of a magnifying glass, as his eyesight was failing. A small edition of 100 sets was offered for sale. They were too brutal for the French. The prints did not sell. He painted miniatures on ivory there as well. The ivory plaques he used were two to three inches square. He used the very tip of his brush. I have not seen the originals of these. In reproduction, they could be full-sized paintings. They are rendered with no sense of minuteness, no loss of detail.

When Goya left Spain for exile in France, he took a room in Paris for awhile before moving on to Bordeaux. He just wanted to explore this city he'd heard so much about. The French police kept an eye on him but soon found it tiresome. They recorded in their log that Goya at age 78 'seems older than he is …' There was at this time in Paris a young painter named Delacroix who had recently obtained copies of the Caprichos and was studying them in wonder. But there was no way for him to know that Goya was in the city just then, and no record of them meeting.

13 April Thursday

She wore long white linen pants that were absolutely see-through. They're like onion skin. Under that a lavendar thong. I notice what appears to be a tattoo of a butterfly on one cheek. A very soft looking and loose fitting blue cotton corduroy shirt. Two heart-shaped jet earrings. Alpargatas, the white canvas-and-rope shoes of the Basques. She's brought some food with her in a brown paper bag, pimientos padrones, and goes to get a plate from the waiter and comes back to the table with it and two glasses and a bottle of albariño.

Is that tattoo a butterfly? I said, pointing.

She turned her ass toward me and looked down at herself.

It's a brand. I got it in Amsterdam. She slapped herself on the ass. Hard to resist, don't you think?

I would say all but impossible.

Che said it's too big.

It's hard, I said … hard to say. I'll give it some thought and get back to you.

Do I look like a slattern today? she asked. I was going for the classy slattern look.

Damn close, I said.

She looked herself over.

Ah well, she said, it's better than havin' to wear a chunky sheepskin all winter like at home.

She sat down.

I like that color, I said of her shirt.

It's called French blue. I've got another one just like it in a green. Teal, I think. Good lord … teal. No wonder people beat us up. But, I looked a bit like a fancy duck in that.

She divided the peppers between us. These are one of my favorites, stir-fried in olive oil, with a good taste, mildly hot for the most part, though now and again, and you never know when, you're liable to get one that is nuclear. I tend to take a little taste of each one before I get at it.

Have you seen Chelo? I said.

He stopped by one night. He's not in good repair. Tatty, I would say. He was so full of brass when I first met him, goin' about his dubious affairs like a dogfox. Always harmless, though. He's more inclined to hurt his own prospects than harm anyone else I think. He did bring good hash with him. Perhaps he'd like his troubles to go up in smoke. Then my landlady came by and wouldn't leave. She doesn't like anybody, and she didn't like him right off, thought him quite dodgy, and he left. He's looking for work in Japan.

They pay well. An' everybody's drunk on their ass there, which appeals to him. He needs to get out of Madrid. His life … he jus' seems to be waiting it out here.

A part of me goes down with him, I said.

Aye. It's dismayin'. She went on: I told him not to come back, she said. It's for the best … for him, I mean.

How'd he handle that? It was me, I don't guess I'd take kindly to it.

Not well, she said. That kind of bleak mystery he's become washed over him again. He actually gave me the finger, which … I don't know. It struck me as funny, though I didn't laugh.

She had started talking flatly just then, wasn't quite there.

I went to see you work, I said.

She opened her eyes wide.

Kevin, too. It was a while back. We went to Truck.

A lopsided grin. It's quite a place, eh? Tawdry or … colorful. It's a point of view thing. I haven't been there for some time. I'm working for an escort service. Or I was.

How'd that go?

Profitably. My clientele quite rich, and generous.

What're they like?

They're pigs. She laughed. Most of them are from out of country. They're here on business. Usually older types. It sorts out some different than what you'd imagine. They don't demand much. They want companionship … and to have beauty hanging on their every word. An' maybe a handjob in the backseat of a taxi.

Did you notice anything about my eyes today, she asked.

I hadn't. There are other things to look at when she's around. But I saw now they were no longer the color of wisteria.

They're gray, I said.

It's their true color.

Sometimes, I said, I think about you, about us maybe … it's not gonna happen, but … it enters my mind. I don't believe it's possible to be around you and not have such thoughts.

I'm not the sort of chap who'd think about that until it happened, she said. But I believe most would have a go, wouldn't they?

That's the problem, I said. You are a chap … though every sense I own tells me different.

She smiled, mirth in her eyes, and something else, and I knew suddenly that things were infused with a burning caused by the way she looked at me. I knew something was very different, and it had changed from one moment to the next—and that, otherwise, I did not know very much at all. To punctuate the feeling, I just then bit into an extremely hot pepper and swallowed most of it before I had time to think what I'd just done. I sat there sputtering, making faces, my eyes watering. I downed a glass of wine quickly and then drank out of the bottle and finally my breath caught again.

She watched me, bemused.

I shouldn't have done that, she said.

What?

I turned up the heat.

I noticed.

Then soon enough I sensed that most of all she wanted to leave, and I didn't want to her to. We had a table close to the front of the bar, and from time to time the sun glanced our way, and her earrings seemed to have a sudden mineral life about them.

I've been studying Goya this past week, I said. He was Basque on his father's side.

I didn't know that, she said.

His tomb is in the San Antonio chapel, down below the rose garden. Only his body is there, I said. He died in France. A souvenir hunter took his head.

A change came over her. She looked at me steadily, her eyes slitted.

Is that what you take me for, Luke? A souvenir hunter.

I'm not sayin' nothing about you. I'm just talkin'—

Aye, but that's what we *do* to one another.

I'm talking about Goya, that's all.

Oh …

But, I said, what I'm thinking is, you're going to leave here today, and I'm never going to see you again. And it troubles me.

Maybe she nodded. If so, it was all but imperceptable.

Is that wrong? I said.

It took her a long time but she finally said, No … I'm sorry, she said. I guess I'm already gone.

This thing you're planning …

She looked away.

Are you okay with it?

I have given myself over to one thing, she said. It's easy now. I just want to get on with it.

Just shortly after this she said very quietly, Do you like it here?

It came out of the blue, but then, she just wanted to change the subject.

I feel pretty far away from where I live, I said. San Ann is different from this, that's for sure.

What's it like?

Down to earth, I said. Red.

Red?

Cracker, I said. An old-time way of lookin' at things. Kinda hardass. Everyone in town is armed and dangerous, but … they're relatives.

Sounds like home, she said.

We sat there for awhile saying nothing. No exact meeting of the eyes. To look at her and be a moment late. She'd just looked away. Then an oblique glance over my shoulder. I turned and looked that way, rows of liquor bottles standing sentry—colors in the gloom.

Then she found me again.

Goya's head is somewhere else, she said. We're like that …

A memory struck her then and animated her.

I'm thinkin' about going to Trujillo for awhile, she said. Down in Extremadura. It's wonderful country there, all cork forests and straw-colored fields. Iker and I went there last September. He had this Brit customer … dropped off his Bentley to get worked on while he went back to London for a visit. We took that … rode in style.

It was our last good time together, before all the trouble started. I've had Trujillo in my mind much lately. My thoughts of it come in brilliant. The old man sweeping up napkins at the churro shop at Plaza Aragón with a broom made of twigs. Or having lunch at

Café Pizzaro. We ordered roast lamb, Bishop's soup, a bottle of Lar de Lares. And of afterwards, when we walked to the top of town—Trujillo is just this big hill out in nowhere—and picked up black figs from the road and ate them, figs and pomegranites bursting on the trees along side us.

There's a little castle at the top. It's a thousand years old. It's like looking over a ledge up there, and all of old Spain spread out on a table below you. And way down below us the swollen udders of the goats in an olive grove. Always fruit in these thoughts and the fullness of the time.

We saw this little nun walkin' the hill on the arm of a boy. He was six, seven years old, and they were both about the same height. She took notice of a peach tree in a yard, the branches hanging over the sidewalk and loaded down. She said somethin' to the boy, and he jumped and grabbed a branch and shook it, and ripe peaches fell to the ground. The old nun got a laugh out of it. She was so ancient, I think she was probably getting smaller each passin' year. An' it was lovely to see her laugh like that.

Our last day in Trujillo was a Friday. At noon we were sitting at Bar La Victoria at the Plaza Mayor having coffee and looking at the fine statue of Pizzaro there. The town had a one time building boom when he and his men came back with their gold. Sittin' there with the September sun on my face coming down through the leaves of an orange tree that had blue morning glories on it. The old men at the next table playing dominoes. And me with a red stone in my pocket shaped like a heart I'd picked up an hour earlier from the grounds of the castle. I thought just then … If I could, I would never leave here.

She looked at me closely.

Sometimes, she said, you get things you don't expect. I'm glad I met you, Luke. She reached her hand across the table and briefly touched mine.

Right, there we are then, she said.

She looked toward the street.

I have to make some money, she said. I'm damn near skint.

She got up, stopped and looked at me as if to say one last thing, then didn't say it but continued on to the sidewalk in front of the bar where she confronted the first decent looking prospect to come along and, in her Spanish slang, speaking as she always did with unaffected simplicity, asked if he wanted a blow job. The man's eyes wandered over her and were slow to leave. They made some arrangement and then walked off together. She did not look back.

I noticed that, momentarily, the bar went quiet, the street also. For the most part, the Spanish only stop talking from sheer exhaustion. I looked around. No one spoke. Nothing moved. It was like the place had gone inanimate. I heard the chirl of pigeons outside. I heard someone out of sight whistling. I smelled gasoline ... beer swill. And her perfume, still settled in her absence, the raw smell of German iris. Then the mechanical howling of the traffic returned, and it all started up again, everywhere, clamorous.

April 14 Friday

I walked north of Sol and stopped at a little second floor gallery called Museo de la Real Academia de Bellas Artes. Displayed there is Goya's Self-portrait in the Studio. It was painted in 1794-95. In it, Goya is standing before a tall easel, brush in one hand, a circular paint pallete in the other, diffused light pouring through the windows behind him. He is wearing a pot hat, a sort of squat top hat, with small candles attached to the brim. He is dressed in a bullfigher's jacket, embroidered, red-braided. Tight breeches. His hair is shoulder length. He's looking slightly to the left, at you, as if you were the subject of his painting. His face a bulldog's mug.

16 April Sunday

Goya died on this date in 1828 in Bordeaux. He was 82, for that era, a very old age. One of the late drawings, done in his funny pages style, is of an antique man walking with the aid of two canes. The title reads: Aun aprendo. I am still learning.

Just to reference a time frame, it was just about then that the first orange groves were planted in Florida along the Indian River.

That night, after Megan and I had dinner, we watched a Spanish movie she'd taped, *Vacas*, which means cows. It's a Julio Medem film set in Guipuzcoa, one of the three Basque provinces in Spain, from 1875, during the 3rd Carlist war, on to the start of the Civil War in 1936. It portrays the lingering animosity between rival families, three generations of them, who live next to each other on farms in the hills. The men of the families are aizcorlari, competition log cutters. It's about family ties and neighbors feuding and also falling in love. It's concerned with history repeating itself, both in family and country, and also how the Spanish are so adept at murdering one another. The film stars a young Emma Suarez, worth the price of admission in itself, Carmelo Gómez and Ana Torrent. The wars, petty rivalries, incest and madness depicted take place in an idyllic setting—the Basque farmland, their forests, houses, haystack, scarecrow—the countryside of dream. The cows watch over all this with dispassionate eyes. They are symbolic, obviously, but my mind simply scatters when I try to pin down what that's all about.

We'd seen the movie several times. I didn't yet know exactly what the characters were saying, but the imagery carries it. It could be a silent movie; it wouldn't matter.

It's a fine movie; however, I fell asleep during it—soon after Carmelo Gómez made love with Ana Torrent, who plays the sister of the neighbor that hated him. He laid down on her in the woods and bleated like a goat. When I woke, Megan had already gone to bed.

I went for a walk. It was after 10, a pleasant evening, the sidewalks thronged and alive with spring in this nocturnal city.

That I wouldn't see Darlen again stuck in my craw. I had money in my pocket I wanted to give her, $500 left over from Shaloo's bet. Maybe she'd be home, maybe not. I had written down my cousin Pogey's address and phone number in Grand Isle and in a short note explained that if she made it to the States, he could help her set up in New Orleans. It would be a good place for her, better than most. Besides that, I was not clear on what I was doing. It's been a complicated balance all along between good intentions and desire. So far, I'd done the best I could with that.

Another tenant was leaving the building, and I caught the door and went in. I walked up the footworn steps. A slight dislocation of time there. History jostling for purchase. I knocked on that solid, archaic door, like one borrowed from a fairy tale, and a crone opened it wide as the latch chain allowed and eyed me malevolently. A rough looking old housewife, ash-colored hair pulled back, dressed in black. A presence from another age, one of Madrid's añejas, the severe, tightlipped face you might see in a photogravure. I was not expecting this and stood mute. She started speaking in a language strange to me—biting, fractured syllables.

Darlen, I said finally.

No aquí, she said, and closed the door.

I looked at the huge lock on the door.

It must take quite a large key to open that, I said. Maybe the giant's got it. I'd put salt over this doorway I thought to myself. Can I borrow your broomstick? I said. I know you're immortal, but some of us have time on our hands. We're in a hurry, say …

On the way out, I dropped the note with Pogey's address and phone number in Darlen's mailbox. I kept the money.

I walked west along Magdalena toward downtown. A block along this route, there's a tall white plywood construction wall you walk beside, the white now all but obliterated by graffiti—the building has been under reconstruction forever—where, because of how the street lights shone, your shadow walked long and thin in front of you. Most nights your shadow broke in two at a certain point as it was thrown against the wall. This time my shadow split into three and walked ahead of me in black triplicate.

I have taken to going down to Café Barbieri in the late afternoons, sitting by one of the windows, drink a few stout, watch the rain, the ghost sky. I can recall only two full days of sun since my birthday.

I feel slightly pissed off for no particular reason, not something you can get ahold of anyway. Perhaps the last remnants of mental health slipping gears. Quixote said: A knight-errant who goes mad for a good reason deserves no thanks or gratitude; the whole point consists of going mad without cause.

From the outside you would not know Barbieri is a bar. There is no sign proclaiming it. The place where a sign might be is caved in. The owners simply won't make improvements. But inside it's beautiful in its oldness. The interior is done in brown and yellow, the latter muted by age and smoke. Ornate wainscotting, Belle Epoch style. Brown metal columns holding up the ceiling beams. The bar is 99 years old. It has an odor similar to that of a very old paperback novel, the pages foxed, with spilled beer on a good many of them.

You enter Barbieri's front door, then push through red velvet drapes, 14 foot tall from ceiling to floor. This day I sit at a small table for two along the windows that look out on an alley, the tabletop white marble. Underneath the table is a container for your bags, coat or hat. Outside my window a sign says Travesia de la Primavera. It's a one-way alley that leads out to C/Ave María, a public garage, big sign, GARAJE PÚBLICO, to the back. I'm looking mainly at a building wall, dirty yellow, an industrial view, a small red car parked there, behind it a motorcycle chained, the bike taken as a pissing post by dogs, a white car behind that. There are frosted etchings in Barbieri's window glass, a flower design. Sconce light, a seashell or clam design, behind me. The light doesn't work. Ceiling fans. They don't work either. Out past the mouth of the alley, you can see the top of Plaza Lavapiés, nine small trees, fresno and acacia, the wind tilting the young leaves. Café Babilonya is directly across the street, red french doors of the apartment above it stand out.

Tom Waits is singing on a scratchy radio. There are two drunks to my right, below the giant clock. One carrying on loudly, drinking Johnnie Walker Red straight, a large glass. The other with his hands over his ears. The talker keeps saying Oiga! A favorite Spanish word. It means, Listen up. Hear me out.

Barbieri is known for its inept waiters. One eventually finds me, even though there's hardly anyone else in the place, and I order a beer. Cars pass by in the alley occasionally. A VW convertible goes by with Virginia plates. How'd that get here? A taxi came down the alley, stopped in front of my window awhile, the cabbie doing paperwork.

I go to the bar and order another beer. When I return to the table, the taxi is gone. Some time later the waiter brought my drink and some salty olives. I started sipping the beer. I looked out the window. A man comes up the alley and stops, facing me, to light a cigar. One of those guys parts his hair close above one ear and combs it over the baldness. A gust of wind strikes the alley, and his hair competely flops off his head. It hangs there like a crow's wing. It looks like he's signaling a right turn.

Then I got lost in thought—many things moving in that stream. I woke up from a dream last night laughing out loud. I don't remember one iota of its content. Thought for a moment of hunting next fall. I have a very clear idea that I'll be spending much time in the woods then. Thought of how in his letters Goya rarely spoke of painting, though he'd often brag on what a good shot he was. Thought of the angled sun of a late Florida autumn morning, of sitting quietly in a stand in the Green Swamp. I held that one for awhile.

Two girls walked down the alley just then, one of them pretty, the other not so lucky.

I thought of the last time Megan and I went to the Rastro. She'd stopped to look at some porcelain. But she'd pointed out that it wasn't right—See this maze of tiny lines? It's called crazing. It indicates pottery. Porcelain hardly ever crazes, she'd said. Thought of all the ancestors in my blood. I often listen in on the bone line. Megan is not blood, but she's so down to earth close to my grandmother I never know quite what to make of it. She is a shiny remnant of Tillie somehow. If we have to go home, and it's looking that way to me, change will come. A whole pocketful of it. I can feel its vibration and warning already. But I'll change little, I suspect, and Megan not at all, and maybe that will save us.

I went to take a sip of beer. My only trouble with drink, besides that it costs money, is that the glass tends to go empty so quickly. The waiter was walking past, and I ordered another. I guess he heard me.

At any rate, my mind was back into the here and now, and I looked out the window just as Chelo entered the alley from C/Ave María. He leaned against the red car, took out a phone and punched in a number. He moves closer to the end of the alley and does it again. He's wearing a blue v-neck sweater, black jeans, unbuttoned navy peacoat. By the glint in his eye and his easy manner, I take it he's talking to a woman. He seems happy. He gets done talking and punches off the line, puts the phone in his coat pocket.

I knocked on the window. All of a sudden he was around the corner and gone. I can't be sure that he saw me. He probably didn't. It's not like they wash the windows here.

April 18 Tuesday

I left the apartment early before Megan woke. I stopped at Pastelería Alex at Lavapiés 39 and bought a baguette, walked past the ruins of the church, Escolapios de San Fernando. It was destroyed during the first days of the Civil War, and I've never gotten a clear story on who burned it or bombed it, or why it just sets there now, a ruin in the heart of the city. It started out, in Goya's time, as a school to educate the children of the poor. An intact part of the church still serves as a parochial school. The dog walkers are out now, the delivery men. Aluminum kegs of beer wait outside for the bars to open. A waiter chalks up the daily special on a restaurant window. Women throwing buckets of water on the sidewalks. The neighborhood prostitutes are coming home in taxi cabs. The fellas who sit around the metro entrance with their tall cans of San Miguel look at you and there's nothing behind it, neither malice nor curiosity. It's like their eyes fire blanks. Sleeping among them is a mime in whiteface with a pet rat in a cage by his side. Then I went back home and back to bed and didn't get up until after noon. Megan was gone by then.

Making coffee, I remembered a short dream during that sleep.

In it, Megan said to me, One of the lambs died. I went immediately to the hallway out of her sight and started weeping. It really hit me hard, which, this reaction surprised me even in the dream, as I hadn't known until she spoke of it that we owned any sheep.

I went to get a paper at the kiosk across from Casa Antonio's, the little standup Basque wine bar. I stopped there for a drink. It was not crowded yet. Dos Santos wanted my opinion on a wine. I tried it and found it a bit heavy and ordered a glass of that Cataluña rosado that tastes like cherries. I asked him:

Do you know Iker Carbó?

He seemed surprised.

Sí, claro, he said. Es de Durango. Y tú?

I know his girlfriend.

Ah, he said and smiled and started making shapes with his hands.

Cómo está Iker?

He's in jail, I said.

Por supuesto, he said. Of course. Too bad, he said in English, but … he's a good Basque man. It won't be held against him.

Then things got abrasive on the way home—the push and shove and be loud at it of this jacked-up city. The sidewalk crowd acted like it badly needed a cigarette. Then I caught it, too. I walked along in just barely controlled fury, waiting for the next stupidity to occur, the next angry horn, or someone screaming in my ear. A white delivery van cut too close to me at a corner as I was waiting to cross the street. I stiff-armed the side of it, made quite a racket. Gilipollas! the driver shot back at me. Asshole! Then back at the apartment, I notice there's a dumpster parked in front of our building. Megan had returned from school, and I asked her about it.

That storefront below us …

It'd been vacant since we got here, been that way for years from what I understood.

… they're going to put something in there, she said. Most likely a bar.

Drilling, sledgehammer work is on the way. As for the workers, what I see around the neighborhood is a sense of true ineptness operating, and little urgency. There's some fellas working in the building to the left of ours. They speak a language I'd never heard before; maybe they're East European. There are three of them, rough characters, always arguing and slapping each other on the head. I've begun to think of them as the Three Stooges. Their glory occurred one day early on when they threw large items from the 4th floor balcony into the dumpster below on the street. Toilets, sinks, icebox, couch, large mirrors, you name it. Sometimes they would hit the mark, more often not. Later, one of them spilled a gallon of green paint on the sidewalk. They made no attempt to clean it up. Now there are permanent green footsteps headed in every direction.

I went and stood on the balcony, observing the theatre below. Olivar is a narrow, one-way street, the traffic heading downhill. It's a street that's been around a long time. The little noisemakers from the elementary school on the next block are heading home down the hill. There are not so many Spaniards among them. Mostly Morocs and Chinese, a few African kids. Most of the Africans in the neighborhood are connected to shops that sell wood carvings, totems, masks. The women dress in tribal costumes and stand out. They're spectacularly colorful. It's hard to know what to make of these shops. There are five, six of them in the immediate area, each chock-full with goods. But you never see any customers. When Wolf was here he attempted to buy a mask. It was crudely carved but striking nonetheless—the face of some dog god. No one in the shop, however, seemed to know quite how to go about making a sale. Draw your own conclusions.

There's a skinny, blond girl lives across the street with her mom and dad and cute little black and white dog. The dog looks, by far, the most intelligent of the lot. The girl is 17 at the most I'd say. She's chatting at the moment with this older fella below our balcony. He's in his sixties, and his right leg acts like it's dead. When he walks, he throws the leg out in front of him, where it waves about like a flag before the foot is heavily planted. He steps gingerly and quickly on it, then goes again to his good leg. It's uncomfortable to watch him go up the hill. But, like I say, they're chatting. They go to say goodbye. She offers her cheek for a kiss as the Spanish do. The old guy grabs her and really lays one on her, full on the lips, and it lasts a while. People walking by seem embarrassed. When I look back at the two, they're talking again. Then, this time, the girl grabs him by the back of neck and slams her face into his. She's frenching him. Then they went their separate ways.

I told Megan about it. She was folding clothes.

The old guy, she asked, that walks around in a sports coat and pajama bottoms?

That one, yeah, I said. He may have started a trend there.

You ever been up close to him? she said. One of his eyes just kind of sidles on him. I thought he was her grandpa. But ... nothing surprises me in Lavapiés. She folded clothes. She stopped that a moment, took off a Stevie Ray Vaughan disk and put on Miles Davis' *Sketches of Spain*. She knows this album calms me, and I'm wondering why she wants me calm.

Finally she said, Chelo came by last night.

What'd he want?

I don't know. I didn't let him in. He asked if you were here, and I said no, and he left.

How'd he look?

He didn't smell like beer, she said. She folded her clothes. She seemed very intent on getting them just right.

I open the door and he says, Hey, friend. I'm thinking, Not on your best day, asshole.

After awhile she said, We had a test in class today. They never do that. All they ever do is lecture. But we've been studying Camilo José Cela's *Journey to the Alcarria*. It's a classic of Spanish travel literature, and the professor explained that someone had asked him a question last week after class that was so moronic he realized perhaps no one knew what he was talking about, or cared. So he told us we were going to have a little test on the reading assignment ... then today during it, he catches this kid with a crib sheet. The

Spanish call them chuletas, for some reason. Chops.

What'd he do about that?

He congratulated him on his ingenuity.

That's surprising.

He was being sarcastic, she said.

I wonder why we call them cribs? I said.

She took a pair of my jeans and shook them out, then sat down again and folded them.

Damn, she said and put her hand to her lips.

What?

I keep biting my tongue.

Look, she said. I need to tell you something.

Say it.

When I send Mercedes the rent, I get a note back from her. She says, thanks, got the money, or whatever. I didn't get a note this time. I just kept waitin' … a wrong feeling to it.

So I called Hollywood awhile ago. I figured I'd wake her up probably, but at least I'd get hold of her. I wanted to, I don't know … just give her a heads up that we might have to go home, what with Aunt Delle and all. Let her know of the possibility at least.

I talked to one of her roommates, and she gave me a number to call here in Spain. Mercedes, she tells me, left California. She got homesick, she hated Hollywood, had a bad time of it with English … I got the whole story. This girl I spoke to is from Madrid, but she's been out there for years. Anyway, Mercedes is staying in Alpedrete at her parents'. I'm going to call her directly. But I wanted to talk to you first. She finished folding one of my black T-shirts and smoothed it flat.

Can we go home? she said. I woke up last night … you weren't here … I woke up … I don't want to lose you to this place. An' I'm afraid that I might am.

She looked as though she would cry, but didn't, as she never cries.

Aw, shoot, honey, I said. I went to her and held her. And after awhile she took me by the hand and led me to her bedroom.

Wednesday

Just before midnight, Megan had gone to sleep and I was reading out in the front room, I started hearing what seemed like pebbles hit the window. There's another one. And another. So I went to the balcony and looked down, and Chelo was standing below on the sidewalk.

Hey, he said.

We shook hands at the door and he came in and we sat down and looked one another over.

Long time no see.

I've been aimin' to get over here, he said, but ... I had some things to work out.

Things?

Like my sanity. Small items such as that.

You want something to drink?

No, thanks. I haven't had a drink since last Saturday around midnight. It was just about then I discovered I was listening to jazz at Café Central with this Spanish couple I'd met for tapas early on. Had no idea how we happened to come to Central. Just blank on it. I'd lost some time after ten hours of high-speed consumption. I got to the point where I couldn't get any drunker, and just kept on. We could have arrived in a carriage pulled by The Three Blind Mice for all I knew. That was enough. I quit.

You can just stop like that?

I have to want to. That's the only key. Then I have a couple bad days, and it's over. It won't last, but ... I never could get into that AA business—Say hello to crowd. Say your name. Say, I'm an alcoholic. I haven't had a drink since I parked my car out in your parking lot ... There's too many steps to that program. About eleven.

He looked around.

Megan asleep?

It's late.

By the look she gave me the other night, I'd guess she hates me, or still angry, one.

I think she only sees your bad side.

Man, I'll tell you … that look coulda skinned a cat.

I don't see that one very often.

Is she doin' okay?

She wants to go home. Since Emilie left, she's had a hard time of it. They had fun together, and she doesn't have a friend to talk to anymore, 'cept me, for what that's worth. She wants to go back to San Ann. Maybe replant one of my grandma's orange groves.

Can you think of any way I could make amends with her?

Not offhand, I said. A lifetime of atonement for starters, I thought. But even that wouldn't do. You cross Megan once, what comes after don't cut any ice with her.

He turned his eyes to mine.

Darlen's gone, he said. She wanted me to tell you that.

I figured. Where to? did she say.

She stayed at my place last night, he said. This morning I walked with her to Atocha, and she caught the Bullet Train to Seville. She talked about going to Ibiza. Or Lanzarote. Talked some about Trujillo, down in Extremadura. Don't know if she was just putting up a smoke screen on all that or what, but she's on the run. She's got something big goin' down, wouldn't say what. I hope she covers her tracks good.

She's probably adept at it, I said. She'll end up somewhere people like her are accepted … Amsterdam, say. But she'll keep moving for awhile I'd think.

Her landlady's up north for Semana Santa, and it's going to happen soon. She didn't want her involved.

The one looks like she's been settin' on a nail all her life? I said.

That's her.

I went over there the other night, I said. I had some money to give to Darlen. She spoke of needing money. She wasn't home. Just the witch.

She sent most of hers to her boyfriend, Chelo said. Sent it through some politician … A moment later he said, She wanted your address in Florida.

Do you know it?

No. I got to thinkin' later I could've told her put Luke Gatins on the envelope, send it to San Ann. That you're probably related to the postman.

That's true, I said.

I didn't know if you wanted it given out, anyway.

I don't.

You happen to have any that cash left? he said. I'm tapped out till payday.

I remembered what Kevin Ray said about loaning money to Che.

Sure, I said. How much you need?

After we got that transacted, I asked:

Did you make love to her finally?

Hell ... soon as she got there she started making herself over. Bound herself up. Hid that body behind baggy clothes. I gave her a haircut to make it even shorter, wasn't much left but stubble. By midnight she was just a boy again. All that sexuality and heat, it was gone.

I must have looked incredulous.

Believe it, he said. We didn't sleep. Kept talkin'. Tell the truth, it was nice. I felt good about it, which is much better than feelin' used up. Anyway, I came over to say I'm sorry, Luke, for how I been lately. I've acted the fool. An' I got real good at that work. I know that's how you learn—get burned. Just, I somehow got rendered stupid in the process.

Don't put more on yourself than you need to, I said. She had me goin' too.

No. I have ... I've been a fool, and I realized it awhile ago and couldn't do a damn thing about it except get angry and grit my teeth at night. Did you ever get so mad at yourself, he said, that you could kick your own ass?

20 April the start of Semana Santa. 21 April Good Friday - 23 April Easter Sunday

Holy Week is the most elaborate and curious of Spanish festivals. The cofradías, or brotherhoods, from each church carry figures of Christ and the Virgin Mary through the streets of Madrid. The men of each brotherhood walk ahead of and behind their floats, dressed in the long, hooded robes of the Inquisition, holding candles, incense, rosemary. They are followed by penitents bearing crosses, many of them barefoot, some dragging chains from their ankles, or with shirts torn at the back and carrying whips. Crowds follow, crowds line the way.

From balconies and sidewalks along the way, spectators sing to the Virgin songs of torment and flattery called saetas—arrows—songs shot to heaven.

The young men carrying the floats pause and rock the big dolls from side to side while the singer finishes this cry of praise. Then the bands in front take up the mournful tune of Holy Week, and the procession moves on.

Anyone with sense clears out, and the city is left to the fanatics. There are even parking spaces available. It is religious ecstasy in the streets. The worship of large dolls. On Good Friday I will find myself in a crowd of a hundred thousand around the Sol/Gran Vía area. Much sobbing and cheering as the flower-laden doll floats passed. The faithful have been telling their secrets to these figurines for centuries. They believe the dolls know all their cares and concerns. Old ladies with red hair bounce against the crowd like pinballs, jostling for a better view. Much pushing and shoving in general, just slightly out of the ordinary really, though there was no place to move. A Madrileño delight. Meanwhile, the stores close, but I have stocked up on cheese and wine, and, of course, the bars remain open for business.

If you still need to feel the odd friction of just how different things are here, Semana Santa is your moment. Religion is the very strangest of things Spanish. Other institutions such as the bullfight and flamenco are much like you'd imagined them, only better, but it's hard to prepare yourself for barefoot penitents with tow truck gauge chains dragging from their ankes in solemn procession through the main streets of the capital. Or for men in self-flagellation, rope whip to bare back, or women walking blindfolded miles on end. Or the adoration, though some may call it idolatry, shown to statuary or divine dolls riding on heavy street floats carried on the backs of twenty or so young men, many of them drunk. It is like carrying a big load of sins or perhaps hell itself on their backs, and they do it willingly, they want to.

It's hard to picture that beneath the KKK hoods, the three foot tall conical hats and long robes, are the same men usually seen knocking each other and you about on any given day along the same streets on their way to a café. Just the notion of collective and very public repentance may stop you cold. And I'm not sure how reverent it all is. It strikes me as medieval and more than slightly pagan, and Holy Week an excellent opportunity for all the true assholes in town to wipe clean a year's worth of mischief with some quick religious ardor. The good citizens in the wake of the floats carry themselves with a mixture of solemnity and pride. However, it is best observed, in my opinion, with a grain of salt and perhaps a small order of boquerones, and through the green coloring of a wine bottle on your terraza table.

Sunday was busy and loud late into the night with cars returning to the city. I gave up on sleep after awhile and worked on this early Monday morning, starting around 4 a.m. When finished, I saved what I'd done. I went back to make sure it was saved, and it was nowhere to be found. I'd racked up 275 minutes on the machine and was rewarded with zero word count.

It threw me off. I walked to Sol. I think maybe this is a holiday also; the streets are not nearly so frantic as usual, the crowd thinner. The city has planted flowering cherry on the sidestreets around Sol. They're in bloom now. Tulips are blooming also, and wisteria. It's spring on the sunny side of the street, dismal in the shade.

I stopped at my tabac shop and purchased cigars and stamps. I have two letters to mail. I put stamps on the letters. The face on most Spanish stamps is that of the King. The trouble with Madrileños, I think, is that, even though they like the King well enough, they feel he has usurped their rightful position.

I dropped the letters into a buzón. I stopped at a kiosk and bought a paper. Moments later a gypsy all but mugged me. She wanted some money for a little red ribbon tied in a bow. You can't cross a street in this area without getting hit up. Like this ribbon, what they have to offer is never anything you would consider buying on your own. I don't want the ribbon I tell her.

Dame algo, she says. Give me something. I shake my head, but she won't take no for an answer. She starts following me across the street. I shout at her—Get away from me you fucking loon! A fella on the corner was playing bagpipes. A strange note got stuck in my ear. I have a dental appointment coming up. These tend to color my mood. I soon found myself walking at an extremely rapid clip, somewhat irate. That is to say, I was one with the electrical crowd.

25 April Tuesday

Cold, inkwash sky. I can't say much for April so far. Megan and I went out anyway, to Retiro, Plaza Mayor, any place with a terraza, including Calle Armugosa in our neighborhood, waiting for the sun to show. At one point it approached a pale straw color. That was the best it got. 500 pesetas a beer in Plaza Mayor now, so we won't be doing that again. To compensate, however, you get surly waiters and have to listen to the junkie/box wine crowd converse across the square. They don't care to sit close to talk. No challenge in that.

Then, toward evening, I was standing on the balcony looking at a grey cat across the street jumping from one apartment to the next, railing to railing, and then back again. Dangerous play, but she seemed to have the knack of it. And a lightning bolt seemed to hit right on our street. It made a huge cracking sound. Soon after this a downpour commenced. Rarely that we have anything here but a drizzle. But this rain came stomping down and brought bad weather behind it.

26 April Wednesday

The dental appointment is at ten in the morning. One of my lower front teeth had crumbled, a big piece falling away. I looked to belong to some primitive tribe that files its teeth into points.

A new dentist once again. He turned out to be a likeable sort, a young Spaniard who had spent two years in Miami. But I had difficulty finding his office. I was looking for 1B on the far right side of the building. Megan had scouted the place. She said, There's something odd about it. The address. I can't remember what.

I go to the intercom, check the addresses. There's no 1B listed. There's a 1B attico. I buzz that and talk to a lady who soon enough starts calling me tonto. This means fool. Talk to the portero, she tells me in Spanish, exasperated with my butchery of the language. Gracias, asshole, I say in return. She seems to think I said ajo, which is garlic. This brings on another outburst from her. Why would I be calling her a garlic? she wants to know. I experience cultural vertigo as she speaks.

I find the portero and he walks me to the office on the far right, 1B, just as Megan had said, but which has a completely different name on it than the one I'm looking for. However, it's my dentist. I'm in the right place he says. He looks at my teeth in alarm. First of all, he said, they need to be cleaned. I can't see them for the wine and tobacco stains. When that was done he repaired the tooth. All this took awhile. Afterward I walked home, walked fast, elated to have it over with. I talked to myself in that deadmouth lisp you get. Down a sidestreet past Callao I felt suddenly lost. Nothing serious, Sol was close by. I just happened to be in an unfamiliar area. I wasn't in the slaglands, those portals to the subconscious I wander into when my thoughts have turned to scree.

The demolition crew is hard at it on the shop below. A cold drizzle continues as I sit here looking out the front windows, heavy sledge hammer blows stunning the room.

The Madrileños have some curious names for this slow rain— chirimiri, calabobo. I decided to hunker down till the outside started acting decently again, but the noise below drives me away. I put on a union suit under my clothes, and raincoat, and a ballcap inscribed with Who Gives A Shit and walk about town. I stopped at a bookstore at Sol. I looked at books for an hour with no intention of buying anything. I just observed books at rest in their quietude.

When I got home, the hammerheads were still at it. Hard to imagine what could be left in there to knock down. It is a small place. I handle it as I do all such events—give my regards to oblivion. Several times during the afternoon, the sun blinked on. When I hustled outside to take this in, it would slip behind a cloud. I leave again to escape the racket. Upon my return, all is quiet. When the workers realize it's me, however, sledge hammer blows commence once again, the entire apartment vibrating. The noise is cumulative. It seems a sure bet at this point they have been employed to drive me mad. Not that I have actually spotted a worker, only heard the work being done. No debris is taken out in my presence, no new building materials arrive. It may only be a machine. A clever torture device.

27 April Thursday
Early this morning, around 4 a.m. Darlen's piso was raided by Guardia Civil and city police. I didn't know it had happened, but Chelo stopped by later in the day with an *El Pais*. He read the article to me, translating:

Police Find ETA Bomb Cache, he read aloud. Anti-terrorist police found bomb-making materials while searching a centrally located apartment in Madrid where it was believed the Basque separatist group ETA had set up an explosives workshop.

Police discovered packets of sodium chlorate, a chemical used in bomb-making, electrical devices, hundreds of 9mm cartridges and a computer during their search. They found plastic explosives in two pressure cookers.

It was not immediately clear who occupied the apartment. The place is registered to a man who's been deceased a decade. There were no arrests made, Chelo said. He read some more without speaking, then: They call it a safe house. That it was logistically important.

Looks like she was more involved than she let on, he said.

Looks like, I said.

I hope she finds her way, he said.

I hardly used this day at all. It's nearly pristine. I went out once for bread and wine. At the entrance to a little wine store I came across a skinhead holding a pigeon. They are called rapados here—those who crop their hair. I'd never seen one in daylight before. It was a touching moment: Falange youth cradling the dove of the city in his tattooed hands. I stopped at a panadería to buy bread, not the one I usually go to, and notice on a portable blackboard that the special for the day is trout cake. It was a three-layer cake with white frosting. *Trout cake*. I'm thinking, Where the fuck am I?

I leave there with my baguette and not half a block later come upon an entire dumpster full of discarded umbrellas. It's curious out here, I say to myself, and hustle back to the apartment. Later Megan tells me she got on a metro car returning from school. For a few moments, she was the only one in there, which happens infrequently, or never. Then seven midget fellas dressed in business suits and carrying briefcases filed in and sat across from her. I felt a bit like Snow White, she said.

Full moon tomorrow. It's already pushing me around.

In the night I have a dream about my mother. The two of us were on a train. She was reading a magazine. What's the article about? I asked. I can't make heads or tails of it, she said. It all seems to be in the devil's handwriting. I was lulled by the isochronal nature of the train wheels, the countryside rolling backward in the windows. Houses flew by on both sides, streaks of sharp light coming and going. Then the train took a long curve, and on the other side of this was darkness. My mother wasn't beside me any more. I had wanted to ask her something, it was important to me I remember, though just then I couldn't get any sense of what it might have been. The train was flying along the ground at excessive speed. Another curve, this one sharp, and then the dream moved on. I tried in my sleep to get back to where I'd been, but there were too many countries in between.

28 April Friday

I tried to read early this morning, Somerset Maugham, Henry James, but for some reason the pages didn't turn so fast on these particular books, almost like they had rusty hinges. When I finally went for a walk I realized what a fine spring day was at hand. A day like this in Madrid makes up for many things.

I went to Retiro and spent several hours there. The Tree of Love is blooming now, similar to a redbud but much larger, with pale lavendar flowers, thousands to a tree. The horse chestnuts are blooming also, and lilac, bridal wreath. They're all out at once, seemingly overnight, and it's a show. On the way out of the park, I saw what I took to be a mother and daughter on a bench talking and laughing. They were bullshitting with each other and found delight in it.

Close by Retiro is the Military Museum, and I stopped in. There's a fine collection of rifles and pistols in this museum, some of them incredible, especially the big-bore rifles. You wonder about the shooter surviving the kick. They have the sword of El Cid. One of his two swords that is; it's name is Tizona. He thought his swords had personalities. He took both from Muslim kings he'd slain. He liberated Valencia from the Moors, 3,000 of his fighters against 30,000. He was the fiercest warrior of his time, that time long ago now—he died in 1099. Yet what strikes me always when I see Tizona is the smallness of the handgrip. It could fit the hand of a child, an 11, 12 year old. You see it also in the proportions of the suits of armor, which have a weird mechanical insect quality to them. They were smaller people back then.

I'd like to make another stop before we leave Madrid, at the Arqueólogico Museum, to visit the Lady of Elche one last time. I'm in love with this beauty, though she is 2500 years old and carved from sandstone.

Goya's Head

I was sitting on a bench in Plaza Santa Ana later on reading the sports pages when this blonde bounced into the vicinity wearing what appeared to be a large doily. She had on a bra but no underpants, and the dress material was quite thin. She was slightly agitated, going around to the old ladies in black there. She'd lost track of her husband, she said, and had they seen him? The old ladies looked away blushing.

The plaza had been spruced up lately, hundreds of flower seedlings planted. In a week the pigeons cropped them. It looked like a herd of rabbits hit the beds. On the street across from me I witnessed a comedy routine—two Madrileños, a middle-aged man and a young woman, ran into one another. I noticed them when they were about nine feet apart, moving fast on a collision course, the wooden look on their faces of those with other things in mind, neither aware that anyone else in the world existed. They clashed heads and both went down. They damn near knocked each other out.

Megan has arranged for a moving company to come give us an estimate. I don't have so very much to take back—our little portable CD player, books, art work I've picked up along the way, hats, shoes, story, notes. Maybe my old wine jugs. My wardrobe for the most part will be staying put. I'll wear my heavy coat to the airport and ditch it there. I've started packing. So far I've only included my hash pipe, corkscrew, and hand-painted coffee mug Megan bought for me in Portugal. I wanted to start with the essentials, get them placed handy. What room I have left in my suitcase, Megan will use. She's a packrat. She doesn't throw anything away, including myself, for which I'm grateful. She'll take everything left in sight after the movers finish. If there's still room in the suitcases, she'll go shopping.

For weeks now I've been getting notes from Shaloo. He might show up for the San Isidro bullfights in May, he says, save a spot on our floor. My thought is, Thanks for the warning. I had started to tire of the panic this news inspired and told him in my last letter that we have a nice floor, but it's the kind that gets hard after a couple days. Now I'll have to tell him that we'll be home soon.

I bought some walking shoes. Pumas. I feel like a big cat stepping out now. There are still shops here that, when you go to buy something in them, the sales people act as if they're doing you quite a favor. This stems apparently from the years after the Civil War, when there wasn't much in the shops and they had the upper hand. Now it's a tradition. The kid that sold me the walking shoes, he could have been handling bananas. He didn't know shit about what he was selling and did so with the least amount of energy expended. I wore my Red Wing boots in there. I wear them mostly in inclement weather and if I don't plan on walking far, as they're heavy. I bought them ten years ago from the Red Wing store on Busch Blvd. in Tampa, and they're still in good shape. I heard the fella who sold them to me died not long afterwards. He knew everything about his product and about feet, knew it all well and seemed pleasantly moved when he got the fit just right. He'd been doing that work for a long time. When I wear these boots now, I think about that guy sometimes and miss him, and all those like him.

Today on one of my many walks—the commotion of the city under reconstruction in full swing, pneumatic drills, sledge hammers on cement, radios of workers blaring, normal car horn madness, plus the loud nonstop talking of the inhabitants—I noted that it's entirely possible to get a headache just trying to purchase a newspaper. I get the paper and stop at a little restaurant for a quick coffee, a waiter there slamming cutlery around. I am, in the first place, taking long walks to escape the noise directly below us, which continues unabated.

I ended up far out near the university on one of these walks, take the metro to Sol to get back closer to home and am rewarded by what I assume will be the last pickpocket attempt against me. This guy was as incompetent as the rest, but he came close just because I had other things on my mind. It was around lunchtime, and the car was packed. I was jammed in there with this guy right to the side of me and slightly in front, a tall, skinny gypsy. I identified him in my mind as a pickpocket. I looked around for his partner, as they normally work in tandem. I didn't particularly spot his partner, though. I thought all this, then spaced out. I was thinking about this and that. Thinking about home, and all that held. We've been in contact with Mom. Megan has talked to her twice. I called Wolf. She knows we're coming home, Wolf says, though she can't keep the details straight. I called my brother also and gave him a heads-up. When I came to again, I see this guy's finger trying to slide into my front shirt pocket. They seem to know where you keep your money; I'm not sure how. I did an American football move on him called the headslap. This knocked him and the nearby crowd about a foot to the left, and I made my way around him and stood by the door, my back to it. I had a couple stops to go. He got out at the next one. As he passed me, I put the hex-eye on him. He gives me in return a palms up gesture like, just doing my job, nothing personal. Fucking asshole. He walked away with his knuckle in his ear.

We're getting Allied to move us. They're coming next Friday, the 5th of May. They pack everything for you. Megan wants to take home her big Persian rug, but otherwise, we're leaving the furniture for Mercedes. Door to door delivery, two weeks, from Madrid to San Ann. Air freight. After the movers come, we'll take a hostal room for the weekend and until the morning of the 8th, when we fly out.

That evening I fell asleep thinking about home, good thoughts, the little screech owls in the backyard at night, the chuck-will's-widow. Then I dreamed. I recognize a street. I'm in Madrid among the jacked-up crowd. How unfortunate, I remark aloud, though my voice seems to have a klaxon quality to it, and people rotate their heads toward me. I turn a corner, the streets here unfamiliar, and come across a hit-and-run scene. There's a young lady down, against the curb. A long black car speeds off, through a red light, it's gone.

The young lady's clothes speak of money. She seems all right, though stunned by the hit, her nose bloody, her eyes open and blank, but what you notice rather is that her legs are spread so. Her skirt's bunched up around her waist. And her cunt's enormous. It's like a picnic basket. A man standing ahead of me several feet takes it all in nonchalantly, his right hand buried in his jeans pocket, his left slowly searching around for his cigarette pack. I understand that he is operating at a slight remove from the scene though I don't know how I know this, or why it is so. I can't see his face well because of the angle.

No one makes a move to help the young lady, as her cunt seems a magnet of sorts, the crowd held in place by it, either positive or negative, relish or horror carved on faces, and only this one man between the poles, detached. But all eyes are drawn there, and more. Bananas, sausages, green wine bottles start flying out of grocery bags from the crowd assembled, ramming into her. She, however, is not paying attention. She's looking at the sky vaguely, like she's wondering if it might rain.

A false nose flies by my head, hits the target. Good god, I say aloud, the false nose people are about! Apparently, once more, I have honked the message. Several faces are diverted and gaze upon me with obvious distaste. I look around my person for the horn. Perhaps I am Harpo Marx just then. I attempt an explanation of this to the codger at my left, who only clicks his tongue. I didn't care for this response. I've been hearing it too much lately I decide. I gave him an elbow, and he spun out of view.

The man ahead turned and observed me over his shoulder in a bemused way, and I notice off-hand that he looks very much like me. A certain hulking manner. A man detached from his immediate location. He is a bit younger, heavier in muscle, clean shaven, but the resemblance is strong. I haven't shaved my beard in some time now and begin to wonder what I really look like. He stared directly at me then, a cold logic in his eyes, and said something. I couldn't hear what, and moved closer. He spoke again. I caught the last part of it ... *not worth the straw it is made of* ...

Luckily, I woke before he could let me in on any more of his bullshit. I understand this as a meeting with my character outside the written page.

29 April Saturday

Megan was doing some paperwork. She'd been packing for days. I'd just finished up, my T-shirts and socks.

School's gonna let out here pretty soon, I said.

I'm just gettin' some things squared away for the students I've been tutoring. There's people gonna take them. These are notes on their progress this year, what they need yet.

Did you teach them any San Ann jargon?

She looked up and smiled.

Turd roller … a few such as that, is all.

Local color is important, I said.

Far as school, she said, I need any more learnin', I'll get Lalo to teach me.

She's speaking of Modesto Aponte, Sixto's only son, called Lalo.

He knows grafting. You ever see that little grafting knife of his? I've had enough of college. It's a good place to hide out, but that's over. You know, the grove by the house, Tillie never used anything on that but cow manure. It's what I want to use, too. It'll take time to get the grove up and goin'. It'll be some before we make money on it.

We'll not be rich for awhile, you're sayin'?

We already are, baby, she said. There is other coin.

Tillie was caught in one of the bank crashes in the summer of 1930, which took what little cash she had then. She got along without. She bartered, paid for shoes and flour with farm produce. Day labor was paid the same. She had Sixto hunt wild hog for her table. Even later on when I was a kid she served game often as not and with the admonition, Watch out for shot. Or trapped a young pig and fed it kitchen scraps and acorns till it was 200 pounds, butchered and cured it. She had her garden, tomato seed passed down the generations from her family, sweet potatoes, and field peas planted in the shade of the orange rows. Chickens for eggs. Honey for sugar. She had a banana patch. Over time she established a small herd of crossbreed cattle. She called them Spanish cows. They weren't much and she never kept so many of them. They interested her mostly for manure, but she'd butcher a steer if necessary. She had one of those washing machines with a wringer on it, hung her clothes out on the line to dry in the sun. She purchased a window unit AC for her bedroom in the early 60s as a concession to modernity.

After the summer of 1930, she was never beholden to bankers again. If she needed money, she went to Aunt Sylvia. Sylvia had foreseen the market crash of '29 and turned her stocks into cash beforehand. She'd worked her magic, that is to say.

Tillie's first grove, on the five acres Megan now speaks of replanting, was planted with seed oranges, the trees not yet bearing when they were wiped out in the December freeze of '34, in what Tillie called the coldest night of her life. She replanted. This time she used rough lemon rootstock and grafted on budwood she obtained from a Bartlett family friend in Webster. They were old-time rust-streaked oranges and uncommonly sweet. At some point she started planting Valencias, which come ripe in the spring, and had oranges on her trees eight months of the year.

The freeze of '34 always stuck with her, and she vowed to be prepared for the next one. She waited twenty-eight years for it, in the meantime stocking up on oil heaters and keeping old car and tractor tires until they filled a large outbuilding. Then in December 1962, a Canadian clipper brought arctic temperatures that lasted four days and froze the oranges solid. The worst night was the 13th. Tillie got Sixto to round up all his people, then drove over to Trilacoochee and hired, as she put it, every man jack and grown child she could find, offered top wages and free whiskey. She even went into the roadhouse there and spoke her piece, the first white woman they'd ever seen in that bar.

They worked through the night using oil heaters and burning tires. Most of her trees lived, she said, but no one could breathe worth a damn come sunrise.

A slow thaw afterwards saved her oranges long enough to harvest and get them to the concentrate plant in Dade City for processing.

It was frozen juice, which came in after World War II, that allowed her to get near well-to-do. By 1975 she owned or leased 200 acres, pretty much the north end of town. But she had some intuition that disaster was on its way, didn't know its identity—hurricane, freeze, her own demise. She didn't know what exactly but felt it coming and knew it would be stronger than her will this time.

Then on the morning of January 19th, 1977, snow came to San Ann and the entire Tampa Bay area. I remember that one. There's nothing more striking than snow on ripe oranges. And that spring Tillie started selling off parcels of land.

Toward the end she got a little befuddled. She became overly concerned about having enough money for her casket. She played it off as a joke, but it was a serious matter to her and one that made no sense to any of us. When she passed, Dad and Uncle Harlen found thousands of dollars cached around the house. And along with the money, old presents she had opened from birthdays and Christmas, admired, and soon after put into drawers and never used, left to wait for rainy days.

All of Sunday and Monday I went through the story making corrections. The spell check on the computer doesn't work, and I spend a good deal of time looking up words in the dictionary. For some reason I got obsessional about it. Megan wanted to take the computer home, but I nixed that. The machine is so beat up it's not worth the effort. By Wednesday at noon I have a good copy printed, erase all my work and in three trips take the computer and screen and printer and set them beside the dumpster outside. Afterward I go to the kitchen and open a beer, then to the living room and talk to Megan. She is trying to close my suitcase and it's way too full, not with my items but hers.

You might could sit on it, she said.

What do I get for it?

Get a hard time if you don't, she said.

When we got that accomplished, I went to the balcony and looked down. It's gone already.

4 May Thursday

I went to the Prado one last time. I went to the section that houses Goya's cartoon paintings, which he did early on and before his deafness. Cartoon refers to that they were painted on *cartone* paper, the design later woven in wool for tapestries. His assignment for these was to amuse the royals, show them what the common folk were up to. Several of them are simply Goya's first masterpieces. I like one of these very much, The Parasol, done in 1777. I've stood before it many times, and did so again this day. The composition balances on geometrical forms—Xs, diagonals, pyramids—a stylistic design Goya would use throughout his life, but you wouldn't know that unless you knew it. What you see is the perfect equilibrium, and the subject matter two young people, an elegant young lady and a boy who holds a green parasol to shade her, and the painting, for lack of a better word, is sweet. Once again I'm taken by his use of color—green parasol, yellow dress, how small doses of red reflect around the scene. If you want to know what silence did to Goya, study this painting awhile, then look to the Pinturas negras.

In 1901, seventy-three years after Goya's death, the Spanish government asked for him back, and his remains were exhumed from the cemetery of the Chartreuse in Bordeaux and buried in Madrid. In 1929, it was decided to rebury him beneath the altar of the chapel of San Antonio de la Florida. They took a look at him then. His head was missing.

No one knows if Goya's head is in France still, or in Spain. It remains elusive.

6 May Saturday

Allied came and went. It took most of Friday for them to pack, and they were steady at it and knew what they were doing. Then their truck pulled up in front, they loaded, and our belongings were headed home. We moved on to Hostal Matute, just around the corner from Plaza Santa Ana, to a small, clean room, 6,000 pesetas a night.

In the morning we caught a bus to a village called Colmenar de Oreja. This translates as The Beehive's Ear, though it's uncertain what that might mean. They have a fair, this year from 5 to 7 May. They set up a bullring in their little plaza, run bulls in the streets. Megan got several hot tips from fellow students in her classes. Go early, was one. We got there at 10 in the morning; they don't run the bulls till 4. The name of the best restaurant in town; it was closed, all the windows broken.

In fact, when we arrived that morning the bars were jumping. Then I got to looking around at the clientele, all with dark circles under their eyes and that stricken look indicating no sleep. The feria started the day before, and knowing the Spanish, they'd spent a couple days beforehand partying, looking forward to when the party began. They were at the moment having a nightcap or two before bed. And things calmed down for good soon afterwards and didn't start up again till around 3.

Colmenar is a farm town, really podunk, which I liked, and Megan was in her element. Things were inexpensive and the people very friendly. There is good local wine, rows of grapes all around far as the eye could see. I had 12 grilled shrimp and roast leg of lamb for lunch. I hadn't meant to order that much, don't know that I did really, but that's what came. The meal was done perfectly, and they all but gave it away. Families were coming in on tractors pulling trailers behind, flatbed trucks. You'd see eight, nine of them, from grandma on down to little grandson, that in the face looked to be exactly the same person.

That afternoon, we got stranded in a street just before the bulls arrived. Barracades were set up along the street, similar to large bicycle racks. It was cold out, I had on my heavy winter coat and soon discovered that I couldn't fit through the bars. You experience primal fear when a bull is coming at you, and I'm not kidding.

Because of the street layout in Colmenar, the bulls can arrive from either of several directions. They come around a corner, and they're on you. I hit the barracade and got stuck there. Megan ripped me through finally. She got a good laugh out of that. We watched the rest of it from the sidelines. So much for courage. They were some cute little red bulls that didn't do any damage in our sector. They ran two at a time. A fat kid near us fainted, too much wine I believe. That was the only casualty we saw.

There'd been one last Madrid letter in the mailbox before we left Calle Olivar, from Wade Bonner, Tampa poet, former bouncer at the Cadillac Lounge, down near the corner of Florida Avenue and Sligh. He quit the bar and is driving a cab now. The job allows him to keep living in the night. I saw him the last time we went home and gave him our address. The letter went to Argüelles and was rerouted. It is as follows:

I pulled up to the guy's house and recognized him right away. Hey Lawrence, how ya doin'? He wants to go up and down Nebraska Avenue because he is looking for a whore, and not just any whore, but the one he is in love with. Man, what a romantic idea. I've been in the romance business and didn't realize it. Up and down the avenue looking for only one girl. I was almost overcome. Well he settled for some rough looking black whore, but what is that up against the once and always great notion that propels the world? He's got his own electrical business and had done some work at a particular motel and would be offered a free room there. So I pulled into the Royal Palms Motel and crossed myself just for luck. It's not that I think Billy Jenks is still there, just why would you take chances with stuff like that. Anyhow, Lawrence paid me 25 bucks, which was a 10 dollar tip and said come back in half an hour. When I got there, he gave me another 10-spot and said come back in an hour. You gotta admire a guy like that.

It has entered my thought lately that I need to come to terms with Billy's passing. The shot that took him out has echoed long enough. If I stay at odds with this, it will keep haunting me. I would like to leave all that behind in Madrid. He is with me because his spirit is irrepressible. He'll always be with me, he will not lose his place. I just have to accept that he is with me now in just that manner and no other. And maybe it is that, when the dead leave here, they leave at different speeds. If you're listening, Billy, it is time to move on. For both of us, it's time. I'll catch you down the line.

7 May

Today the swallows returned to Madrid.

One of the people around the King in the old days was called the Keeper of His Majesty's Hairbrush.

I write this in my notebook to tell you that my thoughts are flaring off now. They are like the swallows in the hard blue sky. They go here and there with no reckoning.

This story has been written from the viewpoint of an outsider making his way through the heavy crowd along certain streets at a place in the mind called Madrid—by a man who felt solitude and tried to turn it to account.

I've been wanting to tell you about this fella across the street from Hostal Matute who comes out on his balcony around noon each day and gives a raucous, expletive-laced, rather too long speech to the world at large. I can't tell exactly what he's saying, but he holds his right hand firmly against his heart …

afterwards

I got a phone call from Chelo Cruz on the 5th of June that year. A day earlier an ETA gunman had assasinated a Durango city councilman. His name was José Loinaz Etxea. He was a member of Spain's governing Popular Party. One shot to the head.

I take it this was Darlen's contact. Chelo thought the same. We may both be wrong. Hell, what do we know?

We talked for awhile that day. When he received his last paycheck, he was taking the night train to Barcelona. After that, his plans were up in the air. I asked if he'd had any word from Darlen. No. Nothing. And it was the last I heard from Chelo Cruz. I have no idea where he is now. I hope he does.

We get e-mail from Kevin Ray occasionally. He's working in Dubai, United Arab Emirates.

You pause a moment in the conversation and a year passes. Megan and I went to Boston this past winter. We stayed five days. Megan is replanting Tillie's original grove, an acre at a time. We can't be away too long, nor do we want to. And five days, that was enough really.

We went to visit Emilie. She lives there with Erik and teaches at Suffolk University. We had a good time with them. They never did marry. She could not pull that trigger. But now that they're together, it's not so important to him. We stayed in the Back Bay area, at the Boston Park Plaza Hotel, which was built in 1927. The hotel is a block or so from the Boston Common and the Public Gardens, and up above that Beacon Hill, steep walking there and good little wine shops and restaurants. We went there toward the end of February, 1st of March. I liked the snow and cold, and walked about as I did in Spain. It's the same feel to the old town there but without all the madness of Madrid. Everyone lives in apartment buildings, many dress in black. I'd stop at the Frog Pond in the Common and watch the ice skaters, the shadows of the old trees pastel blue against the snow. One day I rented skates and tried it out. There's a sign that says Skate At Your Own Risk, but I was not so much at risk as those around me.

I liked visiting the Old Granary Burying Ground nearby. Paul Revere, John Hancock, Samuel Adams, and victims of the Boston Massacre lay in rest there. Only five men were lost in that particular massacre, but … Tom Paine turned them into symbols and set our nation in motion. It's a bleak little place, the modest grave slabs with death heads inscribed on them—a skull with wings. Mother Goose is buried there, also.

I'm reminded just now of a trip Megan and I took to Paris that one winter with Emilie when we went to Père Lachaise cemetery. I wanted to see Jim Morrison's grave. The map at the front entrance, which was made of metal, showed you how to get there, but so many fingers had touched Morrison's name that it had been erased, along with the directions. We walked around a good long while and couldn't locate it. Finally we came to a mime in white face and white gloves, who was juggling three bowling pins. When I asked about Morrison, he stopped what he was doing. He had to think. He put his hand to his chin, went through a whole routine as mimes are wont to do. A lightbulb came on over his head. He described it with his hands. Then he took an exaggerated step to the right and pointed.

We were close on it. I could see people standing around there, a dozen or so young freaks smoking and drinking. Up close then, few of them spoke the same language. They were from all over the world. There was also a cop assigned to it, not sure why exactly, but he seemed pleasant enough. All the headstones that day had several inches of snow on them, the same as at the Granary. That's the way to see them properly I think, with snow on them. It makes it clearer somehow to understand how things here come and go, and afterwards, the finality of it and the sort of hat you get to wear.

I woke in the night once in Boston and noticed the snow was

really coming down, those big wet flakes that make people walk the city streets with umbrellas. The Bostonians, at this time of year, are tired of snow, but it pleased me no end. I went to the window and watched. It was 4 a.m. Across the street I saw lights on in one apartment, and a couple dancing over there. They were doing the jitterbug. They danced unbelievably fast. They had their windows covered with thin yellow shades. It made them appear like shadows dancing.

When we came home from Madrid, we stayed with Mom that first week while I worked on my house and yard to get them in order, the garden gone rank, the acre of lawn a meadow, the dog pen compelely overtaken by blue sky vine and virginia creeper. I went to Mom's for lunch one day when I was done mowing, and she and Megan and I had Cuban sandwiches and, afterwards, I was sitting on a chair near to her. She was in her rocker, which was Grandma Tillie's before her, and now Megan's. We were listening to the weather report and talking. I was looking through the sports pages just then but noticed that her speech had suddenly gone very drunk. She'd been drinking some, but this was extreme. She was slurring badly, and the words did not connect.

Megan called for an ambulance. The paramedics got there quickly. They happened to be in the neighborhood, down on Route 52 anyway. Mom didn't want to leave her house. She insisted she was okay, though that was not the case. They took her to the hospital, and she was never able to return home. She hung on another six weeks, but it was clear how it would go and she spent her last days at the home of a Christian woman in the country outside San Ann, a retired nurse, who takes good care of those in the process of leaving this place.

Mom could talk out of the left side of her mouth. She could move her left hand and arm some. It wasn't easy seeing her like that. She'd blink in and out on you. After awhile she didn't bother opening her eyes anymore. Because of this, you couldn't always tell if she was awake or not.

Goya's Head

Sometimes the dying reach out to unseen objects. One day I was there and she was doing just that. I'd been sitting quietly in a chair beside her bed for awhile. If she was asleep I didn't want to wake her. Watching her reach out in this manner, it struck me what was going on. I take it she was touching little pieces of time from the past, the good times, the best.

She opened her eyes, gave me her lopsided grin, and closed them again. I felt lousy that she could not come back home and told her so. There was no way we could care for her, but to this day I don't feel right about that.

It doesn't matter now, she said. I just had the most wonderful dream, Luke. I was dancing with your father. We were cutting a rug, I'll tell you.

We talked for a little while longer. Then she asked if I would leave. If I wouldn't mind doing that for her. It was the last time we spoke. She wanted to go back to sleep she told me. She wanted to dance some more.

Early this month, May of 2001, I received a letter postmarked from New Orleans. I was out in the yard burning leaves when I saw the mail truck. I went to the mailbox and got the letter. There was no return address, no message. Just a lock of oak-blonde hair, fastened with tendrils of Spanish moss.

I had to smile a bit. She'd obviously gotten ahold of cousin Pogey, but I'd not heard a word from the boy.

acknowledgments

Jane Duke did the first editing of this story. It was hard work. Without her help, I'd have made a fool of myself many times over.

I would like to offer thanks, also, to the newspapers whose articles I cited in this story, *The New York Times*, the *Independent* of London and the *International Herald Tribune*. During my stay in Madrid, they were simply lifelines. Thanks to Ian Herbert for his timely piece on the 'Buckley Goya.' I followed closely two correspondents based in Spain, Elisabeth Nash from the *Independent* and Al Goodman from the *Herald Tribune*. I found in their work, always, good information, well written.

I read a good number of books for historical background. Some were not only informative but entertaining as well. These in particular:

Robert Huges, *Goya*. This is a work of genius worthy of its subject.

Mark Kurlansky, *The Basque History of the World*

John McPhee, *Oranges*

Hugh Thomas, *The Spanish Civil War*

Bernardo Atxaga, *The Lone Man*

Larry Collins and Dominique Lapierre, *Or I'll Dress You In Mourning*

Jan Morris, *Spain*

André Malraux, *Days of Hope*

Gerald Brenan, *The Face of Spain*

Miguel de Unamuno, *Abel Sanchez and Other Stories*

Stetson Kennedy, *Palmetto Country*

Jean Genet, *The Thief's Journal*

Pablo Neruda, *Memoirs*

Ernest Hemingway, *Death in the Afternoon*

Christopher Maurer, *Federico García Lorca, Selected Poems*

And to Heather Galloway, Ana Bustello in Madrid. Jimmy Moore, Eduardo Perez, Glenn Morgan in Tampa. Mark Edmonds in Dade City. Antonio Roman-Perez in White Springs. Joe Taylor in Coatopa. Robert Smith, Willie Reader—parts unknown. They are story tellers. I learned more from them than any book.

Author's photo: Jane Duke

Tom Abrams lived for several years in Madrid. He now lives in Florida with his wife, Jane Duke. He is a combat veteran of Vietnam. This is his second novel.